Volupté

Volupté

The Sensual Man

Charles-Augustin Sainte-Beuve

Translated by
Marilyn Gaddis Rose

The State University of New York Press

Published by
State University of New York Press, Albany

For information address State University of New York Press, State University
Plaza, Albany, NY 12246

Production by Laura Starrett
Marketing by Dana Yanulavich

Library of Congress Cataloging in Publication Date

Sainte-Beuve, Charles Augustin, 1804–1869.
    [Volupté. English]
    Volupté : the sensual man / Charles-Augustin Sainte-Beuve ;
translated by Marilyn Gaddis Rose.
    p. cm.
    ISBN 0-7914-2451-0 (cloth). — ISBN 0-7914-2452-9 (pbk.)
    1. Vendean War, 1793–1800—Fiction.   2. Chouans—Fiction.
I. Rose, Marilyn Gaddis. II. Title.
PQ2391.A8E5   1994
843'.7—dc20
                                94-38657
                                   CIP

10 9 8 7 6 5 4 3 2 1

Contents

INTRODUCTION

For a long time now Sainte-Beuve's minor masterpiece *Volupté*, subtitled here *The Sensual Man*, has been known chiefly by hearsay, even by specialists. Even when it was published in 1834, it was discussed more widely than it was read—hearsay again!

There is little doubt that this was because it was covertly—and correctly—identified as a roman à clef, an exposé of Sainte-Beuve's relationship with Victor and Adèle Hugo. From 1827 to 1834, he had been known as a close friend of Victor's, and also, it was rumored, a suitor for Adèle's affections. Given her husband's womanizing, she would be vulnerable to an ambitious young man. From 1833 to 1837, she was, according to reports, Sainte-Beuve's mistress, though this would have been too late to affect the composition of the novel.[1]

But the novel is much more than a roman à clef. Its autobiographical aspect being then, as it is now, probably its least relevant aspect.

Readers open to the entire novel find that the intersecting triangles form merely the geometric base for a disturbing psychological study, interwoven and sometimes overshadowed by a turbulent historical era. Amaury, a priest for approximately two decades when he begins his confession, loves the wife of his patron the Marquis de Couaën. Amaury, in turn, is fancied by another socialite and treated as a prospective fiancé as by a young noblewoman of his neighborhood. (On prostitutes he is simply besotted.) But his royalist neighborhood is the Vendée of western maritime France plus Brittany and Normandy, and the novel really gets started in 1796 when the Republican armies lift their siege of this region. All threads become convincingly tangled by the time Georges Cadoudal, Jean Victor Marie Moreau, and Joseph Pichgrue are arrested for their plot to kill Napoleon, in February and March 1804, and the novel is essentially over with the victory at Ulm, on October 5, 1805, although approximately two

vii

more years are summarized before the final scenario. The personal
and political continually and jointly compete for reader attention.
Although Amaury worries that his recollections are leading him back
to sinful thoughts, he persists in researching the past he squandered
before he received his calling.

When we consider how successfully Sainte-Beuve weaves together
strands of psychological interest, historical significance—not to mention plot, characterization, and rhapsodic interludes—we realize in
amazement that its various aspects both draw on and contribute to
at least four French fictional traditions: the Rousseauistic personal
confession of mixed motives and misdeeds; the gossipy exposé with
names changed, a genre that Musset and Sand, for example, would
shortly thereafter use against each other;[2] the historical novel of
adventure that becomes a fiasco for a protagonist like Stendhal's Julien
Sorel or Flaubert's Frédéric Moreau;[3] and an examination of memory,
both voluntary and involuntary, that Proust continues, calling his
first sketch of *A la recherche du temps perdu* appropriately *Contre
Sainte-Beuve*.[4]

Was this novel almost too much of a tour de force for its own
continued readership? Possibly.

But just as possibly it may have too little of each. First, although
the narrator and his confessional may be the aspect that will intrigue
readers most now because of its complex ambiguities, the confession
is a composite because the priestly persona is. This persona is Sainte-
Beuve himself and contains elements of his sometime spiritual mentor
Félicité de Lammenais (1782–1854) and sometime friend Ulric Gut-
tinger (1785–1866). It is not a "true" confession of a "real" person.
Second, readers learn few details of his relationship to Victor and
Adèle Hugo, partly because the characters have composite prototypes
and representations and develop by an internal logic. For example,
Monsieur de Couaën, Amaury's royalist patron, stands for Victor
Hugo and, likewise, a royalist acquaintance from the Vendée. Adèle
Hugo is split: Madame de Couaën stands for Adèle during the period
of Sainte-Beuve's infatuation; Madame R. stands for Adèle at a later
stage of their liaison. The Vendée prototypes bring us to the third
aspect, the historical time period itself. It was veritably shared information for Sainte-Beuve's first readers. The abortive assassination
attempt on Napoleon occurred in the year of his birth. For the French
to read of Vendée in 1834 would be like Americans now reading about
the Vietnam War, or Americans in 1890 reading about the Civil War.
Furthermore, in a broader perspective on the Napoleonic legacy, the
Vendée uprising is somewhat peripheral. Finally, as an examination of

memory, Sainte-Beuve was not only limited by the lexicon of the time (no Bergson or Freud, for example, had given names to mental states), he had to write like a priest and express the psychological disturbances in religious terms like "soul" and "faith" or use flamboyant extended metaphors, suitable for inspiring the presumed single reader of this confession. It is germane to mention that Sainte-Beuve was considered such a good Latinist that he was appointed to the chair of Latin poetry at the Collège de France.[5] His French is reminiscent of Latin. His use of language for its etymological meanings in period sentences adds substance to Amaury's unwitting self-characterization, but the antiquated aura achieved posed a risk for continued readership.

This meant that *Volupté* was by design veritably an eighteenth-century pastiche when published in 1834, and would definitely have seemed old-fashioned by the time of Sainte-Beuve's death in 1869.[6]

It could be said that Sainte-Beuve planned the novel's obsolescence. Further, and somewhat ironically, he surely contributed to its being pushed aside or covered over by the masterpieces of Realism and Naturalism. As a major arbiter of public taste, as an independent scholar whose common sense was nearly as well developed as his erudition, he himself preferred writing that observed verisimilitude. For example, he followed Flaubert's career closely; his articles on *Salammbô* and his subsequent correspondence with Flaubert are among our most important documents on French Realism. Naturally critical and intent upon "facts," he appreciated the Realists, who dislodged Romanticism in the novel, and the Parnassians, who dislodged Romanticism in poetry. Thus, *Volupté* became an inadvertent casualty of changing fashions in literature.

He has stayed in the canon as a critic and historian. Coining the expression *"Tel arbre, tel fruit,"* he attacked biography, history, and literature with an instinct and talent for semiotic decoding before the fact. It is not surprising that he could write a novel with psychoanalytic encoding in a style we might now label baroque.

But it is most likely that this novel went into eclipse because the rest of Sainte-Beuve's oeuvre overpowered and marginalized it. That is, the extent and impact of his work as a critic and literary historian simply made this novel an anomaly. In 1852, nearly two decades after publication, Musset reportedly termed *Volupté* "a marvelous psychological novel, one of the most impressive books of our times."[7] The novel stayed in print during Sainte-Beuve's lifetime and was reissued for its centenary in 1934 and for the centenary of the author's death.[8] But when compared with his history of *Port-Royal*, his biographies of women writers, and, above all, his *Causeries de Lundi,* regular columns for *Le Constitutionnel, Le Moniteur,* and *Le Temps,* not to mention his regular contributions to *La Revue de deux mondes* and *La Revue de Paris,* a single novel, a genre he was not to use again, was bound to slip out of the canon.

A writer with such a motto would also inspire his scholars to look for him in Amaury—just as his contemporaries had. He is there more in attitude than in event. Like Amaury, he had lost his father before birth. Unlike Amaury, he had not lost his mother. Sainte-Beuve's mother was a tough, clearheaded lady who made sure her only child received the best education available. She was forty when he was born in 1804 at Boulogne-sur-mer (Pas-de Calais or the English Channel). She sent him to Paris to board at the Collège Charlemagne and subsequently the Collège Bourbon. She moved to Paris when he was graduated in 1823. In 1832, she bought a three-story dwelling at 11 rue de Montparnasse, her home until death and subsequently her son's until his own death.[9] Her death in November 1850 resulted in severe disorientation for the forty-six-year-old author, for she had been the axis of his well-being.

Unlucky in love, looks, and lifestyle,[10] her son loved learning and could tell that the life of the mind, actualized as a career of a professional intellectual, was his path to success. In 1829, at age twenty-five, he published a French *Werther: Vie, poésies, et pensées de Joseph Delorme.* He made the right connections and easily convinced older, influential contemporaries of his brilliance and incisiveness. Writing poetry did not hold his attention, no more than the novel, but writing reviews of the creative works of others did. It also helped with contacts and career advancement. When he was elected to the Académie française in 1845, it was Hugo himself who had the task of receiving him. Richard Chadbourne believes we can read an allusion to *Volupté* in Hugo's address.[11]

We can do better than allude to it. We can remove it from hearsay. It is time to reappraise *Volupté* and reinsert it in the canon. What seemed passé fifty to sixty years after publication, especially in a literature so attuned to the vanguard as is French literature, can be seen over a century and a half later for what it is. (Mallarmé's pronouncement on Poe—*"Tel qu'en Lui-même l'éternité le change"*—is true for Sainte-Beuve as well.) It is a rediscovered, authentic period piece. For example, today we would not be impatient with the dénouement of Amaury's romance, romantic in the popular sense because it is what we might expect in Romantic novels, such as those by Hugo or Sir Walter Scott.

In addition, *Volupté* manifests a theme much discussed in contemporary literature, a theme we have not mentioned up until now but one that permeates Amaury's chief relationships and which leaps out and nearly stuns present-day readers: abuse of women. Its florid style, which enforces close reading, encourages reading across the text and consequently helps us detect this meaning that is expressed only by its opposite. Amaury, as a sixty-year-old priest, is complacently confessing his abuse of women to an erring younger friend. He expresses regret, hardly sorrow, at having abused women. But he couches this regret in what for him and his author is a larger and more important perspective, for us a more damning perspective: these abusive relationships could have cost him his soul and salvation, and he does not want his younger friend to run the same risk. We cannot read this confession as Sainte-Beuve probably expected, but the novel has gained in the process, and here, as often happens, translation has shown the way.

Translation is particularly well suited for reading against the text, even against the author or authorial narrator. This is because the translator while reading the printed text must always look for what may not be expressed but is rhetorically and/or culturally implicit, and, with an older text, what a rhetorical tradition and/or cultural history has inserted in the meantime.

This is why translation tends to bring a writer's strategy to the surface. Whatever game a translator plays with a text, consciously or intuitively, the transfer process enforces analysis, making the translator get inside the text *and* back away from it. However much a translator is enthralled by a text, he or she cannot be lured along, charmed and unthinking, while translating. He or she must check each agreement, each antecedent, each gender—and with Sainte-Beuve, certainly, be on guard for double-entendres that, if unidentified, would damage the tone.

For these reasons, translation represents an opportunity to make new a work long in eclipse, forcing even specialists to look at it again with fresh eyes.

Translator's Note

Any piece of writing poses unique challenges for a translator. *Volupté* certainly does. It is a novel that enjoins deference. The readers must stay with Amaury and indulge his behavioral idiosyncracies, chiefly displayed through verbal flourishes.

The chief lexical challenge is cultural and historical. Inasmuch as this is a psychological novel antedating Freud, Amaury often discusses mental states where a writer of the past century would call on technical language. He relies on elaborate and extended metonymies, conceits, and, most troublesome for a translator, *"âme," "esprit,"* and *"moi."* These words have a referential range that changes with the times and tends to be dissipated. Sainte-Beuve exploits grammatical gender. This can be a help in pairing pronouns and their antecedents. It can also be a trap set by the author, for example, *"amour"* as a masculine noun, referred to as *"il"* and *"lui"* throughout a very long sentence, can modulate in reference and refer as well to Amaury, especially when he is speaking of himself in the third person. The same can happen with *"âme,"* which as a feminine noun can set up a sequence of *"elle"* and *"lui"* that starts referring to a woman. Generally my strategy here has been to repeat nouns when the reference would be unclear in English.[12]

The chief syntactical challenge is linked to grammatical gender. French and English do not decline nouns, and neither language has an ablative case. This lack, however, does not prevent Sainte-Beuve from pushing present participles into service. Nor do French and English really have a proper vocative case, albeit Sainte-Beuve has Amaury indulge in many an apostrophe.

However, where the distinctive voice of Sainte-Beuve's Amaury is concerned, my overall strategy was to err on the side of respect, staying close to the lexicon, sometimes using cognates where they would not usually be indicated. After all, Amaury likes learned words and the Latin meaning. I frequently calqued the syntax. This person is formal and overwrought, staying calm only with great exercise of will.

Far more troublesome was the exercise of will required of the translator. Because of the nature of the testimony, I had to practice the neutrality of a courtroom interpreter. I could not rely solely on Amaury to know what transpired but had to role-play with the victims—or simply the objects of his feelings of superiority—while withholding judgment on him. Amaury sees the other people as both objects for his gratification and subjects with whom he can somewhat identify after the fact. As translator I had to situate myself in the midst of the recorded dialogues and the references of the meditations. I am also the "second reader," the friend being addressed once removed.[13] Above all, the translator must defer to Sainte-Beuve's text and resist the temptation to clarify its ambiguities by overinterpretation. Even if Sainte-Beuve may not have been entirely aware of all that he was saying or what his words would say later unbeknownst to him, his daimon of inspiration—or the demon of his sensuality—was surely clairvoyant.

Clairvoyance is a feature of a minor masterpiece. *Volupté. The*

Sensual Man should sound like a nineteenth-century priest, concealing his passion in eighteenth-century rhetoric, but it is eerily akin to many a Postmodern sensualist whose intense self-study conceals him from himself.

Notes

1. The break with Victor Hugo was complete by 1834. Raphaël Molho, who edited *Volupté* in 1969, believes that the actual affair lasted from 1832 to 1837, with a brief renewal in 1840. In *L'ordre et les ténèbres ou la naissance d'un mythe du XVIIe siècle,* he puts the year of composition as 1831; this would be during the tender friendship.

2. Musset, *La Confession d'un enfant du siècle* (1836); Sand, *Elle et Lui* (1859).

3. Stendhal, *Le rouge et le noir* (1830); Flaubert, *L'Education sentimentale* (1869).

4. *Recherche* (1913–26) and *Contre Sainte-Beuve* (1908–09, published in 1954).

5. He found the students at the Collège so rude that he moved to the Ecole Normale Supérieure where he lectured on French literature for four years.

6. Molho, *op. cit.* argues that Saint-Beuve took refuge in the seventeenth century. Roger Fayolle, a Marxist critic, argues that Sainte-Beuve mythologized the eighteenth century; *Sainte-Beuve et le XVIIIe siècle ou comment les révolutions arrivent.*

7. As reported in Louise Colet's *Lui* (1869).

8. The Library of Congress holds seventeen editions. It holds also *Voluptuosidad,* trans. by J. Huici Miranda (Buenos Aires: Espasa Calpe, 1952).

9. She bought the house the year his affair with Adèle began, but neither that domicile nor his hotel permitted intimate visitors. According to Harold Nicholson in *Sainte-Beuve,* the couple went to shabby hotels. Although he did not live with his mother, he visited and lunched with her almost daily.

10. He was a hypospadiac, but while this condition may have counterindicated marriage, it did not seem to hinder sexual activity.

11. Boston: Twayne Series, 1977.

12. Occasionally I translated *"un amour"* as *"a lover"* or *"a man in love."* A plural that refers to a couple is even more troublesome. In Chapter XVII, Amaury contrasts his silent love for Madame de Couaën with that he had for Madame R. . . , a public liaison: *"Mais il est un autre amour plus à l'usage des âmes blasées et amollies,"* finessed as "But there is another kind of love more suited for the worn and world-weary." *"Madame R. . . et moi, nous étions un peu de ces âmes"* ("Our souls, hers and mine, were a little like that").

13. Peter Newmark, British translation theorist, has named the translator the "second reader," the first reader being any reader in the original language.

Works Consulted

Allem, Maurice, ed. *Volupté*. (Centenary of publication.) Paris: Garnier Classiques, 1934.

———. *Sainte-Beuve et Volupté*. Paris: Edgar Malfère, 1935.

Benoît-Lévy, Edmond. *Sainte-Beuve et Mme Victor Hugo*. Paris: Presses universitaires de France, 1926.

Chadbourne, Richard. *Sainte-Beuve*. Boston: Twayne, 1977.

Derré, Jean-Paul. *Lammenais, ses amis et le mouvement des idées de l'époque romantique 1824–34*. Paris: C. Klincksieck, 1962.

Dechamps, Jules Albert. *Sainte-Beuve et le sillage de Napoléon*. Liège: H. Vaillant-Carmanne, 1922.

Duncan, Philip A. "Pillar and Pool; the Metaphor of Amaury's Bipolar Nature in Sainte-Beuve's *Volupté*," *Romance Notes* 23 (1983): 232–37.

Fayolle, Roger. *Sainte-Beuve et le XVIIIe siècle ou comment les révolutions arrivent*. Paris: Armand Colin, 1972.

LeHir, Yves. *L'Originalité littéraire de Sainte-Beuve dans "Volupté."* Paris: Sociètè d'enseignement supérieur; 1953.

Marechal, Christian. *Le Clef de "Volupté*. Paris: Arthur Savaete, 1905.

Molho, Raphaël, ed. *Volupté*. (Centenary of Sainte-Beuve's death.) Paris: Garnier Flammarion, 1969.

———. *L'ordre et les ténèbres ou la naissance d'un mythe du XVIIe siècle*. Paris: Armand Colin, 1972.

Nicholson, Harold. *Sainte-Beuve*. New York: Doubleday, 1957.

Rose, Marilyn Gaddis. "Translation and *le différand*." *Meta* 35 (1990).

———. "Translation and Language Games," in *Translation Perspectives*, ed. Dennis J. Schmidt, 5 (1990).

Troubet, Jules Auguste. *Souvenirs du dernier secrétaire de Sainte-Beuve*. Paris: Calmann Levy, 1890.

Preface

The true purpose of this book is to analyze a tendency, call it a passion, even a vice, and the part of the soul that this vice dominates and colors, this part—that is languishing, idle, clinging, secret and private, mysterious and furtive, dreamy to the point of subtilization, tender to the point of laxness. In short, the sensual, voluptuous part. Even so, the title *Volupté* still has the drawback of not indicating the sense intended and suggesting something more attractive than is the case. But the title used somewhat unthinkingly in the first edition could not be withdrawn subsequently. The editor of this work decided, moreover, that persons whose scruples would tend to make them stay away from such an equivocal title would really lose little in not reading a piece where the moral, serious as it is, is addressed only to less pure and less wary hearts. As for those, on the contrary, who would be attracted precisely by what would keep others away, since they will scarcely find anything they are looking for, the harm is slight. The author, the nonfictional character of the narrative, died a few years ago in North America where he held an eminent position. That is as much as we shall say. The literary executor, that is, the editor, and, if we may say so, in many respects the rhapsode, but a rhapsode always faithfully respecting these pages, before turning them over to the public, was held back by matters other than those of style and organization. Let us cite one of the questions of conscience he had to consider at length. Such a thought put into writing, detailed for a good, but quite confidential, end, a kind of general confession on a very ticklish point for the soul and in which the grave and tender character accuses himself so often of deviating from the severity of the task, will not such a thought go against Christian intentions, leaving thus the sick breast where the narrator had left it and where he wanted to effect a cure? This delicate course of treatment of such a vice *by its like*, should it be attempted other than covertly and in an especially determined and exceptional case? This is what I have pondered for a long time. Then, when I turned my eyes upon the times we live in, on the confusion of systems, desires, straying sentiments, confessions and exposures of all kinds, I came to the conclusion that the publication of a true story could scarcely be one more wrong, and that for some readers even some good could come of it.

1834   S.-B.

VOLUPTÉ
THE SENSUAL MAN

My friend, you are in despair. You know what the good is, and you desire to attain it, yet you think you are being borne away into a vortex of low acts and bad habits with no hope of return. You tell yourself that the twig is bent, that your past weighs you down and makes you fall, and when you remember an unhappy experience, it seems to you that your firmest resolutions must always give way under the slightest shock, like a door used so much that its worn hinges can only turn this way and that and lack even enough resistance to creak. However, you have confided in me often enough. Your failing is simple; your injury isolated. It is not from false knowledge, arrogant love of domination, or a factitious desire to bedazzle and impress that you have become obsessed. Your tastes are humble. Your modest heart, after the first intoxication of diverse doctrines, warned you that none contained the truth, although there were fragments of truth scattered throughout. You know that disputes cause consternation, that a more productive study for fruitful results must be warmed on a more intimate and viable hearth; that knowledge is not a shifting pile that needs either scaffolding or ceiling. It is an ocean full of perils and maelstroms once it stops reflecting the heavens. You know all this, my friend, and you have often said as much yourself in your letters or in our last talks and said it better than any argument I could reproduce here. Nor do you have any of those stupid artificial passions that are encrusted like monstrous or grotesque superfoetations on the bark of old societies. Your nature is genuine, and you have known how to stay sincere. Achieving at an early age an honorable degree of public esteem through your mind and talents, you appreciate such success at its true worth. You do not look upon that as a stepping-stone for climbing higher, and by no means do you use this fragile handle to try to put your hand on your future. Since you are exempt from so many false beliefs and so many heavy chains, and have such numerous resources, you would seem to be able to reach your destination, safe from shipwreck. Yet you still complain. You no longer believe in your own ability, in your goals, in yourself, and without there being anything for you to despair of, still you have, in my opinion, some cause for apprehension. One inclination alone, but the most perfidious and insinuating, has long led you astray, and you have imprudently succumbed. *Volupté*, sensuality, holds you in its thrall. A corrupted gift from the Creator, vestige, emblem, and pledge of another love, cherished and pernicious treasure that we must bear in holy ignorance, enshroud forever, if need be, beneath our dark cloaks, and which we must, if we are to make use of it, use chastely, like the purest white salt of the altar—sensuality from an early hour has been for you a shining vow, a flower damp with dew, a fragrant cluster of grapes where your desires mounted, the nourishment unique in essence, the crown of your youth. So your youth plucked sensuality. But your youth was not satisfied with this strange fruit, and once drowned in its perfume, your youth ceased to be either fresh or beautiful. Nevertheless, you persisted in pursuing what you had fled, pressing from these calyxes new fragrances that were just as quickly dissipated. Sensuality, which was at first an inexpressible seduction, developed by degrees into a habit, but its monotonous fatigue removed none of its power over you. You know in advance what it is worth, what it grants you after every experience in bitter disappointment and regret. But what can you do about it? It has broken out of the bonds that kept it pushed back in lower and unknown parts of you. It has seized your flesh. It courses through your blood, a serpent in your veins, swimming and flashing in your field of vision. One glance exchanged where it has a role is sufficient to undo the most austere resolutions. That is your failing. The first impulsive act made a place for habit, and habit, after some duration, and when no longer motivated by the violence that accompanies youth, is called vice. You sense the slope and slowly you slip. Hurry to get up, my friend. You must, and you can if you so will. Wean yourself just once, and you will be astonished as how thinkable a cure is. I myself have not always been the person you know now. Before reaching solid ground at the end of errors and developments of my meager faculties, at a destination more in conformity with a higher plan—before that decisive enthusiasm for truth, which you do me the honor of attributing to my nature, and this rude, active yet serene existence which did not come to me by magic, I lived, my young friend, a life undoubtedly rather similar to your own. I went through, like you, a long and cowardly moral malaise stemming from the same cause. The particular accidents which marked and changed its course perhaps resemble yours more than you suspect. After we have lived a little and made comparisons, we find our pride less in the way and we can see to what point our destinies, in their wretchedness, are basically the same. We think we conceal incomparable secrets in our breast; we flatter ourselves that we are the object of singular fatalities, and however little the hearts of others, even those we brush past in the street, are opened to us, we are amazed to see how similar all wretchedness is and how equivalent are our tricks and ruses. At the point of departure in the common flight of a single generation of youth, we seem to discern contemporaneous activities with diverse projections, bound to result in unheard-of differences. But with a little patience, soon we see these diverse curves bending in a kind of uniformity. All the blades of the sheaf will fall to the same degree, some to the right, some to the left. Blessed is the ripe grain that resounds on the threshing floor when detached and that finds mercy in the winnow of the Winnower!

Since the elements of our destinies, my friend, are nearly alike, and any complete human heart, in present-day society, passes through secret phases with only slightly varying forms and caprices, you should no more despair of yourself than you would take pride in extreme situations, deep distresses to which you were reduced in your youth. It is the outcome you should attend to. It is the world of intimate impression that you receive from these irregularities, and the practical morality you infer from them, that constitute our original and distinctive sign, our own merit, our virtue with the help of God. You have sounded me out indirectly more than once, my friend, on the time, already long lapsed, when I went through that crisis, which was salutary for me. I am going to give you a leisurely response today. In this species of forced retreat, where passing circumstances confine me, deprived of materials for study, surrounded by foreigners whose language I speak badly, I shall spend a few hours each day with you. I shall begin one last time to turn the pages of my heart, which are so moving I have not dared touch them for a very long time. I shall sort them for you one by one, without craft, without color, in the somewhat confused order in which I recall them. And, if later, you uncover some profitable application for yourself, I shall consider that I have not completely neglected the duties of my calling during these two or three months of inaction and solitude.

CHAPTER I

I was 17 or 18 when I started going out in society. Social life indeed had hardly resumed, since society was trying to put itself back together after the disasters of the Revolution. I had been isolated up to then, buried in the country, studying and daydreaming: serious, pious, and pure. My first communion had been very good, and during the two or three years following my religious fervor had not abated. My political beliefs were those of my family and province, the despoiled and proscribed minority. I adopted these beliefs in sorrowful and precocious meditation to seek from within my own resources the higher cause, the sense of these catastrophes which around me I heard accused as sudden accidents. It is an incalculable schooling for a sheltered child to be from birth and by the position of his immediate surroundings outside the movement of the times, not to take his first steps with the crowd in the midst of the celebration, and to approach present-day society from the sidelines with contradictory feelings that increase natural vigor and hasten maturity. Children who grow up in the thick of things, and whom all factors predispose to the reigning opinion, are consumed more quickly and for a long time mingle their first fire with the general enthusiasm. The excessive ease with which these young people figure out what will get them their way disperses and dissipates them. Resistance, on the contrary, pushes back, tries out, and makes the will say *I* early on. By the same token, in developing physical strength, it is not a matter of indifference if you are born on some beach and grow up in daily struggle with the ocean.

For me, those chaste years, which make up a veritable treasury, amassed without effort and held in surety against the corruption of life, were prolonged very far into puberty, and maintained in my soul, at the heart of a thought already strong, something simple, humble, and ingenuously puerile. When I think back on those years today, despite the calm God has restored to me, I am almost envious. I needed so little then for the holiest happiness. Silence, regular habits, work, and prayer: a favorite walkway where I went to read and dream towards noon, where I passed (without a notion of making a descent) from Montesquieu to Rollin; a shabby little room at the top of the house where I took refuge away from visitors and whose every object in its special place reminded me of a thousand successive tasks of study and devotion; a tile roof where I eternally cast my gaze, loving the rusty moss more than the green lawns. A corner of sky, wedged in the angle of two roofs, gave me its deep azure in my moods of sorrow as well as a setting for my visions of chaste love! Discreet and docile like this, with nourishment for my growing mind, I should have been sheltered from any evil. It touches me yet, and makes me smile with delight when I remember with what personal anxiety I followed the praiseworthy heroes of ancient history, the conquerors favored by God, whenever they were pagan: Cyrus, for example, or Alexander before his debauchery. As for those who came after Jesus Christ and whose careers had variations, my interest was double. I was on pins and needles as long as they stayed pagan or as soon as they inclined to heresy. Constantine and Theodosius alarmed me exceedingly. Tertulian's false start afflicted me, and I was overjoyed to learn that Zenobia died a Christian. But the heroes to whom I was especially attached with a passionate faith, free from fear, were the missionaries to the Indies, the Jesuits of the Reductions, humble and hardy confessors of the *Edifying Missionary Letters*. They were for me what for you and the other *enfants du siècle* were the glorious and disappointing names that you have cited: Barnave, Hoche, Madame Roland and Vergniaud. Tell me today yourself, do you believe my personages less great than the greatest of yours? And weren't mine purer than the purest of yours? In view of my sedentary and settled life, I had a particular predilection for the story of Monsieur Daguesseau as it was told by his son. And on that subject, let me add that the desire to learn Greek came to me as a result of stories by Daguesseau and Rollin, and because people around me could barely do more than figure out the letters, I attacked it tenaciously, without any help, and while studying it, I lulled myself with the thought of going soon to learn Greek in Paris, the only place it could be done. For me, Paris was the place in the world where Greek would have been easiest for me. That is all I saw in it. In that beginning were moments when I tied all the ambition and happiness of my future to being able to read Aesope fluently, by myself, on gloomy days under a poor attic roof, which would be like my own on one of those deserted streets where

Descartes had immured himself for three years. Now, how in that atmosphere of such regulated tastes, frugal imagination, and wholesome discipline, did the notion of sensuality gently spring into being? Because that was when it was born, gaining ground in me little by little, by a thousand twists and turns and beneath the most deceptive guises.

The master I had for Latin until I was around 13 was a man of extreme simplicity, totally ignorant of the ways of the world, yet highly qualified for what he had to teach me. Good Monsieur Ploa, delayed by a family matter at the moment of entering Orders, had only been tonsured. In mind, manners, and knowledge, he had stopped precisely at the boundary that any complete human being must cross for the human trial to take its course. As for him, by a felicitous exception, in the years where a mere contretemps retained him, he remained effortlessly with the modest tastes, classroom authors, schoolboy virtues, as well as the plainsong he had not given up, and the general opinions inculcated by his masters. No doubt had ever ruffled him, no passion had ever aroused his equable disposition where only a faint stirring of a ticklish and certainly justifiable vanity could be perceived as soon as he took up a meaning in Vergil or Cicero. The Revolution, which confined him for a while to our backwater, let me profit from his instruction. Later, when things appeared to have cleared up, he left us to be a professor of rhetoric at the grammar school in the small city of O———. For my part, submissive as I liked to be and full of confidence in his opinions, I went further, however, than the excellent Monsieur Ploa, and I sometimes ventured, as a point of pride, through readings he had forbidden himself. On this matter, moreover, his candor was singular. Never having read the fourth book of the *Aeneid* up till then, by some scruple abetted by sloth, even though the *Aeneid* hardly had left his pocket or his hands for a decade, he imagined that to read this book more fittingly, he should have me explicate it to him. I managed this perfectly. He even had me memorize and recite it. In this way I translated with him Horace's voluptuous odes to Pyrrha and Lydia. I knew Ovid's *Tristia*, and since I frequently encountered certain Latin expressions that Monsieur Ploa rendered generally as "liberties," I asked one day point-blank what he meant by that. I received the answer that I would know when I was older. I was stopped short, blushing furiously. After two or three such questions that made me bite my tongue, I quit asking. But when I explicated the poets aloud for him, there were obscure and sensually suspect passages which gave me a beaded brow

in advance and I bounded over as if there were burning coals beneath
my feet.

When I was around 15, I stayed for six weeks at the château of
Count————, an old friend of my father's. During that time, when I
was so sad and homesick, I gave in to my dangerous penchant for
tenderness, hitherto restrained by my regular habits. An inexplicable
ennui for my house at home took hold of me. I went to the depths of
the thickets, weeping copiously and reciting the 136th Psalm *Super
flumina Babylonis*: "By the rivers of Babylon, there we sat down; yea,
we wept, when we remembered Zion." My hours rolled by in a
monotonous obliviousness, and they often had to call me for meals by
shouting throughout the park. In the evening in the drawing room I
sat in the circle listening to *Clarissa*, which the estimable Mademoiselle
de Parkes was having her nephew read aloud, and my distraction
continued comfortably through it all as if through languishing and
plaintive music. When I returned home after this absence, I started
reading elegaic Latin authors besides Ovid. The melancholic passages
especially pleased me, and I repeated ad infinitum down my path, like
a sweet tune you hum unconsciously, these four lines from Propertius:/Elegies, book II, 16/:

> Ac veluti folia arentes liquere corollas,
> Quae passim calathis strata natare vides,
> Sic nobis qui nunc magnum spiramus amantes
> Forsitan includet crastina fata dies.

I also repeated without too much comprehension, like an amorous
motif of revery, the beginning of a song by Anacreon: *"Bathyle est
un riant ombrage."* A new unknown world was already stirring in
my heart.

However, I had no opportunity to see members of the opposite
sex who were my own age or near it. I was, moreover, ferocious about
such an encounter, precisely because of my budding desires. The
slightest allusion to this kind of subject matter in a conversation was
torture for me and like a disconcerting personal gibe. I got terribly
disturbed and turned a thousand colors. In the end I had become so
susceptible on this point that the fear of losing face should the
conversation touch upon morality or honest sensuality continually
obsessed me, and poisoned in advance chats during or after dinner.
Such excessive modesty in itself already had something sick about it.
This superstitious shame indicated something reprehensible. And it
was true, if vis-à-vis the universe I repressed these vague and disturbing sources of emotion down to the third well of my soul, I would

return to them entirely too secretly and complacently. I listened all too curiously, spellbound to their murmurs.

From 17 to 18, when I entered upon a somewhat different routine, when I began to cultivate more, and for myself, several of my country neighbors and to do frequent errands, entailing stays of several days in the city, this *idée fixe* on the sensual aspect of things stayed with me. But in going deeper, it materialized in a strange form, completely malicious and chimerical, too singular to be explained in detail. Let me simply say that I came to the opinion one day that I was affected by a kind of ugliness which would rapidly increase and disfigure me. A chilling despair followed upon this alleged discovery. I went through the motions of animation, I still smiled and practiced my expressions and gestures, but in my heart I was no longer living. At times I was astonished that others had not already realized from my face the same alteration which I thought I felt. The glances I received seemed to me from one day to the next more curious or slightly mocking. Among the young men of my acquaintance I was continually taken up comparing the silliest of faces to my own and envying theirs. There were entire weeks when I was doubly irrational and when the fear of not being loved in time, of seeing myself cut off from all sensuality by a rapid onslaught of ugliness, gave me no respite. I was like a man who, at the beginning of a banquet, has received a secret letter announcing his dishonor and who, however, holds his own with the other guests, foreseeing with each person who enters the chance that the news will spread and unmask him. But all that, my friend, was only a particular detour, an unexpected ruse of the siren born in us. She slips in at the beginning and wants to triumph in our hearts. It was only a perfidious means of pulling me abruptly away from the simple images of ideal and chaste beauty, of bringing me more quickly to sensual attraction by showing me the prospect of deformity. It was the least suspect and quite gripping manner of renewing the eternal flattery which impells us toward our inclinations and instilling in me a air of panic without revolting my principles too much. Those debilitating bits of advice to hurry, to gather the first flower in time and to use from that very evening the passing grace of life.

The sole result of this crazed preoccupation was thus to pitch me unawares very far from the point when it found me. My gentle moral regime did not get reestablished. My wholesome habits underwent alteration. That idea of Woman, once evoked in my eyes, remained present, invaded my being and broke the train of earlier thoughts. I felt my religion pale. I told myself that for the moment it was essential to be a man, to apply somewhere (did it matter where?) my faculties

of passion, to take possession of myself and one of the objects that
any youth desires. Of course I would have to repent afterwards and
confess this abuse. One particular difficulty [   ], suddenly revealed
to me by the technical readings I was doing at the time, added to my
embarrassment and complicated it more than I would know how to
express. I was alerted to an obscure but real obstacle at the same time
that the chimeras of my imagination shouted for me to hurry. I have
no fear, my friend, in letting you glimpse these shameful miseries, so
that you will not despair over your own, which are perhaps no less
petty, and because very often so many men who act high and mighty
in the decisive moments of their destiny obey secret motivations of no
more consequence. You would be dumbfounded if you could see,
bared, how many such hardly mentionable circumstances have influenced morality and the first determinations of the most endowed
natures. A birthmark, a club foot, a crooked torso, an unbalanced
figure, a fold of the skin—and one becomes good or fatuous, mystic
or libertine because of something like that. In the state of strange
weakness where as a result of the disorders of our fathers and relatives,
we have received our will power, such grains of sand, scattered here or
there at the beginning of the road, have made us rear up or turn
around. Eventually we cover over that poverty with magnificent
sophisms. In my case, who knows how many hours of burning mania,
at the age of intelligence and strength, I spent alone, heartsick, biting
my fingernails, pressing into my flesh this imaginary grit that I
thought I felt. I, who would have joyously paid then the price of my
eternity for the eradicated obstacle, the easy seduction, the beauty of
the hair and face, repeated with the poet that aphorism of the adulterous Trojan: "The lovable gifts of Venus cannot be rejected." When I
recall how I roused myself from these idolatrous moments of cowardice by short fits and starts up to the effort of the cloister and the
asperities of Calvary! I would have thus experienced in this paltry
disarray of powers of the soul whatever is tossed around inside us in
such monstrous contradictions, whatever is deposited by accident of
the contagious and impure and from which can result our fall, Oh
my God!—I no longer give so much credence to men's pompous
explanations. I am not going to look very high, even in the noblest
hearts, for the secret origin of these miseries that are dissimulated or
exaggerated. But without insisting too much, my friend, on what
would make many a forehead blush, especially without usurping its
mysteries from He who alone can probe our nether regions, I shall
speak to you here only about myself. To that first chimerical disorder,
which no one ever suspected, were attached the principle of my errors

and the deviation in my life which lasted entirely too long. From that moment on, self-love was ashamed of docile simplicity and without undertaking a legitimate revolt, lost no opportunity to sprinkle doubts like so many capricious stones on the revered shady groves where my childhood was nurtured. Gradually political activity took the place of piety, and my personal relationships with the gentry of the neighborhood involved me in the endeavors of emigrés and princes. Thus, by a diversion, I could go about changing myself rapidly to suit my dominant motivation. And when this kind of moral hysteria, which lasted a good year altogether, had dissipated, when I recognized, with outbursts of laughter, that I had been duped by my fantasy alone, my flow of ideas was no longer the same, and the acquired impressions stayed with me.

CHAPTER II

During those frequent comings and goings of my daily errands in the country, I used to like to turn my horse off at La Gastine, a large old farm house, scarcely two leagues away. The Greneuc family that owned it had lived there for some years, and their warm welcome always brought me their way. At the same time I should hardly dare claim that the attraction of that company was to be attributed solely to Monsieur and Madame de Greneuc, a venerable couple, tried by misfortune, displaying virtues of bygone days. They were good to listen to on several chapters of former days. The wife talked about the Mesdames Royales to whom she had once been presented; the husband, about Monsieur de Penthièvre, whom he had served as second squire and to whose sainted memory he made a cult. Monsieur de Greneuc, moreover—his lofty, perfectly preserved frame, his head of the barely bowed white wolf, the steady sweep of his eye, his movements still quick and exact—made a splendid hunting companion who felicitously balanced my inexperience and often wore out my young legs. But what made me seek his company especially, I freely admit, was that this worthy gentleman and his wife were guardians of their seventeen-year-old granddaughter Mademoiselle Amélie de Liniers. There was another granddaughter also, Amélie's cousin-german, still a child, six or seven at most, sweet Madeleine de Guémio, for whom the older girl acted as governess and mother. The parents of both orphans had fallen victim to the furious turmoil, both fathers, even Madame de Guémio herself, on the scaffold. Madame de Liniers had survived her husband by two years, and her dying eyes at least could rest on her daughter, already blossoming, sheltered from the storm. Thus, two old people and the two children made up that household. A revolution had swept between the extremes of age and youth, and the generation in flower meant to join the two had been swept away.

Four heads in the family, but the best-developed and most whole, had disappeared. It was a sight full of charm, lending itself to fertile reflections, to see Mademoiselle Amélie standing between her grandparents in their armchairs and little Madeleine on her low chair, unceasingly taken up with either the two elder or the younger, with unalterable patience and good nature, whether answering the child's questions or paying attention for the 100th time to the ceremonies of 1770 or the alms of Monsieur de Penthièvre. I can still see that dark, low-ceilinged room on the ground floor (the building had only one story), even lower than ground level because you went down two steps with leaded casements overlooking the garden and the iron benches outside. In choosing this rather uncomfortable place for their residence, Monsieur de Greneuc, whose fortune had remained considerable, had wished above all to avoid the risk of a more imposing dwelling, given the far from stable circumstances. When I would enter this familiar room from the back threshold at each visit, I could admire the contrast of such fresh youth in the midst of so much decay, and the genuine harmony of virtue, calm, and affection which reigned among these beings united by blood, and brought closer together than was even natural, by recent misfortunes. When I went in, my chair was already out ready to receive me, its back to the door, vis-à-vis Monsieur de Greneuc, to the left of Madame de Greneuc, to the right of little Madeleine, who separated me from Mademoiselle Amélie. It was she who would hear the horse's hooves in the court, although there were no windows on that side of the room. She would pull out the chair and take her seat again so that when I appeared, I was always expected and no one would rise. In answer to my deep bow, she would point to my place with a graceful gesture. Welcomed like that, on a footing of gentle familiarity and affectionate habit, I felt from the first that we were simply continuing the conversation started the day before or the day before that. I related the recent news from town, the important political and military events of which there was no dearth, or the active schemes of our friends in the environs. I would bring a few books to Mademoiselle Amélie, books of devotion, travel or history, for she had a solid and cultivated mind. Thanks to the care of her dying mother, her first education had been extraordinarily fine, although of necessity quite simplified in this solitude. After a quarter of an hour passed in these novelties and exchanges, it was usually our turn to listen to the grandparents' stories and reenter into the detail of those olden manners and morals. Mademoiselle Amélie and I enjoyed this; we even encouraged it a little by a conspiracy that had a hint of mischief. In this kind of conversational game in which we were partners, our venerable interlocutors did not suspect any trap, and since their memory found only too much to talk about anyway, they could hardly complain. But when as one thing led to another in their expanse of memory, Monsieur and Madame de Greneuc touched upon macabre circumstances where so large a part of themselves had been rent, there, gradually, every smile faded and every question faltered. United in the same feeling of ineffable mourning, we listened as if down on our knees. Tears rolled from every lid, and only little de Guémio could break the awkward silence by some sweetly innocent and naive remark.

Do not be surprised, my friend, to glimpse me already in a light so different from what my age and present state would allow you to suppose. I knew the common lot of man. Aside from having been withdrawn from society, passing without interruption from the first studious retreat of childhood to successive engagements and to the formidable stages of the ministry, aside from having been reared, educated, and dedicated in the same enclosure and never having known as a pleasurable extreme, after the divine joy of the altar, anything but two handball games a day and long walks on Wednesday. Outside that, I hardly can conceive of cases of frailty which, almost all, in their movement and their beginning resemble one another. It is difficult for a feeling organism in its shortest encounter with society not to receive tender imprints, not to bear some kind of testimony to objects. Once the eyes are directed to this kind of attraction, the rest follows. The awakening has begun. The heart becomes involved while flattering itself that it is staying free. It is soon a self-exacerbating wound. Soon it triumphs, or in other words, is cured only by more wounding. And you find yourself thrown far from the light, gentle, and carefree beginnings.

Madamoiselle de Liniers was not one of those beauties whose mere appearance overwhelms and stuns the senses, although she was a genuine beauty. Noble in bearing, with regular features and a clear complexion, she brought to the society of her grandparents, and to her care of little Madeleine, a perfectly gentle submission of her entire person, and very early on she had taught her own passionate sensitivity, innate enthusiasm to obey a severe inner law. I appreciated these inner merits and the charm I felt in seeing her grew. Sometimes, when I had come early in the morning to take Monsieur de Greneuc hunting, I glimpsed the granddaughter on her knees, lacing the old man's gaiters. In my eyes, that momentary pose expressed completely her life of duty and simplicity. There were other times, too, at the same morning hours when, arriving by a fresh September sun, with my rifle on my shoulder, I had come upon her in the garden with her beehives, not yet dressed to receive. The domesticated bees swarmed around her, blond above her blond head, and seemed to applaud her voice. But my dog, who had followed me into the garden despite my order, recognized her and bounded joyously barking towards her, jumping heedlessly, trying to snatch the swarm. Instead the swarm twisted, buzzing twice as loud, rising in a slow cadence into a beam of sunshine.

What made our relationship attractive was that it was undefined, and the delicate bond that floated between us, having never been forced, could go in either direction, be ignored or felt, could escape, as desired, in the mutual enjoyment that favors budding tenderness. Most often when we were chatting tête-à-tête, we did not use each other's names, because none would have been in tune with the vague yet special feeling we had. In front of other people, the accent was always in place to correct what was too ceremonious in imposed usage, and a slight affectation that we put in the tone seemed to imply that between ourselves we had a right to less ceremony. But once alone, we were ordinarily guarded, dispensing with any name, happy to follow singly, side by side, the thread of our conversation, and that very ease, which, to tell the truth, was not without some embarrassment, was one more grace granted in our situation, a mysterious nuance. Few people came to La Gastine and only rarely. Such a life of peaceful isolation would not otherwise have been so prolonged, and excitement from the outside would have quickly extracted what future passion it was hiding. One day at a hunting party at Saint-Hubert, some 15 persons of the environs had met at the *rond-point*. Some women, including Mademoiselle Amélie, had come in riding habits. The movement of the trail, the morning freshness of air and sky, the momentum of conversation rising and falling every moment, the self-confidence that is awakened so lightheartedly in such circumstances, a trace of rivalry that, after all, is inevitable in a group of young men and women intoxicated me, emboldened me to the point that I seized a moment when the galloping company had slowed down a little to try, with a rather gauche pretext of sudden jealousy, to force a change in what until then had remained implicit and obscure between us. But she, instead of listening to me seriously as she usually would, and making me ashamed if necessary, excited also by the wanton atmosphere of the occasion, abruptly spurred her horse on ahead of me and escaped as soon as she realized what I was leading up to. And every time I tried to start the conversation again, her horse lunged forward by my third sentence. The wind carried away the rest. This teasing, modulating into bursts of laughter, finally exasperated me. Towards evening, when we returned to La Gastine accompanied by several members of the party, I played the haughty and indifferent and acted terribly taken up with talking to the young lady from Breuil, to whom I had attached myself. Mademoiselle Amélie, at that, serious and almost anxious, passed back and forth in the little drawing room where we had withdrawn from general conversation. But I for my part let my fingers roam distractedly over the clavecin where I was standing, thus covering my idle conversation so that she could not make out anything. But this manuever seemed too pathetic to me, and I returned to the room where almost everybody else was, and since there was only one free chair, which Mademoiselle Amélie indicated to me for a seat, I proposed it to her with an expressive glance. At first she refused. I insisted with the same glance. She sat down immediately, as if subjugated by a rapid thought, pronouncing "*oui*" under her breath. A quarter hour later I moved to get up and leave. She came over and said in a gentle, steady voice, sure of being obeyed: "You shall not leave." And I stayed. That was the only answer I ever got from my questions that day. Those were her vows.

I only wanted, my friend, to tell you about my youth with its principal crises and results in a way that would be profitable for you, and now I see that from the first steps, I let myself be carried away by enchanting flights of memory. They were slumbering when I thought they had vanished. But at the least movement in the crannies of my consciousness, the least beam of light directed upon them made them rise like dust of innumerable atoms demanding to shine. In any soul that began living early, the past has deposited its debris in successive tombs which the lawn on the surface can consign to oblivion. But as soon as you plunge into your heart to scrutinize the ages, you become apprehensive of what it contains. There are so many worlds within us!

At least, these memories that I catch myself pursuing into their tender flirtations, are they not entirely too guilty for a man who has renounced life and do they hold no more peril for me, O Lord? Is it never late enough in life? Are we never far enough advanced along the way to be able to turn our head with impunity toward the life we have left, without having to fear the softheartedness that insinuates itself, that slips in during one last glance? With my pretension to standing tall and strengthening the youth of someone else, shouldn't I instead keep one eye on my sealed scars, keep my two hands on my chest and stomach, for fear of some violent assault, always lurking in ambush? There is no doubt, Lord, that the heart where You dwell contains no ferocity. It overflows with tenderness and loving tolerance. The heart is commanded to love. But this must always be in view of loving You. But when it happens that the heart reaninates the shades of people who were dear and expands in memory toward the past, then serious repentance will inevitably blend its tearful intercession with the involuntary sighs that our weakness keeps alive. Prayer then must drop its purifying dew. At this price alone is the Christian permitted to give in to remembrance, and I can justify only in this way the return I am undertaking this once for the last time, my God!

During this period, when my heated brain, emerging from an uncomplicated childhood, had suddenly filled me with gross fumes, I heaped up pell-mell many a dream, and strange ideas of love came to me. At the same time, the fear of arriving too late set me secretly on fire with brutal and immediate desire, which, if it had dared to manifest itself, would have hardly been embarrassed by choice. On the other hand, I indulged in refining the most romantic projects. I considered subtle passions drawn from all kinds of enticements. But at no moment in this vacillation did permissible feeling, modest and pure, have a place, and I gradually lost the obvious idea of locating happiness there. The effect of this state was cruelly felt in the attachment I have just been discussing, my friend, an attachment so appropriate, it would seem, to hold a heart like mine, reared in pious solitude and a novice in the ways of the world. Whatever increasing charm I might find in cultivating that attachment, tightening the bond day by day, I quickly realized that my definitive vow would not let itself be chained to it. Beyond the horizon of this star so dear, behind the vapor of this cloud so white, my anxious soul still glimpsed a destiny full of storms for the future. Now I did not say to myself that my life could get along without Mademoiselle Amélie and still be crowned with happiness. But while lending myself to a pleasant hope of union and the imperceptible habit that would nourish it, in my thoughts I postponed the date until after unidentified events. The very virtues of that noble creature, her natural prudence, which enveloped her as needed by some reserve, everything that would have made her actually desirable to a man who deserved her, had instead the opposite effect on my imagination, which was already so fantastic and perverted. The peace of marriage, preceded by an uninterrupted harmony in love, in no way matched the inebriating tumult I had called forth. To delude myself about my motives and to give an honest disguise to my disordered impulses, I would object that Mademoiselle de Liniers was very rich through her mother and her grandparents, much too rich for me, who with little inherited wealth had, in addition, no acquired steady income yet, no personal distinction to offer. Thus my sorriest side was decorated in my own eyes with a veil of delicacy, and when from time to time this veil did not quite cover my ulterior motive, I did not fail to find other convenient sophisms to add and many another reason equally slippery and false.

"What I wish, what I have to do to prove to myself what I am," I replied to Mademoiselle de Liniers, as we walked along the enclosure of the flowering orchard one May evening. "What I need is an opportunity to act, a test that shows me what I am worth and shows others as well." She was walking bare-headed next to me, pushing little de Guémio ahead of her. She was stroking the child's brown curls with a hand silvered by the moon. "I need a foot in the world of action and turmoil, on this vessel of France which seems to have vomited us out. How is our youth going to be spent? The earth trembles. The nations clash without respite, and without us. We cannot be either for or against France. One moment, and that was a fine moment, we opened the battle. There were two sides: Cazalés spoke; Sombreuil offered his chest. We could have died. We who were too young a few years ago but who are full of vigor today, what can we do? The kings have fallen, and from the depths of exile their people's voice no longer reaches us. Our fathers, who were to give us counsel, failed us on a single day and have no tomb. We are no longer hated, just forgotten. Contempt cuts us down, not the axe. Instead of the rumbling thunder of battles, we oppose plots made of spiderwebs and whispers. Oh, Mademoiselle Amélie, tell me, isn't it shameful to live beneath this sweet sky when, invested with gigantic spectacles, we cannot breathe out our share of soul and genius in any skirmish, for any cause, either by word or blood?"

She smiled sadly at this overflowing enthusiasm, applauding in her heart what her lips called madness, and whenever I expressed this impetuous thrust to action and glory, she would repeat in a plaintive tone, like the refrain to a song she would have sung beneath her breath without paying too much attention to the sense: *"You'll have the chance, you'll have the chance."*

Then my ideas, excited by the hour and by their own momentum, would gush forth, spreading over a thousand objects. Because nothing is so delightful in youth's idle hours as this torrent of plans and regrets, you introduce a kind of simulacrum of action that doubles the delight and justifies the enjoyment. At one moment, the love of knowledge, this thirst for holy letters which had stirred me since childhood, had me take up the dispersal of the cloisters. I imagined myself working tirelessly in a bookish asylum for 60 years. I seemed to be requesting eternal and mortified labor for myself. Then, turning with a jealous hope toward more public and tender works, the palm of poetry tempted my heart, inflamed my brow. "I think I feel within," I would say, "many things which have not been said like that before."

And to this ambition, Amélie, who had been silent on the subject of the cloister, picked up more sharply, rather mocking, I believe, and no doubt impatient at seeing me put so many distant desires ahead of her: *"You'll have the chance. You'll have the chance."*

When I would come back down from the ideal to more concrete alternatives and more practical details, I would see other obstacles to my début, in a personal sense, given my lack of patrimony and the nearly complete ruin of my family. Then, however, she could not contain herself and at the mention of personal fortune, she would let escape in a charming manner, as if the refrain carried her away: *"Oh, well, we'll have the chance!"*

I heard her! The moon was shining, the fragrance of the flowers wafted over the enclosure. At that very instant, little de Guémio cried out gleefully at the sight of a glowworm in a bush. That entire evening is still present in my mind. While Mademoiselle Amélie was stroking mechanically the curly head of the child who let her keep countenance and save face, I spied on her finger the ring her dying mother had given her. It gem sparkled in the moonbeams. I pretended to notice it for the first time. I asked to see it and took the opportunity to remove it from her finger and try it on mine. The ring fit me, but I gave it back. All this happened in silence. A few moments later, when it was time for me to leave, I came out on my horse with Amélie nimbly preceding me to the barrier, which she closed behind me. And from the outside, above the hedge I skirted up to the turn, I made a final bow.

Love, budding love or whatever approaches it, a wavering voice that sighs and sings in us, a blurred melody recalling Eden, at least once in our lifetime the Creator sends it on the wings of our own springtime! Choice, avowal, promise; happiness offered and granted, none of which I wanted. What heart upon reflection would not have been troubled, would not have drawn back almost in fright at the moment of rushing and seizing such love! Scarcely had the crown of beech trees around La Gastine faded from view, the first spurt of the ride quieted, than I would enter the heather and let go the reins. Reverie would gradually take over. "What! tie myself down!" I would say, "down there, even in happiness?" And vis-à-vis that solemn notion, I shuddered from head to toe. A sorrowful presentiment, almost to the point of faintness, rose from the depths of my being, and in its quite intelligible languor warned me to wait, that for me the hour of decision had not tolled. The world, travel, numerous accidents of war and study, those mysterious combinations so prodigal in youth, opened before my eyes with the perspective of infinity and assembled, swimming in mobile forms according to the play of pale light in the brush. I loved these emotions, even the foreseeable misfortunes. I would say, "I shall return to these grounds some day after having taken my part in distant affairs, after having renewed my soul many a time. Rich with comparisons, matured by precocious experience, I shall pass by here again. The gentle moon, like this evening, will light up the heath, the bouquet of hazelnut trees, and some whitened sheepfold, over there beneath the dark grove. Light and sadness, all these reflections today, all these vestiges of myself will be here.—But the beloved, will I find her again, will she forget me?" And these obviously bitter vicissitudes, which I mulled over with a tear or two, smiled at me from that distance and made me feel life in the present. It was through such labyrinths of thought that treacherous inconstancy, so dear to human hearts, led me astray.

CHAPTER III

At that last hunting party I spoke to you about, my friend, I had the opportunity to be introduced to the Marquis de Couaën, one of the most important men in the region and whom I had wanted to meet for some time. Despite the distractions of that madcap day, I had found a moment to discuss with him the sad state of humiliation and futility we had sunk to. I had lamented my frustrated faculties in his presence, and while listening he distinguished me by an attention much greater than my age seemed to warrant and this immediately won my loyalty. He repeatedly invited me to visit him at his property of Couaën, some two leagues away, and I did so at once. My entry into the affairs of the world and society properly dates from that day. Throughout the countryside a sentiment of respect and expectation clung to the manor of Couaën and its owner. In fact, the place seemed to have become the center of much secret activity and frequent gatherings of the nobility. It was a short distance from the sea, near a very rocky and deserted coast, at a range of nocturnal communication with the islands, and fishermen whom rough weather had pushed on these banks said they had more than once seen in the cavern of the cliffs some craft that did not belong to any of them. The life of the Marquis himself lent itself to conjectures. Long absences during his first youth added to both his imposing reputation and the somewhat ambiguous reservations people held toward him. He had served early, had fought at Gibraltar. Then travel had distracted him. It was known that he had stayed for a long time in Ireland, where a branch of his family had been established since olden times. Having rushed home to no avail at the rumor of the royalist insurrection, he had found the first Vendée expiring in its blood and returned to Ireland again. He did not return until 1797, this time bringing with him a charming young wife, already a mother, strange and wonderfully beautiful, they

said, who for three or four years now had been living in complete
seclusion at that manor where political intrigues appeared to be
brewing and where I was invited.

You reached the chateau of Couaën partly by long and narrow
paths along hedges, partly by covered and hollow roads, veritable
ravines, barely dry in summer, impassable in winter. The castle and
its grounds, which you could not see until you entered, occupied a
spacious back part of beautiful greenery, magnificently planted. Behind, on its other side, it was defended from the winds of the sea by a
rather elevated coast, which for more than a league extended in divers
undulations up to the bank and broke up into a cliff. Every aspect in
the appearance of the building indicated a fort, which in the remote
past had served as a refuge for the people of the countryside against
pirate attacks. A massive, round brick tower with a pointed tile roof
rose above a curtain of tall trees surrounding the gardens. Once you
crossed the farm courtyard and reached the second barrier, the house
appeared on your left. Then you crossed a kind of bridge, which was
no longer a real bridge, since on one side it was level with the garden
and separated by a grill. But on the right, a moat, only partially filled
now, for use as a pigsty or a kennel, bore vestiges of the old usage. At
the upper end of the bridge, once you crossed the vault which was still
crowned with a little tower, you entered the vast inner courtyard,
divided by a cloister. The first half next to the service rooms was used
for daily tasks. In the second half, free and separated, there was a
brilliant lawn spreading beneath the windows of the single-story
dwelling and the large corner tower, which was in the center of a
slightly square platform and had a view of the property leading to the
sea, as well as of the avenue that graced the way up to the summit.
When you approached the edge of the platform and the support walls,
you realized you were on a rampart—a rampart carpeted with peach
trees and vineyards, overlooking meadows, tree nurseries on the lower
slope, and on gardens, formerly moats, but which had not been
judged appropriate for raising animals as in front, so that this part of
the property preserved the old arrangement. I am making this description less for you, my friend, who have not seen the place, or who, if
you had visited, would be able to get a grasp of it from my impressions
and coloring, than for myself, going through them again with details I
must apologize for. Do not spend too much time trying to picture
them for yourself from this description. Just let the image float lightly
past you. The merest idea will suffice. But for me, you see, when I
think back about it, I can never dwell enough on the contours of the
scene. I have to prove to myself, like a blindman verifying the stones

in a wall, that it is there, always standing in my memory and calquing in lines like these, even in cold words, so deeply painted in my mind, of my best known house and my most faithful landscape.

So there I was one day making my way towards that calm dwelling, curious, excited, with a secret feeling that my life was going to find its orientation, receive some defined propulsion. And since, given the bad state of the road, I was often obliged to slow down or even dismount and lead my horse by hand along the enclosure and over the hurdles, I was smiling at the thought that I was choosing a bizarre route for breaking into society. That of Versailles surely must have been broader and more commodious for our forefathers. But this very contradiction, what was incredible in such a detour, going to seek a point of departure for my flight in the depths of the most hidden valleys, plucked another sensitive cord in my being and responded to one of my deepest weaknesses. Because if the glorious and famous openly prefer the dazzle of a royal access, the romantic and voluptuous love mystery. And into our innermost instants of ambition and projects of pride, mystery, silence, retreats of nature and shade combine to cast a spell on us, bringing the hidden presence confusingly to us in a gracious vicinity: the possible apparition of what is dearer still than any ambition, bewitching fame in our eyes, our fugitive nymph Galatea or Armida.

When I reached Couaën, I found the Marquis with only his wife and their two beautiful children in the vast and ancient reception room where the windows on one side opened onto the platform of green lawn I have already mentioned, and on the other, overlooked from rather high up, the gardens I had glimpsed through the left grill when I came in. My heart was beating, my eyes hardly observing, when the Marquis came over to me and, introducing me to his wife, established immediately a cordial conversation in which I was quickly launched. Then after sitting down for a half-hour, he offered me a tour of the gardens where I could see the groves and appreciate their disposition and vantage points. The tower struck me most; he led me over. Only two of its floors were lived in. The first, on the ground level, or only a few steps higher than the level of the salon, which it joined, formed a lovely room for Madame de Couaën. I did not enter but only glimpsed the door. There was still another room for the children and a deep study or office, completely hollowed out of the thickness of the wall. The next floor was composed of a single, large, high-ceilinged room, three-quarters round with a study likewise entirely set in a wall. This was the Marquis' study and library, his bedroom, perhaps, because a majestic bed filled one of the corners. From there

you had a three-way view: an open, dominating, seignorial view of
the platform of the rampart and the back of the mountain; an enclosed,
shaded, two-sided view of the gardens in the middle and those below.
The garret of the tower, a kind of granary provided with a stout door
with a triple lock, enclosed a multitude of rats, whom the Marquis
could hear from his library at any hour of the day. The lower cavity,
which must have existed beneath Madame de Couaën's room and the
subterranean chambers, which probably were attached to it, had been
completely eliminated. Here is what I learned, what I saw on the first
day. I questioned, I guessed, nothing escaped me. I have always had a
fondness for interiors. Others have their eyes turned from childhood
to the wondrous plains of the heavens and the starry steppes lured by
contemplation to unravel marvels. Or the ocean calls them, and the
monstrous wave that lures them from the bank is like a mistress for
them. Others are pursued relentlessly up to their domestic hearth or
ancestor's armchair by wild forests and the ways of ancient peoples.
Oh, lend an ear, listen! Be neither too prompt nor deaf, find the
underlying voice in your passing caprices. Pray, pray! God has often
spoken in these familiar suggestions. Kepler, Columbus, Xavier, you
knew something about this! I did not wait, did not pray, did not
discern. My taste lay in intimate habits, private agreements, household
details. A new interior to explore was always a pleasant discovery for
me. From the threshold I felt a certain commotion. In the bat of an
eye, if I was attracted, I seized the framework, I constructed the
smallest relationships. It was a gift I had, a sign where I should have
read what Providence had in mind for me. The guides of the devout
soul in daily situations, those spiritual directors, untiring with their
gentle bits of advice, who spoke from the retreat of their cells or
through the confessional grill, virginal, greyhaired old men who can
probe so far into the paticularities of our secret life and its most
circumstantial detours, were no doubt marked by no other sign. They
possessed the gift to a higher degree but not, I need to believe, more
clearly than I. And what a consoling use they have been able to make
of it. Tender St. François de Sales, I was born to walk toward salvation
in your fragrant footsteps! But instead of controlling uprightly my
natural talent or finding its goal early, I went about misusing it for
quite contrary ends, sharpening it into an art that was both futile and
nefarious, and I spent a good part of my days and nights skirting
parks like a thief and lusting after the women's quarters. Even later,
when Grace had touched me, there was no longer time to go back to
that. What would have seemed the best route in the beginning had
become my reef. I had to avoid this faculty, even curbing it violently

so as to apply myself elsewhere. Less spellbinding parts of my heredity claimed my attention. Breathing heavily, but serene beneath my cross, I climbed other paths on the holy mount.

If the place and the simple arrangement of the manor held me as much as that, you can imagine, my friend, that the Marquis himself preoccupied me no less. I missed none of his expressions. He was around 38 then. His noble face already lined, his forehead repeating the curve of his brows, a benevolent mouth keeping the projects of the soul. His aquiline nose was finely chiseled. He had a few faint wrinkles in the transparent skin of the temples; they were wrinkles etched by neither the fatigue of marches nor the weight of the sun but from the inside, I judged, from their tender roots and transparency. His manner was superior and suave, appropriate for leadership. He was one of those men who bear within them their principles of action and home, a man, in short, in the loftiest sense of the word, a man of character. The look from his perfectly clear, hard blue eyes called for my gaze in return but made me avert my eyes. Fixed and immobile at times, he was never calm. When he turned toward the beautiful countryside, he did not reflect it. The azure fields of his eyes reminded me of an unbroken desert scorched by unrelenting desolation. When I knew the Marquis better, my first speculations on his history became more precise. He had ambition, active talents, great incisive boldness. For a long time he had roamed outside the theater of events through various countries and over seas, consumed by his wanderlust. A romantic passion, violent and belated, had detained him in the backwaters of an Irish county at moments when his role was singled out everywhere else. He was impelled to make up these years, and it was his judgment besides that the times had become more propitious to his cause. The revolution seemed nearly to have spent its fury. In his opinion it was exhausted by anarchy, and living at the moment only in one head which needed to be taken care of now. His secret communications with illustrious military leaders on the inside demonstrated to him that the consular office, imposing from a distance, could crumble when the signal was given and break the idol. Like most enterprising men with a very keen appraisal of material obstacles, he set little store by lower-class resistance; general opinion had no distinctive personification whatsoever. He believed that at any given instant a political result could be produced if the men who forcefully willed it knew how to conquer the opposing leaders. His thought was not, however, that right would die in a single day vis-à-vis might and that the affections and beliefs of the population could be suppressed with impunity. But he separated the vacillating opinion of the populace from real and ancient customs. The former hardly figured in his calculation, and as for the customs themselves, he considered them easily destroyed in a rather short lapse of time, unless someone came along to avenge them. In a word, Monsieur de Couaën paid little heed to what is called the progressive force of things or the power of ideas. For him the sense of success depended in the end on the adeptness and decision of three or four noteworthy individuals. Aside from that, below, he saw only a pure teeming mass, a crushing fatality, suffocation. His most burning desire was to become one of those crucial individuals who for a moment in history have a part of the world in their hands. He was not unworthy in his capacities, assuredly, but on the periphery, without a striking prior act to his credit, without long standing alliances built up, he was left out of the principal positions. What he could do with his own resources was to support with a vigorous uprising in his own province the blow others would strike at the heart, and he had arranged everything beautifully for this aim. The little castle of Couaën was the stem and knot of an extensive network, which penetrated in twisted lines into the interior of the region. Among those who were employed under his direction close by, whose determination to succeed seemed sometimes to border on imprudence, I was not slow in realizing that regardless of the perfect welcome he accorded them, the Marquis counted on few real auxiliaries and did not really depend on any, but through them he reached various points of the population, and this was enough for him. Once the signal was given, he expected support only from the brave population and himself.

With a mind of very high calibre, which at a certain high level operated with ease in any subject, the Marquis still had had a very uneven education. In working with him, you could be astonished by what he did and did not know. That struck me from the outset despite my own incomplete command of subjects at the time. You could see that detoured most often by circumstances and feeling his destiny elsewhere, he had looked in books only for recreation and as a last resort. He presented, then, a mind and general observations formed from sequences of rather solid knowledge, which were interrupted by large spaces that were completely fallow. His culture was composed chiefly of politics and some history. I compared it in my own way to fragments of a Roman walkway in a vast and barely subjugated land. The first day I went to visit him, when we went in his library, a recent book lay open on the table. I looked at the title and looked for the name of the author, who would be subsequently famous.

"Who is this gentleman from Aveyron?" I asked.

"Ah! one of my boyhood friends in the Midi, a deep thinker and very opinionated! All the moral and political theories of our philosophers predicated some kind of wildman from Aveyron, and would not have been upset to bring us to that point. But now Aveyron has found them a gentleman who will show up the philosophers and wildmen." These were his very words.

As for Madame de Couaën and how she seemed to me during that visit and the following, I have little to tell you, my friend, except that she was in fact extremely beautiful, but one of those strange and rare beauties that our eyes have to get accustomed to. After a six months' acquaintance, my opinion of her was very tentative, in a suspension of feeling, which, far from being due to indifference, came rather from a refinement of respect and my excessive scruples in questioning myself on my feelings for her. When I was with her, I greeted her without addressing my remarks to her very openly. I replied to her almost without turning towards her. I saw her without gazing at her, the way you do around a young mother who is nursing her baby in your presence. She was some kind of chaste forbidden image over which my regard spread a cloud on entering, and in leaving, I drew the curtain on the memories. But who can tell what ruses of malign intention and connivance take place in us? Perhaps the cloud and curtain were there only to save disturbance in the beginning and to permit habit to multiply its imperceptible seed in the shade.

I went to the castle of Couaën often, but in the beginning, especially, I spent little time there. Whenever the late hour or some storm made me spend the night, I left very early the next morning. I was quickly informed about the people seen there and into the secret weaknesses and pretensions of everyone. What I thought was a considerable initiation from afar, when seen close up, was only a rather noisy game whose masks diverted me by their confusion when they did not overwhelm me. Only the Marquis was superior among these men whose narrow-mindedness, for the most part, was as great as their sense of justice. I attached myself to him more and more.

My errands at La Gastine had slowed down, although without interruption and with a show of courtesy. I had an excellent excuse for my delays in my attachment to Monsieur de Couaën and my assiduous attendance of his counsel. My conformity of principles and political allusions kept me from being disapproved. Mademoiselle de Liniers, in her delicate pride, personally enjoyed my success with the most authoritative personage in the region, and like women in love, placing devotion on the most trivial things, she happily sacrificed seeing me as often as at first to what she believed to be the road of my advancement. Our conversations, even when we were alone, leaving by degrees the habitual twilight and the confines of our own feelings, had become more varied, less in low voices, more studded with piquancy and verve. The abundant material I brought them from the outside world did not let them grow sentimental or languid. I used to give amusing pictures of the personages and their conflicts of self-esteem and the false alarms they gave. I always painted a noble picture of Monsieur de Couaën and his clearcut poise in the midst of these heated disputes. If I kept quiet about the Marquise, Mademoiselle de Liniers took it upon herself to break my few reticences on the subject that attracted her more than the rest. The appearance of the young woman, the character of her beauty (Amélie had not met her yet), her manner and use of her time with people with whom she had little in common, the age of her two children, which was the handsomer, whether the daughter looked like her mother. What else did she ask about? Did she still have a foreign accent? Did she speak our language like us? Did she like to share family anecdotes and memories of her first fatherland? A thousand such questions followed one after the other from the lips of Mademoiselle de Liniers without idle curiosity, without the least awakening of rival coquetry, with a genuine, well-meaning interest, like everything which came from such a decent person. For myself, I could not forgo satisfying so many natural desires, and once on this subject, I forgot myself in gossip and developments. Since she herself pulled away the veil with which I imagined I covered over this gracious corner in my mind, I felt permitted in such moments to launch some glance which made a truce with my self-imposed constraints and to profit from an opening for which I was not responsible, to see just what my memory already contained. At least, my conscience murmured low, it was not I who brought up the subject. It was not I who began. So I went in, I penetrated, and I never stopped talking on the subject. La Gastine was no more than an echo of the secret marvels at Couaën. If the feelings I subsequently was afraid of tried at that time to form some distant and dark points in my mind, it must have been by means of similar conversations where my speech, full of its subject, and urged to elaborate, determined the first contours.

CHAPTER IV

That winter, long as it seemed to me, passed. When spring came, my trips to the manor increased and could no longer be counted. Our acquaintance spanned an entire cycle of seasons. I had become an old friend. The room I used from now on, no longer just for the night, but sometimes for a whole week or more, overlooked the gardens and farm courtyard from above the entry arch. I would spend my mornings reading, thinking over metaphysical systems that my restless skepticism favored and that I extracted for the most part from works by English authors from Hobbes to Hume, which the Marquis' uncle, a free-thinker, had added to the library. I also got my hands on several very contrary works of Saint-Martin, the self-styled *Unknown Philosopher*, but I didn't attach much importance to them at the time. This questing curiosity held a perilous attraction for me, and under the pretext of an honest zeal for truth, succeeded in actively breaking down my remaining beliefs. When during these ruinous speculations on man's moral freedom and the more or less fatal concatenation of motives, some breath of spring reached me, when a torrent of penetrating smells and stamen pollen was carried to my window by the morning breeze or when alerted by the grating of the garden gate, I saw from above the Marquise with her women, in a flowing gown, going down a sanded path to drink the ferruginous waters of the spring down below as she customarily did at eight o'clock in the summer. At that sight, amidst these perfumes, in the fleeting lights of these images, I was suddenly thrust back into the world of the senses. I found that left to myself, I had no resources. My understanding, lowering my brow, had nothing to gainsay in the idleness of my heart, the book no place in my sighs. No more faith in the way to salvation, no more familiar recourse to Love permanent and invisible, no prayer. I could not pray for anything but my desire, could not petition for anything except its blind goal. I was like a captured soldier who holds up his arms. All the philosophy of the morning (note this triumph!) ended usually in some half-understood English passage which I made a point of querying Monsieur de Couën about at lunch. The Marquise, who was often present, sometimes took the trouble to have me repeat the passage in order to explain its meaning and improve my pronounciation.

Politics, which had first inflamed me, interested me little, except when I chatted tête-à-tête with Monsieur de Couaën and we gradually rose to the overall theater and to a comparative assessment of events. As for the enterprise in which I saw him embarked and where I was resolved to follow, it seemed all the more risky when I knew its strengths better. Monsieur de Couaën himself felt how little he was in charge and was consumed by it. Isolated in his thickets, in the most remote corner of the scene, the initiative had to come from somewhere else. He could do nothing without the requisite signal, and the least upset at the center, London or Paris—Pichegru's bad mood, Moreau's indecision—made delays last forever. However, he had to keep his own maneuvers ready without being noticeable and keep to a suitable quantity the easily exaggerated or faltering ardor of his chief aids. The talent he employed in this narrow operating space was prodigious, and I suffered for it as much as I admired it. My patience, certainly, did not go so far as his, and during most of the vehement conversations that he led with infinite serenity and ease, I escaped as best I could on the foot of a frivolous youth, sometimes leaning on my reputation as a philosopher, which some of these gentlemen granted me. At dinner, rather than put up with these remarks I had heard 100 times, I would happily settle down with the children, who usually ate with us, unless there was a large group. And since the serving plates had in their centers large blue flowers or little blue flowers or none at all, the anxiety of these dear little ones was at its peak to know whether the good Lord would send them a plate with flowers, either large or small. That had become a way rewarding their behavior during the morning. Thanks to lifted eyebrows of their mother or me, providence in the form of the old servant made few mistakes. For my part, I much preferred these giggling anxieties to those of our dignified guests and their tumultuous outbursts on more serious but no less defined subjects. Naturally Madame de Couaën showed the same preference.

Love had not entered the picture yet, my friend, no, not yet. Before evening I would plunge into those woodlands with a book in my hand as a pretext for solitude in case of an encounter. In my silent periods after dinner, during that autumn of the day when the dazzling

fires of the sky display a bright light, reflected over so wide an
expanse, and which the secret voice of our heart is the most audible,
freed from the weight of noon and the innumerable desires of morning, in these moments of reverie, on benches in the arbor, in the
garden at the back, and on the banks of its limpid fish-pond, wherever
I roamed, I murmured no name, I had no letter to carve, I carried no
image with me. Madame de Couaën pushed away Mademoiselle de
Liniers without installing herself. Other apparitions figured there.
Each one disturbed me. A peasant with his lass seemed like a king to
me. Thus, because my affections had no precise object, I desired any
object all the more wretchedly. The simple pleasures of these hours
and sites were only more corrupted by my overflowing sensibility.
There comes a time in life when a beautiful place, a warm breeze, a
slow stroll beneath the shade, a loving chat or reflection is a matter of
indifference; any will suffice. The dream of human happiness can
imagine nothing finer. But in the heat of youth, all natural boons
serve only as a frame and an accompaniment to a single thought. This
thought, when it remains unfulfilled, this creature whom God had
permitted most of us to seek, when this woman is not found first off,
the heart can too often be led to blasphemy. You suffer aggravation,
you are distraught, you crush the new blades of grass beneath your
feet, you tear the humble flowers as you snatch the budding branches
along the way. Your inflamed nostrils repulse the cooling breeze. You
insult with your desperate looks the magnificent gift of the twilight.

These gentle spots, these warm havens, which at the age of
extreme sensibility looked vacant, burning, embittering, deserted, and
which later fill our sensitivity when it begins to decline, leave no
impression more durable than the first. As soon as they become
sufficient for happiness, they follow in succession, blend together,
and are forgotten. The only ones that stay alive, perpetually enchanting our memory, are the ones that often seemed intolerable at the age
of burning impatience.

At the age I was then, which you, my young friend, have already
passed, love and the senses are all the same to us. You desire what
touches the senses; you think you can love whatever you desire. I was
blinded by that illusion. In such a crisis the heart is so full of faculties
without an object and without a known range. The life outside and
our own are quite entangled. A flight of phosphorus lights our gaze;
radiations escape in sparks and rain on things around us. As soon as
the voice of desire rises and unless another sovereign voice cuts it
short, the entire being shivers with a magnetic movement; on the faith
of so many signs, you cannnot believe that love is not there with us,

ready to follow with its inexhaustible enthusiasm those ever-new perfections in its repertory, its eternal promises. But if you let go, lowering yourself to these lures; if you do not prevent desire from letting the word of evil enchantment insinuate itself; if you do not seal your senses forever with the inviolate bandeau of the mysteries, offering your senses as a burnt offering to the unblemished union with the divine Bride; or if you do not confine them early in the human and secondary order in the sacred circle of marriage but still under the eye of divine Love—if, then, you let go and try a few of these vain delights. How quickly and inevitably the divorce between love and the senses occurs! Pain and disgust as the deep division of the senses and love makes itself manifest! As the senses advance unbridled, true love dries up and draws away. The more the senses become prodigious and facile, the more love holds back, impoverished or miserly. Sometimes love clearly divides in two, and breaking all bonds with the senses, takes platonic refuge, exalting on an inaccessible summit while the senses sink into the valley of thick currents and gross vapors. The more, then, that the senses hold on to their pasture, the more love, by a kind of reprisal, subtilizes into its essence. But this contradictory activity is disastrous. If the senses act too much as the opposite of love, different as they are, they ordinarily kill it. In expending themselves they rarify our capacity to love. Because if the senses are in no way the same thing as love in man, there is in this world a passing but real alliance between love and the senses for the secondary end of natural reproduction and the legitimate harmony of marriage. That accounts for the apparent confusion they offer at first. That accounts also for the excess of sensual diversions and, past a certain limit, for the destruction of our power to love. Otherwise, as for an absolute alliance, an identity among them, there is none whatsoever. In a good number of stormy sensibilities not led by religion, but which vice and vanity have not entirely lost, it is when the senses have tossed their first spark and their violence makes less noise that the sick soul discerns more clearly, beneath the voice of the senses, the voice of love, the voice of the need to love. This voice, which is heard off to itself, especially during the second youth, is far from possessing the fresh melody that the senses lent it during their mutual confusion. A little harsh from now on, changed and suffering, no longer as virginal as on the threshold of chaste nuptials, no longer insidious as at the banquet of false pleasures, but grave, disenchanted, true and un-adorned in its lament, it reclaims on this earth a heart that we love and that loves us forever more. Oh, against that voice, my friend, if a man knows how to hear it, if he knows how to translate its real meaning, I would not know how to be very severe. It comes in the interval of respite between errors and obduracy, a supreme call of the infinite within, a mournful protest, in human form, of our immortal instincts and power to love. For the man who warms this voice on his breast and listens to it speak at length, it can become the signal of the blessed return. Either the soul does not find on its path the incomparable soul it seeks, and the soul, weary but courageous, passes beyond and, in its disgust of all diversion, in its growing thirst of loving, detached, repentant, does not stop until the higher fount in which it can plunge; or by a very rare encounter, which in this pilgrimage is the most refreshing of benedictions, perceiving finally the soul it desires, moves forward, has itself recognized, admitted, climbing with and through the soulmate to the regions of true Love. In this case, human love is like an unspotted step on the stairway to the incorruptible throne. But if this destiny is fine, praiseworthy, and gentle even in its sacrifices, you should not hide from the hazardous obverse. As a result of wanting to be each other's support, you may well fear to become a reef instead. If you want to know whether the human love you feel remains pure and worthy of trust, whether it continues to make you grow mature, wholesome, and alert, then repeat these words of the gentle Master: "Love is circumspect, humble and upright; it is not weakened, frivolous nor given to vanities; it is sober, chaste, stable, full of quiet, keeping sentinels at every gateway of the senses, *et in cunctis sensibus custoditus.* Repeat again: "Love is patient, prudent and faithful, and never acts for himself alone, *et seipsum nunquam quaerens.* Because," adds the gentle Master, "from the moment a person acts for himself, that is the moment he falls from the grace of Love."

That is what you must ask yourself, my friend, and this is what can alert us at each step if the human love one pursues approaches Divine Love and if this love is on the way leading to it. Others, I admit, are more rigorous than I, and without hestitation pluck such a man from the paths of salvation. But after so many trials, I cannot keep from being indulgent with him. One day during a week of pious retreat Laura's lover, the learned and gifted Petrarch, thought he saw the great Augustine enter, and his revered patron spoke to him. And the great saint, after having assured the trembling believer, began to question him. He examined this life like a concerned director, and he bore his advice into each part: honors, study, poetry, fame, all in turn passed by, and when he came to Laura, he rejected her. But Petrarch, who had assented to each of the saint's decisions, cried out in pain and begged on bended knee the man who had wept for Dido, to leave him the image of Laura. And why indeed, oh most tender of scholars, oh most irrefutable of the Fathers, why did you let him have that? Is it truly and absolutely forbidden to love as an idea a creature of one's choice, when the more one loves the idea, the more disposed one feels to believe, suffer, and pray? When the more one prays and is uplifted, the more one is inclined to love the idea? What is wrong when that unique creature is already carried away by death, when for us she is already on the other bank of time, next to God?

Divine Love, from which all good comes, and by which all is sustained, can be represented to us on the altar that none has ever seen from the front or ever will, in the midst of skies and worlds. And from there Love darts, beams, shakes. Love penetrates to different degrees and moves all life, and if Love reached our hearts in this mortal world pure and solitary (*merus*), it would not intoxicate them, nor dazzle them. Love would make them shatter like crystal. And Love would melt and drink them as its pleasure even if they were invincible diamonds, a little the way the sun, Divine Love's pale image, would burn our globe if he darted his naked rays. But like air, there in nature, marvelous and almost invisible, welcoming the sun, clothing the earth, distributing to earth the fires from on high in varied lights and tolerable warmth, likewise in front of pure Divine Love for faithful hearts here below is Charity who knows neither void, nor relapse, who embraces all mankind, puts them between God and the fellowman, and operates in the sphere of human souls this beneficent distribution of saints and burning fountains. Entirely too often, it is true, what was vitiated at the outset, elements where evil has infiltrated, seeds become corruptible, ferment and burn in the transparent air from the heat of the sun; from that come storms, thunder, and lightning. In the same way, at the heart of darkened charity, exhalations of pride and passion engender hatreds and wars. There are, however, beautiful souls, so tenderly endowed, so strongly nourished, that they receive Divine Love, quick and unalterable, at every instant, through millions of rays of that immense charity, and give it to their fellowmen in a thousand loving ways, in plenteous tears upon all wounds and in sublime devotions. And if, at some sad hour, they sense those rays, too numerous and too scattered, expiring without an object, they can get them back in spirit if they only watch them all leave, as at their source, from the breast of the merciful Pontiff, once dead and always present, from that luminous and sweet breast of John the beloved. But other souls, my friend, are less prompt and less serene. They are neither so firm at their center, nor do they have the diffusible speed of the rays. They would faint from wanting to embrace so much directly, and in the darkness, where the world beyond customarily appears to us, Divine Love reaching them only by universal charity, would make too uncertain an impression on them. Charity, besides, to be all-powerful in a heart, almost of necessity claims its virginity, and many souls, capable of loving, sullied themselves when they started out. Such souls, then, in their return to the feelings of the Saint, can consult, in my opinion, a closer and more circumscribed mirror where the supreme Love can be symbolized in their eyes: some dear shining brow beneath his torch, the sight of a heavenly eyelid in which he is reflected. Such souls can chastely use their one and only love to climb the steps to the love of all and the Love of the Sole Good. Ah, if they succeed by this route, if what they feel is neither exclusive egoism nor cumbersome idolatry, if in passing through the veil of the beloved face the sacred rays do not break as if against a stone, if at no moment do they become cutting like swords or piercing like lightning, if they remain recognizable through the living disk that must give them a focus and center, enlarge them, paint them on our weak iris, ah, all is well, all is safe, all is repaired. And when the beloved creature dies before we do, when the rays of holy Love reach us henceforth through that glorious transfigured form of the beloved and her incorporeal sheath, we have still less to fear that they do not deviate, do not break, and are neither dangerous or deceptive. The presence at our side, the descent into our nights of the angelic Shade, makes only more tender, veils with more softened reflections, unceasingly changes and renews in our exile that light in which she bathes, with which she is clothed and which, thanks to her, begins here below in the vale of tears, our immortal nurture.

But where am I rambling now, my friend? I was taking you, as I recall, into the woodlands of Couaën, where I forgot myself. I was pursuing in her myriad forms the phantom that enveloped me in her mist, that lay heavy upon my brow and eyes but whose face I could not make out. Nothing was more nefarious, I was saying, than this continuous fixation upon such an object. Brooded over, fused covertly by a heated thought, love and the senses drag our other faculties and all our principles into their dark melange. The process slowly ravages us on the inside and like a subterranean dissolution, when first discovered, it gives us grounds for panic. While in a truly chaste young man who tempers his thinking, all the virtues of the soul, like all the tissues of the body, are strengthened and in this person honest gaiety, openness to simple pleasures, energy of will, inviolable faith in friendship, cordial sympathy towards men, restraint of oaths, frankness of speech, and even some rough edges which usage will polish— all compose an admirable naturalness where each quality has its rank and where everything is supportive. Here in illusory chastity, by the effect of that prolonged liquefaction that it favors, the most intimate foundations are submerged and weakened. The natural, Christian order of virtues enters in confusion. The very substance of the soul grows soft. We keep up the exterior, but the interior is drowning. We have committed no act, but we prepare ourself for universal infraction. This deceptive chastity, where warms a collection of all leavens, is without doubt worse in the long run than would have been a first incontinence brought under control.

Other ideas, more reasonable, perhaps, more consistent, at least, had their part in my pensive excursions. I had come to Couaën to open my access to life; to climb, as I made a breach, upon the active stage of society. Despite my confidence in my noble guide, I was beginning to think I was mistaken. I sensed that I had gone into an impossible, false path that would not end. It seemed to me that all the trouble we were taking, imagining we were advancing, could be compared a band of shipwrecked men marching along a perilous shore. As we dragged ourselves along our tongue of sand, from rock to rock, watching the lighthouse, dreaming of a way out, without wanting to recognize that we were turning our backs to the land and that the rising tide of the century, which much earlier had cut off our sole point of return, at every moment was gaining beneath our steps. The inexpressible sadness that at certain hours of the evening I had seen extend and double in the more bluish network of veins on the Marquis' pained brow, made me suspect that despite the decisiveness of his kind of character, he was not without anxiety himself and that among the diverse chances of the future, he was bitterly aware of the nothingness of his projects. Above all else I empathized with the rips and tears of such a stout heart, and I was far from regretting having involved myself, but I suffered also on my own account in my frustrated faculties, in that need for peril and renown buzzing in my ears, in those multiple aptitudes which, exercised in time and depending on the occasion, would have made of me, I dared believe, a political orator, a statesman or a warrior. My habitual thoughts of enjoyment and love, which covered all the rest, eroded them little by little, but did not destroy them in a single blow. In bathing in my overbrimming lake of languor, I frequently stumbled against some sharp point of these rough coastal rocks.

One day, when I was indulging myself like this, bruised by bumps and watered with tears, after having plumbed at length the defective crannies of my destiny, I had invoked for my entire succor that unique, absorbing sentiment, which would have been in my eyes the ransom of the universe and my supreme compensation. It was a day that I had wasted in the most abundant sighs; I had stripped more buds and stems of the blooming reeds, held out the most suppliant hands to some invisible ring of that chain, which to me seemed like that of Plato's gods. That day, the sixth of July, if I remember, burdened with the entire weight of my youth, I came out of the woods by the square plot of the terraces, my hair in my face, my eyes on my feet. And floating at the back of my mind was this: "How long must I wait for her? Where should I look for her? Does she exist somewhere? Is there someone beneath this sky meant only for me?" Suddenly my name was uttered in the silence. I raised my head and saw Madame de Couaën sitting at the window of her tower room. She was beckoning as she called. In two leaps I was beneath that blessed window I could almost reach with my hand. Her charming head in that ivy frame leaned toward me: "Uncivilized as you are," she said, "you can still retrieve my ivory needle, my embroidery needle, which fell there, do you see it? Somewhere at the bottom of this peach tree or in its branches. If you would please bring it up to me right away; and then if I may be so bold, I will request your company for another tedious chore of mine."

I picked up the object without seeing it; I crossed the garden gate, entry vault, and inner courtyard almost without touching the ground. In the space of a second I was at Madame de Couaën's door, where, before turning the key, I waited one or two seconds more so I would not look as if I had been running. I even knocked lightly a couple of times as if I had feared to surprise her, and it was only when I heard her answer that I opened. A fragrance greeted me. I was entering this private room for the first time. Everything there was simple, but everything shone: polished antique furniture, a guitar hanging on the wall, an ivory crucifix to the right of the bed alcove, to the left a mantelpiece decorated with rare porcelain, some Irish crystal, and a small medallion portrait on each side. Still seated in the window, she was facing me. There was a chair in front of her for her feet, and an embroidery hoop was on her knees. One of her elbows rested on the embroidery which she seemed to have forgotten, and in her obliviousness she had turned her sweet, noble, and sparkling face to the sky. She didn't budge at first, and she barely looked at me: "Here's what's involved," she said, taking the needle from me. Monsieur de Couaën will be gone all evening, leading back those gentlemen. I think I would like to go to the mountain chapel Saint-Pierre-de-Mer; it is a duty of devotion. Will you go with me? It will take an hour at a slow pace, but there's enough sun left." And without waiting for me to say yes, so wrapped up was she in her thoughts, she stood up to get ready, and we left.

I gave her my arm. The walk would be long. I had an entire evening of happiness before me. Moments of delectation when you ask nothing, expect nothing, even think you desire nothing! How much affectionate concern I dared to show her in the least of movements and without assumed servitude! How my arm, timidly supporting hers, begged it to lean on mine! And when we crossed the meadow where the dangerous bull was grazing, and when we crossed the little bridge over the ferruginous brook, and when we climbed the coast heaped with pebbles, how many natural and discreet attentions enclosed her! I was extremely clever in sparing her steps, I made her a winding path. It seemed that by myself, with my own hands, I placed her feet in the softest places and that I stretched a magic carpet beneath her steps. She received these attentions graciously, sometimes with a faint smile. Most often she took advantage of them without appearing to be aware of them; meanwhile, by way of recompense, she chatted to me about her family and fatherland. Her baptismal name was Lucy O'Nelly. She had lost her father when she was quite small, and her loving mother had reared her. Her elder brother, a fiery patriot, had seen in the French Revolution an effective means for emancipating Ireland. He had dedicated himself to it. He was one of the first to join that generous league of the friends of Ireland, led by his relative Lord FitzGerald, who came to such a sad end. Monsieur de Couaën's stay in their neighborhood occurred at the height of that period of heroic frenzy. Between him and his beloved's brother, violent differences of opinion had broken out. For a long time the republican gentleman, as head of the family, had refused his sister's hand to the foreign adversary. More than once their quarrel on this subject nearly came to bloodshed, and it had required all gentle Lucy's firmness and affection and all the mother's inexhaustible and overflowing love to dull the shock of those two prides and let love triumph. However, they had had to leave this mother who was so good and already in bad health. At first they received news very seldom because the war was going on. Later, only for a few months, they received news more frequently, but it was very sad and gave little grounds for hope. Madame de Couaën had received a letter that very morning, and this excursion we were making to Saint-Pierre-de-Mer was a pilgrimage to leave a prayer.

She explained these circumstances with a naive volubility, sprinkling her words with unexpected and picturesque turns of phrase and nuancing her succeeding thoughts, without ever marking any passion but love. We had reached the height of the coast and were walking on an uneven plateau, bristling with broom, where here and there reared up some spindly, wind-twisted trees. The bank, a mere half-league in front of us, was wrinkled and somber. Although the sun on the horizon almost touched the Ocean, setting it on fire with a 1,000 splendors, the closest waves, which surrounded like an angled bay the high masses of boulders, were already covered with the muted hues of evening. This solitude, at this moment especially, presented an idea of savage grandeur. She appeared struck by it. After a rather long silence, I saw she was more pale than usual beneath her jetblack hair, and her keen eyes, fixed at the horizon of the waves, penetrated beyond the horizon with the indefinable expression of a girl of the sea.

"You're looking for your Ireland, aren't you?" I asked, "but isn't it really here with its heather and beaches?"

"Oh, no," she cried, "the green and white aren't the same here as they are there. Over there it is less rough and more distinct. My fatherland is quite moist in the morning, gleaming green from the grass and shimmering from the fountains. The crests of the hills and the lakes in Ireland sparkle in the sun like the crystal in my room. Oh, no, there's no Ireland here!" The sound of suffering when she uttered these last words alerted me that it was less the places than the distant persons that her glance was seeking. In going down through many rough spots in the terrain and following the broken tracks of a stream that ran to the shore, we reached the chapel where she was to pray. Although this chapel had been without a priest, or even a caretaker for a long time, it was not in ruins, as might have been expected, or even devoid of ornament. Madame de Couaën had seen to having the tile roof repaired and sent someone over once or twice a week to see the upkeep and cleanliness and maintain the altar light. Moreover, the devout fishermen and the coastal dwellers, who had made vows in times of danger, had hung up offerings, which the holiness of the place sufficed to protect, even though it was completely open. I went in the humble nave with her for a moment. But when I saw her kneel, some kind of modesty made me leave, fearing to mingle any alien movement to so pure an invocation. It seemed better to me that her sigh, like a dove's, should ascend to Heaven alone. When I did that, I was concealing from myself the virtue of this divine act, which Jesus taught to the least of us. I forgot that any prayer is good and acceptable, and that prayer, even from the most blemished of men, can add to that of an angel if it comes from the heart.

This is a thought that has bothered me many times since. If at that moment of crisis I had knelt to pray with fervor for her and her mother, would some of those evil accidents that I did not know how to ward off have been changed in my future life and perhaps in hers? Would not a meritorious act of that sort, set in the beginning of my feelings, have been able to regulate my use of it differently, to direct its course better? Because good prayers, even when they do not achieve their direct goal, reverberate in other good effects without our knowing it. They often strike in the depths of God some hidden spring, which needed only that blow to move, imprinting a new turn in the conduct of a soul.

But, although by the effect of the sight, the walk, and the impressions of the evening, I felt myself truly more devoutly disposed than I had been for a long time, I did not follow through with that religious feeling. Leaving Madame de Couaën kneeling in the chapel, I went over to the remains of a stone watchtower at the border of the cliff: space, the roaring abyss, the reddened disk of the day star now half drowned, everything plunged me into reverie. Now reverie is not the same thing as prayer at all, my friend, but takes its place in the souls of this century, the vague sensation conveniently dispensing with any show of will. When you dream, you know all too well, there is nothing you will. You scatter the present sensation to the chance and accident of things and spread yourself disportionately through the universe, blending with each object felt. Prayer, on the other hand, is willed. It is humble, withdrawn to clasped hands, and even in its dearest demands, crowned with disinterest. It was above all this disinterested effort I lacked that evening and that prayer would have given me. I veiled, I enveloped my personal chimera in a thousand ways. I dispersed it to the winds, upon the waves. I confided it to nature and took it back. Not for a single instant did I immolate myself. The sun had entirely set when she came back out to me. The absence of the sun left the burnished masses of the shore and the rising waves breaking there more gloomy than before. A trace of tears still bathed her lashes, and she moved forward in all the beauty of her pallor. I was poignantly moved, and taking her hand, since we were only two paces from the abyss, I began to speak to her more than I had ever yet dared, of what should console her, support the trials of a heart like hers, of what would watch over her from on high, what surrounded her here below and who would love her. She listened to what I had to say with that particular glance fixed on the horizon, and all she said was, "Oh, it is so good to be loved!" and with that response we resumed our silent trek.

It took us less time to return. Once we reached the coast, we only had to go down. Since there was still some daylight, we soon distinguished Monsieur de Couaën on the chateau platform. He had recognized us and was watching us come, the only creatures stirring on the mountain, preceding the shadows of evening. We hastened towards him, sending signals, she especially by waving by its ribbons the broad-brimmed hat she had been wearing. When we were nearer the lodging, the trees and a turn in the road blocked the sight of us. At the moment we entered the courtyard, Madame de Couaën nimbly ran ahead to meet him and anticipated his questions by some words I did not catch but which explained the purpose of our excursion. He received slowly her hurried justification, appearing to appreciate it. He was motionless, smiling, a little stooped, his whole person expressing very tender shared pleasure. After she had finished, he put his arm around her like a contented father, and raising her almost up to him, kissed her on her hair because she bowed her forehead. A sudden blow from a sword would not have struck me any differently. My heart and my eyes, through the twilight, had missed nothing of that chaste scene. My insensate reign had come to an end. I understood bitterly what I had only dimly felt up till now, what, from that very evening, became the piercing goad of my nights, how far behind the least caress of love, the most indifferent familiarity of marriage leave the keenest advances of friendship. Therein lies the eternal punishment of the indiscreet friendships we begin. It is the gnawing, corrupting worm. Invasive youth, which wants nothing halfway, is exasperated by an inequality where his pride has as much a role as his senses. Youth stirs, youth turns and returns to that jealous thought. From that thought to the more dangerous is just a case of letting ourselves be pushed. We are on the slope of slanting paths.

CHAPTER V

The next day and the days following, my disposition seemed altered. My very pain was a sign that I was thinking it over hopefully. All my sensations, all my vacillating ideas began to stir, to move in a certain order. I had emerged from my state of nothingness. I was in love. A faint whiff of superiority, my proud satisfaction with my heart, which for so long I had thought arid, was uplifting during those first moments of discovery. Instead of being sad and dreamy, as people ordinarily are when love hits them, I showed a bizarre gaiety. The woods saw less of me. I stayed in company and joined in discussions with verve and persistence unusual for me. Madame de Couaën watched me with astonishment. A genie was waking up in me, because I am one of those men, my friend, whose strength is tied to tenderness and who expects all his inspiration from love. At night, when I had retired to my room, a more acute suffering, but less desperate than before, put a stop to my reading and took over my dreams. When I woke up my first impulse was to plumb my soul to find my wound again: I would have feared a cure too much.

But you get used to wounds that do not heal. If nothing renews or revives them, you soon uneasily discern them among your other fundamental affections. You are tempted to believe they are losing strength, when, on the contrary, they are working underground. After another week had rolled by, I already had doubts and an uncertainty that brought back all my languor. I was saying to myself, "Is this really love?" Since the hour when I had painfully felt love coming to life in my chaos, wherein I had greeted it in my bosom with the trembling—and almost the pride—of a mother, I had learned scarcely anything else new on that score. My life resumed its customary dreary routine. It is true that I saw Madame de Couaën alone and cheerfully accompanied her, but these were scenes more or less the same, repetitions that were always delightful, when she was present; always futile and effable when she was absent. This love, which did not exert itself, at times could not even recognize itself. My friend, my friend, what can I tell you? I do not have to recount episodes. At that moment and still later even, it would be eternally the same, a subtle, monotonous life, blank pages, empty days, immense intervals of nothing; anticipations so long and consuming that in the end they made me stupid; few acts, endless feelings; a mass of commentaries on a graceful distich like in the days of the Decadence. Thus I lived; thus passed the fertile years. I saw little directly; put little into practice; I started nothing head on. But I skirted the principal sites of a certain number of existences, and my own I skirted more than I crossed or filled it. I conceived and imagined a great deal, although with a kind of aridity of reproduction as when we do not vary the experience by ourselves and we shine a long time in space, speculation, and solitude.

Five or six hours of seclusion for study and reading each day (this is a routine I have kept up in the midst of the most hostile distractions) sufficed to maintain the natural gift of intelligence that God did not want to let perish in me. The rest of my time went into fantasy and the hazards of leisure. I mentioned that the woods were less agreeable. In fact, when I now felt like wandering alone, I was more likely to choose the mountain or the beach. She had sown on these boulders a memory that I could inhale. Sometimes we both returned there. I would accompany her also to the canal of the mill that was in the meadow beyond the tree nurseries and the orchards. The foamy fracas, not to mention the swimming ducks, amused the children a lot. In such a spot considerable watchfulness was needed with the little ones to prevent an accident. I did not rely on the women; I kept a constant eye myself while she, relying on my supervision, could work, carefree, pensively following my argument, which was often interrupted. Or she would make judicious and deep remarks on matters of the soul, because her imaginative turn of mind in no way interfered with her perfect judgment. She presented a picture of a disposition simultaneously romantic and sensible. I now was as avid to watch her expression as I had been to avoid it earlier. I brooded over that noble and gentle face; I penetrated that rare and singular ingenuous expression, which had not struck me at first. In a way I was spelling out each line of that great beauty, as if it were a somewhat difficult sacred text that some friendly angel would have been happy to hold open for me.

She remained calm, serene, patient beneath my glance, even when it was blank and fixed upon her brow. She let herself be read and understood. In her innocence she found that simple and good. But one day beneath the willows of the canal her little girl, who had stayed quietly beside us, said after some serious thought, "Why do you always look at Mama like that?"

You asked, beautiful child beneath the willows of the canal, why I looked at your mother like that. And if you had been old enough to understand me, I could have almost told you because so much respect was in the purpose of that glance. It is because beauty, any kind of beauty, is not an easy matter, accessible to anyone, intelligible at first blush. It is because above and beyond common beauty, there is another that requires initiation, to which you accede by steps like a temple or a sacred hill. In our world there is beauty for the senses and beauty for the soul. The first is carnal, opaque, immediately discernible. The second, which is perhaps no less striking, but which requires the elevation of the viewer, lets its transparent substance be penetrated and its veiled symbols seized. Idol and symbol, revelation and lure, this is the double aspect of human beauty since Eve. Just as we have love and the senses inside us, so there are outside us two kinds of beauty to correspond to them. True beauty, more or less mixed, more or less complete, is often difficult to feel in its purity. We notice it late, just the way we are slow to identify true love. A child does not understand beauty; it is just so many brilliant red colors that capture his attention by composing a strange picture. An adolescent who pursues and adores beauty is almost always mistaken. In his blind, impetuous fury you see him fall to his knees, embracing rough stones along the way, just as he would embrace the porphyry statue of a goddess. Most often the senses have to be already a little blunted for us to receive a distinct sense of beauty. Then happy is he who can appreciate this belated beauty, who can still dedicate himself to it in time and make his heart worthy to reflect it! The sensual man who senses and enjoys beauty is really its scourge! His homage profanes it. He intends only to degrade and obscure it. Instead of raising himself up to it, he revels in bringing it down to lascivious love affairs. He sacrifices it, knocking it off its pedestal forever. On the contrary, noble beauty, when the soul who inhabits it has remained faithful to its principle, will not perish with its terrestrial shell. Such beauty will deserve to continue elsewhere, rectified by truth, purified by love, and in this new form that will never change, the person who served it here below will still be permitted to love it. We need this hope and nothing, my dear Lord, forbids our believing it.

Novice that I was then and totally unworthy, even if I was not clearly aware of such distinctions, I sensed them in part, at least in her presence. I made progress each day in the inner knowledge of that soul and of the perfected form that expressed it. I seized the symbol ever more completely. But did I avoid the trap altogether? Did I, in studying the lamp beneath the alabaster, not dwell too long on the contours? Did my fixed and avid glance seek solely to understand? Was my glance not trying sometimes to be understood and to question? Did I never withdraw my glance, rebuffed by the calm, untroubled brow which I received like a rejection? Was I never exasperated when the inattentive child could call my glance singular while the passionately cherished object seemed to find it so simple?

And then the most equable and best maintained beauty here below has inevitably its dull and absent hours. A beautiful woman does not unfailingly show us her portion of the ideal and eternal in a steady light. There are seasons and months when she is subject to languor. She gets up in a cloud that stays with her, hiding her in a treacherous warmth. Her eyes swim, her arms hang limp. Her entire body is oblivious, falling into unbelievable poses. Her flattering voice goes straight to the heart, making you want to die. When she is near, emotion takes over, the disturbance is contagious. Each gesture, each word from her seems like a favor. On one of those days you would say that her hair, carelessly heaped on her head, would come tumbling down, covering your face. A fragrant sensuality is emitted from her body like the stalk of a flower. Inebriation and poison! Run away! At certain moments every woman is a seductress.

At such moments, in fact, I wanted to run away. Sometimes I even did so and stayed away from Couaën for several days. Then I would think about marriage again. Could not a virginal love, mine alone and duty-bound, outweigh the enervating attraction of these sentimental friendships with young women? I threw myself into this fantasy. I pictured my foyer, its serious repose, its strong, permissible sweetness. The gracious preludes I used to know at La Gastine came to life in my reveries and rekindled a growing flame of a chaste and blushing tableau. Two poor lines of my own poetry, which I still remember, were associated with that vague epithalamium:

> And with their eyes the lovers could adore,
> Beneath parental eyes which could ignore.

But, bizarre subterfuge! Instead of heading off at such moments to Mademoiselle de Liniers, who was already found, and to whom I regarded myself at heart as so close to engaged that I would not have taken on a relationship elsewhere, I went on to imagine a marriage with some one of the young women I had glimpsed in one of the chateaux of the neighborhood. Then, when I had concocted a total fantasy, which I felt protected my heart like a cuirasse, I would scurry to Couaën to consult the judicious lady. She lent herself indulgently to these contradictory projects, to these mad plans, which I pursued chiefly to skirt her love more closely and blindly, to let her introduce me to a thousand intimate details of which she was the constant target. When we had a leisurely conversation on these country beauties among whom I was trying to choose, she would laugh and put herself to work to give me an occasion to meet them. These captious friendships are so sure of themselves that they never know jealousy. A half-league from Couaën lived a singular country gentleman, small and old, a widower with a seventeen-year-old daughter said to be beautiful. Madame de Couaën took me to visit them one day. I already knew the father, because he attended our political meetings and would sometimes get carried away, although his habitual retreat after each remarks was "As for me, gentlemen, I am no conspirator." Aside from his somewhat impatient royalism, he was a worthy man, a complete contrast with his turbulent neighbors and offering a picture of peaceful and meticulous tastes which natural infirmities had encouraged early. His first education had been very scanty, had left him disadvantaged, even in orthography. Nevertheless, Monsieur de Vacquerie loved to read, made excerpts and copied out the beautiful passages, especially the emotional ones. He received Delille's works in their first run. Every two years a trip to Paris brought him up to date about a multitude of little inventions that had aroused his curiosity. At his house, to give visitors a good welcome, he had a Barbary organ with new tunes and extra cylinders, an opticon with prints representing views of the capitals, a microscope with fleas and other insects, a game of solitaire on a table in the salon, and finally his rosy-cheeked daughter, an interesting miniature. You should have heard Madame de Couaën and me as we rode back, gaily inventorying the dowry that heiress was going to bring me. Add to all that a pretty woodland that covered almost half a parish and two gamekeepers as a showcase. For her part, Mademoiselle de Liniers, whom I still visited, although more seldom, was not so carefree. But her innocent suspicion was not directed at Madame de Couaën. Rather, my other relationships began to worry her. A deceptive situation for our three hearts! an illusion that mocked all three of us.

My love wound through these sinuous by-paths, like a stream hidden beneath grass. I lost it from sight. I could only hear it rustle. Sometimes I would have thought it had vanished completely, if some accident had not alerted me. Since this love never tried anything directly regarding the beloved, it came to my attention only in conflict with other strange sentiments that could cross its path. The strongest proof I had of this nature was my steadfast resistance to the unambiguous intentions of a woman in the neighborhood. She did everything she could to attract me. In a rather grim marriage, I think, around thirty-six and childless, she was prey both to the boredom of too little to do and the extreme desires of her second youth, now nearly past. She had singled me out on various occasions. I saw her intentions in her insinuating, disturbed expression and her vague, platonic conversations where she tried to ensnare me. My senses quivered, but my heart was repelled. A few months earlier I would have gleefully surrendered. One day when I had let myself accept one of her invitations, reading to her in the garden as she requested, she interrupted me wantonly, snatched the book out of my hands and ran off, scattering rose petals she snatched from the bushes as she went along. Surprise made the peril great. I was careful not to expose myself again. The strength of my resolve on this occasion made me well aware of the mysterious altars where I worshipped.

However, impatience with my situation subjected me to frequent sudden attacks. Then all disguise fell away, all subtlety flew away like a light sail under the gusts of a storm. I pulled on my chain, I shook it with pride, I neither wanted to break it nor hide it. I wanted to bear it away to the desert. How often that adored chain seemed to drag at my feet; I thought I heard it drag noisily along the beach where I was walking against the wind, breathing in the salty rain that hit me in the face, and adding my inarticulate cry to the barking seagulls and the waves! With my eyes turned West, facing the ocean and its sterile furrows, I liked to rest my gaze on a bare little islet that reared up close to a nearby promontory. Once, they say, it was the site of a college of Druids, then later, a Christian monastery; today, deserted with the exception of a few wretched huts. As a result of seeing it I imagined myself staying there alone, cultivating on that bare boulder my eternal, sterile thoughts and going to visit the living object only once a week at most with the devotion of a pilgrim. So one morning, saying I had to be absent and without telling anyone, I took a canoe to the island. At first I went through all those ruins, escarpments, and monumental boulders with a nearly savage joy. I walked completely around it several times. As long as the sun shone on the horizon, all was well. But when night fell, the place seemed dreary and mournful. The day and evening following doubled my anguish. Mortal fears obsessed me; dark desires, unclean thoughts came to me everywhere in this austere site where I had promised myself purity and constancy of soul. On this limited space I prowled in the same spots until I was dizzy. I did not know where to flee, what bleeding god to frighten with my lack of character. I pressed my hands and face against the granite blocks. That haughty stoicism of the night before had roughly instigated an abject contempt of self. I finally fell asleep under a fisherman's roof, but it was sleep that was disturbed, thick, agitated, heavy as a tombstone and just as streaked with painful figures and emblems. Oh my God, the evening of life, and, above all, the night that follows, would the cowardly sensualist find it like those nights on Druid Island? Oh God, if it is thus, have mercy upon us! I want to bathe myself in You before that evening, pray to You while the sun still shines with whatever strength is left to me. I want to surround myself with good deeds, with many a pacifying memory, so that my last sleep will be gentle and sweet, so that a happy dream, peacefully deployed, will lift my soul from the arms of the throes of death and guide it to the lights on the shore.

I had hardly recovered from my projected retreat on the island when I moved my sites further off. I contemplated a less restricted and harsh solitude behind a larger arm of the ocean. Madame de Couaën had often spoken to me about her native home, a mile out of Kildare, in the country of the same name. She had lived there until she left Ireland, and her mother lived there still. From having her describe them in minute detail I knew the sites, their least peculiarities, the long roadway between the double bush hedge which led to the entry grill, the huge elm trees in the courtyard, and on the side of the garden, that dear library whose arched windows were surrounded with honeysuckle and roses. Always present in my inner eye were the pots of fragrant carnations, the boxed myrtles on the circular terraced steps of the entry lawn, the music of the birds, two steps away in the hedge border of the bowling green. From side to side, dense thickets of shade, and opposite in the middle, a clearing through the seedbeds, with the Curragh river animating the distant vista. It was there in that green setting that my love imagined sweet little Lucy in a white dress, bareheaded, giving her arm to her sickly mother, making her sit down on a bench in the sunshine, putting her long cane in her hand when it was time to get up and walk. "Oh, yes!" I cried out involuntarily, imagining that pious daughter when I witnessed her panic and anguish, "yes, Madame, I will go live with your mother over there, I will bear your tenderness, console her for your absence, take care of her for you; I shall have a closer bond to you than ever; for her I will be another you." And I had her tell me again, as if to a confidential messenger, each object in detail, beloved flowers, benches the most caressed with warmth, the places touched by memories. She smiled in these moments of trust with incredulous sadness, but still grateful. But I took my thoughts seriously. I planned one way after another to carry them out. Only my conviction of the peril that would leave Monsieur de Couaën in was able to hold me back. After reflecting, however, that an important intrigue was just then getting underway in London and that by going through I could be of major usefulness to our friends, and that besides an immediate outbreak appeared less and less likely because of the truce with England, mixed in, I really believe, with these reasons—without even confessing it to myself, was an obscure will to return, my last scruple did not hold up, and I waited earnestly for the inevitable opportunity.

And it came. One evening towards the end of autumn, under cover of fog and darkness, a boat arrived from the British Isles with three men and secret dispatches. Monsieur de Couaën had been absent for several days visiting the former governor of ———, who lived more than twenty leagues away, too far away for us to have had time to warn him because the boat was leaving the following night. We could nevertheless turn over a sealed packet that he had had the foresight to entrust to his wife before he left. During the day I spoke with these men on his behalf, and there was no difficulty in getting them to agree to taking me back with them. I wrote a long letter, especially addressed to Madame de Couaën, but so expressed that it served as an excuse and explanation to him. I revealed my plan, my feelings for both of them, my deep vow to hold on to human society, indeed to life, just because of them. I depicted the disorder of my soul in poignant but disguised terms. I spoke of returning, with certainty but without a fixed date. Once this letter was written, I put it in an obvious place in my room, and as midnight neared, I went back to the craggy beach. The high tide to bear us away was nearly in; however, our men, who were snatching a little sleep to regain their strength, were not around. We had at least an hour yet to wait. So I sat down while waiting at that precise shelter near the chapel where I had come the day when she offered prayers. The same thoughts, magnified by an infinite number of others, rose in my breast. The waves, the shadows, my soul; all intensified the depth and infinity within me and around me. It was a dark, cold night, cloudless where stars cast little light, where bounding waves moved like a black herd, where the palest sliver of a crescent moon pierced the sky like a magic symbol. At that hour for solemn, nearly tender farewells, the Genie of the place was revealed to me with more authority than ever, and without any abatement or laxity it became imperceptibly personified in the divinity enshrined in my heart. Times gone by of miracle-working priestesses, the eternal and sacred bond between Armorica and Ireland, those confessor saints who, they say, made the trip, barely wetting their sandals on the flattened crest of the waves, I felt all of that like something present, familiar, like an event in my love. Innumerable nebulous circles, in the visible expanse of the Ocean and the Ocean of the ages, vibrated around a single point in my thoughts and sur-rounded me with a potent charm. At the strongest moments of that formidable harmony, where I continually drowned only to find myself, it seemed to me a voice arose from the wind and waves, calling my name. The voice approached and from time to time was distinct. There were intervals of deep silence. But I heard one final cry, a cry which named me in distress, a human accent, real and rending. I rose, seized by fright. What did I see? A wandering woman, cloak blowing, unbelted, hair disheveled, running towards me, frenzied yet still noble, waving something white at me. Soul of these shores, fateful beauty, immortal Velleda. On that autumn eve, beneath that waxing moon, was it you? Only the golden sickle was missing.

It was she. You already guessed, my friend. It was she, none other than she. She before me at that hour, on that deserted cliff where already our hands were joined. She, calling me through the heather as she looked for me! I was speechless. I thought I was under a magic spell. It took me several minutes to understand. Here is what had happened. Throughout the entire war news from Ireland could only reach us indirectly through these risky communications sent from London. Since the peace, family correspondence had been open. A few letters, however, by force of habit, had followed that former detour. That evening, however, before going to sleep, Madame de Couaën had a compelling intuition that this might be the case and she took a chance on opening the packet that she had not looked at the night before. Immediately she was struck by a letter addressed to her. It was her brother's handwriting. Her mother was dead! With this fatal letter in her hand, she ran to my room but did not find me. Someone had seen me go out. She did not ask anything else, and either by a vague instinct for a path she knew, or a sudden conclusion that at such an hour I could only be at the place of embarkation, she felt compelled to come after me. Her feet had carried her to me almost by themselves.

I calmed her. Her breast was heaving. I got some answers and tears from her. Having forced her to sit down for a moment, I dared stroke her feet, cold as marble. Then we came back at a gentle pace, as we had so often before. To better staunch her pain, to show her how much at the very moment of the dire news, I was already entirely committed to her departed mother, I told her about the plans her arrival had curtailed. She read the letter I had written. She was greatly disturbed; our souls mingled. "Oh, promise me you'll never leave," she said, "Monsieur de Couaën holds you so dear! You are indispensable. My mother is dead. I need you just to be able to talk about her and those things you listen to so well."

The next day, after an exhaustive conversation about her cherished mother, she cried out suddenly, without any apparent transition, looking at me with that long fixed look that was hers alone, "Say you will stay with us forever, that you will never marry!" My reply was choked with sobs; I wept on her hands as I kissed them.

CHAPTER VI

Monsieur de Couaën returned home the next day. The communiqués were serious and more critical than we could have imagined. A break with England appeared imminent. Our friends were planning to land a series of small groups. Additionally, all plans were closely tied to Paris. Monsieur de Couaën himself, needing to go there anyway, announced that he would leave right away. But on reflection he agreed that to disarm suspicion, he would take along his wife and children and have me accompany them. That way everything would look like a family trip. An old retainer, François, would be in charge during the fortnight. The eve of that expeditious departure, Madame de Couaën was busy with preparations, so I took the path to the hill, which was now luminous in the full moon. I had never climbed it with so light a step, so bounding a heart, with so much wind in my face and hair. My inner life was finally teeming. The outside world of action was going to open up. I had never experienced such a sense of this double life within and without. However, my worries about the approaching enterprise stimulated my emotions a little, and even though there was mixed in the prospect a thousand desirable opportunities for service and devotion, I could not hide from myself the idea of a happiness unfulfilled, dear but unknown, peaceful and increasing the more I became involved. The Marquis in particular I could not understand. Of course, I could conceptualize my own lack of foresight. I followed both of them in their fate. But he, what was he following? What raging fatality kept him from enjoying what he had? It was clear that he was going to ruin himself somewhere and more or less break us at the same time. I did not dare make conjectures in advance on what concerned him, on what reef or in what accident he would shipwreck. While I was considering her and him and placing inevitably as at the onset of any appealing project the silent enigma of that noble face, I noticed as soon as I reached the heath that he was there himself, walking slowly back and forth, stopping frequently, his hands buried up to his elbows in his back pockets, his head sunk to his chest like someone so absorbed that he is oblivious of his surroundings. I was at his side before he heard me, so deeply was his attention turned within, so much was the sea wind blowing against us, chasing away all noise, and so much was the fine heath grass muffling my footsteps! When I greeted him by name, he started, straightening up, as if his wound had been seen. He continued with more studied posture, but the bitterness of his blue eyes, the signs of pain on his damp temples, made the state of his soul quite obvious, and beneath a rather abstract and general guise, in the conversation he broached he was following his thoughts aloud.

I have noticed many times, my friend, that men of action, strong, resolute minds, even the least learned, when they have recourse to pure ideas, make true breakthroughs. They latch on and jar unusual angles and do not let go. Thrown into metaphysics, they straddle it strangely and cross it by oblique shortcuts, by quick and bold pathways. Since the number of serious questions in human experience is not infinite, and the number of solutions still less so, it gratifies my curiosity to see the eternal subjects of meditation recast to fit a life of action, to see the rough energy of a heroic mortal cut a belt to his own measure as he passes through, instead of weaving an idle and subtle web of Penelope like dialecticians and philosophers.

Monsieur de Couaën, in a voice that was not usual for him, held forth in this melancholy discourse with the following direction and meaning.

"Amaury, Amaury, life is a rough arena, a bruising heath. That is what I was telling myself as you came up. There is probably a law, some absolute order above our heads, some vigilant and infallible clock of stars and societies. But for us men, these distant accords might as well just not exist. The hurricane heaving on our shores can have a marvelous tone in a higher harmony. But the grain of sand twisting in the hurricane, if it has thought at all, must believe in chaos. Ever since man emerged, as they say, from the oak tree, he is not less dependent upon the north wind then he ever was. Here beaten down, stunted, sterilized (and he struck a knotted and meager holm-oak with his cane); there, further down, majestic, dominating and fully leafed; yet look, the vigor of the two trunks is the same. Men's destinies do not correspond to the energy in their souls. Basically this energy is entire in each man. Nothing is done or attempted without it. But between it and the development it needs, there is arid space, the reign of things, the accidents of time and place, and human encounters. If there is an overall result that humanity must accomplish en masse with relation to eternal law as a whole, I would be scarcely concerned. Individuals do not know what this result is to be. They compete blindly for it, some falling, some walking. No one can say that he is more fit to help than his neighbor. There is such an infinity of individuals, such as infinity of throws of the human dice, who could take care of this goal with diverse compensations, so that the end is reached despite all apparent contradictions? The phenomenon continually belies the law. The world turns, man suffers, the species goes on its way, and individuals are crushed!

"No, where individual human destinies are concerned, even where the principal events and personages of history are concerned, I know of nothing I can proclaim necessarily and regularly coordinated. I know of no one, who in my opinion, from the vantage point where we are now, could not just as well have been someone else and offered a different scene and figures."

And he chose a salient example which has always stayed with me. "Perhaps you judge the fall of Robespierre and his men, the 9th of Thermidor, as a necessary event. In a sense there is some truth in that. People were tired of monsters. And yet, if on that day in Thermidor, the Commune and Robespierre had won, which was materially entirely possible, Robespierre would not have fallen. Who know what new turn events would have taken? He would have managed the transition himself; the hypocrite would have tried moderation. He would have parodied Octavius to the end, and it would be he instead of the other, he the old triumvir, whom we would have to conquer today and who will, perhaps, conquer us. . . .

"I gladly subscribe, my dear Amaury, to a supreme, absolute law, in a universal order or fatality. I still believe in the individual energy that I feel in myself, but between the sovereign and sacred fatality, that of the group, the brazen sky of harmonious spheres, and that energy belonging to each mortal, I see a vague, nebulous, inextricable field, a region of contrary winds, where nothing is united for us, where every human combination can or cannot be. In the absolute order, I do not know whether everything holds together, if the inside of our earthly ship is bound in its least movements to superior vicissitudes. When rats stir at the bottom of the hold, is that tied to the phases of the moon, the monsoons of the ocean? Whether that happens with men in reality, no link of that kind is perceptible. We are such a numerous crew in the face of this earth, we have to straighten things out by ourselves. Hour, rank, circumstances, a cable here or there between the legs, a multitude of varying causes we can call *chance* combine with the energy of each man to help or hinder him. This energy sometimes triumphs, sometimes succumbs. There is only luck and loss, it is as simple as that. . . .

"When you feel strong in your soul, fully adept and vigorous, and yet lack a propitious destiny, you would at least like your destiny to be nobly and grandly contrary. Not having a burst of fame, you would claim painful misfortune and frantic rigor in order to experience nothing by halves. But no, even that, oh man, is asking too much! To the largest hearts, misfortune itself is mediocre, obscure ill luck wears you down. Instead of thunder, we have fog. You experience a slow and partial disintegration, not a great ruin. . . .

"Look over there," he cried, pointing to the sea, which beat the point of the promontory. From time to time a higher wave broke in foam against the point and sent its whiteness climbing into a corner of the setting sun that pierced the overcast sky. "See that shining wave aiming at the crest of the boulder like a marine divinity. That is the great man, the man who reaches the summit, but at the price of how many others whose plans aborted! Many waves will press forward with the same ambition, just as strong and powerful. No eye will espy them. No voice will call them divine. Some fall back growling in that mobile breast they swelled for a moment. Others will die in a hidden cove, in a cave on the beach, like some ordinary seal. In order for one wave to dart and surge from its pedestal, how many vanquished gnaw the base and serve to launch higher the one that is blessed and triumphant. So it is also with the ocean of men. A single difference. The happy wave is launched at the target all at once, while once above the common level, human energy, repressed up till then, reacts, unfolds, steps where it pleases and holds sway. . . .

"That man who mounts and magnifies each day, that man I admire and hate, whom tomorrow, if order is not restored, his victories will crown Caesar; that man whose glove I would kiss, if I were not reserving a blade for his heart—you believe him without an equal in his epoch. The public roar greets him. Listen. Already he is proclaimed unique, indispensable, the giant of our age. He has his equals, Amaury, I assure you. They are few in number, I admit, but they exist! They are even in the crowd that rears beneath his balcony. Some who will die as sergeants in his army—or colonels perhaps. Some will die hating him and will be unable to conquer him. Some will live long enough to support him to the end of his pride and dementia.

"Young people like you, Amaury, are of the age of action, which you expect soon, and with your exuberant enthusiasm you don't feel this way. You do not count, you do not measure. You giddily accept the universe and your rivals, relying on yourselves, and without worrying about the risks! (I don't need to tell you here how mistaken the Marquis was about me.) You grant them the better position. Provided the fight starts immediately, what differences does it make that the sun is in your eyes? Whatever the result, it strikes you in advance as justice itself, and more than adequate to right all wrongs. But later, at the approach of the rainy season, when fate has unabashedly jeered, when the battle was postponed at dawn and you are harassed by exasperating incidents, you ge morose, reasonable, and severe. It is hard to see opportunities slip away one by one, to see our equals drop anchor and get established, to see new generations pressing us, and to see the bark of our fortune, like a black dot on the horizon, take off before we boarded, and vanish in immensity, quantity, and oblivion.

"Such a man seems bizarre to you, taciturn and displaced. You have lived near him, with him. You have accosted him many a time. You have met him at the waters two summers in a row. For two winters he dined with you at the garrison table. You think you know him. You have passed judgment on him: an incomplete and atrabilious nature, you say. And now he is cut from the high ranks. But do you know what that man has in his soul, what he could become if he were not barred forever by certain things, if he felt that he was ever so little on his way, if one morning it was granted to him, in coming out of his thicket, to see his destiny face to face?

"Because, once they have arrived at a good stopping place, people exaggerate or amplify men after the fact. They are made into gigantic trophies or mannequins. They are decked out with almost supernatural ideas, credited with twenty kinds of systems, petitions of dreamers and dialectics for posterity. All that is idiocy and deceit!—Well, good people, remember this, there is in the world such a sullen person, mudstained like you perhaps, but made of the same stuff as your demigods. There are many virtualities without *exertion* (a very good word that we don't have, Amaury—and that the Marquise would pronounce much better than I), many such seeds that abort in obscurity, or stop at immature stages, for lack of opportunity, a fresh breeze, and sunshine."

As I saw the Marquis was turning the same idea over obsessively and getting plagued with exhaustion, I took it upon myself to interrupt him.

"This multiplicity, this loss of human faculties in this world," I said, "is both consoling and sad: sad for such and such individual no doubt; consoling for the group. This shows that the gross part of the human species today is composed and recruited from noble and precious matter, and that the species is no longer at the mercy of the first Nimrod upon the scene as before. I prefer this numerous, repressed, and groaning lucklessness to a level of dormancy. I prefer the heads of princes, captains, and orators, stuffed and struggling to swim, to a peaceful flock of animals led by one or two shepherds."

But he did not understand the matter in the sense of my conclusions. All his irony against the individuals outside the line did not turn to the thought of the greater number, to the consideration of increasing and soon dominant importance of a mass moved thus with the most generous ferments. He simply was devoured and outraged not to be one of the exceptional mortals who confront and break the straws of fate, one of the hunters of people, if that was called for, or shepherds. Monsieur de Couaën lacked a feeling for modern times.

Night was falling. We both climbed down that dear and eternal mountain rather heavyhearted. The sky was nearly at that very moment of decline as when I had come down the first time with her, a little more than a year before. And at this advanced season beneath those cold autumnal tints, the memory of that serene evening was brought back by the very contrast of the least details. To the full conversation earlier had succeeded a few rare, insignificant words that indicated the fatigue of prolonged thinking. The Marquis, more and more somber, was following his own thoughts within. As I raised my eyes at the turning of the descent, I perceived near the angle of the rampart, the very spot where on the first occasion he had seen us coming, the woman I was leading then. She in turn was watching for us from the lodge and glowed on her distant platform like the apparition of a chatelaine, white against the shadows calm and merciful.

"Look," I couldn't keep from crying out, as I touched the Marquis' arm, "look, wouldn't you say that is Hope?" *Lucia nimica di ciascun crudele?* (Lucy, the enemy of all cruelty). That is Dante, the poet of the proscribed and strong souls like yours, Marquis, who said that." A sardonic smile flitted over his lips; he immediately covered it over with some affectionate words.

Can you clearly visualize, my friend, the course of the slope and the turning point of the avenue where these events took place? Have you noted well in its simplest rough spots that the route is always the same? Have I brought you there often enough for you to paint it? If you visited it, would you recognize it? If I die tomorrow, will this deserted spot of the world be preserved in someone's memory? Or have I instead worn you out futilely on tracks with no terminus? In following me, did you not find the climb very slow, the contemplation very long, and the return much too ponderous? Have you not been put off by these problems I love and this monotonous grandeur? If that is the case, my friend, patience! we are now finally going to leave these sites. . . . Three weeks from that moment, Couaën would see me briefly one more time, but not the mountain. I was to go back to the mountain only more more time, the final and supreme, seven long years weighing upon my head. That visit was to mark the next day or evening of the most formidable and agonizing of my hours here below. My profane destiy would close, sealed forever beneath the stone. A bent and bleeding pilgrim, I will be seen bearing the ashes of sacrifice to the top of that very hill where my desire was born. Each leaning on the other, the Marquis and I will mount this hill together.

And yet an ineffable regret blends with the thought of the first charm. Men whose youth and adolescence are spent dreaming in deserted paths get attached to them, and leave behind gentle parts of themselves when they go away, the way lambs leave their whitest fleece behind in the bushes. Thus, alas, I left a great deal in the heather of La Gastine, and especially in the heather of Couaën. Dear beds of heather, solitary brambles who stole from me as I imprudently returned, what have you done with my linen vestments and the blond fleece of my youth?

CHAPTER VII

The trip for me, my friend, was what that first trip outside your own canton, a trip with the woman you love, always is. First of all, the intoxication of feeling yourself moving, rapidly propelled, outside your own volition, towards your encounter with destiny. Then there is that naive pride to be looked at, envied, by those stay-at-homes in front of their houses as you pass through the villages. There is the happy holiday confusion in taking care of the most ordinary acts of life; a curiosity like that of a child held between the knees, whose joyful shrieks you share even while affecting nonchalance. Many of those hills you climb on foot by the shortest path with a show of habit but with the thrill of new discoveries; endless conversations, by the lowered glass, beneath all the lights of the sky, but which double in intensity when the risen moon idealizes the landscape and sleep is out of the question. And then when sleep descends, the silence you enjoy when you are keeping watch; the fantasies you attach to the passing trees; a faint notion of danger which you cherish; a thousand precious, unsuspected inconveniences, which you assume and which the carefree accidents of supper and bedtime interrupt. All that magical variety of the road would expire the evening of the fifth or sixth day, in fatigue, mist, and tumult, when we reached our faubourg in Paris.

We stopped quite close to Val-de-Grace, in that same dead-end street of the Feuillantines you have heard me mention so often and that the childhood of one of your illustrious friends had made dear to you. What memories you unknowingly brought back to life for me when you uttered the name of that place in the belief you were telling me about it! Madame de Cursy, Monsieur de Couaën's aunt, formerly Mother Superior at a convent in Rennes, lived there in a community with several nuns her own age. She was expecting us and received us in her home. Monsieur de Couaën believed that on this occasion we could accept her hospitality without compromising her. She was a truly devout woman, nearly sixty, short, her face wrinkled, yellowed, crushed, but with a glow of unchanging dawn. She was one of those creatures whose contrite flesh took on early the image of our crucified Savior and a reflection of that glorious shroud made her luminous in darkness, like one of the holy women at the Tomb. Happy are those souls who pass here below beneath a veiled sunbeam and in whom a loving inner smile always animates, yet never dissipates the perpetual cloud! Her face, indeed, had something of her nephew's haughty expression, but it was corrected by sweetness at every moment, and the underlying nobility of her manners blended with her humility as a handmaiden of the Lord. This friendliness put everyone at ease in her presence. She already knew Madame de Couaën, whom she had received on two earlier visits, but she had not yet seen the children. They took to her at first sight and, following our example, called her "Mother." I was welcomed as a member of the family. A copious meal restored us and as we did not know how to stop our stories, she took it upon herself to remind us we were tired. Hardly had she led us to our bedrooms, to our beds protected by crucifixes and blessed box-wood branches, than I felt the profound silence of that house separate us from the distant roar of the huge city, and for the first time I dreamed on the shore of that other ocean.

The next day was Sunday. Around eleven o'clock in the beautiful morning sunshine, after a mass heard at Saint-Jacques-du-Haut-Pas (because that of the little convent was said before we got up), we started off for glittering Paris, which I had seized only by its nocturnal murmur the night before. Oh! when the bridges were crossed and the repopulated Tuileries appeared before us. When, in that too-narrow court I saw, gleaming and bounding, generals, aides-de-camp, con-sular guards and the young women at the window to greet them; when the First Consul himself came out on horseback at the stroke of noon, twenty martial bands played *Veillons au salut de l'Empire* all at once. When the chargers reared and whinnied and in the undulating crossing pattern of plumes, manes, helmets, and standards, a thunderous acclamation reached the clouds, . . . oh, wretchedness, I saw how very small and puny I was, more crushed in each of my limbs than dust beneath the horseshoes. I could hardly breathe. At that moment I remembered what I had read in Plutarch about the crows that dropped dead from the insane Greek acclamation of its presumed liberator. Glancing at the Marquis, who was standing next to me, I saw that he was in an even more deplorable state. Livid desolation beat and battled his brow, as would the wing of an invisible vulture.

He was biting his pale lips. His eyes were full of hatred. He left us almost immediately, recommending a stroll in the gardens. I myself did not feel hatred, but rather a jealous regret, an internal bleeding, suffocating with no foreseeable release. The feeling of precocious abnegation, against which my generous sap was mobilizing, was long, you will see, in getting established and acclimated in me. In the course of the idle years which would follow, it was frequently complicated by suppressed rages. They made my other wounds burn and sting, irritating them often.

But when you are young and in love, you first give all your attention to love. All suffering is enriching, any passion, even strange, is poured in to increase love. Ambition complains of being indigent only because it would like to offer love a throne. Curiosity, which enjoys new sites, only seeks out new retreats, and in imagination chooses shady places. You, who are twenty, imagine envy and desire. Enlarge and change your horizons. Fan your flames of war, please your eyes! The end of desire, the end and the reward of effort is always love. If I had had love then, love in its truth and certainty; if the creature too pure to whom I vowed a fire without fuel and sparks had never made me doubt, to my very depths, the sovereign phrase "Je t'aime"; if in these unexplored Tuileries, beneath the leafless chestnut trees, around the solitary green rug that Atalanta tramples, a few fatal, eternal words had dared ignite and escape; if, finally, guilty and fiery as I was then, I had believed steadfastly in my evil, ah, at least that evil would have seemed better than anything else to me! How it would have eclipsed everything else! Gilded groups, resplendent morning of the century, consular constellation, how superior I would have felt to you! The man who loves and is sure of loving, if he passes to one side of the inebriated and glorious crowd, is like the avaricious Jew who would carry a priceless, solid, and limpid diamond, set in his heart, enough to buy 100 times over the tawdry feast he disdains both those who give it and those who admire it, since he with a simple glance at the magic crystal can discover whenever he wishes more conquests than Cyrus, more luxuries than Solomon.

Although my love was never to come from such a transparent crystal so marvelously endowed, although it was drawn at most with a few wavering, trembling, and confused lines, the movement it was subjected to and diverse shocks helped it grow and gave it more substance and reality. The change and variety of place, especially when you begin to love, work to the advantage of love. Since everything encountered is its tributary, it is like those bodies of water that swell faster in flooding. If you go from a long time spent in a calm residence to one abruptly strange, you become very sensitive to the strangeness. All the vague parts of our soul, which were rooted in the former place, are now detached, widowed, folding back and taking root in our obsession. My overexcited senses and overheated imagination for which the groves of Couaën offered me little enough protection and that the daily sights, fatal for my scruples, had just doubled in me, came from another less delicate source of passionate accelerations. That, alas, was the principal and most blind. I have to insist on this even though I blush with shame! I will tell you here only the ravages it caused.

You could only have a weak notion, my friend, of the Paris of those days in the opulence of its disorder, the frenzy of its pleasures, the display of its exciting scenes. The fall of the old century, joining the adolescent vigor of our own, formed a rapid, turbulent confluence, with spattering slime and bubbling foam. Our idle armies and the multitude of foreigners from every nation, coming in during that brief peace, were like a sudden swell that makes a beautiful river overflow. Of course, I could merely glimpse and guess the extent of the tumultuous inebriation during the first two weeks of my first stay. However, although I went out little and usually accompanied Madame de Couaën, my glance quickly formed a picture. Passing through the squares and down the streets, I did not follow wise Solomon's precept, but let my gaze wander and stray: I let myself look at everything. My sideways glance, which probably looked indifferent, crossed corners and pierced walls. With Madame de Couaën on my arm, I appeared to be completely absorbed in taking care of her, but I had taken in everything. Once or twice in the evening, after having walked with Monsieur de Couaën as far as his political meeting near Clichy, where I left him, I returned by myself, and from the Madeleine to the Feuillantines, I crossed that sea of impurity as if I were swimming. I plunged in running to the furthest quarter, to increase the few free moments I had for my unleashed curiosity.

"The shadows are deep, the crowds are unknown; the flickering evening lights dazzle without revealing. No eye, I fear, will see me," I said in my heart. So I went in, launched by a wild fury. I got lost but always found my way. The narrowest passageways, the most populous crossroads, and the most laden lures appealed to me most. I discovered them unerringly, led by a morbid instinct. They were strange, inexplicable circuits, a twisting labyrinth like that for those damned by lust. I passed by several times, panting at the same angles. I seemed to recognize in advance of the deepest ditches because of my fear of falling in. Or else I would come back to skirt the peril with the horror-struck face of flight. A thousand honeyed or besmirching propositions welcomed me throughout the passage. A thousand fatal images struck me. I bore them away in my palpitating flesh, retracing my steps like a cornered stag, my forehead dripping, my feet broken, my lips dry. Such fatigue quickly brought its own brutalization. I scarcely kept enough lucidity and nerve to pull myself away from the diseased attraction, to break that enlacing spiral of the sudden slope which ends in ruin. And when I had crossed to the other bank, when I had escaped from the shipwreck to my new mountain and reached the little convent where the good nuns and Madame de Couaën were finishing supper, I would find that my consuming race through these worlds of corruption had lasted no more than an hour.

The sight presented as I entered was so calm: that frugal spread, the salt and oil of the dishes, those pious faces to Madame de Cursy's right and left, in silent repose, that good odor of the Last Supper emitted there, and those shared blessings of the end of the meal. All that refreshed me somewhat as I stepped in, and dissipated the thickest flushes on my cheeks and in my eyes. However, no healthy fear was reborn; no sacred founts reopened. I still had a culpable aridness, an unsatiated memory, which I kept alive all evening long beneath that chaste and merciful regard. The beams of that modest lamp, which should have gleamed only on a heart veiled in scruples, shone unbeknownst on profaned regions.

One December morning lightly touched by frost, Madame de Couaën and I took the children to the Jardin des Plantes, for they thought about the menagerie even in their sleep. After many a walkway and detour we sat down on a bench while they ran around us. We were enjoying the beauty of the first frost, the tremulous brilliance of the sky and the instinctive lightheartedness it inspires. "This must be the way it is in life," I was saying, "when all is stripped bare within, when we walk down avenues of leafless trees, there are days like these when rejuvenated hearts sparkle like springtime. The first tinklings of freezing old age arrive like a joyful angelus. Is this a delusion, a lost echo of youth on that slope leading to death? Is it an annunciation and promise of a sojourn in the beyond?"

"It's most assuredly a promise," she answered.

"Yes," I resumed, "it's some distant call, an affectionate reminder to hurry, to have confidence at the beginning of the darkening days, those days termed *non placent*." And I explained to her, with all the sadness I attributed to it, what *non placent* meant. But near us on the same bench, two women of a rather respectable age and appearance were talking, and since the expression *infernal machine* came up

frequently, we listened in spite of ourselves. They were talking about
the assassination attempt of Nivose, exactly two years to the day.
Their naive horror made me break out in a cold sweat. Madame de
Couaën herself, usually indifferent to such subjects, blanched. What
kind of plot were we engaged in after all? Where did it lead? with what
kind of men? what kind of means? and what would be the public
judgment? That last thought struck both of us. We had no need to
express it. A long silence cut off our blithe speculations of the moment
before. She said she did not feel well, and I took her home. As for
myself, agitated in my darkest ideas by what I had heard, I could not
stay inside, and I returned alone to the very same walk in the Jardin.
The two women had left. Two others had taken their place, one of
them in a showy and provocative ensemble. To my confused vision,
she looked beautiful. Glances, whispers, slow and sinuous pacing,
shrill laughter; as treacherous as the whistling of a fowler, the whole
rigmarole soon began. From a distance I paid more attention than I
should have. Culpable thoughts replaced dark thoughts. At these
moments of perplexity and bitterness, if God is absent, if there is no
altar of good council, if it happens in the squares and streets where we
try to take refuge, sensual diversion easily replaces and removes moral
concern. The near future that gets in the way of foresight, the whole
of eternity itself disappears in that ticklish point of the present. The
wild fruits of the hedges seem good because they fill us up; man acts
like a baby animal. If I may use, my friend, strong, chaste comparisons
from the Scriptures, at first we are a lamb who gaily follows a ewe that
is not his mother, traipsing along like a morning game as if promising
himself to turn around at any moment. The turns and twists are long,
cheerful, and flowered at the beginning. The distance is reassuring.
First this walk, then another. At the corner of the next hornbeam
bower, there will be time to turn around. You pass the bower and keep
on following. Little by little the mechanical compulsion takes the
upper hand. You stop frisking; you no longer say, "I'll leave at the
next corner." You lower your forehead, the paths grow narrower, one
heavy tread leads to another. The feckless lamb has grown like the
stupid steer led to slaughter. That is where I was, my friend. I gave in,
head down, when a sudden encounter that these frivolous creatures
had at the turn of a gate bore them away. Noisy shouts and jokes
apprised me that I had been spared and delivered. My first reaction, I
confess, was bitter and silly resentment. I felt all the fluster of evil
without having reaped the gross benefit. However, remorse followed.
When I had returned to Madame de Couaën, when I saw her again,
still pale and teary-eyed, still obsessed by the morning episode, when

she said, "How peculiar it is. This is the first time I've seriously thought about these things. Only today did they appear to me in their true light. What those women said was a sudden and dreadful illumination. We are engaged—we and our friends, my husband, these dear children (and she kissed them tremulously)—on a path of ruin and crime. How did I never see that before? But I didn't. My concern with my poor mother and our sweet, sheltered life over there hid it all from me. I've never been able to be absorbed in more than one thought at a time."

Hearing her sigh like that, I could not find the means, both inexhaustible and tender, to salve her wound. My soul was no longer a pure fountain at her feet, reflecting and drowning her tears. My feeling, sincerely moaning, withdrew from the meaning of my words. Even while uttering them, my mouth was sullied by its intentions. I was ashamed of myself, a very different kind of shame, I assure you, than after those bad evenings where I had wandered aimlessly. Because here it was a distinct face, the first of that kind I had noticed and followed—and in broad daylight!

This took place on Christmas eve, two days before we were to leave. Monsieur de Couaën had made sufficient arrangements with the leaders of the party. I myself had not gotten involved in any direct relation. Christmas day we used for rest and worship. The little convent was filled well before dawn with hymns, lamps, incense. Those aged Carmelite voices seemed to have gotten young again. Still, we went in the morning to Saint-Jacques-du-Haut-Pas to enjoy a more elaborate celebration of the solemn rebirth. Madame de Couaën's impression had not dissipated; her suffering, which had assumed a mask of calm, reappeared in the insistent and deeply affected manner of her prayer. Filled with this sight, entreated by such touching surroundings, inwardly convinced of my humiliating fragility, the idol of my reason could not resist. For a moment the beams from the divine crib, the manger of Bethlehem, touched me. Once again I was back with my strongest days of faith and grace, with an inexpressible sense of their flight. I wished to recapture them. I held out my hand to that redeeming cradle which offered them to me. Oh, if only that suppliant hand had remained outstretched, that it had not grown wearied, that it had dried up before falling back. Where were you, angels in heaven, my good patrons, to hold it up? I had weakened up to then, no doubt; I had wandered dangerously off course; I had lusted and caressed the reef. But there was still room for a simple return. That Christian year, just beginning, could have taken me in its course like the floods of high tide take back the skiff abandoned by the earlier tides. I would have reformed before my total fall. Nothing absolutely mortal had been consummated. Alas, however, it was not to be; I was already too much within the mortal grasp, too much on the brink of my loss, for any effort besides a desperate effort to have extracted me. I knelt and agitated vainly on the slope. That momentary gesture towards the shining crib was less a sheltered and sure ark at the entry to the deluge of immense waters that I invoked for my future salvation than an innocent basket of delightful and regretted fruits that I greeted with a passing fancy. My will did not will it. The grace from on high glided by like a gleam of light. How many other Christmases like that would have been spared me, how many Easter penances would have been changed for me, but after having already rolled to the bottom, degraded, Oh my God, forming impotent vows, resolutions contradicted every hour, proposing to me, Lord, loci of support and moments of solemn pause in that insensate and repeated fall, sometimes hanging from your crèche, sometimes at the angles of the holy tomb, imploring to hold one of the nails of Your Cross, crying out, "From this Easter—or this Christmas—henceforth I pledge myself to death and rebirth; I swear never to fall again!" And my deplorable, enervating facility seemed to redouble with my efforts, until that day finally when will and grace mysteriously accorded, like two equal wings lighting together, to carry me to an asylum of tenderness and stability, that solid rock with the spurting stream.

We left Paris after long farewells to Madame de Cursy, who made us promise to come back soon. Our return amidst continuous rain was dreary and cheerless. Madame de Couaën remained pale and preoccupied. The Marquis was silently absorbed in the plans he had just explored close up, and I, besides my habitual restlessness, had my own disorder, blazing and struggling at all inner points. When I concerned myself with the children—the only ones still carefree—my eyes met those of Madame de Couaën, fixed on her children and overflowing with bitterness. In that short trip, so charming in the beginning, and during which nothing apparently substantial, nothing materially perceptible had happened, how much peace was destroyed, never to return, illusions forever flown! The infirmity of our sights and desires! A little more enlightenment here and there, an horizon a little larger beneath our glances sufficed to break the spell.

CHAPTER VIII

However, our gloom was, to tell the truth, only a disturbing premonition somehow anticipating things, like a color change in waves announcing proximity to dangerous depths in the sea. Events would soon justify this premonition. On reaching Couaēn very late in the evening, we learned that for a few days several detachments of soldiers had been encamped on the neighboring coasts and that our own, Saint-Pierre-de-Mer, had just been occupied. They appeared to have wind of some proposed disembarkments they wanted to forestall. But at that moment I could hardly investigate the details. A message, delivered in the course of the day, informed me that my uncle, paralyzed by a stroke, had probably only a few hours left to live. I took off on horseback before sitting down in the salon and left Couaēn in the anxiety I shared. I was crushed with presentiments on the cloudiest of nights as I rushed towards my own sorrows.

My friend, you have sometimes crossed through these inevitable crises. You have lost some cherished creature, closed someone's eyes. Like me, you have rushed along the road at night in some chilling anguish, not knowing whether the dying man would already be dead when you arrived, slowing the trot suddenly when you approached the windows and touched the paving stones of the streets and courtyard, for fear of waking that dear soul, perhaps resting that very moment in a light, refreshing sleep, or perhaps for fear of provoking his eternal slumber. You have been present, I imagine, during the affliction of a mother who does not want to be consoled. You have grasped in a mute clasp the hand of a proud and grieving father who has buried his sole male child. Chance or pity has surely led you into some hideous hovels of misery. There you have seen, on the pallet of gaunt mothers in childbirth, suckling infants crying with hunger, or an aged paralyzed couple, one who still speaks unable to walk, the other who still drags around, unable to make herself understood. You have breathed in that sweat on the limbs of the poor, more vivifying here below to those who sponge it off than the incense angels burn, and you left ready to confess to the Cross and charity.

At midnight, waking with a start, perhaps you have seen your chamber red with the glow of fire, and barely clothed, tongue thick with saliva, lips black and dried, you ran straight to your stricken old mother to carry her away from danger. You put her down in a safe place and returning alone, with no hope of aid, calculated the disastrous rate of the conflagration, the time it would take one section of wall, then another, to burn, then the roof, wondering where you yourself would sleep the next day.

Poverty, too, perhaps because it comes suddenly in our times of trouble, caught you unawares, and you formed strong and pious resolutions to work to support your dependents. Finally, my friend, you have certainly passed through one of those sacred hours where human life opens violently beneath the brazen rod and where the real depth is revealed. Well, in such moments, tell me, in these hours of true life, life rent and profound, tell me if the idea came to you, if the senses and their flattering images and pleasures appeared to you. Tell me, how low, shameful, perverse, extinguishing all spirit and all passion, and to speak plainly, how vicious in their intoxication and brutalizing in their sustenance! Yes, if during an evening of the Toussaint, beneath the marble porticoes of the most beautiful Sicilian cloister lapped by the waves, when the procession of monks moves barefoot over the flagstones, singing the prayers of deliverance--if suddenly through the grills of the air-vents came a rotten blast from the sewers of our large cities—the effect would be no different from that of pleasures and sensuality, when they come back to us at those moments where severe sorrow, death, love in its eternal aspect triumph and bathe us again in the reality of the things of God. Each time that from the heart of these mobile, contradictory waves where we wander in error, the arm of the All-Powerful plunges us back into the secret, icy current, in that kind of Jordan which moves in rigorous waves beneath the warm and corrupt currents of our ocean, each time we feel that same shiver of disgust aroused by the idea of the Siren, and we vomit the joys of the flesh. And if that affects us in this way, because a purifying pain comes to us when we witness the death of others, we may often wonder, "What will it be like at the brink of our own death? What will it be like afterwards in the formidable shock of the shore?"

When I reached the house, my poor uncle was still breathing, but there was no longer any hope, and his final rattle was the sole sign of life. For several hours, he had not raised his eyelids, He no longer murmured, and gave no sign of hearing anything. His last words had been to see whether I was coming. Standing next to the bed, I gently clasped his had and told him who I was. I thought I felt a light pressure in response. A hint of a smile at the angle of his lips finished his thought, and until the last breath, whenever I spoke, that pressure of his hand responded; at least he had recognized me. And so I lost the person who had loved me the most blindly and trustingly, who had loved me like a father.

I had lost my father and mother when I was very young, as I forgot to tell you in the beginning. My father, a naval officer, had died on the bridge of his frigate during an accident in maneuvers. My mother, who followed him shortly afterwards, had remained at the threshold of my memory like the distant azure of a recollection. I see myself in a tiled antechamber where they used to bathe me on Sundays and holidays. I was naked in the tub, and the sun coming through the door opened to the courtyard fell on the square, forming long lozenges I can still draw. But suddenly I heard military music in the street announcing the passage of some troops. I wanted to see and shouted for someone to carry me to the windows of the next room. The women there were either hesitating or refusing when another woman, pale, clad in black, entered abruptly, carrying, I think, a large bouquet of red flowers. She picked me up, wet as I was, in a coverlet, and took me over to see the soldiers pass. That woman in black, by my reckoning, must have been my mother. But the scene itself, the bath, the martial music, all that was perhaps only an image, stimulated after the fact, touched by the stories I was told daily. I was told a lot about my mother. My uncle, her own brother, whose retiring nature, sensitive and somewhat talkative, could not get over some impressions of the past, had nurtured me on the purest domestic milk. Although of a station quite inferior to my father's, she was so renowned before her marriage by her glowing pearlescent beauty and smiling demeanor that almost no one considered it a misalliance. Their meeting had been like a novel, considering the scruples of the girl and the passionate pursuit of my father, who ran over from Brest whenever he could and prowled beneath her window, seeing only a vague shadow through the window panes and curtain, and sometimes for only a half-hour at night. All these attentions conquered her heart; and one glorious afternoon, the beautiful bride was taken by launch through the road-stead of Brest. She nimbly climbed the gangway of the frigate *Elisabeth*, where a gallant ball awaited her. To that trip and the festivities of those days, my uncle loved to return. Or rather he had never returned, and up to the end he saw in its novelty his sister's grace and triumph standing out against that setting of rope and rigging.

Well, go ahead, dear maternal uncle, start over fearlessly, always for the only time, never often enough, start over until I can remember as much as you, until I imagine I saw it myself. The child's imagination is tender, facile, and faithful. The mirror is virgin and free from tarnish. Engrave it with a diamond and revive its pure imprints a hundred times over. How memories relayed thus make us enter the flower of earlier times and gently push our crib backwards! How memories like this are the clouds of our dawn and the chariot of our morning star. For us, the most alluring colors of the ideal are stolen from these reflections of an epoch slightly earlier, when we are rocked by the family tradition and think we really witnessed. My own ideal, when I had a human ideal, was illuminated by many a flash of lightning from these years, from which I could garner only echoes. In the midst of those bannered returns of d'Estalog and Suffren which unrolled in my fantasy, I often imagined the main staircase at Versailles, where my father would have presented me in one of his trips and where I sailed amidst chimeras; it was always in one of these hunting lanes of the royal forest where I unerringly transported my first interview with Monsieur de Couaën, but with a Monsieur de Couaën powerful and honored, as he deserved. Didn't you do that, too, my friend? Doesn't it seem to you that you have lived with the new pomp of the times I have described to you? Those regal purple morning ceremonies of the Consulate, didn't they exert the fascination of reminiscence, although at that time you had not even been born? Have you never noticed that the era we should have preferred to live in is the one that immediately precedes our own?

Although my parents were dead, I lacked none of those affectionate attentions that develop our youthful nature. My uncle, who lived in a country area where he had some property, and my mother's entire family, scattered throughout the countryside, made me the object of a thousand indulgences. My father, who had left me only a few distant cousins and some friends, whom the Revolution was still dispersing, never lost sight of his name and blood in my person. To the great store of gratitude for the good family that reared me, I joined—shall I confess?—a secret conviction of being superior. But none of that showed externally, and when I was later negligent, acting like an ingrate towards many of those good relatives who loved me and had cherished me since childhood, so wretched a thought in no way contributed to my obliviousness. I was simply too much a prey to the currents bearing me away. Indeed, these relatives on my mother's side, who watched tenderly over me in her memory, and whom I almost brusquely stopped seeing when I came of age, I loved them, I thought of them only with emotion. They count even now in the back of my mind. But they are unaware of it and were unaware of it then. Their feelings were hurt, and they complained. This is because youth is naturally ingrate, fickle, and unstable. We turn our back on the games of childhood, the green hedge of the home grounds, that nurturing field where we looted for honey and ate the fruit. At that age, we go away one morning like a swarm of bees that is not to return, like the raven of the Ark which did not return with the olive branch. We keep the flower of the past and sow it along the way. Rejecting with an expression of injury everything that youth denied us, we want the special bonds of youth, friends and acquaintances which are youth's alone, which we have chosen. Because we feel, with youth in our breast, treasures that will buy hearts and streams to water them. We find ourselves infatuated for life with friends unknown to us yesterday, and promising eternal love to virgins barely glimpsed. Always excessive and rushed, we show little understanding for what we leave behind. We tear what we pull off. We break old roots rather than let them fall. As we scar towards our pleasant preferences, caught in youth's imprudent chains in the home of the strange woman, we despise the good natured who love without knowing why, because we are more or less blood relations.

I hope you grasp my simple idea, my friend. I in no way blame youth for being expansive, for not wanting to take root in the paternal threshold and go off to meet other men. I know that we no longer live under the ancient law, in the shadow of the patriarchal palm trees. I know that the words *unknown people* and *foreign woman* no longer have the meaning they did in the time of the Sage the Apochrypha, and that it would be truly impious to repeat with him, so much the communion of the Lamb has changed everything, "Remove thy way far from her, and come not nigh the door of her house; Lest thou give thine honour unto others, and thy years unto the cruel: Lest strangers be filled with thy wealth, and thy labours be in the house of the stranger" (Proverbs, v:8–10). There is more to this. This unbounded transport of youth, this detaching of the bonds of blood and race, and the meager acceptance of them, could be precious aids for the new alliance and intermingling of men. But we must not dissipate this expansiveness, so rich and zealous, into a crossing of error and inconstancy, capricious and sterile predilections. Besides, certain in-alienable virtues of the family order should never disappear, even under the law of universal brotherhood, when Christ will rule on earth.

With my loving nature, which, well directed, would have sufficed both for earlier bonds and new adoptions, I managed to be both indiscreet in my external attachments and ungrateful for those I was leaving behind. My greatest, genuine misdoing of that last type, over which I still feel sharp, concerned a fine woman, my mother's relative and godmother, who had transferred to me the same feelings she had for my mother, increased by what age and the memory of the regretted deceased can add. There came a time in the height of my affairs and diversions at la Gastine when I visited her less frequently, and after I was taken up at Couaën, I stopped seeing her altogether. Her home was not very much off the road leading from Couaën to my uncle's, but I didn't pass directly in view of it. Once the first awkwardness was created, I waited, I postponed, I no longer dared. At first she was indulgence itself. She asked my uncle about me and attributed my behavior to projects and new duties. But when after months, seasons, even New Year's day passed without my stopping, she let herself complain, saying one day, "Will I never see Amaury even once before I die?" I knew she said this, I promised myself I would go, and did not do so. Partly false shame, partly blind distraction Mademe barbarous. What did you think of me, my mother's old friend? What did you tell her when you joined her in heaven? Did you really think I was a spoiled ingrate? Did you decide I was prouder and harsher with age? That I was suddenly contemptuous of those who loved me? At that final hour, when you would have blessed me like a grandmother if I had been present, did you harbor harsh thoughts against my inexplicable neglect? And today, when you can read in me, today when I have so often prayed for you and uttered your faithful name with each sacrifice in the commemoration of the dead, beloved benefactor, in the joyous breast of Mary, have you forgiven me?

How petty are human friendships when God has no share! how they exclude each other! how they follow upon each other, pushing other on, just like waves on the sea! My friend, see it and take note. I had deserted the shelter of my mother's godmother for La Gastine and then La Gastine itself went too far away. Will the Couaën that took over stay in view? We are, alas, getting close to departure, and during the years that followed I tried to forget it. What wretchedness! That house, where you went morning and evening, which seemed like your own, even better than your own, for which all previously favored sites were abandoned, well, if God did not intervene at the threshold and accompany you there, that house, you may rely on it, would some day fall in your eyes. You would avoid it as if it were nefarious, and when by chance your travels brought you close, you would make a detour to keep from seeing it. The more acutely sensitive you are, the truer this will be. You will go then to another house, then to a third, like a wandering guest who tries to settle down, but you will not return to the first. And the one that will hold you in your last years, to which you seem most faithful, will simply be due to habit, weariness, your final apathy, to your powerlessness to go further and begin again. And the feeling of flight and inevitable displacement in purely human liaisons, when you have already lived through two or three, often grows so strong even if we are still young and anxious to pretend we are in love, that we no longer have enough faith to seriously undertake new searches. The simulacrum of duration, which embellishes any attachment in the beginning, no longer charms us. So we climb the stairs of today's friends, saying to ourselves that probably in a year or two we shall climb some others. And the day when that omen hits us, our hearts are dead for that friendship. There is nothing durable and in place beyond the reach of things, the trial of absence itself, of violent separations and shipwrecks but these friendships, to use the happy modern parlance, *through which God loves us* and which love us through God. On these, in stormy hours, faith descends in the same eternal objects like a lifesaving rope, and in calm hours, recognize and follow the same guiding star from the East. These are diligent friendships whose first act is to deposit a noble form of themselves in the celestial treasury, where they can subsequently find and unceasingly study to emulate it.

As long as my uncle's last moments and funeral obligations retained me, I had only the Couaën news I sent for each day, but the day after the interment I could go to spend a few hours myself. I learned about the occupation of the coast in more detail. Soldiers stationed themselves in the recesses and did not display themselves, but let no one approach. They avoided lighting fires and maintained a rigorous watch, especially at night, as they were hoping to surprise rebel landings. The commanding officer, said to be of high rank, seemed to have very precise indications on the place, although less so on the date. Monsieur de Couaën did not seem very disturbed to me. Either because of the need around him to keep calm, or because it is the familiar countenance for energetic characters when danger threatens, or because of genuine conviction, he supported us with the greatest imaginable composure, insisting that the mine was not discovered, that the indications had to be false, that the very movements of the troops two or three months in advance proved it. He absolutely refused precautions of personal safety, and all that I could do was get him to gather all his compromising papers in a secret cabinet in the tower, with permission to destroy them in case of emergency. Fortunately, we had not received the arms and powder that had been promised. Our other friends and noisy conspirators in the neighborhood were probably not so secure. Monsieur de Couaën had received no news from anyone since his return; that was how this sudden alert had dispersed these amateurs! Kind Monsieur de Vacquerie, who was no conspirator, was the only one to give a sign of life; not personally, the poor devil! but at least through his two gamewardens, who on his instructions came and went, getting information, delivering warnings, on a continual alert. They came to Couaën twice on his behalf during a brief visit I made one afternoon. When Madame de Couaën saw them, sad as she was, she could not keep from returning my smile. She was truly sad, pale, lethargic, lost in obsessive thoughts that kept her nearly in a stupor. One notion, which I would not dare call superstitious, oppressed her, and she was happy to have someone finally to tell it to. The "blues" did not respect our dear chapel Saint-Pierre-de-Mer; they had settled it from the first as a kind of headquarters. Even Christmas morning, old François, who had come from the coast two evenings earlier, leaving things as usual, had found the place invaded, the lamp out—or broken—and the soldiers camping in the nave. From certain features of his tale and various other bits of information on the troops' hour of arrival on the point, Madame de Couaën concluded that it was the morning of the day before Christmas that this violation occurred, and she imagined that the symbolic altar light, which had kept watch so many years, must have been put out the very moment on the day we were sitting on that bench at the Jarin des Plantes, hearing those women whose account had stung her on the spot. That is the only way she could explain her electrifying agitation there, that bitter blood vessel that ruptured in her chest, that sudden and icy chill that had blown on her happiness. Her mysterious explanation affected me, and even while trying to dissuade her, I was preoccupied by it. I have thought about it again seriously since. I would never be the one to deny, although never favored at any time by this kind of strange communication, these mediating harmonies, to which God occasionally has recourse and from whose flight good and evil spirits can, in passing, extract exact or propitious analogies.

There are times and clusters in our life when after a long period of inactivity, events crowd together, as if congesting a narrow exit. A short week was not enough for all the accidents. Monsieur de Greneuc, sickly and bed-ridden for several months, died during our trip. Madame de Greneuc decided to leave that residence in mourning for another property in Normandy. I said my goodbyes only at the last moment. The worthy lady was gloomy and silent. Mademoiselle Amèlie, tranquil, attentive as usual, had grown perceptibly paler, and her voice, its gentleness increase by its simplicity, had gained, even in the lowest tones, a liquid sound that went to the soul and caused pain. How many tears had been shed within to penetrate and discipline that young voice! She was near the door to the room when I entered. The sudden blush, which betrayed her when she saw me, immediately faded, marked better her customary pallor. I myself was awkward, inhibited, piteous. I relied on the banal resources of condolence and courtesy. I broached nothing. She took pity on my embarrassment, and put me at ease in the old strain of chatter with questions about Couaën. She had me tell her about our trip. Since Madame de Greneuc had left us alone for a moment, I tried finally to approach the essential point, feeling that it was now or never, but at the same time was neither able to go more than halfway, nor dared to do so either. Oh, it is hard to move forward with a firm step when the long grass of a nearly forgotten path has become slippery and viscous like snakes! Wherever she went, I said, she could count on being always in my deepest thoughts, on my loyal concern, which would accompany her to her new home and the problems there. Besides, this separation could not last; we would surely see each other in a little while, and until then, she should have faith in the vigilance of my thoughts. I was still turning around in this rambling circle when Madame de Greneuc returned. Wretched words, and yet as devoid of artifice as my cowardly and equivocal intention could manage. I tried simultaneously to express what I really felt and to appear to express what I did not feel, to be sincere with myself and deceitful with her. Or, rather, I was trying only to get myself out of a painful episode, without intending even to give a false impression of the real situation. For that indicated only too clearly: "Count on me as I do, but don't count more than I do. I belong to you, if ever I can. I would like to want to, but I don't." Mademoiselle Amèlie, listening, had remained patient, unaffected, accepting me on my terms, only following where I was going, showing neither spite, nor surprise, nor outraged persuasion, nor self-mortifying resignation. At one moment, when I held out my hand, she touched me. Emboldened, however, by Madame de Greneuc's return, and wishing to reach some kind of conclusion, I began to speak animatedly of the political circumstances and uncertainty that would still surround the existence of young men for a rather long period, two years at least, and I returned with some emphasis on this period of two years, during which any kind of definitive decision had to be postponed. Mademoiselle Amèlie, picking upon the two years, showed that she understood and agreed.

"You are right," she replied, "for at least two years, nothing is possible in private lives because of all the agitation. It would make little sense to establish any lifelong project now." And she added, "But be prudent; your friends entreat you. Be more prudent than in the past." On that I rose, taking advantage of her smile. I took leave of both her and Madame de Greneuc. I kissed them and I took my leave. She accompanied me to the barrier of the courtyard as she used to, even though snow was falling. What girlish superiority she kept to the end, and what generous dignity! Those were my final farewells at La Gastine. That is how I left, never to return, embarrassed, ashamed, my head not held too high, my heart not too faithful, not able—without some inconvenience—to be anything more. How much this humiliating departure differed from the earlier departures! Where was that lulling, ideal evening of my daydream triumph? And what had I gained since, what had I dared that was so great, and what had I tasted that was so sharp it made me disdain and crush all those virginal promises?—I stopped short at that thought and repented having had it. Enough ingratitude, my soul. Lament and weep over what you lose, but do not disown what you have found!

Entering the lodge after that visit, I first met one of the two ubiquitous gamekeepers of Monsieur de Vacquerie. The latter had been in town at the moment when Monsieur de Couaën, who had also made a tour, had been arrested by a superior order and directed immediately to Paris. Good Monsieur de Vacquerie had instantly dispatched one of his gamekeepers to Madame de Couaën at the chateau and the other to me. These humble men had never been so useful. I reached Couaën before night. The police officers and magistrates left town at the very minute of the arrest, but encumbered and delayed in the snowy ravines, arrived an hour later. The dangerous papers had already been destroyed. Madame de Couaën received these people with a kind of calm and let me do everything. They seized some insignificant letters, which I had left out on purpose. The following morning, she and I and the children were on the road to Paris. Whether or not it was proper for me to be the leader at my age, we could not hesitate. I was the most intimate friend, the only one present, the others lost in flight or fright. She accepted my offers, not as offers—without objection, without thanks, absorbed and sorrowing as she was throughout the trip at the thought of danger to her family.

It was that way throughout the trip. She received my care passively, like a docile child. I was both touched by this sign of naive friendship and perhaps wounded a little in that part of egoism that is always mixed with devotion. However, I was acting without reservation. Her anxiety was mine, too. Occasionally I asked myself with terror what would become of her if I was arrested, too. An overwhelming need to arrive consumed us. Our unending conversation, this time devoid of charm, was comprised of two or three questions that she repeated endlessly, and my vaguely reassuring answers, which I varied as best I could.

CHAPTER IX

The first night we stayed at the little convent. Except for the first night, Madame de Couaën wished to stay elsewhere, for fear of making our presence a source of anxiety. Madame de Cursy was categorically opposed. But Madame de Couaën and I had agreed that regardless of the reasons advanced by our good aunt, as we called her, before the end of the week I would find some hotel nearby in the quarter. Besides my required absences in the evening, we could use my morning study as a pretext. As soon as we arrived, Madame de Couaën sent two letters: one to General Clarke, her compatriot and a family friend of long standing; the other to a special friend of Lord Fitzgerald, an influential and rather prominent person in the new regime. Monsieur de Couaën, during his first trips to Paris after returning from Ireland, had formed some ties with him. I delivered the letters myself the next day. General Clarke was absent on assignment. He was expected in two weeks. As for Fitzgerald's friend, he received me cordially, had the whole affair explained to him, and took it to heart. He gave me some useful pieces of advice on conduct and for his part promised to act without delay. On his advice and with a note from him, I sped to the Police bureau to see Pierre-Marie Desmaret, who could enlighten me better than anyone on the nature and gravity of the charges. He was a courteous, firm man, whose severe manner did not displease me. I was indeed astonished when he appeared already to know me after reading my name on the note I handed him. He was in fact very well informed about us and declared that he had strong moral misgivings on our score. I felt, however, quite relieved when he told me that the affair would turn especially on the papers seized at the chateau. New searches had been ordered and would have been completed by the time we spoke, and if nothing turned up more damaging than what was found in the first visit, he thought he could predict, even guarantee, some flexibility in the arrest conditions, at least partial and reassuring. After a few ironically paternal observations on my talent for confusing my pursuers, a talent, moreover, in which I should not place undue faith, I finally came to believe that on one evening, towards the last of our earlier trip, Monsieur de Couaën and I had been followed by some spy. When we had separated just before Clichy, the honest spy had preferred to follow me, and my singular course through Paris, which he managed to follow only in the beginning, had impressed him as the most skillful strategy. I burst out laughing in the street when that idea hit me, already forgetting what I should have recognized as inevitable confusion. And since my mind is naturally inclined to moralize on everything, I thought that there must be many probable and author-ized interpretations in history hardly less farcical than that one.

My reassuring report restored Madame de Couaën's composure. She saw Fitzgerald's friend; I took her to see Desmaret herself. Soon the Marquis ceased to be incommunicado. We could go comfort him every day as neighbors at the Sainte-Pélagie Prison, where he had been transferred at our request. The first time we saw him again, he struck me more than ever by the coldness and extent of his contained affliction, by the features hollowed in his face, by his majestic brow, still higher as his hair receded, by the outrage invading his temples that grief inhabited for so many nights. Because it is there, always there, where the temples and eyelids meet, where my eye can first read the true state of a friend just like a pane of glass. Evidently, in that virile soul there had been a final, complete annihilation of ambition and hope, burying any notion of the fame he had never had. That noble heart of a Charles V without an empire had taken on a hairshirt inside, but a hairshirt without religion. To me, who was attached to his thoughts like Caleb, his mute mourning seemed durable, indelible, equal to the character of any dispossessed con-queror. Some abyss had opened within, in that surd convulsion, an abyss veiled from view, but which nothing can fill anymore. Besides, the Marquis was open with us. He was tender. "Well, you see me cured," he said, keeping my hand in his "heroically cured! And you, Lucy, and those two poor children, and you, dear Amaury, from now on you are my life, my horizon. Let others have the arena!" And since we were not precisely alone, neither on that occasion or on the following, the conversation could not continue in depth. I brought him books. Madame de Couaën spent around an hour embroidering in front of him. We chatted on inconsequential subjects just for the satisfaction of conversing, and for the rest, we were patient. Desmaret had almost promised a rest home for spring.

Madame de Couaën found again, from time to time, serenity and security, which gave her distraction and reverie, although the bad effect on her health did not vanish with her anxiety. The more I saw her, the more she became an enigma of sensitivity and depth, a soul so disturbed, then suddenly so somnolent, so buried in herself or so pulled by the two or three creatures of the environs, sometimes immured in a particular anguish, sometimes engrossed in mysterious apathies, and her eyes fixed on the blue of the clouds. With all that she had no taste for going out, seeing things, no care for society, entertainments outside, nor for friends. She had none except a young woman whom she knew from having met at the home of Fitzgerald's friend and whose husband, secretary to Upper Magistrate Regnier, was actively working for us. This young woman, of an interesting and melancholy disposition, had taken to Madame de Couaën, and two or three times at her insistence, we had gone to her house.

At that time I customarily imagined the two souls of Monsieur and Madame de Couaën, whom I could contemplate at leisure each day as a large allegorical painting. Here is what I mean: it was a calm, somber landscape, green and empty, reached through craggy and bare gorges, beyond mountains, ravines, and bogs. At the heart of this landscape a lake of considerable extent, although not immense, one of those pure Irish lakes, stretched from beneath a tall, immutabale boulder that dominated it, hiding from it entirely a side of the sky and sun, the entire East. The lake was smooth, smiling, without foam or discernible depth, with no boulder but the sole gigantic one. This boulder, besides commanding from its face seemed to enclose the lake in its arms. It seemed even to have engendered the lake from its ribs. Two young streams, brisk and bubbling, spurting from clefts in the boulder, made distinct trails across the beautiful lake that held them back, gently stemming their course. They overflowed the lake in waterfalls. My pleasant role was to navigate the lake, skirt the immobile boulder, measure it for hours at a time, cover myself with its thick shadow, study its severe and strange profiles, wonder what this giant had been, what it could have been if it had not been turned to stone. I loved to row slowly across the expanses of this unruffled lake, to reconnoiter and follow beneath its somnolent mass the thin current of the two pretty streams up to the spot where they came to overstep the bounds and escape to the lawns. But while I was rowing, what marvels beneath my eyes and all around me, how many mysteries! From time to time, without there being a breath of wind from the sky, all the waves of this limpid lake, furrowed and stretched to a point, agitated with an incomprehensible emotion that nothing in the surrounding nature nor atmosphere could explain. It was never wrath. It was an internal trembling lament. The two pretty streams would then stop and retrace their course. The lake pulled them to itself with the panic of a loving mother. And then these same waves would fall back, suddenly becalmed, and become again a lazy mirror open to the stars, moon, and nighttime splendors. At other times a mist no less inexplicable than the earlier tremor could cover the lake beneath a tranquil sky. Or else you would have said—strange spectacle—that this milieu reflected more stars and lights than the celestial dais presented. And also, at certain times, the most cheerful spots on the banks opposite the boulder, the willows and the tufted outcroppings of the shore, ceased to be reflected in this water that seemed struck with magic obliviousness. The bird passing over the surface, almost touching it with its wing, left no image. And it often seemed to me in my almost fatal discouragement that I was slipping on a wave that would not notice and would not reflect me!

But to return to the real situation, my friend, here is how we lived. I had lodgings next to the little convent. I went there regularly around noon, that is, their habitual morning meal was over. Rain, snow, or blustering winds, usually on foot, Madame de Couaën and I went to the prison. On sunny days the children went with us. We were back by three, and after a bit more conversation, I usually left, not to return until seven, towards the end of supper, unless I ate supper there myself, which happened at least twice a week. Madame de Cursy and some of the nuns kept us company during the first half of the evening. But after they had retired and the children had gone to bed, we would stay up very late, very far into the night, near the smoldering hearth, in a thousand kinds of reasonings, remembrances, unending conjectures on fate, the oddity of encounters, situations, the mobile in human drama. Astonished over the least details, wondering about the whys and wherefores, extracting the spirit of each item, returning everything to two or three unchanging ideas on the invariable, invisible, and inner triumph of the soul; never wearied by this mutual echo of our conclusions, always natural, or our subtle analyses. It always had to come to a close, however, so with a light and friendly "bonsoir," as if I had only passed into an adjoining study. I suspended the unfinished conversation, the way you pause before the end of a page of a book you are reading. In a couple of leaps I had slid to the bottom of the stairs, crossed the court, and left, closing everything behind me with the key entrusted to me so as not to keep anyone up for me. The

noise of the door I closed, my key in the lock, the resounding of my
steps outdoors along those isolated walls, awoke and vibrated within
me, alas, at that moment, as would a familiar clock at one's bedside.
In the short interval between the little convent and my lodging,
sometimes the clocks of Val-de-Grâce at Saint-Jacques would strike
one, a toll penetrating and brief, even more solemn and nocturnal to
the ear than midnight. What sensations came together, what plenitude
I experienced during those few minutes, so often rainy or freezing! I
did not swagger; no living eye espied me anyway. On the contrary, I
was calm, pleased to leave her alone, perhaps thinking of me. Inwardly
fulfilled by her words, which came back to me with a delightful after-
taste, in harmony with myself, not imagining that this happiness could
change and desiring no more than that. Oh, these moments were by
far the best and loveliest of my life then. After all, the hearts of
fortunate lovers hardly have any better, and at least this memory does
not embarrass me too much. Whatever good I did by way of sacrifice
for her was repaid, I have to believe, by these brief and lucid moments.

But that did not make up my habitual state. These two or three
superfluous minutes, tossed in at the close of my days, did not make
enough of an impression to modify my life in any respect. My arid
heart soon drank in all that dew. So where was I with my feelings
then? in what new nuance? beneath what reflection of my growing
and diffuse cloud? This is what is harder for me to trace, my friend.
Because while advancing continually but losing the limit points which
served as my reference, I am little by little isolated, as if on an ocean
when the shore is left behind. Days, sights, horizons blur and blend.
Only a few tempests, one or two encounters, still help me make
distinctions among that monotonous sweep of waves and errors.

After our last episodes, when real worries and actual anxieties had
assailed me, I had pushed my intimate thoughts a bit to one side.
Inevitable trouble and material agitation had taken precedence. Nothing from reality had mixed with the soft region of my soul. That point
had been obscured by an active fermentation in the rest of my being,
a noisy intoxication by unaccustomed things, a great movement of
limbs, blood rushing to my head, and a thousand objects in my eyes.
My mind, improvising in the midst of these problems, had managed
with sufficient vigor and adroitness. My devotion to my friends in
trouble had not faltered. But this devotion, even limited to itself, had
often been chary of smile and affectionate speech, a devotion serious,
somber, anxious, and weary. When after the first shocks we resumed
a regular life and I returned to probing and examining myself, I found
that my previous disposition had come undone on its own. I had

already passed that marvelous scene on the cliff, that holy promise in the midst of tears to remain forever self-abnegating. Back again was the persistent desire of the slave who wants to escape. It had all come back imperceptibly in those last days, simply by the exposure of my dominant activities, through the atmosphere of these new places, where every breath you take leads to ambition or the senses, and also through what I believe I glimpsed of Madame de Couaën's indifference and unconquerable delight in other, more permissible thoughts. To feel I was relegated in her heart to a place which was neither first nor second, but perhaps fifth! That was an intolerable calculation; why was I doing it? Nor can this question be avoided. It imposes itself every minute in such friendships. In probing, I would say to myself that I had to go to the end, serve loyally and without expectation of recompense, since once at liberty, Monsieur de Couaën would take my place, and I would be launched to find my way on my bark alone. In the meantime I enjoyed the late hours of our long conversations. As for her, she was just what I have told you: the lake where I represented her was her perfect emblem. To be sure, she had a store of deep sensibility, usually fluid and somnolent, sometimes strangely fixed on an object which could even become an *idée fixe*, a passion, with all the accidents, all the distractions, and a naive blinding of passion that completely ignored the rest of the world. I had already seen her like that on the subject of her mother, and since our walk Christmas Eve in the Jardin des Plantes, this exaltation had been transferred to her children. The succeeding events no doubted justified a great deal of anxiety. Yet this anxiety from its onset and through its development remained no less singular, unbounded in its passion and as if outside normal motives. After our first two or three days in Paris, this kind of violent tension in her soul, this upheaval of sharp inner pangs had brusquely ceased, more brusquely even than seemed possible in a situation still so shaken. Madame de Couaën's common sense, which never left her, came remarkably to her aid in these lapses of perception. She would remark judiciously that it was much better that the Marquis had been arrested earlier rather than later, and that he would have risked more punishment if the affair had actually been underway. If, indeed, he had been arrested a year later, in the general imprisonment of Moreau, Pichegru, and Georges, I don't know how his head could have been saved. Once calm, Madame de Couaën managed to see in the prison an effective and truly fortunate guarantee against worse perils. And although beyond the grills and bars that perspective would sometimes make for less smiling twists and turns, she customarily dwelled on the tender projects of a life henceforth retiring and prudent which would follow her husband's release. Now, at those moments I saw her staring, distracted, but no longer acting on stimulus from without. Like the ancient nymphs, she had plunged again into her mysterious realm beneath the fountains. Oh, on those bright February days, what was she doing in her room, seated next to her window panes, when I arrived a little late, around one o'clock? What object did she follow so attentively? What phantom was her floating yet powerful faculty creating among the clouds? It had been lifted up twice on completely different points; did it have nothing at its disposition today? There was no sign or manifestation on her part at such moments. The children, who stayed downstairs with Madame de Cursy after dinner, made no demands on her. What was she thinking about? What infinite, invisible world did her mind wander through? It was not our world. Our varied sights, festivals, and landscapes did not figure there. Nor did the pomp, color and gold, the very coloration of the fields affect her. In her indifference to things, in the sovereign sway of her fancy, there were days of mist and rain, she dressed up early in the day with studied artlessness, and days of brilliant sunshine, where she forgot until she was ready to leave that she was still in her housecoat. When I would first arrive, I had trouble getting her attention, getting her to break or direct towards me her stream of silence. And when she escaped in speech, it was deep, continuous, elevated, unending. She stayed sickly, and her face had spots of affecting pallor. But she complained little and seemed oblivious. I noticed that only on the days of extreme pallor she was more subject to tender devotion. Then she would read and pray, and her prayer did not fulfill her. When I would come in and see her like that, I would readily imagine her some nun in the South, a Portuguese, for example, motionless in her cell, watching the sky and the Tagus, waiting eternally for the lover who would not return. I imagined still the most saintly of lovers and the most loving of saints. Teresa of Avila, at the moment when her chaste heart took fire, would cry out: "Let us be faithful to Him who cannot be unfaithful to us!" And realizing soon that the pale, white rays came from the February sun, that instead of the orange trees and the Tagus, we had only a little garden on the north exposure, completely stripped by winter, and that the creature whom I fashioned into this dream was a wife and mother, I would smile inwardly at my own fantasies. And if I greeted her then, whether I was coming in or going out, and it was *bonjour* of *adieu, monsieur* that she uttered mechanically, she froze me in my tracks, as if I had dared to presume to too much intimacy. That word *monsieur* was so strange, so thoughtless; it went straight to my heart,

and I felt suddenly weak, as if the oar fell out of my hands when I saw
the lake did not reflect me. But there were many other more precise
and clearheaded moments when she seemed, on the contrary, to
remember me. She counted on me; she named me expressly in all her
plans. She made me sit down again more than once before I left, and
she would say when I rose to leave after many long hours, "You are
always in a hurry to leave me."

One day, being somewhat indisposed the night before and hence
getting ready later than usual to go get her for our visit to the prison,
she came by to pick me up herself, because the weather was nice.
There was a knock at my door. It was the maid with her son, whom
she had sent to see whether she could come up. I rushed to my little
stairway to receive her. She came in for a moment, made a tour of that
simple chamber, praised its cleanliness, the atmosphere of learning,
the discreet lighting. She sat down a second in my sole armchair, and
these places became sacred to me.

Puerile behavior! tedious idolatry! sighs! disturbing images that
return in spite of myself, that hover around my pen when I write, like
the crowd of shades hovering around Virgil in the *Aeneid,* around
Charon who passes them by! Flowers too light, too fragrant, which
rain unexpectedly on my foolish head along those paths of yesteryear
where I expected to find among the cypresses only a few tombs and
warnings in the dust! These are memories that almost go against my
goal, my friend. What is my relation to them now? Do I have to efface
them? Should I nevertheless push on and finish so that one day you
can read about them? If I welcome in detail these souvenirs too
strongly etched in my memory, if too often you think I am complacently adding to the picture as if I held a brush, if I grant them a place
they would merit as much, perhaps, as certain great events in society,
but a place that becomes more perilous because of its intimacy, is it
because I truly regret the first emotion? Do I miss something in those
times I must repent? Or do I not attach myself to their spirit narrating
them? Would it not be the breath of pure love, scattered among these
meaningless moments, which has preserved them?

But what seen from afar may form in its ensemble a rather pleasant
cloud was, at the time I was living in the midst, so scattered and empty
that the least flattering conjectures about the future pursued me in my
leisure. Once the Marquis was out of prison, he would leave Paris at
once and would go bury himself at Couaën or elsewhere for the rest
of his days. His wife and family, momentarily isolated and without a
guide, would reenter his life forever. Was I myself to reenter his life
also? Was I to take a place in his entourage, a shameful and spineless

rival, settle in and evaporate in his shadow? In these odd moments of reflection I certainly uttered beneath my breath the vow of escaping these bonds that were too smothering, of approaching society on my own, and trying out my youth beneath the sky, of acting in Paris like the intractable cabin boy who, once arrived in an attractive port, hides so that the vessel, when leaving, will not carry him back. All the recent activity which had developed in me, as I mentioned, goaded me as well to this emancipation that was half pride, half sensuality. Often, during moments of her greatest kindness, when I had just shed tears on her hands, and when I called myself blessed, I raised my head dry-eyed and cold. I would have liked something else, not something from her but something besides her. First of all, my freedom. And I couldn't say what else or what next. I was tired of this role, exasperated and jaundiced at the threshold of that happiness to which I loudly gave lip service. That is, after all, what the hearts of men are like. The more tender and delicate they are, the more quickly they are blunted, disgusted, at the end of their rope. Which of the lovers among you, the most gratified, at the heart of overwhelming favors, has not felt bored? Which of you, beneath the very blow of mortal delights, has not desired something above and beyond, has not imagined some capricious, inconstant diversion, and at the feet of his idol on perfumed terraces, has not perhaps wished for some gross exchange, some vulgar creature passing by, or just to be alone for his own rest? Human love at the very places where it seems as deep as the Ocean has sudden undiscovered dry spots. The poverty of our nature does that. Human nature, daughter of Adam, raises a hideous head through access to us and looks like a vagrant old woman offering debauchery to the prodigal son who drinks in golden cups and forgets himself. In the love of God, which also has it sensuality and inebriation to fear, the greatest saints have indeed experienced such salutary periods of drought.

So it was as a function of the effect of these sudden arid spells peculiar to our nature, and mine in particular, and by my increasing propensity to glimpse a future outside my circle, and by my genuine respect for the absent noble and for her through her distractions, and her frequent absences in herself, it happened that in this new life of greater, private familiarity, I observed the same restraint as before. The same veil, always indefinite for me, impenetrable for her, floated between the two of us without my using the occasion to push it away or part it more often.

CHAPTER X

But as the Sage noted a long time ago, better a passion hopelessly bared than a love concealed. Can a man keep a flame burning in his breast without his clothes catching fire? My friend, I could not protect myself. If from the time of the first trip to Paris, the characteristics of the disease were well advanced, what was I to feel during this new, protracted sojourn? My mornings remained pure enough, devoted to work, divers readings, noble natural instincts, to the upkeep of the intellect. Starting off the day well is not rare. Then she took over. I went to her. My life filled the air she breathed in, I lived the air she breathed out, and my affectionate thoughts still stayed pure. But when I left her, I was idle and overwrought during those vague, dragging hours. If they had been productively filled, they could have been calm and contemplative, but too often, like the weighty years of life which correspond to them, they have lost the freshness of morning matters and succumb by degrees to a material invasion. In those long hours that ended the day and preceded my return to my rooms and the shelter of evening, what could become of me? Usually in crossing Paris I lost myself in the quarters of the area. I preferred to dine there when I was not expected at the little convent. And before dinner and especially afterward, I procured the emotion of my palpitating excursions to my heart's content. In order to be sure of putting any spies off my trail, in the event I still had one following, I never failed to make in the beginning three or four turns, so abrupt, so cunningly broken, so elusive, so dedalian, that they would have detached, shaken far away the most determined wasp. Even on the days of brightest sunlight it seemed as if it was all my shadow could do to follow me. This first sly trick filled me with bizarre joy and jeers. A useless detail, linked to a peculiarity lost in the beginning of these pages, still made me postpone the day of my defeat. The prolonged emotion, which I had in the heart of peril, was then inspired by a kind of precarious security and a false vestige of innocence. It was always in that same ruinous way to push to the end from the inside, to let mature, even rot, almost inside me, the thought of evil before the act, to heap up a thousand mortal ferments before anything happened. But many a time, while I skirted by running to the brinks of the precipice, I was all the more audacious, saying, "At any rate, it will not happen today." Many a time my feet nearly slipped, vertigo disturbed my vision, and I would soon be plunged headlong despite my sullen resistance.

One day, when any objection had probably finally vanished, I left my lodging with a violent resolution. That day, nothing particular happened to me. When I saw her in the morning (alas, do I have to bring her blessed name into such narratives in any respect at all?), that morning, I was saying, she had been neither too distracted nor too attentive. She had neither disturbed my senses nor bruised my soul. Nor had I, if I remember correctly, any ulcerating spectacle for my ambition nor a quarrel with anyone, nor an outburst of anger, none of those petty wrongs or disappointments which make us out of sorts with ourselves and lower us to drunkenness, brutal satisfaction, as indemnity and oblivion. So nothing compelled me that day, just my dementia. I wanted to put an end to it; that is what I said to myself as I got up. A singular sarcastic lightheartedness was visible in all my movements, my gestures, vibrated metallic in my voice. It was like the hissing serpent getting ready to strike across arid rocks. My consciousness of the certain evil I was going to consummate lit up my forehead and glittered in my gaze. A good hour before dinner I passed into the other Paris. While walking, I struck my heels more sonorously on the hardened pavement of the bridges, and I lifted my head still higher toward the sky sparkling with bright flecks of diffused frost. Here and there, to the right and left, I looked about proudly, as if applauding myself. Whom was I looking at like that, O my God? Why did I show that joy and that sinister radiance, when all should have been veiled? And what made me leap and bound? I held on to purity by the last material link, and this weak link weighed on me, and I was proud to be on my way to breaking it, like a violent man marching to his vengeance. It is because sensuality, which quickly produces humiliation, begins also with pride. Love of pleasure is not everything with sensuality. Vanity also, emulation in evil, revolt against God are there like one more exasperation on the threshold. A small boy of Israel, who was docile and pure, wants to become like a giant. Thus I, who would have blushed to be seen and followed by anyone in particular, gloried in advance, vis-à-vis all those unknowns and myself.

Although it was still broad daylight, I immediately began to walk through the usual streets and places. I noted, but with a more critical eye, those reefs which at first sight had all seemed gracious and smiling. There was hardly a one that kept its power to dazzle. This time my heart beat stronger, the thuds closer together and harder. From time to time I stopped to try to calm it. Not wanting to decide on anything before evening and already very weary, I darted into a café, where I dined alone at the back. I went out, stuffed, overheated, into the sharp mists and night lights, once again dedicated to my errand and my search. Just as burning although less difficult to please, I shortly began my rapid, excluding turns. Rather little delicacy remained for the choice, and some distinct scruples. I had only that vague idea that none of the creatures glimpsed would have a soul worthy of the transports I was going to offer, so at least I should have carnal beauty, perhaps Venus herself. Thus I prolonged this demanding search beyond measure and contrary to my aim, and soon, as usual, I panicked, losing all pretense to clearheadedness, so that in the end, worn out by my exertion (what marvelous good fortune!), I fell absurdly, without choosing in any way, without any attraction, in some mediocre spot, solely because I had sworn to fall that day.

From that fatal day forward, once the foul gutter was crossed, a powerful element was introduced into my system. My youth, held in for so long, overflowed. My unleashed senses were prodigal. We each have two periods of youth, my friend, one coming after the other. The first, ascendant, exuberant, always self-sufficient, not believing in fatigue, keeping no accounts, embracing all opposites at the same time, sends all his coursers into the fray. There is a second, already weary and forewarned, who looks very much the same on the outside, but to whom an inner voice often cries, "Whoa!" This youth hardly ever gives in to anything without regret, repents quickly for having given in, and no longer manages a style equal to the mind and body together. At that time I was fully immersed in the first. My double life was henceforth organized. On the one hand, an inferior, submerged, engulfed life; on the other, a more active life of head and heart. In the morning, my spirit and intelligence ordinarily took up my studies with excited and eager revenge over the debasement of the night before. The evenings too, on my return, the subtle life of the heart, next to my special friend Madame de Couaën, immediately took the place of the heavy disturbances of the preceding hour. Sometimes, hardly out of the slime, while I was looking about at the serene moon

and stars as I returned through the squares or along the quays, my
thoughts cleared up also. Beneath that sensual and weakened spell, I
saw better, I felt nature, the evening sky, our transient state more
keenly. Like the old pagans, I let myself be rocked in the light foam
to the surface of that abyss. I brought melancholy from a guilty stream
to the feet of that woman who made all reverie sacred.

So this heart, which had palpitated so roughly in evil, this
contradictory and fickle human heart, which should be described like
Ovid's Centaur in the *Metamorphosis*, a chest where two natures come
together, this deplorable heart shook off shame in an instant. It turned
its role around and changed suddenly from gross convulsions to
platonic aspirations. I killed my remorse, at will, and instantly I was
lost in subtle love. An abusive facility! A versatility mortal both to us
and to true love! When the human soul is subjected to that fatal
routine, instead of being a hearth of persistence and vitality, it soon
becomes a clever machine, electrified by countercurrent, at the mercy
of divers circumstances. The center, by dint of going from one pole to
the other, no longer exists anywhere. The will has no more support.
Our moral person is reduced to being only an unbound compound of
currents and fluids, a mobile and shifting pile, an accommodating
setting for a thousand games. It is a type of nature I will not call
hypocritical, but which is always half-sincere and always vain.

After the first shock was dissipated, as well as the first fires, I was
able to gain considerable savoir faire, a refined knowledge of good and
evil in that double way I practiced, sometimes in the hurlyburly of the
crossroads, sometimes on ethereal clouds. A mysterious analysis, for
which I certainly paid dearly, instructed me each day in some new
particularity of our double nature, on my abuse of one and the other,
on the secret of their very union. A sterile science, isolated and
impotent, an instrument and apportionment of punishment! I understand better what man is, what I am, and what I leave behind as I
become inured and walk further into the paths leading to death.

First of all, I learned in my lascivious routine to discern and
pursue, to fear and desire the type of beauty I will call nefarious,
beauty that is always a mortal trap, never an angelic symbol, beauty
that is painted neither in the mirror of the eyes, the delicacy of the
smile, the nuanced veil of the eyelids. The human face has nothing, or
almost nothing, to do with this beauty. The eye and voice, combining
in sweetness as neighbors of the soul, have no role whatsoever with
what one desires. This is real beauty, but overwhelming and entirely
carnal, and seems to go back in direct line to the daughters of the first
fallen races, not judged face on, in direct conversations, as is appro-

priate for man, but rather from afar, upon the accident of the nape and back, as a hunter would size up wild beasts. Oh, I understood beauty like that.

I learned also to what extent that such beauty is not true beauty, that it is contrary to spirit, that it kills, crushes, but never attaches. Despite inflicting the most ravages upon the senses, it has the least effect in the soul. Because, through these maleficent currents so far as such beauty is espied, how everyone trembles! how everyone blanches! I break into sweat. Am I going to rush forward or grow faint?—A little patience, my soul! Take hold of yourself and say to the quivering body, "This evil beauty, to which you want to surrender blindly, which you have glimpsed only from the front, tomorrow or sooner, its imprint will be replaced and erased when another woman passes by. You will be disgusted by the first without even having enjoyed her, and so with the next, and whoever follows her. Why disturb me so much? Just learn how to wait and resist your first glance."

I learned in this way that damage comes first through the eyes, and the severe precepts appeared to me in the perceptibly exact truth: "Moderate your glance, put blinders on your eyes like those on mules to keep them from stumbling! Eyes are windows of the soul, and faces enter and leave through them!" My own example made me often recall St. Augustine's story of the fall of Alipe in the Circus games, when he heard a loud shout and, despite his resolution not to look, could not keep from opening his eyes. In that involuntary blink all the cruelty reentered his heart. Thus cruel, bloodthirsty sensuality often reentered my heart, despite my efforts. Oh, the prophet Jeremiah expressed my lamentable dispersion, my defeat on all points from a soul at the mercy of the eyes: "Let mine eyes run down with tears night and day, and let them not cease: for the virgin daughter of my people is broken with a great breach, with a very grievous blow" (14: xvii).

I learned at that time, my friend, that true love is in no way located in the senses. For if you really love and desire a pure woman, when you come across an impure woman, you will suddenly think you love her; the latter blocks out the former. You move on in pursuit, exhausting yourself, but at the moment that what the impure woman inspired has vanished like smoke, and in the extinction of the senses, the image of the first woman beings to appear again more desirable and beautiful, lighting up all our shame within.

At the most intense moments, when I seemed to give in to an unconquerable fatality, I learned that man is free and in what sense he truly is, because man's freedom, which I was experiencing intimately then, consists chiefly of whether he will or will not keep out of the turbulent range and clutches of objects, depending upon how susceptible he is—too much or too little. If you find you blow hot and cold for charity, run and find the poor! If you know you are vulnerable and fragile, avoid every perilous corner!

I learned that sensuality is the transition, initiating sincere and tender dispositions into vices and other low passions they would never have originally suspected they were capable of. Sensuality made me conceptualize drunkenness and gluttony, for in the evening of certain days, harassed and far from satiated, my inner self, usually sober, would make me go in cafés to order some strong liquor, which I would gulp down with fire.

I learned that for man each morning is a reparation and each day a continual ruin, but the reparation becomes less and less adequate, and the ruin keeps increasing.

I understood profoundly, and I crushed to the marrow that dictum of the sacred texts: *"Ne dederis mulieribus substantiam tuam"* (don't throw away your goods on women); don't toss to all the grasshoppers of the desert your fruits and your flowers, your virtue and your genius, your faith and your will, the dearest part of your substance!

And another dictum of an Ancient, which I had read without paying attention, came back to me forcefully: "I have killed the wild beast within." Yes, the ferocious beast is inside us. It triumphs during this first, wicked youth. It devours the entrails of each, like the wild fox gnawing beneath the gown of the Lacedeamonian child.

I learned that if sensuality and the excesses it causes usually produce humiliation, its absence easily evokes pride. A reverse relationship, in effect, a singular balance of our two capital vices: the active, ambitious, fame-seeking, clamorous external vice and the flabby, idle, furtive, savorous, mysterious, hidden vice! Have you ever noticed this double game, my friend? When sensuality decreased in me, and I succeeded in repulsing it, then pride, gleeful and proud satisfaction, increased by that amount. But as soon as the other took the upper hand, there was gradual prostration, surrender, and self-contempt. With any man, one of the two vices is likely to dominate, but not to the total exclusion of one or the other, although there are certain monstrous, extreme cases where a single one fills the soul. They are like the two poles at the farthest limits of inhabitable earth. Most men float in the intervening space and incline more or less here or there. The soul, which would establish its dwelling in one or the other extremity, would be affected by moral death, and would become stupid on that point. The pole of pride is the most inhabited nowadays. I have known several Nebuchadnezzars. There has even been an effort to bring sensuality to another aggressive passion, and to group the two in a chimerical hymen. Don Juan, deceitful idol, belongs to a century in which there is much more pride than love in pleasure. But in leaving the Don Juans, all pomp and braggadocia, and restricting my comments to what I have felt, it is a constant that these two vices are linked by an inverse and alternating movement. At the moment of extreme sensuality and the selfabasement it brings us, pride is far away, its lofty reef has disappeared. Then we cry out, "Oh, if I just weren't a sensualist!" in the belief that this is the only vice we must battle. But if you do battle for a while, if you seem to be winning, satisfaction enters the picture. The heart begins to swell. Jealous pride, the desire for praise and prominence among men, stir inside you and become a pressing enemy. Do not applaud yet; do not say, "Oh, I don't have that vice anymore," for just let some woman pass by; from the back you can only make out the brown hair piled on top of her head. But already your desire has come back to life and runs on ahead. We have to keep doing battle.

If it is true that pride is the most frequent antagonist of sensuality, even more is self-love the enemy of love. I learned, however, that when we lack the strength to take for our supreme auxiliary pure divine Love and lean on it, when we fail to consider, as we should, that the body is the temple of the Holy Spirit and that our limbs are the limbs of Christ, it is good at least not to purge human love of all human respect and self-love. Because if the love for the beloved woman is too humble, too contrite, too sacrificing, it can, for lack of divine Love, leave the senses to their own devices, and in that way, it permits and receives irreparable defilement.

I learned finally (and this is where, my friend, I may take too much comfort in this tenebrous science; this is the sole aspect that was immediately fruitful), I learned to weigh, to correct what ancient Solomon, in his royal satiety, said about women, to cherish the merciful unknown philosopher, this modern Solomon, invisible and mild. I began to understand, practice, should I confess, what Christ showed us with the Samaritan woman, that is, not to curse woman. Solomon, who had found woman more bitter than death, proclaimed, "One man among a thousand have I found; but a woman among all those have I not found." (Ecclesiastes 7: xxviii). Louis-Claude de Saint-Martin, who called himself the unknown philosopher, wrote also in a moment of holy fright that there is no woman. For him, the matter of woman appeared more degenerate and fearful than that of man! But remembering that Christ, engendered by Mary, came to earth, he added these consoling words: "If God could have a measure in his love, he ought to love woman more than man. As for us, we cannot keep from loving and cherishing her more than ourselves. Because the most corrupted woman is easier to bring back to the straight way than a man who might not have taken more than one step in evil." And so, I never cursed you, creatures whom we walk over and never name; nor you superb and wild creatures who boldly carry off the passer-by; nor you discreet and perfidious creatures who, slipping along the shadows, seem to say, "Hidden streams are sweetest; the stolen bread, the tastiest!" I have not cut you off from humanity, you who make up an immense, unbridled population! I often found you better than I was in the harm you did me. My inner misery, my infinite fickleness helped me explain yours. Whether you were laughing, ulcerated, or repentant, I felt sorry for you. I saw myself in you and lamented myself in you. How much the abyss in your hearts, the opprobrium in your senses were mine as well! Women of Canaan, I do not throw the first stone at you!

But do not let this pity for the creatures be, I pray, indulgence for their work! The way our century judges on this score, as on so many others, is based on a kind of indifference (which, besides, makes use of this work as it pleases) and a tolerant contempt, self-satisfied, eyes closed. Materialists (and these days most men are, at least in practice) envisage the fact of sensuality as almost independent of the rest of their conduct, as acting simply in our animal nature through fatigue or stimulation. Most physiologists will even speak to you about a reputed advantageous reaction in the brain. Fathers, elder brothers, tutors, in the advice they give on the subject commonly make it a matter of hygiene, economics, regularity. In all that, there is a deep obliviousness of the most essential and delicate side. The head of the Empire, who during the camp interval was not upset when our Capua absorbed the superfluous ideas of his warriors, glimpsed the real truth better. There is, indeed, no external or superificial act by which the inconvenience of rather poorly dissimulated disorder of the senses is betrayed. Soldiers, salesmen, or courtiers will be none the worse for the next battle, the boulevard promenade, formal-dress tête-à-tête, financial or bureaucratic skirmish. But if we enter into the vital and spiritual sphere, the realm of ideas, there the counterstroke is disaster, perdition, decadence. From that point of view, which is in no way imaginary, I assure you, who can tell in a large city, at certain hours of evening and night, how many treasures of genius, beautiful, beneficent works, tears of tenderness, fertile whims, detoured in this way before birth, killed in essence, thrown to the winds in insensate prodigality, periodically dry up? Someone who was born capable of a sublime monument will clip his thoughts each evening in such pleasure and will launch only fragments in the world. Someone whose sublime spiritual creation would have come to fruition in severe continence will miss his moment, the passage of the star, the burning hour he will never meet again. Someone naturally disposed to kindness and charity, charmingly tenderhearted, will become cowardly, inert, or even hard. This character, which was basically consistent, will remain dispersed and flighty. This imagination, which tomorrow would have shone with a soft velvety glow, will never be cloaked like that again. A heart that would have loved late but much will waste along the way its faculty for feeling. A man who would have stayed upright and incorruptible, if he dissipates his strength for these delights at twenty-five, will learn to waver at forty and accommodate the powerful. And so many consequences will stem from this single infraction, even if repeated only in moderation. In such limits, hygiene has no role. Who knows? The positive man may be the better for it. But what is more subtle and vital in the matter, thus thrown off, killed for a bad end, no longer in us, like a rich divine spark, for running, climbing in every sense and being transformed, this *blood soul* the Scriptures tell about, in going away alters man, impoverishes his secret virtuality, strikes him in his superior, hidden resources. The inscrutable ways of justice! solidarity of all our being! the very mystery of life and death!

Do not take fright, my friend, do not feel shame! I will say nothing more on the subject now. I shall not spell out my thoughts on the matter again. You know the place of the fall, you can measure the extent with a glance. I will not bring you slime by the handfuls. I am not unaware that repentance itself should go over such memories with circumspection and trepidation, often closing its ears and eyes. Bossuet pointed out this vice, favored by the human species, which you cannot even think about without risk, even to blame it. Christian preaching points it out only from a distance—and does so obliquely. St. Paul desires that it not be mentioned among the faithful by any of its thousand names. This case of saintly reserve is in no way, regrettably, our own. More direct intervention suits us. So I, a sick man, somewhat cured, speak solely to you, a sick man made desperate. These pages form a confession from me to God, and from me to you.

Oh, at least in my immense ill-conduct I never had any distinct and express attachment. Among so many phantoms piled up, none in particular comes to mind. The only name I utter is always blessed. Images of those days, multiply once more the confusion! Shades of former evenings, seize your scattered objects, make them all return, if possible, to the same cloud!

She, she alone remained for me the incomparable being, the shining and inaccessible goal, the ideal and excellent good. My life took its course all the more necessarily alongside hers by certain kinds of tenderness and adoration, while I felt on the other hand the corrupting flood separate me from her more. My discontent with myself henceforth produced between us more imbalances, passing shocks. And, at the point where we were, each new shock tightened the bond. Perhaps also I was approaching the intimacy with her more aggressively, since I was assured of the ruinous safeguard. At the least exasperation, the least stir of too strong an emotion, through disgust or through ardor, I went off wandering, making use of my routine of the time, and I returned calmer, considering my senses numb at her feet.

CHAPTER XI

We were into spring. Monsieur Desmaret kept his word, and the Marquis was transferred to a rest home neary Passy. Madame de Couaën decided to more immediately to Auteuil to facilitate her daily visit. What made her choose this spot, other than the advantage of the woods and fresh air for the children, was the obliging young woman I mentioned, Madame R———, wife of Desmaret's private secretary. She usually spent her summers there and was to move in a few weeks. Her immediate desire to have Madame de Couaën for a neighbor forestalled any of the latter's hesitation. I kept my lodgings near the little convent, but I went to Auteuil every afternoon. When it was a little late, I went directly to the rest home, where I would find Madame de Couaën already settled in. We would eat as a family. I would escort her back at dusk and would then return to sleep in my own faubourg. In this way I served as a continual messenger between Madame de Cursy and her niece.

As I mentioned, my morning hours were quite taken up with reading and study and taking advantage of the numerous resources for learning which Paris offered then. That active age of youth embraces everything and suffices for everything. I frequented several times during those 10–day Republican calendar decades Monsieur de La-marck's natural history courses at the Jardin des Plantes. This instruc-tion, whose paradoxical hypotheses and contradictions vis-à-vis other, more positivist and advanced systems I was well aware of, still exerted a powerful attraction for me because of the grave, primordial questions Lamarck always raised and the passionate, almost painful tone he brought to science. At that time he was one of the last representatives of that great school of natural philosophers and general observers who had reigned from Thales and Democritus to Buffon. He displayed his mortal opposition to chemists, to experimenters and analysts *en petit,* as he put it. His hatred, his philosophical hostility against the Flood and Creation stories in Genesis, was no less. His conception of things had much simplicity, starkness, and much sadness. He constructed the world with the fewest elements, the fewest crises, and the most duration possible. According to him, things made themselves, by themselves, through continuance by means of sufficient lapses of time, with neither passage nor instantaneous transformation through crises, cataclysms or general commotions, from or by centers, nuclei or organs prone by design to aid and duplicate them. Long, blind patience was his Genius of the Universe. The actual form of the earth, to hear him tell it, derived solely from the slow disintegration by rain water, daily oscillations and successive displacement of the seas. He admitted no great stirring of the entrails in this Cybele, nor renewal of its face by some passing star. The same was true in the organic order. Once the mysterious power of life in its smallest and most elementary form was admitted, he imagined it developing by itself, composing itself, and diversifying little by little with time. Deaf need, the sole habituation in the diverse milieux, made organs come into being eventually, in contrast to the constant power of nature to destroy them. For Monsieur de Lamarck separated life from nature. Nature, in his eyes, was rocks and ashes, the granite of the tomb, death! Life intervened only as a strange and singularly industrious accident, a prolonged struggle with more or less success and equilibrium here and there, but always vanquished in the end. Cold immobility would reign after as before. I loved these questions of origin and end, this framework of a dreary nature, these sketches of obscure vitality. My reason, suspended, somewhat leaning over these limits, enjoyed its own bewilderment. I was assuredly far from welcoming these hypotheses that simplified far too much, this uniform series of continuity, which, despite my lack of knowledge, I refuted with my boundless sense of creation and tumultuous youth. But the bold strokes of this man of genius made me think. And then, in his opinionated resistance to systems arising on all sides, to new theories of the earth, to Lavoisier's chemistry, which was destruction and revolution also, he reminded me involuntarily of Monsieur de Cou-aën's comparable, imposing obstinacy in another realm of activity. When he bitterly denounced the alleged general conspiracy of fashionable scientists against him and against his works, I saw him conquered, gagged, unhappy like our friend. He at least had had time to become illustrious.

In the following this course given by Monsieur de Lamarck, I had occasion to meet a worthy and intelligent young man who attended assiduously. We liked to talk over the ideas of the lecture and dispute philosophical matters. He was older than I. He was a product of the Oratorian schools in the first years of the Revolution and quite versed in recent writings and personages. He discussed knowledgeably the opinions of Cabanis and Destutt-Tracy, and the Auteuil circle, which he told me about and where he had been introduced while Madame Helvétius was living. I enjoyed listening to him, I asked him a lot of questions, and he anticipated a request I would not have dared express in offering to introduce me at one of the philosophical dinners which still took place every tridi, the third day in our old 10–day Republican calendar, although their ideologue and republican tendencies could bring about their demise from one moment to the next. A few pages on the analysis of imagination I had let him see pleased two of the philosophers extremely and served as a passport for his request on my behalf. He bestirred himself, fortunately for me, and I had the honor of attending what I believe was the final *tridi* dinner. It was held at a restaurant on the corner of Rue du Bac, on the bridge side. I was overwhelmed with respect and overcome with silence in the midst of these serious men, all more or less celebrated, and from a perspective so different from mine. I did not let a single word of their escape. Their words were simple, of unwavering logic, clearcut, ingenious, completely precise and well-spoken. Garat alone had some aims of brilliance. Politics, glimpsed like a shadow behind the diners' gaiety, broke out like a storm only at the end. Someone's remark against the Empire's appropriations broke up the philosophical discussion, which had been rather restrained until then. Cabanis and Chénier were eloquent. New accents proclaimed the words of republic, liberty, and fatherland. This was the only time I saw these men whose tradition is not unfamiliar to you, my friend, and whom several survivors have described for you far better than I, who had no opportunity to be acquainted with them. In my concern for the divine portion of our nature, which they neglected, you have never heard me pronounce anathema against them.

When I used to go to Auteuil or the rest home straight from these studies and lectures, my head was full of them. I talked a lot about them, even to Madame de Couaën. I pointed out to her Madame de Helvétius' house when we passed it on the square. She smiled at what she called my infatuation and scolded me for my novelties in systems. If I tried to explain to her the formation of the terrestrial surface by rainwater and sea displacement, she listened intently, at first making an effort to understand, and soon would shake her head with a mien of common sense that seemed to say, "How can you believe such tales?"

However indifferent I imagined she usually was to me, there were moments when she paid almost anxious attention to my manner of being and thinking, and these slight fears on her part, combined with my secret discontent and my consciousness of being wretched, disturbed the habitual resignation of my love and ruffled our incomplete harmony. I remember one April evening in Auteuil. We were walking alone down a little winding path where the ground was red and tender. The season was so young that inside the hedge there were thousands of those little leaf tips, still not quite budding. Throughout the length of the pathway we had a clear, cloudless sky without a tinge of red or any stars. We were heading neither toward the side of the setting sun nor to that of the rising moon. Something vague, fleeting, tentative, a dispersed Chiaroscuro, composed that view and that moment. A soft, russet, vegetal haze hovered around us. Instead of being happy and enjoying this beauty, a simple thing, letting our hearts take it in, we had a small altercation. Madame de Couaën pressed me more than she had ever done on the symptoms of fluctuation and divers tastes that the current stay in Paris was bringing out in me. For a while now, she said, she saw me in a new light. She read in my mental enthusiasms and increased acquisitions only a sad prospect of future change. If, tomorrow, we were allowed to leave, would I be comfortable again, dwelling at Couaën and making humble pilgrimages to Saint Pierre-de-Mer et de la Colline? I had trouble making her understand that eagerness to learn is distinct in us from faithfulness in love; that man has a great anxiety to learn, a need to wander, to get outside, in order not to be devoured from within. I said that lacking a stable faith as I did and with my senses largely open, I received all ideas through my receptiveness to intelligibility and plausibility. I must seem to believe them, to espouse them pellmell, frenetically, while what I was really doing was learning them completely and figuring them out energetically, with the reservation of judging and discarding them once I had understood them. The names of Lamarck and his predecessors were often on my lips, and she was tired of hearing about them. Something else should be noted. The night before I had gotten to the rest home later than usual, having paid a call on the way to young Madame R———, kept in Paris by some indisposition. This visit, which, under the circumstances, Madame de Couaën considered futile, was at the bottom of this general reproach she was addressing to me. Her insistence bore more on that point than on anything else. Was she in fact suspicious? Was I at fault? What was wrong? There was nothing that could have been given any name at all and yet, when she had insisted and quarreled a long time on the heights, she suddenly fell back on this grievance, ashamed and distressed by the slip, wounded by the somewhat bitter tone I used. She cried, "Shush," in pain, stopping my explanation for a while: "What an unheard of tone you are taking!" I could not keep from replying, "It's what you're saying 'Shush' to, much more than the tone!" We broke off in silence. A moment later I found still another means of being harsh à propos of the children's education. Where that was concerned I was deliberately harsh, severe like someone who already knows the corruption in the heart. She was indulgent, trusting in natural goodness and innocence. We parted on bad terms, or at least I felt on bad terms with her that evening.

Tomorrow she will have forgotten about it, I said to myself as I walked back to take my mind off of it. And I walked on, partly annoyed by the pain I had inflicted, partly exasperated by the thought of her faculty for obliviousness. The next morning I was at Auteuil earlier than ususal. When she saw me come in, tears came to her eyes.

"I was wrong," she said, "to reproach you, but your manner was a little curt. I was quite wrong, however." And she accused her own character while praising my friendship. She blamed her gloomy spells for disturbing the best moments.

"Oh, don't," I cried then, "It was my fault entirely. Promise me that you believe that."

And when she agreed, we went out to walk in the woods in the sparkling dew, each of us with tears on our lashes. While we walked, I squeezed her hand and murmured in her ear, "How good you are!"

"Oh, I'm only that way for you," she replied, tenderly teasing, "I wouldn't be so kind, you know, for anyone else."

Then she withdrew her hand. Her eyes were suddenly dry, and she reentered her peace of innocence and apparent insouciance. We spent that whole day together. I accompanied her to the rest home and brought her back early after dinner. More than once that day, I noticed her face was pale and changed and studied her intently. But she smiled tranquilly beneath my gaze and did not complain. That evening we were once again at the walk of the night before, united and spellbound, engaged in all sorts of topics, like the view of the sky and the path, sweet, nuanced, fleeting, without a living star, with neither too much sparkle nor too much shade, but delicate as well, just a shade below oscuro, a somber, indefinable hue scattered over the sky like that vernal russet scattered over the woods against a serene backdrop. Oh if only those past tête-à-têtes, that sanded pathway I see again in my mind's eye, be not counted among those other paths leading to eternal ruin! If only I may be permitted instead to see through my tears one of those special little roads Dante depicts, which the souls who will reach heaven climb at nightfall!

The drawback of those fleeting instants, which seem to take part in invisible happiness, is that you cannot humanly hold on to them. The beloved has to die or be continuously separated; the cloister or altar has to rise between her and our desires. Religion must be present, in a word, to perpetuate that chaste nuance and keep it from denaturing. Unless you are one of those who weep, repent, fast, pray, spending their nights and days in self-sacrifice to attenuate any suspect impulse, you have soon crossed the permitted limit, if, indeed, it can be observed. I had scarcely come away from our tête-à-tête that evening, peaceful at first, not keyed up, reliving that infinity of tender feelings, contemplating a pure golden sand at the heart of my thoughts. But when I reviewed the more moving evidence of the morning, which on her part was followed with such placidity and her usual even-tempered disposition, I soon found myself discontent. In part I weakened them in essence, in part I exaggerated these signs of affectionate indulgence. I tortured them to find what was lacking. I concluded that she had undoubtedly in no way attached the equivocal value I now would have liked, although at the time I had in no respect desired it. From one irritation to the next, aided by the darker night and the city tumult, I shook off the safeguard of that pure day, keeping myself less remote from the cesspool I was passing and losing all my precious memories there. In the thick apoplectic sleep which punished that culpable return, no lighthearted, crystalline dream carried me back to the russet path beginning to green or opened my soul to chaste mysteries.

Two or three days later, when she and I returned to our favorite walk in the woods, we found it greatly changed. One of those warm fertile rains that bring on spring had fallen in the night. The largest leaves clothed the trees in abundance. The earth was vaporous. Little round clouds dotted the skies. A turgescent sap oozed from all the branches. At the lodging the chimney fires, which the night before had still sparkled, were going out without the strength to overcome the heavily warmed atmosphere. The air carried pungent odors. Our bodies were oppressed also, and our chests swollen with ennui.

"Oh, it's not our walkway anymore," she cried with surprise at seeing it all sprouted out. "Do you feel like me? How does it happen that I like it less this way?" And soon getting tired, she asked to go back to the convent.

External nature, no more than the heart of man, can pause . . . long at those angelic nuances that appeal to another sun. This rural nature so often praised in certain cases is the aid and accomplice of corrupt internal nature. Ordinarily a good inspiration, and conversing freely with us about God, external Nature has, however, her days of evil counsel. She becomes pagan once more, still subject to old Pan, and entirely populated with Hamadryads. Solitude with too many flowers and too many tufts is often a dangerous companion for a young man by himself. Jerome needed against himself first the frightening desert of Chalcus. In many a place he recommends the harshness of the desert choice. The great Christian painter Raphael, by an instinctive feeling of harmony, like modesty, never placed on the distant trees of his landscapes, behind the heads of his Virgins, more than a few leaves, so rare that they can be counted.

CHAPTER XII

In a package from Couaën there was a letter, by then already old, that Mademoiselle de Liniers had written me on behalf of Madame de Greneuc. The women expressed concern about my welfare, about what might have happened, given the dangers my friends and I were running. These few simple words, which had forced their way through a rebuffed and bleeding heart, this pure letter, which nowhere betrayed a trembling hand, reawakened a thousand echoes of a past that had almost sunk into slumber. I was alarmed that I had changed so much since then and lived through so much. Madame de Couaën read the letter and was touched in her own way by its discreet essence. She added a few grateful lines in her own handwriting to the response I wrote.

Madame R———, the young married woman, had finally gotten installed in Auteuil. Her husband, much taken up with his concerns, came only occasionally and would stay only a few hours. Although he was a likeable man, perfectly correct in his attentions with her, you could see that some deep cause of estrangement contributed to keep their relationship considerate rather than tender. Without being entirely abandoned, she seemed quite disillusioned, sad, and in some respects, widowed. In her daily visits to Madame de Couaën, whom she tried to oblige in every way imaginable, she scarcely ever spoke about herself. She seemed to view our intimacy without envy, with a silent, gentle smile. Generally when I arrived and got seated, she would leave after a few moments on some pretext.

This regulated life of ours continued for several months. It was at the very end of August or perhaps at the beginning of September when, one day, Madame de Couaën was indisposed and stayed in the house, and I went to the rest home alone. The Marquis was not in his apartment. I discovered him after some effort at the far end of the garden in the thickest part of the grove. He was walking up and down with another person whom I had never seen before, and it was obvious to me from the attention they paid to my approach that I had interrupted a confidential discussion. This person was nothing if not natural and open. Still young, robust in build despite conspicuous *enbonpoint,* confident in manner, he had one of those physiognomies that impose through a blend of distinction and roundness. His voice was pleasant. His protruding eyes were clear and decisive. The Marquis, although always in control where the will is required, had at that moment, for me who knew him so well, a noticeably altered complexion and voice, as when his deepest cords were touched. Before the person had spoken of taking leave, he requested that I wait there at the same place in the garden, and both continued their conversation as they moved away. When he reappeared after a few insignificant words that did not distract us from our preoccupation, he said beneath his breath, clutching my arm violently, "Do you know who just left? Georges, General Georges Cadoudal who joins us from England!"

At that time I was overwhelmed, too, and exclaimed, "Surely you're not going to reembark on some enterprise?"

"Eh, no, do I have to reassure you on that again?" (and he accompanied his response with a discouraging sharp laugh) "Don't you know that well enough? My own life is finished. I will not ressuscitate it. Georges came for some information that only I could give him. I won't be seeing him again."

The Marquis' sardonic disposition pained me. He became milder as soon as he had expressed the feelings agitating him. I questioned him first about Georges. He got carried away by the subject, and I learned a great deal.

Georges, as I was already well aware, was not a common conspirator nor a desperate bravo, as can be found in all causes. Several details in his corespondence with the Marquis had already given me a sign of his capacity for grandeur, planning, and vigorous conception. But the last two years especially had matured him. Men of all ranks whom he had trained and organized during his exile were, from this point on, ranged over vast scale at his disposition. The need to wipe out that assassination attempt of Nivôse (December 24, 1800), which was certainly his idea even if the precise plan had not been, weighed on his mind and stimulated him to form some grand design. The design had germinated. It had taken form, and the moment of execution had arrived. Since the war between England and France had broken out, Georges had landed with some of his men. Others would follow, all steadfast, all chosen by his hand. He was as sure of them as he was of himself. Rallying this elite group would be time-consuming, taking two months, perhaps longer. But what difference would that make? Georges and his officers' temerity went hand in hand with so much prudence, and besides, this prudence used temerity as one of its means. When all would be ready here, Pichegru would arrive in his turn. He and Moreau would agree on final points. If the Count d'Artois dared risk his person in the enterprise, that would be best. Georges was advising it, almost demanding him to ennoble and "loyalize" the immediate realization. But whether or not the Prince deigned to reply to the call for a meeting, it was no longer a case of a murder or assassination. The shock, this time, would not be blind and infernal. They would take up their swords as military men. Georges and his three hundred men, at the agreed-upon hour, in an unevenly matched, chivalric encounter, would assail the First Consul, who would be surrounded by his men in the full light of some ceremony, at the threshhold of the Pantheon, the parvis of Notre-Dame, or the esplanade of the Invalides. Once he had fallen, they would present the army with the name of Moreau and present the people with the name of the Prince. That would be the expiatory triumph, Georges' revenge, the adventurer achieving the hero's sublimity.

In unfolding this magnificent hope, the Marquis' forehead appeared lit by lightning. His animation made him appear to believe in it. For a moment I had a flash (which nothing ever discredited) that he had told Georges to alert him, if need be, and that he would swear to be one of the three hundred swordsmen.

I was fired by the plan when I heard it. One project after another crossed my mind. Then, as I began to think again particularly about the man, I was astonished. I tried to explain to myself so much character in the person I had seen such a short while before. We acknowledged in him one of the finest loyal and valorous natures, all the qualities which proceed with flair and reknown to destinies in the outside world. "But he is only an admirable general and war hero," said the Marquis, solemn once again. I joined his train of thought in defining Georges as one of those men whom Cesar, in passing review, would have designated by a glance to command his tenth legion, a man he would never have feared, it seemed to me, to meet on his way to the Senate.

At that point the Marquis pulled from his wallet a carefully enclosed letter. He said, "Since we're talking about heroes, here's another. Read this. Georges, who saw it, wept with admiration."

The paper, which the Marquis gave me to read and which he had never mentioned, was a letter from a former Georges officer, Monsieur de Limoëlan, one of the two who had directed the frenzied attack in Nivôse. A man of pleasant appearance and austere devotion, he had completely accepted the means in view of the ends. But having miraculously escaped, he saw in the aborted catastrophe a sentence of God made manifest. A bad end turned his action into a crime. He had considered himself worthy of serving as an instrument of blood, and he had been crushed upon the stone and rejected. In deep self-hatred, he resolved therefore never to reappear to the members of his party, to shame himself vis-à-vis society, to live here below as a holy criminal, to take his punishment. To this end, having found a berth as a common sailor on some ship, he had succeeded in reaching a foreign shore, Portugal, I think, and a convent took him in. It was from that convent that a first letter written to his sister reached Jersey and was brought to Couaën among the papers addressed to the Marquis. He had unsealed it, thinking it was his own correspondence, and since the envelope had been burned immediately, as was the custom, he had had to wait to learn where to send it. At the time of the arrest, the original of the letter was seized. Monsieur Desmarest, touched by its contents, promised to have it sent to Limoëlan's sister. Monsieur de Couaën had received authorization to transcribe a few passages which I later obtained from him. I should like, my friend, to cite one of them:

"I was insensate to go against the Supreme Design that I presumed to be serving," wrote Limoëlan. "That man for me is truly untouchable, the Lord's annointed. At the very moment where I watched for his appearance, at that fatal corner, I prayed for him, and I begged you, O Lord, to save him against us, if your people needed him. There will never be enough evening vigils, enough signs for me to pray for him. And yet this man was an anathema to me, and I judged him the greatest obstacle to your design, Oh Lord. At night in my dreams or in desires you seemed to send me through your angels, the idea of crushing him recurred without reprieve. I am condemned forever for that. I have girded myself with the cord of the prisoner. I have fasted at length to deserve to be the most vile instrument of your works. I have put on the criminal's smock, I have gathered stones from the mud, I have driven an infamous cart as the hangman's helper. And then when the hour arrived, I shunted the honor of consumation off on another, and I watched from behind a roadmarker like a spy. It was an error! It was human frailty! I have thus put myself against God and against my innocent brothers! I shall spend the rest of my days washing the flagstones with my tears and beating it with my brow! . . . You alone, my sister, who love me still, and worry about my fate, you will be my last link with the living. None but you will know me breathing beneath my penitence. Because I am really dead to the world and crippled in my limbs, my sister, with all the innocent men I struck with stupor, deafness, and death. Poor souls I must answer for, whom I sent to God unprepared. Often in my novice's cell, in order to exert myself as on the day of the crime, I hold the same posture I had at the Rue de Malte for half-hour stretches: my neck craned forward, my body bent, folded, without support, touching the wall with a single finger so as not to fall. To the point that soon I became deaf and blind, numb like those I deafened, blinded, paralyzed with neither an idea nor consciousness of anything, like those whose intelligence I undermined. I am becoming a pillar of salt as punishment . . . I no longer sleep. But if towards morning I happen to drowse off a few minutes, I always wake up with a start from an ear-splitting explosion."

"There is a saint," the Marquis said when I had finished reading. "That is a martyr! Georges is a hero, but what am I, Amaury? Georges, aventurous, determined, will carry his round curly head to the guillotine blade with aplomb if he has to, or he'll fall in the thunder of the melee. Limoëlan, bruised, does reparations, curing himself in his own way in his hair shirt. But what am I doing? Do I have a road, do I have a feasible issue for my destiny? What do I expiate? What do I attempt? Do I have the Cross? Do I have the sword? Do you know, Amaury, how all this pompous shipwreck will end for us? Some sleepy city in Touraine or Maine will be assigned to me for a haven—with a farmhouse and poultry yard. What a merciful fate! From now on even my cliff at Couaën would be too good for me, where I could grow white counting the waves and breathing in the tempest." The Marquis spoke to the point. He had guessed the likely outcome. Monsieur Desmarest had already let me hope as much. As for that comparison in which he was pleased to efface himself vis-à-vis Limoëlan and Georges, I agreed that he differed notably from both, but that he had indeed otherwise more mental capacity than either. The only role that would satisfy his nature was whole and complex; I classed his idle genius in the race of the most noble and ardent ambitious politicians.

How I tried give him examples that would make him feel my own judgment of him, to raise his mourning and honor his rare wound in his own eyes. As I was speaking volubly, moved by the earlier circumstances and as he, however, was silent, no longer responding as if he had ceased to follow the conversation, while we walked I got carried away to the point of shouting, "On that Couaën heather that you fear you will not see again, opposite that beach without a port, without ships, on that theater of a religion long since vanished, I shall go up to some shapeless stone from Druid days. I will consecrate this stone, meditating on its site, and I shall pronounce these words: 'To great unknown men!'

"Oh, yes, yes," I continued (or in words to this effect), "to the great men who did not shine, the lovers who did not love, that infinite corps of elite who had no visits from opportunity, happiness, or fame. To the flowers on the heath, to the pearls in the ocean depths, to the fragrances known by the passing breeze, to the thoughts and tears men confide only to themselves in the depths of the night!

"It seems to me that all the great men checkmated here and there compose a mysterious choir, silent on its cloud, sparing in its sighs. Don't you agree? It is another funereal Pantheon. I can envision it from today on, a mute Limbo where those great, meritorious souls of unknown mortals dwell. You will often introduce me here, O You whom I venerate! I shall expect to learn in those immense catacombs, much better than beneath the narrow vault of the other resplendent Pantheon, human misery and profundity."

And in that burst of ideas that his silence encouraged, I added "There *is* no Pantheon here below. There is no true Capitol for any mortal. Any triumph in this world, even for the shining brows, is never more, I imagine, than a defeat, more or less disguised. Putting aside two or three men, once identified, of any type, two or three nearly fabled lives, which in their plenitude are more like abridged allegories for humanity, ways to express their dreams—beyond that, in reality, dreams, plans, hopes, in all respects seem to me like a body of fresh troops, who start out in the morning to pass through a long mountainous defile, between the two ranks of inevitable, invisible archers in ambush. If before evening, the chief of the troop and some decimated batallion reach the next city with some semblance of a flag, we call that a triumph. If, in our plans, ambitions, love affairs, some part has suffered less than the rest, we call that fame or happiness. But how many desires, vows, secret ornaments—and some of the most beautiful, that no one knew about—had to be left along the way! Oh, for the person who takes the law into his own hands, for the person who reads his own heart after the triumph as before, for God who sees the depths and who counts the dead in us, it can only be truly said, I am sure, 'Human triumph does not happen!' "

At these last words, the Marquis, finally moved to answer, gently placed his hand on my shoulder and left it there awhile, "Ah, well,

Amaury, you too, you know these things already—and so intimately!"

But the words from my lips were more mature than the state of my soul and made me seem more mature than I was. When God is not within us at all times to confirm our speech, nature makes young men pay dearly for their precocious wise words. I had hardly left the Marquis when I was afflicted by his malady. I carried away secretly in my soul the ulcerated disposition I had just fought and perhaps relieved in his. This irritation at my own fate increased with every step. All my old pictures of the future, all my powerful illusions started to stir. At that moment I saw pass away both all that I had planned fondly since childhood and the remaining plans that spoke of their realization. Beneath an infinity of forms, under a thousand reflections of the sun and a thousand flags, love affairs, ambitions, an aggregate of desires, tender affections binding people together, thoughts turning the world, rushed to come to life in my valley, like noisy recruits in an limitless army. I embraced them with my glance like Xerxes from his high observation point, and I wept—but from rage. I wept to hear my thoughts cry *battle* and not be able to fight on any score, to hear them cry *hunger* and not know how to get food. My reasoned reflection, wherever I applied it, came to bolster that none too imaginative vision. France with England, then with Europe, was beginning its turbulent shocks. I had in those days what thoughout my youth I called my inactive cowardice. Divers studies, the search for pure truth, interlocking systems I devoted myself to, the way you surrender to luck in gambling just to lose your senses, these occupations so necessary for my mind did not fulfill me. Besides, it was evident that if I gave in to this side too seriously and vigorously, Man the eternal obstacle would know how to put things straight. Love, for which I was born, made me feel only its languors or its bleeding points. Pleasure let me drink only the dregs. The two young women whom I frequented on a daily basis, and whom I always conjured up when we were separated, appeared in graceful poses in the midst of the woods I had reached. The woman who was my cult was in a reserved, inaccessible place. If only she were less sacred in my eyes, I dared say to myself. If only she was as well suited for the place of the other who paled and sighed from *ennui*! My sole friends, whose destiny controlled mine, would be sent off tomorrow to some stifling, tedious city. I could not see myself living far from them, detached. Nor did I see how I could follow them. So I was just as I used to be, getting carried away, just to escape my remote brambles—first planning a retreat to the Island of the Druids and then a flight to Ireland.

I threw myself into Georges' plans. I resolved to find him, offer myself, to force him to accept me. I said to myself, "If the Marquis is part of it, how can you not be? if the Marquis isn't, if he stays with his own household, at least you can take part. Take part so you won't have to live far away from them later, so you won't have to see such a beautiful friendship fade so quickly, to die in a burst of glory so She and he will weep over you!"

Now I had to find Georges again. Any direct question would have made the Marquis suspicious. But inferring from a passing remark that he must be lodged somewhere around the Parthenon, I chose a spot near that square, near which he was bound to pass often. By crossing these environs at various hours, I would certainly see him and I was sure to recognize him. As simple and well founded as my reasoning on this plan was, carrying it out took long patient efforts and for nearly a week, I ran through tedious tacks in that crossing. All my free hours were devoted to it. My friends had already noticed and reproached me for my anxious, abridged visits. I was running out of all pretexts. I soon saw that unless I spent an entire day on the project, there would be too little for me to hope for. So, warning my friends that I would be absent for a whole day, explaining as best I could, I sharpened my gaze and vigilance. Not until dusk of that slow day, when work stops and working men and women going home give rise to a certain unusual bustle on these unfrequented squares and streets, did I espy among the horde of passers-by a man with a splendid bearing and promising pace. At the moment I got in the best angle possible to see his face, I began to follow him amidst the others going the other way. I passed him casually, almost touching him. I let him pass me in return. No further doubt. It was indeed the guide I was looking for, the heroic brigand, Cesar's sworn foe. At a corner where we were nearly alone, I quickly crossed over to him. "General ————," I said, saluting. He shuddered and moved his hand to some hidden weapon. I hastily muttered Couaën's name, as well as our preceding encounter, and he repaired his brusqueness with a glance. The Marquis, as it happened, had identified me to the General upon walking out with him. I told everything without preambles. I told him how I owed to the Marquis' confidence my passion for the future tourney. To the well-meaning picture he presented of the serious risk and the lack of need for my services, because I was not a trained military man, I replied with a succinct but moving confession of my situation, my *ennui*, and my impatience for action. He could well see that it was the chivalrous use of my strength that tempted me, rather than the satisfaction of political hatred. My frank story touched him.

He held out his hand, promised to mention nothing to the Marquis, and that if the shock occurred, I could assuredly take part in it. In the meantime he required that we have no steady communication, because compromising myself would be a pure loss. Before separating, however, I got him to accompany me a few minutes to my room, which was quite close, so that he would know a safe haven in case of need.

Once this was taken care of, I felt great calm and complete contentment. I was rid of the inner burden that weighed on me the most, of the vague concern of the future. A kind of column, dazzling or dark, but huge and deliberately placed, dominated my horizon. It seemed to me that from now on I had the right to live, to frolic in the plain and multiply. All the energies of my age, all the radiant beams of youth shone again. My friends saw me more attentive to them, more expansive, more adept at pleasing them. I could now attend parades, military reviews without hatred or bitterness. My glance was that of a rival who is getting ready and assesses, when passing the height of the enemy camp, with a kind of pride. As a simulacrum and prelude, I started going to a fencing school and went back to fencing passionately. In my love of contraries, my studies too gained in this new lightheartedness. My reading had never been so varied in type, so fertile in reflections and memories. It seemed as if a finer daylight shone on the pages beneath my fingers. That was about the time, I believe, that like a dream of Endymion, Bernardin de Saint-Pierre's paintings showed me the milky mildness of their sky, the whitened groves of their landscapes, and the melodious monotony like the sound of a flute beneath the moon in the forests. The quite recent writings of an already celebrated compatriot, Monsieur de Chateaubriand, struck me much more than those of Saint-Pierre, and perhaps at first appealed to me less. I was often offended and disconcerted by so many efforts at brilliance. But one evening, when I finished reading that beautiful episode *René*, I wrote in my diary a tumultuous judgment beginning, if I recall, by "I read *René*, and I trembled; I recognized myself completely." How many others in the twenty years since have trembled like that as they thought they faced themselves in that immortal portrait! Such is the property of those magic mirrors, where genius has concentrated its true sorrow, that for generations all who approach to look in see themselves in turn. And yet my malady was really mine, less vague, elevated, and ideal than that of my hero, and beneath its diverse transformations proceeding from a more definite motivation.

To love, to be loved, to join pleasure to love, to feel free while remaining faithful, to keep my secret chain even in passing infidelities;

to perfect my mind, to adorn it with enlightenment and grace only to make me a better lover, to give more to the object possessed, to explain the world to her. That was my definitive purpose in a gentle life, and I attached all happiness to that. Such was the morbid cure which would have satisfied me. As for the rustles of a writer's or warrior's fame, which I heard from time to time, once fulfilled in love, I would have made fame keep still. Any woodland zephyr would have chased away my regrets. Ambitious actions I would have easily pitied. Study? I would only have plucked the flower. The slave of love finds it sweet to cultivate oblivion. Religion, alas? I would no doubt have made it accommodate also the wish of my heart and senses. I would have borrowed from religion whatever I needed to nourish and lull my stale remorse, and used it as a profane crown for my tenderness. Here you have, from one daydream to the next, the state of abandonment I had reached. Aside from sensuality, my friend, I never wanted during those days anything for itself. When I seemed to be willing and acting in some other domain, underneath it was always from that secret impulse. What the philosopher Helvetius said about the sole motivation for man generally, couldn't have been truer for me.

And aging, which comes so quickly for lovers, and the serious years, and death, what was I doing about them? What idea did I have of these terrible envoys? Well, in my plan of earthly Elysium, I never saw either my idol or myself surviving the flattering years very long. However, in the slow decline of a beauty one loves, in the many memories attached to that half-faded sparkle, there is a sad sweetness I foresaw well enough to want to experience to the end. But when this final melancholy was inhaled, somewhat before the extreme end of that autumn of youth, I supposed always (seeing myself present and on my knees) the lingering last illness of my beloved in the breast of a forgiving religion. And after a few years of romantic widowhood and restless solitude, I would pass away piously in turn, around forty-three at the latest. That was the outside limit I could bear imagining myself on this earth. A refined mishmash, wouldn't you say? Epicure-anism, faith in the soul, forgetfulness and awareness of God! A perfidious image which, however, was not entirely false and where was pictured, as you will see, an inconceivable light on the future! And for my novel of happiness I had no need to believe it capable of realization because it continued to float in my mind at the very moments when I was hoping for a different outcome altogether.

But to return to my reading which I mentioned, no doubt this contrasted the most with the turbulence and agitation of that crisis and called me back to a rather high moment towards the invisible region. I was reading some things by a theosophist whom I quote to you rather often because he had had a great deal of influence on me. The books *On Error and Truth* and *Man and Desire* introduced me with some confusion to several precious dogmas blended, nearly dissolved in a medium of mystic perfume. Saint-Martin's response to Garat which I found in the *annales* of the Ecoles Normales sent me to these two works which I had already leafed through at Couaën but without paying much attention. The response itself where the Sage gives his simplest enumeration of his principles, that calm, basic style so opposed to brilliant language and, as the author himself says, so opposed to the crackling fusillades of his adversary, that prudent tone, always reverent with ideas, put me easily on the paths of spiritualism. I should say that on that point I was a wandering wayfarer rather than a deserter. One truth touched me acutely among all others and was a revelation about myself: this is where he says that "man lives and breathes in thought."

Many truths which we think we know and cherish, moreover, if they reach us expressed in a certain unexpected way, appear in reality for the first time. By reaching us from an angle that we had never encountered, they light a spark. That is how that aphorism worked on me instantly, as if scales had fallen from my eyes. All that was visible in this world and nature, all works and creatures, beside their material signification, at first glance, of elementary order and use, seemed to acquire a moral signification through thought—some thought of harmony, beauty, sadness, pity, austerity, or admiration. And it was in the power of my inner moral sense, which I could use to interpret or at least detect divers signs or at least catch whiffs of the fruits of that mysterious orchard, to gather some syllables of that great language which, fixed here, wandering there, trembled through nature. I saw in this process exactly the contrary of Lamarck's discouraging world with its mute and morbid base. Creation, like a once sullied vestibule, was reopening to man. It was ornamented with sonorous vases, bowing stalks, full of friendly voices, insinuations which were generally favorable, and probably peopled in reality with innumerable vigilant spirits. Beneath the animals and flowers, the stones themselves in their gross form, stones of the streets and walls were not without some participation in the universal language. But the more matter became light, the more the signs became volatile and ungraspable, the more penetrating they were. For several days while I walked in the spell of that impression, along deserted streets, my face in the clouds, my brow swept by gusts of air, it seemed to me that I was truly feeling thoughts flutter and glide over my head.

What is surprising is that one can be a man and ignore that altogether. One can be a man of worth, of special genius and human merit and feel in no way whatsoever the undulations of the true atmosphere bathing us. Or, if one cannot not avoid being touched at some moment or other, one knows how to remain closed, to guard oneself as if against foul air, closing the higher channels of the mind to those loving influences which seek to nurture it.

So there are a large number of men, and men of various talents, who, it can be said, never live in thought. Among such men, there are those gifted with all kinds of physical types, of logic and tactics with narratives of deeds and histories, with the observation or expression of phenomena and of that first mask called "reality." But do not ask anything of them beyond the immediate senses. They cut themselves off early from the aerial horizon. They have settled on the floor they consider the only solid ground. They will not leave it. The precise vacuum that they make around themselves with respect to the divine atmosphere weighs upon them and successfully attaches them to those more or less ingenious works where they excel. Who would believe, seeing such examples, that thought is the natural food of spirits? If a few thoughts circulate around them in conversation, they join in only to deny or restrict them. Or else they keep quiet until the thoughts have passed. If thoughts surprise them in their beds when they awaken, listen to their confession! They hasten to shake them off not because they are sometimes stormy, which might be prudent, but because they are like waves, wildly stirring and importunate as thoughts. What a crushing idea these men, rare after all, have of the human nature they ornament. If you cried out to them, like Descartes to Gassendi, "Oh Flesh!" they would be honored by the insult like the latter and would rail in return, "Oh Spirit!" Whatever they possess, my friend, of character, habit or system, let us thank heavens that we are less negative than that. You often have the delicate and preparatory nourishment for these souls; don't despair! If it suits to temper the nourishment in use, as being too intoxicating for this life and a little cloying without faith, it would still be mortal to be weaned from it. At certain moments, which the sincere heart can first discern, let us welcome thoughts without apprehension and try out the sources from on high. Let us open ourselves to that dew which rains from the clouds. Grace itself is only a fecund drop.

The instant attraction that the reading of Saint-Martin held for me gave me the quite natural desire of seeing him personally. I would never have dreamed of approaching him; he was so humble. Or of questioning him, he was a man of prayer and silence. I simply wanted to catch sight of him. Having inquired about him from my ideologue friend, I learned that during the summer he preferred to live at Aulnay, in the house of Senator Lenoir-Larouche. One September day, just on a whim and full of the predisposition just mentioned, I undertook that little pilgrimage. "If I should meet him on some path, I will divine it, and the very doubt in which I will subsequently remain will add to the impression he made." I went and by a sort of restraint fitting my object, without wanting to question anyone, I took off through that narrow little valley, that wooded slope, which the sweet old man regarded as one of the most pleasant spots on earth. I prowled in the thickets of the gardens, I thought I discovered the turns he preferred to climb; in sitting down at the top, I imagined that I was occupying a place familiar to him. But I had no encounter that could have contributed to my fantasy. This timid tracking in the woods on the pious man's traces left me an interest, cheerful at first but soon solemn and scared. After less than a fortnight, I learned that he had not been at Aulnay at the time of my visit, but that he had returned since and suddenly died there.

It was perhaps later, although I should like to mention it to you now, that certain passages in Vaugenargues agreed so perfectly with my train of thought and conduct, they gave me an inexpressible sensation. When he wrote to his young friend Hippolytus about fame and pleasure, I heard him, that thirty-year-old philosopher, consumed, ripened by pain like Pascal, and from day to day more Christian, I heard him address that advice to me in an enchanting tone. They would be just as appropriate if I said them to you: "You have a sweeter error, my dear friend, would I dare struggle against it, too? Pleasures have enslaved you. You breathe life into them; they touch you; you bear their irons. How would they spare you in the flush of youth if they tempt even the reason and experience of advanced age? My charming friend, I pity you. You know all they promise and the little they hold. You are aware of the disgust which follows sensuality, the carelessness it inspires, the deep forgetfulness of duties, such frivolous worries, such fears, such insensate distractions!" I know that sentence by heart. I repeated it often with the same inflections of melancholy that as a child I used to put in the lines of Propertius. I blushed with confusion at those grave words, as indulgent as a mother's. And if, still addressing his young friend, he wrote him on the subject of fame: "When you are on guard on the bank of a river and rain puts out all the fires during the night and permeates your clothes, you will say 'Happy is he who can sleep in a cabin far from the noisy waters!' When day breaks, the shadows fade, the guard is changed, and you go back into camp. Fatigue and noise plunge you into a gentle sleep and you awake more serene to eat a delicious meal. On the other hand, a young man reared in virtue, whom a mother's tenderness keeps inside the walls of a fortified city, even at rest is anxious and agitated. He seeks out solitary spots: holidays, games, shows hold no attraction. The thought of what happens in Moravia fills his days, and during the night he dreams of combats and battles fought without him." How this return to Moravia came naturally to my lips to express my jealous suffering in inaction, far from the victorious frays! Even the merest consonant touched me, and I heard a discouraged harmony.

Now you will think, my friend, that there were not hours enough for such diverse occupations, that such a contradiction of act and thought could not cohabit, that at least during the days of these noble meditations, gross pleasures had no place, that all these objects of my narratives followed each other at a distance perhaps, but did not coexist! You are mistaken. Just look at yourself. Think of what man inexplicably takes into his life, especially of what that marvelous age embraces and condenses. I ran into the valley to search the Sage; I returned to the city on the trail of a warrior and conspirator. I called for the bloody shock, I launched my soul into the most fluid azure of the sky. Then, some thick form of beauty dragged me back. And behind all that a faithful thought, a veiled feeling, drawing from its languor, exhaling, finding itself again at each point: desire without hope, a lamp without glow—my love!

CHAPTER XIII

That prodigious burst of energy which followed my meeting with Georges was thus dispersed in every which way and rather soon expended. Little by little I fell back, as was my natural penchant, to weighing the difficulties of the undertaking, its delays, and probable failure before it had even begun. This new vision made me confront my own stalemate, my customary boredom; and a few involuntary exasperations made my elation shortlived. And if She, usually so accepting and indulgent, perceived these changes in me, if she seemed to worry (as she often did) to see me different, to hear me complain and threaten in a vacuum and wish to leave—or die—if she would then reproach me gently of not loving enough, above all else, to be inconstant and desirous of whatever was least, valuable, I would reply, seizing her own words and accenting their intent, "But would you love beyond compare, would you love above all else, above your husband and children?" It was on the days when I had sensually strayed the most that I showed what a brutal egoist I was. Then her concern for her husband and children would aggrieve me. At the least indisposition of her children, at the idea of her husband's next furlough, I would find her preoccupied by something besides me. The throne I lusted after in her heart appeared to me, I might as well say so, grossly usurped by these people. Oh, how intolerant and injurious human love is the moment man gives full rein to his passions! At those moments when man's love aims at conquest, when he changes, embittered by obstacles, I would compare a man in love at such times to those Asian despots who cut the throats of their near and dear to make their way to the throne. Thus, brutal and despotic love, if allowed to act from instinct, to remain barbarous in its jealousy, and if untouched by Christianity, would gladly cut throats to sacrifice all other loves on that altar. But when I expressed my demanding egoism in this way, with some veiling of the terms, although my basic meaning was sufficiently clear, she did not understand me. She could not acknowledge my ferocious exclusiveness. She could not conceive that love was the enemy of loving, and that from the diverse and related loves there had to result something other than an emulation of ardor and tenderness. All true loves, in her eyes, sprang from the same stem, like branches of the golden candelabra in Exodus. I could see my unbridled pretension made her suffer and worry.

Then, other times when my senses and ego were less in view, when recent evenings had been better, and when my genuine love was somewhat dissipated, then I would become gentle and tolerant around her, sacrificing my share of happiness, effacing myself. And she adapted so quickly when she saw me like that, she blossomed in that easy atmosphere, and we got along so well. One afternoon when I got to her apartment, I found her in her bedroom surrounded by a large number of opened letters. Some scattered on the tables, some on the chairs, and there was a chest still full to one side. These were the old love letters of eight years earlier, the secret correspondence she and the Marquis had before their marriage when they were separated by family difficulties and her brother's rage. That dear chest, taken away from her when Couaën was first seized, had been returned to her several months ago. But on this day she had begun to go through it at random as soon as she woke up and she had kept on reading until I arrived, having forgotten to dress or go down stairs. One letter succeeded another. Scenes, joys, and ecstasies of earlier days had left that fragrant coffer one by one like a garland long since faded, like the trim of her first nuptial garment which had been enclosed also and was half pulled out. The years of the family, the fatherland, virginal love, had all risen up to encircle her. When I entered, she did not budge. In the spell of her present emotion, she remained where she was, tears in her eyes, her head tilted back on a cushion, one letter on her knees, her arms hanging limp. She let me touch these sacred letters, explaining the circumstances and occasions full of alarms. I could even read two or three he sent to her but not a single one she sent to him; her modesty opposed it. I admired the tone of that trembling and submissive love from a man whose contrary traits of character I knew so well. The letters I managed to read bore specifically on the tender promises he made to control his resentment of Lucy's brother and to refrain from arrogant behavior in general— because she apparently had reproached him for his bitter disdain of other men and his opinionated pride in his blood. As I finished reading the letter *sotto voce*, I saw the nuptial garment mentioned and asked if I could take it as a token of inviolable confidence. She made a gesture of consent without seeming to pay much attention and at the same time relying on the benevolent state of my disposition, she said, "Soon when Monsieur de Couaën is released, oh, we will be at peace then, united for a long time. We shall bless his unhappiness, we shall alleviate it. Ours will be a country life of absolute isolation. We shall see Couaën again one day, whatever you say. You will be with us. My children will grow up, formed by your care. My own childhood will bloom again. We will practice our religion. We will celebrate the anniversaries of my mother's death. We shall do good works. That is the sure way of removing the hatreds which poison our hearts. Already you are calm and resigned. I see you less often taken over by those ambitions rages vis-à-vis inaccessible things. You will not detest anyone, will you? That is how it will be with him. We shall force him to give thanks for his misfortunes. We shall all believe in another life, for this one will never be suffice for our affections and happiness."

That was a pure woman speaking, and I listened, speechless with enchantment. The pure woman believes in such plans for the future; she would be capable of conforming happily to that end. And for that reason I judge her superior indeed to man. But a man in love who hears such felicitous arrangements fall from a persuasive mouth, and believes in them for a moment, and thinks he is capable of devoting his life does not really have the strength to do it, whatever he may think. While the beloved woman with the honest, trusting heart, free from desire, is sufficiently fulfilled to see her friend at her side and to let him hold her hand for a moment and to treat him like a brother, her cherished brother, the man, even if blessed by Heaven like Abel or John, inevitably suffers in secret from his incomplete and false position. He feels wounded in his secondary nature, rumbling, scolding, aggressive. Moments which are apparently the most harmonious quickly become painful, perilous, shameful. From there come the exasperated and cruel reversals.

But if what is an internal sacrifice extends in power, if what is naturally feeble and secondary gradually fades and expires, if man succeeds in loving purely as the pure woman can do, if Abel and John's modest tunic gradually envelopes him, from head to toe, if we imagine the bitterness, the corrupted senses, the envy and impoverishment of an exclusive love, fought, conquered bit by bit through pity, vigilance, recourse to another life, generous activity expended for the beloved creature, and the benefits around her at every moment, in her name, then we would certainly have on earth a shadow of the great love that reigns in the beyond and of that unanimous embrace in the order of God. Because in that desired order the separate hearths and centers of the tenderness preceding are maintained, as I hope. Mother, sister, sanctifying friend we do not cease to recognize and name in the celestial gaze. The transported soul finds again in more beautiful proportions his good love affairs, each of them being only an encouragement to the others, an unending flight to Him who both crowns and justifies them.

In the peaceful light of moments like these, we embrace in advance reflections of these depths we imagine realizable here below. Binding projects press upon our lips and multiply our speech. And these were the gently joys that made her bless God for her lot and be thus surrounded, and which afterwards, in solitude, kept her in a perfect state and perhaps still exalted, but for me, once by myself, I quickly undid and corrupted this state.

Autumn was ending and its days of prolonged adieu are the most savored and felt. We enjoyed them as long as possible, until in the end the woods were almost bare, the last trembling leaf waiting only for the approaching winter wind. Then we had to leave Auteuil for Paris. The Marquis had been granted the choice of a private hospital on a nearby boulevard in our faubourg. Madame de Couaën settled back in the little convent to her own great satisfaction and that of Madame de Cursy, the children, and everyone else. Our *modus vivendi* thus was little changed. Only (is now the time to bring it in?) the absence of young Madame R——— made me notice her more when she came. If she remained until evening, I usually escorted her back home. And when I left her, to cross again by myself that sea where I knew only too well how to drown, a mocking voice reminded me *sotto voce*, in a tone of worldly wisdom, that I was bored to death with friendship without possession and possession without love. I tried in vain not to dwell on that treacherous idea. It still occurred to me, every time she came to visit, to look more favorably on the side of that faint star which shone in Madame R———'s eyes.

One day when we were gathered at Madame de Couaën's apartment, Madame R——— was present. While other people were chatting, I approached her where she stood in the embrasure of an arched doorway. By way of compliment I asked whether she had news of a young woman in the provinces whom she talked about sometimes and who was in her confidence.

"Do you know what that little person took it upon herself to ask yesterday? She was insistent upon knowing what had become of *my friend* Monsieur Amaury."

"Well, aren't we?" I rejoined. "Since you doubt it, let us agree to be friends from this day forward." I held out my hand to seal the commitment. She laid her hand on mine, repeating my last words. This happened without any affectation, and no one noticing the gesture would have been astonished. Later, in escorting her home, I shook her hand as usual and said, "Now you haven't forgotten that we're friends now" or something like that as I waited for her door to close behind her. If I had followed my impulse, I would have paid her more calls than I could have given reasons for. At least I profited from every opportunity to be nice to her. But this was no imperious compulsion to which I really surrendered. I was only trying out the singular attraction that is mixed in with these burgeoning complications. After a tender adieu, which escaped me this way and which a soft "oui" had welcomed, on my walk home I often felt a stirring of pride that I could give my heart to one, my smile and word to another, to satisfy them both, while my desires were not fulfilled. And then this futile contentment was mixed so quickly with remorse, uneasy scruples aroused by the idea of Madame de Couaën, secret excuses and little accommodations that I had some trouble bringing about. With such second thoughts I would almost have returned to Madam R——— to ask, "There is nothing wrong or duplicitous in what I am doing, is there?"

I still did not know what Georges was doing, although I had tried on various occasions to meet him, and the Marquis hardly appeared to know more about it than I did. He and I conjectured that the two or three hundred men needed for the group had not been collected and that in being dragged out this way the plan would lose what chance it had. Our fears for Georges and his men were acute; I drew at least half of my anxiety from the Marquis. It would have been urgently in the interest of his own security that his removal to Blois or somewhere else be decided as soon as possible and before the discovery of a royalist conspiracy, which would undoubtedly risk compromising him in the judgement. But such a removal could be so harsh an insult of his honor and would be so dreadful a wrenching for us—and a painful trial for our own friendship—that I did not dare risk promoting it aggresively to Monsieur Desmaret or Madam R———'s husband. Every time that likely outcome was broached, the Marquis spoke with such disgust, almost horror, about the grimy prison awaiting him. That showed me plainly enough his firm intention to be in Paris for any occurrence. On the contrary, Monsieur Desmaret, whom I continued to see from time to time, was clearly anxious to have that solution carried out. From certain intimations, perhaps uttered intentionally, I thought I caught his sense of something in the wind. Such intimations hardly made me any more calm.

The last months of the year rolled by without any salient event, perhaps because affairs really did languish, perhaps because I simply do not remember them. I was kept very busy, homesick as the dreary weather began, immersed in a life that had little to be proud of. All Saints Day and Christmas, now that I think back upon them, had nothing remarkable about them that year. These are strange lapses of memory. To the dazzling fortnight that the meeting with Georges began had succeeded a kind of fog and eclipse. How does it happen that there are patches in distant memories that are so clear, so distinct in the most insignificant circumstances? while some related memories are so cloudy and indistinct? That, my friend, had less to do with the circumstances themselves than the essential state of the soul when those circumstances occur. They are lighted by the degree of active illumination in the soul as it receives them flowing through. We remember the past through and with our soul of today, and it should not be too foggy, but we remember our selves in our soul of bygone days, and there have to be patches of memories where this soul can gleam in the distance like a silvery river, like a stream in the meadows.

May I say a few words on the subject of memory here, as it affects me, and I have felt a great deal on the subject! If memory for most souls in situations like mine is a rude temptation, for me, my friend, it is more a persuasion, recalling me to the good, a solicitation almost always salutary in its vitality. Is that, perchance, an excuse I was looking for amidst those thousands of flowers and thorns where I am treading again? In truth, my God, I do not believe it. Others especially need at least to dwell on their past. As soon as they have redeemed it with enough tears, then they must detach themselves and break with it. Sturdy hope raises them up and pushes them forward, assiduous workmen of prophecy. They have Saint Jerome's burning example. But without it being, I think, a contradiction with immortal hope, and in all that is within the human order, I myself have always had memory rather than hope at heart, the feeling and lament for things past rather than an embrace of the future. Memory, in my moments of equanimity, has always been the most restful, most blue backdrop of my life, my familiar door of return to Heaven. In brief, I have constantly felt I was the most pious when I had the most memories and the most balanced ones. At the same time, even in the most turbulent and ambitious years, I owe to memory a major part of my deep impressions. In the divers ages I have lived through, as I prematurely anticipated the experience of ideas and the disappointment usual for the succeeding age, I lived little from actual enjoyment, and it was through memory that the most refreshing reparations came to me. When I was savoring a moment of true happiness, I needed, in order to complete the experience, to imagine that it was already far removed, and I would pass again one day in the same spots, and that it would then be delightfully sad to remember this happiness. That is how I was in my external view of events and my judgments on present history. The feeling of a past still warm and recently buried wrapped me round with strong sympathy. In my faubourgs, on my favorite boulevards, the cloister walls of deserted communities, the back grills of abandoned gardens, I put together a world I imagined as if I had really lived in it. When my young male lips burned to greet new dawns, something in the heart of me wept for what had passed. But at certain hours, on certain days, especially on Sunday evenings, that impression grows. All my old memories awake and come to life. All the broken rings of the past begin again to tremble in their course, to seek one another out, lit by a gentle, magic light.

Today, this very instant, my friend, is one of those Sunday evenings, and in the strange land where I'm writing, while a thousand joyous bells ring the Salut of Ave Marie, all my past life comes back in a marvelous feeling, all my memories answer, as they would beneath the heavens with the old echoes. Since my uncle's farm, that first blurred glow I have kept of my mother, how many points gradually light up and stir! how many isolated bits of debris, rather unremarkable, unmotivated, it would seem in their reawakening, and yet so full of hidden life and austere feeling! Oh, not only you, inevitable creatures who were everything for me, for whom I must pray and bleed one vein a day; not only the scenes where you are standing blended together and whose image stays with me forever; but also minor scattered incidents, accidental pebbles along the way, the thresholds I crossed only once, the faces of girls or old men that I only glimpsed, some dear creatures who think they are forgotten or who always thought I was indifferent, others whose existence and histories I have known only through friends lost themselves for a long time, and the most unknown of all, those souls to whom I often pay my De Profoundis because my mind stubbornly retained their name after coming across it on some tottering wooden cross in a cemetery I was wandering through. What others are there? Several apparitions, also less pure in origin, but veiled however in a reassuring gloom, everything comes back and speaks to me. Times and spaces come together. Some inexpressible feeling, and nothing if not religious emanates from that vast quivering field. But what could have taken place in the two or three months in question is no longer clear to me.

It was only toward the last half of January that one evening, when I had returned rather late and was ready to get in bed, I heard a hammering on the outside door below, breaking this sluggishness, as it were, and plunging me back into active life. Given the disposition of the house, which was like those in the provinces and had only two floors, and considering that the other tenants lived very retiring lives, I was sure that a visit at that hour was for me. I went down to open up, and my candle lit the face of General Georges. I welcomed him as much with surprise as with real joy. He came that very evening from a trip he had made to the coast to receive Pichegru and other important personages who had landed. After he left his companions in a safe place, he himself had started toward his old retreat. He had remembered me and turned off his way expressly to pass beneath my window. When he noticed the light through the blinds, either through a friendly caprice or curiosity to know what in their daily relations with us the police had been able to extract from recent suspisions, he decided to ask me for shelter that night. I thanked him as if for an honor, some benefit. My impetuous hopes crowded around, agitated, ready for assault. I showed him my sword and the other arms I had procured for his inspection. Since I lacked powder, he told me not to worry about it. After the first preparations for the night, which I wanted to get over with as soon as possible, after we made up the bed for two, we had a conversation that lasted as long as I could have wished and was frank and open. What I discerned from his discourse was a sense of rectitude that would not stray, a confidence in judging acquired from handling men, his contempt for many men and principally those in party leadership. But with that he had an unswerving resolution to serve this party as if it were his own cause, after all, and not solely that of the princes and other men of power he meant to serve. And, to be sure, the absolute spirit of conservation, to maintain his right and his custom, his thatched cottage and his hedge, like the King his throne, and the noble his dungeon, that is what Georges' politics came down to. He considered that in the midst of these gentlemen whose company he hardly enjoyed, these princes who decked him with orders without following him, he was serving his own ideas and the common defense. From thence the usual source of grandeur. He aimed at the result obviously and at the fact much more than the fame. In difficulties of reasoning, at junctures where good sense is found wanting, his faith came to his aid, and he entrusted himself without further thought, to use his favorite expression, to

God's care. He had more than one trait of the experienced and dedicated sailor of our coasts—the person who can do the impossible during a storm but leaves the rest to God. Beneath his frank and cordial manner, beneath his rounded, nearly attractive forms, I was not slow to discover from two or three slips something rude, barely tamable, something of ancient ferocity, if I may put it that way, which I discerned of his ancestry, which many of my compatriots have inherited from their great grandparents, and which I have not gotten rid of, I fear, but at the expense of my strength of character. But why should I regret it? That in the Christian there should be no remnant of the Celtic, Sicambrian or Hebrew? He questioned me closely about Monsieur de Couaën, whom he regarded highly but knew only by his correspondence and by that recent visit he paid him. Because before the pacification of 1800, the Marquis, only recently installed in the country, had not had any occasion to have dealings with Georges. As I attempted to explain my own views of the Marquis, of his outstanding faculties and their unfortunate frustration, it took Georges a long time to understand and follow along with my distinctions. These concerns for power and glory seemed superfluous to him who was intrepid and devout. These are the anxieties of intellectuals and strong personalities, he said, as he listened to me describe that melancholy. According to him, action and danger should be a distraction from anything. "Is he held back by his wife or his children? . . . If not . . . what is holding him back when he is so stouthearted?"

This basic assumption of our friend's courage confirmed my suspicion that the latter had agreed to serve in case of a coup. Whatever that might have been, I kept up a spirited explanation but with rather little success. A singular gradation of minds between them! The Marquis who seemed chimerical and transcendent to Georges would have appeared justifiably positivist, down-to-earth, and too intent on action in the eyes of the theosophist or poet. In the end, when I had thoroughly exhausted my analysis and comparisons on this chapter of the Marquis, when I had shown him young in his numerous voyages, declaiming his thoughts to the winds of the seas and sowing on the arid plain, when I came to the end, following him to his disenchanted vigil on his seaside heath, Georges, who for some moments had stopped listening, interrupted. "All right," he cried, "now I think I understand you. You mean he's a William Pitt who never had a portfolio."

And on the subject of Madame de Couaën, as I slipped, depicting her with evident pleasure and spending more time on her than was really necessary, he broke in, "Oh, you're just a bit infatuated, get on

with the subject!" His tone of voice showed the brusque manners of a
military leader and the puritanical severity of a believer. My delicacy
was offended. I felt the touch of an iron hand. What I told Georges
about Monsieur Desmaret's vague suspicions in no way alarmed him.
The plan was nearly ready to carry out and would continue in the
open. The group, because of the inertia of a large number, would only
count some fifty men, myself included, he said, sufficient in a pinch.
Within three days Pichegru would join with Moreau, and it was to be
hoped that as two men of war, they would talk little and let us
act quickly.

It was getting late and I wished Georges good night. He showed
me that it was his habit to sleep with his faithful pistols under his
bolster. I noticed that he knelt a few moments to pray.

In the morning, somewhat late, we were still sleeping when a
knock on the door of my room awoke me. I rose, hastily covered
myself, and as I hesitated to open, Georges ordered me to do so. I
nearly burst into discourteous laughter when I saw that the visitor was
none other than Monsieur de Vacquerie in person. Having come for
the winter in Paris where this once he had brought his daughter, he
came first (and alone, of course) to pay a morning call and inquire
about all manner of things. I received him at the door and warned him
that the room was in disorder since one of my friends who had gone
to a play with me had stayed overnight. Then, after I went back to
inform Georges, I introduced him to good Monsieur de Vacquerie. He
did not fail to conduct the conversation on a plane of felicitous
prudence, and he dwelt at length on the point that you could be
discontented and be frank among friends without being conspirators
for all that. The Marquis' arrest gave him ample opportunity and he
did not spare lessons of wisdom for young men like us. Georges, who
stayed in bed, kept quiet, and I saw him sometimes smile in pity,
sometimes quiver with contempt, and finally with rage. I began to fear
an outburst. To ward it off, I tried to keep Monsieur de Vacquerie
talking about his daughter, his forthcoming purchases, Delille's last
poem, and Landon's latest prints and engravings. Thus I saved him
from the lion's claw, which the dear man never knew he was so close
to. But he had scarcely gotten out the door when Georges lost his
temper; his indignation against the petty nobility whom he had
counted too much on knew no bounds. The ferocious plebeian who
was not always pleased with his noble lieutenants was fully bared to
me. He was terrifying. Despite himself, he had some of the rebellious
peasant in his rage. Georges, I have often thought since, was the cause
you served with such implacable ardor really yours? Didn't your

courageous instincts make you blunder badly? As a carpenter's son, weren't you thrown from the first into the ranks of the bluebloods? You would have replaced Kléber. You would certainly disputed with Ney, that other hero of the same stamp and blood, the privilege of the brave.

Georges was up, ready to leave. There was something austere in the leavetaking. He made me repeat my promise and my oath; "Within eight days," he added imperiously, "you will hear from me. May God watch over you!" In case I was out, a simple card with a place and hour of rendezvous slipped beneath my door, would alert me. On that he left. I stayed on the threshold, watching him until he disappeared. From that moment on I did not really belong to myself. I was completely at the orders of General Georges.

CHAPTER XIV

The adventure, seen from this short distance and from this degree of detail, henceforth showed me its dark side. I continually felt anxious and oppressed. I was enveloped in a sinister project. The morally suspect side of any political enterprise or plot was not obscured by any blinding conviction on my part, so I saw its every detail clearly. I saw for myself the pleasure of staking my life to an assassination plan, compromising the Marquis' future, which was not, perhaps, what I casually imagined, and poisoning with certain pain the gentle heart who loved me, violating all gratitude toward Monsieurs Desmaret and R———, and as a reward for their kind treatment, making them responsible for my ingratitude. I had neither hatred nor fanaticism as an excuse. The need for change and extraordinary emotion which impelled me was not, to put it bluntly, anything more than the most demanding delirium of egoism. That is what I could not hide from myself. On the eve of a conspiracy, as for a duel, you can try in vain to keep it quiet, but at the bottom of your heart you feel that you are not on the true and just path, and yet human honor binds us and we continue. So as I muttered these things, I did not repent.

Two days after that memorable night, Madame R——— sent us a box at the Theatre Feydeau and Madame de Couaën asked Monsieur de Vacquerie to let his daughter go with us. He himself, a country dilettante, despite loving arriettas, did not like to go to the theater on principle. I accompanied these three ladies by myself. And in the narrow box, during the melodious hours, how many veiled palpitations, diverse nuances, sympathetic or rival were to appear and grow in our hearts! I am not counting Mademoiselle de Vacquerie, who rested her elbows on the railing and was all ears and eyes, as would be expected in a girl for whom the performance was so novel. Next to her, Madame de Couaën, nonchalantly leaning also and half-turned

toward Madame R——— and me in the second row. Madame R———
——— intercepted our glances indifferently and I myself, although not
equally, divided my attention between the two and received their souls
in turn. This for us was the real stage that evening. The music, the
songs, the action on stage, the packed, agitated theater, the dazzle and
the murmur were there only as an echo to our words, favoring our
silence and framing our reverie. Madame de Couaën was the only one
without an ulterior motive. She was happy and trusting, surrounded
by her favorite friends, enjoying all the desirable flowers along the
paths of duty. I read that in her oblivious expression, in her fleeting
smile that replied to questions and glances, in the flat monosyllables
that she let fall if I inquired about her pallor. When I had shown
enough solicitude, I turned as if with her consent to Madame R———
to keep her from being too jealous; one moment I had caught a very
sad look on her gentle face and saw a tear only partly hidden, which
seemed to say, "Oh why am I not loved like that." At that moment
my secret desire joined hers. And I especially remembered it later in
my nocturnal reflections. The attention I had given Madame R———
seemed less guilty now, considering that my life was precarious and
subject to imminent accidents. Before I died, I had to hear "Je t'aime"
from someone's lips. This was the sole expression, I told myself, that
shows you have lived. Now, in looking exclusively for the relative
opportunities I could expect from this brief exchange, I found no cause
for hesitating between Madame de Couaën and Madame R———. It
was on such calculations of superficial vanity and satisfaction that I
spent those troubled nights which might have been my last. A turbulent catastrophe was only good for inspiring a preparation worthy
of it.

During the evening of the play, Madame R——— had spoken to
me about a ball that was to take place two days later at one of her
friends', and she offered to present me there. I had hardly given any
response at the time, but in my new frame of mind, I sent her note
that I accepted and would escort her. Nor did I fail to do so. She was
beautiful that evening in her adornment, her complexion enhanced
and clear, her mood animated, her presence surrounding me in a
completely new light. Her melancholy languor had given way beneath
the candle glow to gala sparkle. I myself, in my heady state, piqued
her laughter and gaiety even though they went against my ulterior
motive and made her constantly escape my spell. In the midst of a
contradance where I was her partner I tried to insert a few mysterious,
dark words on my threatening destiny. They had no effect. She was
more open to my other remarks but responded in a tone that was half

tender and half mocking, which showed she did not take them seriously, either because she did not really believe they were serious or because she enjoyed letting me carry on that way. When my remarks became too clear and pressing, she adroitly maneuvered in a third party or got us separated by the crowd. At the end, when I was seated near her so that she could not avoid me, she first treated it as a game and then took it upon herself to strike my arm and the arm of the chair with rapid taps of her fan, as if to put a stop to my words. And soon she rose, gliding amidst scattered groups, graceful, adroit, triumphant. I was watching the metamorphosis of a fairy. I was fascinated and frustrated. My borrowed gaiety vanished immediately. Shortly thereafter I led her back the short distance to her home, in almost complete silence. I went back to my own lodging in great internal turmoil. At the same time, whenever I returned home now, I couldn't open my door without a certain emotion in case the decisive card had been slipped underneath in my absence.

My friend, I did not intend to speak to you about myself except where our sickness is the same. I wanted especially to use my example as a lesson, and basically intended to spare you and forbid myself embellishments of too worldly a nature. But as I proceeded, my plans wavered, and I put myself to marking once again all my days and hours on the sundial of yesteryear. My memory opened up, and the floods of the past dragged me along. Is it really appropriate for you to read all this? Is it appropriate for me to persist in retracing it all? The lure which leads me to tell everything; isn't it a treacherous lure? Won't it be a futile or even nefarious legacy, addressed to a friend, with rare bits of advice lost in frivolous envelopes emitting enervating perfumes? Conscience, to which I hearken, voice of the praying heart, I hardly dare ask you to give me counsel.

The morning after the ball, around eight o'clock when I was still in bed, entirely absorbed in figuring out the turbulence caused by the night and Madame R——'s behavior, a note from her husband, delivered by an orderly as fast as he could gallop, summoned me to go see him at the ministry immediately. (He had not made an appearance the evening before.) The coincidence was abrupt and surprising, but upon reflection, I could not suspect that it had to do with anything but our political situation. And, indeed, this is what I learned from his own mouth when I got there. Suspicions, vague but emanating on all sides, had increased the last few days. Without knowing anything precise, there were still hundreds of signs that some kind of machination was brewing. That very night, after a sharp debate with his counselors, the Premier Consul wanted to put an end to these worrisome doubts by issuring the sentences of four or five Royalists already detained on earlier charges. By incredible good fortune, Monsieur de Couaën was not among them. But if his name had come from the Consul's lips, the die would have been cast without any possible recall, without any means of stopping legal consequences. It behooved his friends then to put him in a sheltered place as soon as possible until the storm blew over, and there was no other effective measure at present besides transport to Blois, where he would live under surveillance by the high Police. Monsieur R——— offered me his minister's signature, having spoken to him about it. The order seemed like a rigorous measure, but, according to him, it was simple precaution and prudence. I shared his opinion and with many more reasons. I did not hesitate in urging him to render to the Marquis and to all of us this incalculable service. It was agreed that he would try to have a transport order for five days hence signed that very evening. As for myself, I rushed to alert the Marquis and prepare Madame de Couaën.

The Marquis received the news without surprise. When I noted the importance of not being actually implicated in a legal action, he burst out bitterly, "All right, all right. Why shouldn't destiny treat me this way? I'm nothing in nothing. I won't leave my name anywhere, not even on a court record. It is a parody; you know of the Romans' Capitol and the Tarpian Rock. You fall undetected from a dovecote to a dung heap." I brought him back to preparations and arrangements for departure. I explained to him, somewhat nervously, that it would be difficult for me to accompany him. Without guessing all my reasons, he anticipated some of them, such as how useful I could be to him by staying behind and being present, even if it were only to maintain contact with our brave friends. "After a few weeks that will seem very long to us," he added with a downcast smile, "you will come, I count on it, to rejoin the exiles." Madame de Couaën was more difficult to convince: "It is our salvation," she cried, "our deliverance, let's leave as soon as possible. Our dream has come true." She could in no way understand my somewhat gloomy expression. My reasons for delay touched her only slightly, and in the end I had to exaggerate the Marquis' danger to make her consent to my staying behind. My promises, my oaths to join them had to come in every sentence. When the news of the sudden departure made its way around the little convent, there was general dismay. The good nuns surrounded Madame de Couaën, and Madame de Cursy tenderly held on to the children and kissed them. It was decided to have a mass said each morning of the three final days for the Marquis' safety and the favorable outcome of his affairs.

The afternoon was wearing on. I became extremely impatient to find Georges to tell him what I knew and receive some kind of decision. I did not know exactly where he was hiding, so I passed through the places where I had run into him before. For two long hours I crisscrossed the terrain in my attempts. My brain was agitated by this futile waiting. I would think I saw certain prowlers passing back and forth like me, undoubtedly with less benevolent intentions. I came back worn out at nightfall, and when I found neither card nor note beneath my door, I went off in a cabriolet to see Madame R——— to distracat my feverish mind. She was alone, wearing a coat over her white dress, rather altered from the night before and quite different, as unresponsive now as she had been lively before. I felt unsure of myself and stayed only a few moments, rushing off post-haste to our distant boulevards. Gross delectations still had a place in that time of quite opposite concerns.

When I reached the Marquis' room, he was writing, his back to Madame de Couaën, who was sitting on a kind of sofa next to the fireplace. I threw myself down at her side, and full of cold, aimless frenzy began to speak to her like a desperate man prey to violent depression: "A moment ago as I went down those deserted sanded paths I thought it would be, God knows, convenient to kill oneself there a little later when I returned. It would look as if one had been assassinated. Human honor would be preserved; at the same time one would be over and done with a loveless life." Why was I saying all this? What did I expect? How did they come so baldly from my lips, since I hadn't thought them over in advance? What devil was moving my tongue? There are days when you really have to believe you are possessed. The Marquis did not respond, and did not even pay attention because he was occupied with something else. But her cheeks became crimson, tears filled her eyes, and she couldn't keep from seizing my hand, which she twisted in her fingers. I do not remember what words I stammered to counteract the others. But she came nearer, leaning in an increasingly suppliant position. I brushed her waist with my other hand and nearly pulled her against my chest. A moment later she got herself under control and tension fell. The Marquis had finished writing. It was hardly late, but she rose to leave, vaguely hinting at some indisposition. Her unstrung countenance certainly supported this. We were scarcely on our way and alone when she asked, "Do you have some grudge against me today? What is this about?" And when I assured her that she had hurt my feelings in no way, she responded, "Then you were acting like an utter ingrate." Don't ever talk to me that way again. It will make me go mad from friendship." I was frightened myself from the brutal effect I had produced with my gratuitous outburst. At the door of the little convent where I left her, like a sign of complete forgetfulness, she made me promise to come get her early the next day for errands and purchases and visits, so that we could freely talk at length over the future.

But instead of remaining filled with so many marks of affection and stopping at that last impression, behind which lay the perilous slope of tenderness, here is what my malign disposition brooded over, like some kind of strange animal that on certain accursed days stirs and gnaws us. The image of the other woman, alternately fleeting or languishing, appeared in all its charm. The pride of moving thus two women at the same time, of making two women's happiness depend upon my whim alone, the growing desire, the thirst before dying of hearing "Je vous aime," uttered by one or the other as soon as possible—those were the wretched struggles I carried into my night. The absurd result of this new discord was writing Madame R——— a long letter, dated midnight, which was not to be given to her until the very day the enterprise would be carried out, because in my beclouded thinking I was still counting on it. I told her that a great duel, which she would certainly hear discussed, would claim my arm and that I was sure to perish. But I wanted beforehand to declare myself and reveal the hidden portrait hidden in my heart. Then followed myriad confidences, memories dredged up and interpreted. And the imaginatnion in this activity is so flexible, the heart so bizarre and deceitful that as I gushed out like young Werther I convinced myself. Once this letter was written, sealed, addressed, I put it in my billfold, certain that its delivery, would strike one more blow in someone's breast. Having thus exhausted all the incoherent excesses of my situation, harassed and worn out by these ideas, I was still long in getting to sleep. Oh, how hollow and empty these turbulences in life, these swollen and bruising torrents. They do not leave either a thirst-quenching drop or fresh blade of grass behind them! And how much better, my friend, a gentle and just thought, a chaste memory expanded in absence, a healthy maxim flowering within on our solitary slopes fill a day than these devouring conflicts!

After I got up, and while I was getting ready to see whether Monsieur R——— had more information, his orderly brought me a note from him. The transport order for Blois had been signed. I didn't see him at his ministry, so I went from there to Monsieur Desmaret. It was arranged with the latter that the departure would take place two days later, around six in the evening, from the courtyard of the

Conciergerie. A regular chaise would be used, with a lieutenant from the gendarmerie holding a seat until Blois was reached. With these details taken care of, I was back at the convent before noon for my appointment with Madame de Couaën. Because the children begged to the point of tears, we took them with us. The sky was beautiful, and the frost sparkled in the sun. We went down to the entrance of the Tuileries and walked slowly along the bustling terraces. In discussing this painful departure, I could not or would not dissimulate as I had the night before, and it was easy for Madame de Couaën to infer that I was not at all sure I would be part of their future there. She justifiably took offense at such vacillation, and she persisted in questioning me about my motives, having no fear of showing me her incurable need to be loved, to be loved exclusively, as she had been by her mother. And I replied, more openly than ever before, "And you, would you love exclusively?"

And since her eternal circle was, "But you have certainly come with us up to now; why would you not continue? why, unless you no longer love us as much?"

Pushed then into my last refuge, I said to her in words to this effect: "Why? why? If you absolutely must know, Madame, I will agree to explain it to you, even if it means displeasing you. Only bear in mind that you wanted it that way. You see in my uncertainty of joining you only a proof that I love you less. Could you not just as well read in that a fear of loving you too much? Kindly imagine a moment when someone would come to fear loving too much a creature of purity and duty, beyond all reach, and who would absolutely never think that she could be loved in that way. After you have done that, then see if such wounding contradictions of conduct and will are not explainable. Although an upstart with very little firsthand experience, I have reflected in advance on the course of passion, which I know as well as if I had verified it 100 times. I found recently in a consummate moralist a tableau that will paint you a convincing sequence of feelings that I fear in myself. When a man of upright heart first discovers that he loves a chaste creature, forbidden and beyond hope, he feels a great disturbance mixed with a mysterious happiness, and he certainly forms at the time no other desire but to continue loving in secret, to serve on his knees in the shadows, and to spread through sheer zeal a thousand mute signs of affection. But this first blush, if he fails to pay attention, is soon deflowered and withered. Another mood takes over. This is when disinterest ceases. He is no longer content to love, serve, and dedicate himself without wishing for anything more. He wishes to be seen and noticed. He wants the beloved eyes to guess and decode the hidden motive without anger. If those indulgent eyes are not angry, this in itself we see as smiling encouragement and gratitude. We realize that probably not everything has been guessed and want to test the limits of tolerance and show the feelings stripped bare. Until we have uttered, without circumlocution, "Je vous aime," we are not at rest. But in the first moment of utterance, we demand, at least we think we desire, nothing but a hearing. Patience! the word escaped trembling; it was heard without too much anger; it is pardoned and permitted. The lover begins to dig another hollow in his heart. The vow, now repeated every hour, is it really heard in all its force? Is it simply tolerated, or is it supported *sotto voce?* How can that be known if it receives no vow in return? And this is when we solicit the other's vow! Oh let it descend, if only to animate and embellish. The other vow hesitates. We lure it, snatch on the wing. It comes more timid and tremulous than our first vow. We tame it and soon domesticate it to sing and sigh. But by then, it is already no more than an expression and we get tired of that. What proves that the vow is true, no matter how sweet it is? That is what we keep saying to ourselves, murmuring as nature presses us, wanting in everything to touch and see. There must be proofs. But the proofs themselves have their frivolous and reputedly meaningless side. Because they never go beyond certain limits, they perhaps are only an accommodation and a sop to compassion. To be convinced at that point we claim serious proofs. Once that stage is reached, you must expect confusion and delirium."

"But this has nothing to do with the matter," she cried, almost withdrawing her arm in a movement of fright. "No, your suppositions are systems. You torment your life and ours with the philosophers you read. Is it not true that at this moment you have no such desire and are happy like this?"

I assured her that indeed I was happy and at present had no such desire. I was, however, going to continue my perceptive distinctions when in pressing against my chest the arm she was trying to pull away, I felt the billfold where precisely I had placed my letter to Madame R——— the night before. Shame and disgust with this entire factitious, half-false discourse rose up in me like a wave of nausea. We were reaching an exit of the garden near the quarter where Madame de Couaën had business, and I directed our steps towards it. But she herself said that there was nothing pressing in her errands and that she preferred, if I were agreeable, to walk a bit more. I made a promise to myself that very instant not to do anything with that perjuring letter, and, somewhat raised in my own eyes by my silent decision, I happily let myself go in the prolonged action of the gentle penetrating sunshine and those closer rays reaching me with fresh breath. I gradually retracted my preceding words, as she wished. I granted her that these were fantastic suppositions, veritable games like those of the skaters on the lagoon who liked to show how skilled they were by alarming movements. The children who walked ahead of us hand in hand were paying close attention to the scene we were approaching, and they kept turning around with peals of laughter to get us to admire it too. Then Madame de Couaën, finding me docile, her voice calm again, repeated in happy triumph, "Well, what was the point of all those scaffoldings you erected? You can see now it was all for nothing. You love us the way you always have, or, if for a moment you loved me in the wrong way, you are already over it. Besides, if there had been any danger, I would cure you. Monsieur de Couaën has complete confidence in you, and my own is immense." She did very few of her errands planned for that day. When we went by Madame de R———'s, she was, fortunately, not there, and I wrote down Madame de Couaën's name without adding my own. We wanted to put off visiting Mlle de Vacquerie and the others until the next day in order to be able to take the same walk again.

I was hardly back in my room before I burnt the letter to Madame R———. Seeing it burn made me feel unburdened and absolved. The ease with which I lost track of the object itself for sometime showed me better the folly of my exaltation and how much false ardor we create in our brain through deliberate caprice when goaded.

Our walk the next day was very similar to the better half of the first and passed, as wished, over the same tracks: white sunshine, brisk temperature, fresh frost, a return to the propositions of the day before along the sanded paths we already knew. There was still in the beginning some discussion on the way in which I, too, needed to be loved. She granted that she loved me on a par with and as the eldest of her children. That was the glorious part which kept me from complaining while in no way appeasing my desire. Every time I spoke about my difficulty in maintaining the permissible nuance and without repeating my argument of the day before made some allusion to it, she cut me short with more insistence and replied in a rather mysterious and confusing manner, "Oh, as far as that goes, I have indeed reflected on your words yesterday. I've thought of a way to prevent anything bad, and I think I really know a possible way out of it." And when I asked what marvelous means she had found, she evaded answering. In the end this reticence piqued my curiosity. But it was only during the last rounds of the walk that, pressed with questions and a secret wish to tell,she decided to do so, not, however, without much charming embarrassment and with many a request not to make fun of her. "I don't know anything about these subjects," she stammered, "but since these desires, which are increasing, so you say, on the contrary, decrease and pass (this is what you said yourself) once they are satisfied, why not suppose in advance that they have already been satisfied, a long time ago. Then you can assume immediately the simple, sweet feeling that would survive?" Before finishing this speech, she had turned every color of the rainbow.

"Is this your great method," I asked. "Do you think one can suppose these things at will, child that you are?" But it seemed to her that such a supposition could always be made.

"Well, do not be alarmed," I interrupted. "I know a more effective method than yours. I have noted that desire, in what it contains of the permanent, habitual, and incorrigible, is always to some extent a dependent on hope. It is always hope where desire finds its dark and secret nourishment. Without that it would perish by inanition and from a feeling of its futility. Desire is scarcely more than bold, blind hope, disguised and plummeted forward by chance like a sentinal lost near the enemy camp. But he senses behind him, supporting him, a group of other hopes. Now where you are concerned, Madame, I would persuade myself of the nothingness of all hope, and thus I would discourage my desire."

"Well, that sounds like the solution," she said. "I was sure there really was a means available, and you have found it. Besides, it will only be necessary to be on guard a few more years. Age will come soon enough and take care of everything."

It was through such ingenuous and subtle exchanges that in those last moments of mutual illusion, our hearts dilated and blossomed.

At Monsieur de Vacquerie's, where we stopped midway our walk, something relatively trivial had been said about Madame de Geneuc and Mlle Amélie. This made a painful impression on me, as did anything that related to that time and that history. My notion of my old wrongs confirmed my resolution to at least make no more new ones. I seriously kept coming back to a life of sacrifice. Mlle Amélie's image naturally inspired that. I said to myself that if the Georges affair left me free, as became more probable every moment, I would go to live at Blois, devoting my entire future to adorning the life of my friends. Any hold Madame R——— had over me had disappeared. To strengthen me better in my resolve and to remove even the pretext for honorable scruples, I decided to write the Marquis when I returned to my room. In this letter, after much effusion and concern for his injuries, I touched on the state of my poor heart and certain vague anxieties I had and the inevitable hasty passions of youth. Then I asked him whether he saw any disadvantage to anyone in this increasingly intimate relationship he proposed to me. I would never have undertaken discussing this subject with him face to face. Besides, I would have been in no way sure I could do it with the requisite delicacy. For that reason, I preferred to write. And was there not also in that singular project an unavowed ulterior motive to be freer from now on as the occasion dictated and more nonchalant regarding him, since I had in some respects warned him? I really think that no such mean finesse was mixed in; however, nature is so torturous and so filled with hidden folds that I would not dare affirm anything. That very evening as I took leave of him, I gave him the letter somewhat shamefacedly. I asked him to read it and give me a response the next day.

The next day was the day for departure. At 8:30 in the convent chapel, along with Madame de Couaën, the children, and the entire community, I took part in a mass dedicated to entreating a safe trip and untroubled stay in Blois. Instead of my missel, like a simple believer, I had brought a volume of the *Imitation* to read. I expected to meditate, rather than pray. But this excellent treatise, in combination with the solemn impression of the narrow enclosure, the recitation murmured by the priest, followed by hymns loudly sung from time to time worked on me covertly, inspiring keen remorse. I read in that precious book all kinds of direct answers to the mute questions agitating me. For example, "Do not be familiar with any woman but with the others recommend all honest women to God." And if I countered that this maxim applied especially to nuns, I found soon this other one that I could not gainsay: "Oppose evil at the outset because there is a progression from a simple thought crossing the mind, then a strong image that takes root, the pleasure one graduation takes from it, and the movement to a bad end and abandonment." And further on, regarding the vain delights that one pursues in disorder and gathers with bitterness, I read again and repeated with fervent adhesion (I would have beat my chest, if I had dared): "Oh such delights are short and false, all unbridled and shameful! And at the moment when, racked with this wretchedness and seized with a new burst of energy, I cried within, 'Why can't I persevere in this train of thought?' " As I picked up the book and opened it at random, one of the morning rays beamed through a blue corner of a stained-glass window and fell expressly to illuminate in my eyes this balm-giving verse: "Someone whose life is passed in anxiety and who frequently vacillates between fear and hope, on a certain day, beneath

the weight of sorrow having gone to a church, knelt in prayer before an altar and murmured to himself, 'Oh, if I knew that I should persevere from henceforth!' and forthwith heard within the divine oracle replying 'If you knew that, what would you like to do? Just do now what you would have liked to do then, and you will find peace'."
It seemed to me that I was precisely that *someone* to whom the infallible rule was addressed. I felt the influence of that beneficent advice throughout that day and several following. You will see whether it lasted.

When I went to see the Marquis in the morning, he received me with genuine marks of affection of such an immediacy and delicacy that they alleviated my embarrassment. "My dear Amaury," he said, "I want to thank you for your inexhaustible consolation and heartfelt confidence. I, too, had thought about some of the disadvantages you indicated, and I have not been convinced of them. Above all, in the end it is you yourself you must consult. But I entreat you do not put yourself to tormenting with your anxious thoughts a simple situation guaranteed by every good and loyal sentiment. Sometimes we create disadvantages merely by thinking them up and dreading them, the way you puncture a beautiful piece of fruit to verify its condition. That is a fault you should guard yourself against, my precocious friend. Don't imitate people who consume themselves! If you should want to know, after all that, my opinion and hope, I shall say that yesterday I was counting on your customary presence at Blois soon, and today I am counting on it no less."

I was too ill at ease on this subject, too moved by this tenderness from a strong man to reply at any length. Besides I would have been afraid, if I raised my eyes, to surprise a blush on his severe, chaste cheek. I shook his hand at once, mumbling that I was at his disposition, and we changed the subject.

Since the departure was not to take place until nightfall, we all dined together at the little convent. The Marquis had obtained permission to be there, and the farewell banquet was celebrated with all present. We sat down around three o'clock. It was slow, circumspect, silent. At first we chatted only about details of the trip, but a deep feeling settled in, uniting all thoughts. We were twelve, I think, and no one was untouched. Madame R——— herself, arriving before the end, was seated to one side. Although during the last hour, there were several conversations going, Madame de Cursy and her nephew spoke of days and persons gone by. From where I was sitting at the end of the table, I could study and interpret all these faces in the fading daylight. What choice creatures were gathered in that dark little refectory! I thought to myself, what virtues! what suffering! Wasn't human life itself entirely represented there? On Madame de Cursy's face furrowed with wrinkles, with no trace of color, as if dead, appeared celestial calm, deserved here below, the acquired possession of the imperishable port in the heart of a storm. Next to her and her nuns, the ideal face of her niece still depicted pure love for me, love, however, not yet doing without human simulacrum and support, but by means of this support from the heart it claims, making itself also in this life a port, a cloister, a holy security, a profound ignorance. Then two handsome children who enjoyed the gaiety of their age and the mobility of innocence; in them, in them alone among us, the grace and tremulous promise of the future! Beneath and by natural contrast, the thunderstruck brow of the father, like a proscribed, shipwrecked king, who sits at the table of a loyal abbey and whose mourning betrays his bare, despoiled state. And Madame R——— also on a chair on the side, a melancholy representative from the outside world, for frail, lukewarm, abused, insufficient affection. Oh, what choice creatures of sorrow! I repeated. A meeting on the outskirts of life. How many bleeding passions, how many naked souls! As for me who sat there to interpret the tableau as I passed from one character to the next, who was I and what did I want? Oh, it was not the world and society which attracted me towards their objects. Between the interesting sadness of Madama R——— and the serene austerity of Madame de Cursy I would not have hesitated one minute! I would have said, "God and solitude rather than the world!" But what most attracted me and my vow was the prospect of lightening the anguish of the shipwrecked king's heart, of aiding that other tender heart who needed a human mirror to serve her in purely disinterested thought and reflect the depth of heaven.

Please share my feelings of those days, my friend, share the enhanced impression I find again now. You who have followed me so far up the Hill, do not be too weary to take a seat. It takes little to make this banquet, which I attended almost in silence, represent the whole of my first life and be in its most worthy parts an expressive figure. Day falls, the lamps have not yet been brought in, the whitening light plays over all these brows. Count this small number of persons one by one. They are the ones who have influenced me most. Pull Madame R———'s chair a little farther away; imagine another at the same distance where Mademoiselle Amélie's white gown can be glimpsed. Let Madame de Couaën glow resplendent in the shadows! Let a few vague shapes, a few familiar sighs attest to the hovering presence of my dear parents, lost so soon! Those five or six nuns whose faces blurred for me are like a veiled choir of good souls one meets upon his way. Don't we see there, my friend, a depiction of my entire life? Don't you have also in your memory some darkly solemn banquet, some indelible frame where the principal characters of your youth are gathered? Who hasn't had the Passover pilgrimage? Who has not had, some evening, a reflection of the supper at Emmaus?

The talk continued, and perhaps my dream as well, when the police officer charged with accompanying Monsieur de Couaën to the Conciergerie was announced. We immediately rose, and after that ensued only the confusion of preparations and adieux. The Marquis and his escort soon climbed into one carriage; Madame de Couaën, the children, Madame R———, and I followed in another. It was a heavy night. The lanterns lighting our wait were gloomy. When the gendarmerie lieutenant assigned to the trip finally appeared, there was nothing left but to kiss and send short hopeful messages: "We shall see you in three weeks," I cried, waving for the last time. And I moved away slowly, giving my arm to Madame R———, whom I escorted back to her door. We were both filled with the leave-taking and had no words to discuss anything else.

My youth had not quite ended. In fact, in the eyes of society, it seemed only to be beginning. One would have thought it full of promise, brow turned toward future joys. And yet, my friend, the finest part of its course was all over. The most to be regretted had gone. Let us pause for a moment to mourn my youth as if it had died because it had received its mortal wound. Today I can repeat with the great penitent Saint Augustine: at that moment my childhood died while I remained alive. The ages we live are like tender friends whom we hardly distinguished. We love them. We inhabit them. They are one with us. Their familiar arm is around our shoulder. They are our Euryalis, and we are their Nisus. But once fully on our way, these charming ages are so many tired friends who stay behind little by little, and whom we ourselves leave behind as too slow or from whom we are separated by some irresistible torrent along the way. These first cherished friends expire, falling along the wayside, younger and more innocent, and we pursue our journey with new friends in a career less and less happy and simple. My childhood knew me pure. What would it say if it saw me so full of intrigue, so capable of trickery, and from time to time so sullied? What would Euryalis say if he saw his Nisus, who had forgotten him, perjuring virtue, wearing out his strength like a coward on the body of some female slave? We should repeat often: oh, how our former ages, like friends dead young, would blush to see us so fallen if they came back to earth!

So my childhood was dead, dying rather late, and if I wanted to show you its last day, it would probably be at La Gastine, the day I first felt uneasy seeking that sweet face. That threshold, so often trampled since, is like a tombstone over the last day of my childhood. What remained of my childhood in my beginning adolescence expired there, and I became a more emphatic adolescent, a young man. Now if I next look for the day the last glow of my adolescence faded in the dawn of my youth, I believe it was on the pale heath, returning from La Gastine, the evening my inconstant heart found the consequences of that virginal vow repugnant. It was there that my good, loving, pastoral adolescence, which dreamed only of eternal fidelity in a thatched cottage, left me, for I was already much too ambitious and subtle. My adolescence left me beneath the moon, across the broom, like an injured sister who walks away weeping silently, and there was perhaps in my delightful melancholy a feeling of farewell toward that indecisive age which was escaping. From that hour began my full youth, and I had only that for my assiduous companion. But if that age has two successive genies, each blunted too quickly, it seems to me that the first, more shining and fresh (although soiled itself) is already afflicted by a nefarious blow, a schism which will make the first genie languish and will let the second, less charming companion take its place. Woods of Couaën, slope of the Mountain, and, you as well, sanded path of Auteuil, Tuileries terraces, frugal convent table, recent objects of so much love and affection, will I ever feel you with the same soul as in those intense days? If I were to see you again as early as tomorrow, would it ever be in your colors of yesterday?

Thus we fulfill one phase after another, thus our inner ages unroll silently and separately. Basically we are like a place filled with successive inhumations, like a funeral banquet hall where rest all the phantoms of the ages we have lived. And they disturb one another, troubling us, groaning or sleeping fitfully. Happy are we if, as a result of our efforts of expiation, they become pure spirits, reconciled as they keep watch within and sing in concert imploring a common deliverance!

If the successive ages we pass through are like friends—the first falling by the way, the more aggressive replacing and supplanting the more tender—it follows that the later ages are only like friends we meet late in life and with whom we never weave so close and tender a bond. The fresh bark of the heart is closed over and hardened. They did not know us when we were getting started, they never enter our innermost recesses, and we return their indifference in the midst of the very active interchange where we seem to be together. So these middle ages leave us few intimately engraved features. To correct this indifference and this natural chill of the last ages, we would have to have each age in dying bequeath its memories to the next, torch-lit, as it is said of generations in the beautiful poem by Lucretius. We would have to have each defunct age either enshrouded and honored piously by its successor or redeemed and expiated by him. In this way our successive ages would not be strangers either to one another or to us. They would keep up and perpetuate the spirit of the same life. We would reach old age facing a friendly age, which has received from its predecessors the tradition of our childhood and whatever else will keep us in men's memory. Then we will live with this old age, ordinarily discouraging, as with an old saint who would present us our cradle every day.

As I was telling you, it seemed to me that the genie of the tender years had just received a blow. But at least its pain responded by grave and pious promises. Would either this genie or I know how to keep them? If this genie's union with me had up until then too often been spoiled of weak character, shameful desires, sensual surrender, egoistic ruse, and overrefinement, this last day had been repentant and concerned with good behavior. Is that enough for a vow made in the morning to deserve facile fulfillment? Oh, there were too many bad seeds germinating in me, too much corruption had contaminated my heart. Acquired tastes wanted to follow their course. If I had remained chaste, my friend, if I had remained chaste in fact, and also in thought, as much as that is possible in keeping oneself under observation, it is to be believed that in that delicate and ambiguous position which no doubt would have been my only escape, I would, nevertheless, have had the strength to nurture my beneficent nascent inspiration and bring it to term. What would such an inspiration have been? What would it have advised me in so complicated a conjunction with virtue itself? Would it have been, in fact, to go to Blois, to subject myself as soon as possible to a residence full of discomfort, attraction, and vigilance? Would it not rather have been a regular and curative return to Mademoiselle de Liniers? Would it have been already the abjuration of the world with sacred study and the high avenue of the priesthood? If in such moments I had been sufficient master of myself, my will, and my acts to bear them in humility to the feet of God and wait without infringing upon anything, what would have emerged as a complement of His Grace? I do not know. But one thing is certain: the new diversion you will soon see me thrown into will be the contrary to what would have been a good course of action. It was vain for me to be humble and open-eyed about my love and seek a forthright outcome. In the most wretched vice to which my eyes refused to close, I lost in a single moment the entire effort of a day of sincere self-examination, and would have ruined a superior equilibrium if it had been on the point of being established. Despite all the caprices of conscience, all the transports and sighs of a higher origin, nothing sustained, disinterested, and pure was practicable with that shock of the abyss, with that frequent and concealed crumbling. How can it help to keep watch from the front of all the towers, interrogating the stars, if the traitor and coward open the subterranean gate at any moment to the penetrating waters?

You will not be contemptuous, my friend, of these explanations pulled from my very depths, nor of the private motives I have shown you. The more closely I clutch my evil and show you its source, the more chance there is for you to say, "It's that way with me." And you will take heart, remembering that I made my way back. It is not petty morality really (no morality is ever petty) that makes me give you this confession where my soul expresses your soul. It is the sole, universal morality. After all, great events in the outer world that refer to so-called general interest are translated in every man and enter him, so to speak, by twists and turns that always have something peculiar to him. Those who seem to disdain these details the most and who speak magnificently in the name of all humanity, consult as much as anyone passions which concern them alone and private acts they do not confess. It is always more or less a case of the ambition to be at the forefront and lead, the desire for acclaim or power, the satisfaction of crushing adversaries, belying the envious, to play to the end an applauded role. If we weighed only the love of the good, what would most often remain? And as for the results from such diverse motivations, I find that vague social influences, courted and exercised by chance, must lend too much to temerious applications and dubious consequences. That great adventurous morality which is not stopped from the first by some ill causes here and there, does it necessarily end with some good? But without presuming to deny what is also brought into this way partly by generous conviction, without contesting the free speech and honest audacity of someone who believes he has the truth, how much, in my opinion, the gradual perfecting, inner healing—and what stems from it—prudent, continuous, and effective action around oneself, good examples who breathe and bear fruit, leading more surely to the aim, even to the social aim so often proposed! When we throw ourselves into social action before having been healed and pacified inside, we run the risk of irritating many an equivocal motive. Jesus purged the temple before preaching to the crowd. Let us turn now, my friend, in all earnestness, to cleansing and illuminating within. True human charity leaves from there or leads there. Purity for oneself, charity for all, that is individual and social morality, the generating of virtues withhin. If purity begins and does not bring charity to life, it will not remain pure very long; it becomes dull and dark. If charity begins and does not procure purity, it means it is only the flame of a moment with little warmth. I would not know how to explain to you how much this instant link between the two seems necessary to me. Isolated early and thrown to one side, prey to a long internal struggle, I could have listened to myself at close range, and I felt always the sources of good, even general good, the roots of the universal tree stir and move even in my most secret recesses. When we try to heal ourselves within, we are already thinking of others; we are already doing good things for them, even if it is no more than giving more power to the heartfelt prayers we address on their behalf. The complete moral code of Christianity has confirmed me in this belief.

End of Part I

CHAPTER XV

Yet before I continue, my friend, I need to set down briefly my present situation for writing. I had hardly embarked—as rapidly as possible—on my way to the new world where God has called me. The cliffs of Brittany had disappeared behind us two days earlier. Ireland, where that other part of my heart lies, had been sighted on the right. The high seas were in front of us. The weather, which had been rather bad up till then, became more threatening and whipped us towards the Scilly Islands. Soon we were in a furious storm which lasted three days. Our brig, in distress, finally reached this Portuguese coast. It was veritably a shipwreck. Now, since the tempest kept the idea of death before me every moment, I found all the images of my earlier life coming back to life, not only the idealized and weeping forms which can be separated out and erected like holy statues along the Bridge of Sighs, but the tempest had stirred also the bed of the old river and the oldest silt deposited there. All the dust, all the ashes trembled in my tomb like the approach of judgment which, even for the most confident and tender, appears very severe at close range. When I was thrown there upon the bank, nearly drowned, my mouth still full of bitter ancient gravel, and my thirst more quenched by repentance than by waves, I had scarcely dried my vestments in the old monastery shelter than I thought of you. I thought of you, my young friend, jaded in your pleasures, of the comparable bitterness, more poisoned perhaps, which was reserved for you. I had already imagined your peril, and I promised I would write you, if I came out alive, some letter of ultimate advice. Here time was long. Given my unfamiliarity with the language, my conversation with these good fathers was short. I decided then to narrate at a leisurely pace a history of my youth in the form of memoirs. We had at least a six-week delay, and that added to the crossing provided a sufficient interval of time.

Besides, it seemed to me that in this unexpected respite I had received
in this corner of the old world, I was permitted, almost enjoined, to
apply myself to memory by extracting its moral for you. I have read
that the celebrated Monsieur Le Maître at Port-Royal, rigorous as it
was, took pleasure and devotion in having each of those solitary
survivors tell him the spiritual adventures and inner upsets which had
led them to that retreat. In my case, dear friend, it is a man already
used to retreat who by his confessions has been found not repentant
enough. It has been the older who has confessed first. It has been the
confessor who has kneeled before you and accepted humiliation. Oh,
please try to keep this narrative from being completely in vain! Justify,
absolve me by profiting from its complacent reconstructions where I
have wavered. This milieu has also greatly influenced me and has, little
by little, introduced beneath my pen an entire section that otherwise I
would have kept back. Limoëlan must have lived in this country, on
this coast—perhaps near here? Would he be living here still? Who
knows? Would he not have found a haven, I thought, like mine? the
very roof I am under? one of those calls where in the evening I espy
lamps aways dim but never dying? Would his poor bruised body sleep
perchance beneath a flagstone in the chapel where I pray, calling upon
god's mercy for him? The desire to join to my narration a destiny so
strange in its expiation and martyrdom made me include all those
conspiracy details that were less relevant for my own story.

Up to this point, then, I could have dated all these sheets from
this hospitable monastery. I often wrote them during serene mornings
on the terrace overlooking the sea, or the massive balustrade of the
window, in the breeze still warm from the setting sun. I penned several
during the height of day at the end of the plane-tree promenade, the
only shaded path when the rest of the garden is comprised only of
dried aloes and rosemary. I brought together these pages without
artifice, taking my time, perhaps too leisurely a pace, and the nascent
taste I felt increasing as I proceeded reminded me of the time when I
dreamt of writing down everything but I abstained, for I would have
enjoyed it too much. This unseemly complacency in such simple work
is going to come to an end, however. We are reembarked, my friend,
and from now on I begin my narration on board. We are leaving
tonight at the first high tide. I will continue then to the rolls of the
vessel, and perhaps another storm will cut me short. If I reach my
destination, I want to have brought my story to a close—before
reaching that shore where all these waves must expire. The interval
until then is a blank page that I can still fill without losing sight of the

heavens. But once I sight the great banks, I will drop my pen, for I must devote myself to the new work.

My friends' departure had left a deep vacuum that could only increase during the following days. At first I kept myself rather commendably in the line of abstinence and sacrifice, where those last scenes had directed me again. Poor science, the neglected books to which I returned, helped me. I spent the evening in my room. The misfortune of many men is to not know how to spend evenings in their room. Pascal said something to that effect. What concerned Georges aggravated the dark complexion of my feelings. His presence had just been discovered in Paris. All the barriers were immediately closed, and an extraordinary complement of police kept the city in an uproar. I seldom stopped by the home of Mme R——— and then only at times when I was unlikely to find her in. The first days thus found me taking precautions with serious interest, resuming study, and beginning good habits. I was already enjoying the premises of that resumed faith and hearing from the depths of my ennui, like in a dark thicket before dawn, the cheerful murmur of renewed chastity. But what I have experienced only too many times since happened quickly enough, and it finally made me desperate and deplorable. After a week or so of looking after my heart, arming my eyes, maintaining scrupulous purity, praying before I went out, choosing the places where I would pass, looking straight ahead exclusively, and especially without taking pride in my efforts, just at a detour where I expected it least, a familiar appearance entered my soul and knocked me over, like a lead soldier, or a house of cards in a child's game. Oh, this facility for falling, which does not let up until the last limits are reached and you have crossed the sacred Jordan, is the same in all sensual men in every stage of the stuggle before total conversion. This facility made me understand how much half-willing does not do and how much willing completely is necessary, and there again how much willing completely is not enough unless this will, which is our own, be granted, blessed and willed by God! Our will alone can do nothing, although without it Grace is unlikely to descend and certainly will not persist. St. Augustine himself, slave of repeated lapses, paraphrased the Scriptures: Continence is a gift. Oh will and Grace! It was in these moments that I felt most your eternal mystery stir in me but without ever disputing it. And why would I have disputed it? This duel, I dare say, is a stumbling block for so many learned and holy men. Calling it a religious mystery would not embarrass me. Every time I fell so unmistakably, without there being anything resulting from my fault,

I felt free, still responsible for my own acts. In a fall there is always enough of our will, enough guilty, mute intervention, not to mention enough old or originary iniquities accumulated to explain and justify in the eyes of the conscience this refusal of Grace. On the contrary, all the times I succeeded with much effort and pain, I did not feel my will alone but I felt favorable, succoring Grace hovering over me. There is always in the most attentive and steadfast will enough inadequacy and imprudence to require for moral victory the continuous intervention of Grace. I venture to say that it is like the harness attached to children when they are almost ready to walk. If they set out and do not fall, even if the harness was not needed, it was still there floating behind them and their steps vaguely felt it is a support. If they fell, even hurting themselves, the harness being loosened at their request, that means they counted too much on themselves and did not ask to have it tightened soon enough. They did not sit down in time of their own accord, keeping still and showing how little they still were. So long as man is on earth, he is always like that, on the verge of walking by himself. But if he walks without falling, still he never walks without a harness held on high. The holy are those who walk with such balance and agility that to see them from a distance you would not know whether they walked from the velocity of their own feet or with a support, a continuous lifting of the harness, because the double movement you see in them is so harmonious that it makes a single movement. The harness is always with them, incorporated, attached to their shoulders like immutable wings. Let us try, my friend, to be like those happy toddlers who are always ready to walk alone and in effect make the entire way on foot, but do it always beneath the eyes and in the grasp of that supreme tenderness. They are no longer puling and kicking sucklings. They will never become arrogant men. Death will overtake them still trying out their harness, always pushing forward but always docile, walking but born long, working until the end and giving thanks with each step.

Certainly, you are no more distant from that model now than I was then. After those hours of backsliding, I ordinarily rushed to get back to Madame R———; I would go there the very evening or at least the next day. I was impelled there, not by any real or material desire so blindly satiated, but by a need for distraction and spurious excitation, to stun myself, to recover and repair in some way my brutal infraction with the help of some less gross, although more treacherous, infraction, which occurred more in the mind than in the senses. An hour or two seasoned by gallant propositions and deceptive amiabilities were sufficiently intoxicating. It seemed to me that my unbridled heart was ennobled by being transported into a more delicate sphere. If the poison reached me in an imperceptible form with subtle perfumes, it would become a worthy enough nourishment for the soul, and I had less to blush over. A hypocritical and sophistic view of things! For, if sometimes after a week of retreat and meticulous purity, I went to see Madame R———— and found her beautiful and amiable, I would indulge in the same propositions, the same smiles which in the preceding case seemed to me like a felicitous and fragrant distraction. But in the new case my feeling of innocence and fidelity grew weak and confused. When I would leave, I was less careful to keep this feeling as if I no longer possessed it intact, and I would readily succumb. Thus, it is all of a piece. All infractions connive to lead to one another. If the gross fall engaged me once again in laughing and perfidious duplicity, the delicate fall in its turn sent me once more defenseless to the most repetitious temptations.

And then, after two or three days, when I had had a few sound sleeps, when I had forgotten the circumstances of my evildoing and taken myself more or less in hand, I would write some letter to Blois to restore me in fact, to bind and elevate myself through my adoration of this ideal creature whose chaste affection I sought. It was she, not he, to whom I wrote my letters most often. There were no politics, as you can imagine, or if so, only what was public knowledge. For example, "They've just arrested Moreau, Pichegru has just been arrested; the gates are still closed; they're still looking for Georges." But the background was the story of my life, details of my boredom living by myself, hiding all my shady behavior. I gave the bulletin of the little convent, quite a pious picture, softened around the edges, somewhat naive although not very faithful. I ran on shamelessly with my enthusiasms and my laments, even declarations metaphorically expressed. Sometimes she was the willow on the bank that kept me from being carried away by the river; sometimes, the golden mooring ring that kept me on the better shore. The names of Beatrice and Laura slipped in by themselves, but all that was bathed, even drowned in a hue that gave no light either for suspicion or offense. She wrote one letter for every three of mine, usually short and friendly, showing common sense and simplicity. But the conventions of epistolary courtesy, the appellation *Monsieur*, like a strange voice, made me sad, bringing me back to reality and retracing in my mind's eye the austere boundaries I would have liked, if not to cross, at least not always to see. I always kept her last letter with me until I received another. I would sometimes get up in the midst of work or stop in the street to unfold and reread it, to seek beneath the kind words that invited me to come a sign of something more tender, to recognize beneath the inflexible word and in the manner it was used, the nuances that the voice and glance would have used in speaking.

Five long weeks rolled by like this. Political affairs followed an inexorable course. Towards the end I expected every night to have Georges, who was tracked on all sides, come to seek refuge. I would awaken with a start, believing I heard walking and calling beneath my window, and once or twice I went down to open up. But he did not come. In these extremities, rather than compromise anyone, he preferred to have recourse to forced asylum, which he obtained violently from strangers. His arrest the evening of March 9 put an end to my fears. However, Paris was still not open. I had promised to go to Blois for Holy Week, and it hardly looked as if I could. It would have been unwise to call attention to myself by trying to leave so long as people were not free to circulate. Both Monsieur Desmaroet and Monsieur R——— advised me to postpone my trip. So I had just written, on the Saturday before Palm Sunday and under the effects of the assassination attempt at Vincennes, all my sorrow at these obstacles and my promise to double my meditation on their behalf during the week of holy mourning. At my visit to Madame de Cursy in the afternoon, a visit that I always made longer when I was in one of my spells of fidelity, I had picked a book at random from her library. It was a volume of Pierre Bourdalou's *Pensées*, which I took into the garden to read, profiting from the sunlight through the trees that still had no leaves. I loved that little garden, dreary and humid, beneath Madame de Couaën's old room. I imagined it, I do not know why, like that of Saint Monica in her home at Ostia as she leaned out her window, a few days before her death, to discuss heavenly happiness with her converted son. While walking besides the box-wood, the principal greenery that would be used for the branches on Sunday, and conjuring up the image of my absent beloved, I was struck by a chapter that treated friendships in depth, those presumably solid, those presumably innocent. Concerning the latter, friendships of the heart, which make so special an impression, which touch the heart and arouse its overflowing affection, I was astonished to read the following. It was like holding up a mirror up to myself: "We have a thousand ideas, thoughts, memories of the person occupying our mind. We return a thousand times to reflect on a conversation we had with her, what we said to her, and what she replied, on a few kind words from her, on the honesty, some sign of her esteem, her good qualities, engaging manners, agreeable disposition, her gentle, accessible nature, in short, on everything offered to the imagination when it is struck by a pleasing and fulfilling object. When you are in the person's presence, you feel a certain complacency in your heart, certain quivers which make you pause, inwardly titillated, excited, your soul overflowing with an unceasingly novel joy. In your conversations there are terms of endearment, deeply felt expressions of ardor, animated protestations, repeated a hundred times. You seek each other out. There is hardly a day when you don't pass several hours together. You treat each other as family, although always decently. You confide in each other. Often you even discuss God."

I saw myself on every line of the pamphlet, and I stopped in my tracks, persuaded, "Oh, yes, " I cried, "you speak truly. You knew all this, too, Pierre Bourdeloue, austere Confessor. Where did you get these secrets I thought were mine alone?" Yes, we speak of God, of the very things the most obscured at such moments, that is, the death of desire, the sacrifice of the senses, and the vigilance of chastity. And while we speak so well, our own malice, which without our being aware of it wants to seduce, seduce the woman who listens and ourselves as we speak, often brings copious tears to our lids. When these tears mix with our words, they are rendered more melodious. But let us say then, "If she were less young and less beautiful, less attentive to the sound of our voice, would we like to talk to her for hours on end about discreet friendship and inviolable celibacy? Would we be so prone to weeping around her, if she were less prone to weep?"

And returning to the thoughts of this Christian moralist, I found, "How does it happen that you stand so close to the flame and suffer no burn? How can you walk on a slippery path and never fall? How can you remain invulnerable amidst slings and arrows? Is there anything that escapes us faster than our spirit, anything that carries us away more violently than our heart, anything we find harder to restrain than our senses?"

Fathers, physicians, orators. You who burst out in the pulpit or you who vowed silence, old hermits in the desert and cloisters, oracles all too rare of a Christianity in eclipse, the world today tries to believe you strange and savage. But if you leave the grotto, the cell where you sleep, emerge from your dust and your silence, you still tell man his secrets and his hidden motives, making him blanch with surprise! And I do not want to speak only of the great penitents in your midst, of the converts whom the world of their time had first dragged down. I want to speak of those who remained unchanging and simple since their youth. These are the very ones who have known how to scrutinize their passions and impulses, and imagined what is barely made out after centuries of oblivion and what we thought we had discovered recently. Oh you who sailed straight into port, tell me, how did you know about the storm? Because the storm is everywhere. Because the desert is also the world of man's thought. Because the rock of the faith, as high and firm as can be found, receives through certain winds the scattered foam of the waves. The same movements beat stronger or weaker and spend themselves against all hearts in all weathers. The same essential moral circumstances occur with little variation in each of us, or at least they can end in circumstances which no one escapes entirely. Bourdaloue, Jean Gerson, or Jean Climaque, our spiritual masters, you used the same lamp as Christ and the Wise Virgins when you read the common nature of Adam in your separate eras. You light the steps of whoever studies human nature after you. Because every evening, every morning, at any hour of day or night, during years without number, you visited every little corner and crevice of your soul, like a prudent handmaid inspecting every hall and turn of the house before going to sleep. Oh, dear God, may we learn the depths here below without ever leaving our hearts!

This striking piece, when added to several others read earlier, as if adroitly arranged by a maternal Providence, jostled my ideas a great deal. They had been improving, taking my salvation more to heart for some time. Still they would sometimes turn around, stopping along the way to savor the sweetness of a friendship presumed to be innocent. I suddenly realized that this friendship was cultivated entirely too intimately, and the stations toward salvation were not on the same slope nor along the same path. I realized that this meadow that was so soft and warm in the moonlight, its grasses so inviting, enveloped in white Elysian mists, certainly was not leading to Calvary. I was perplexed all over again. I was weighing the arguments with application and care, when the next day, a Sunday, I learned that the last three conspirators had been arrested. The barriers had been lifted, and the last extraordinary measures removed. The trip to Blois instantly became feasible. My soul was so unstable and characterless that I could not think about anything else. Perplexity, equilibrium, everything was shaken or suspended. I flew, ready to leave in a few hours, and Monday morning early, I was on the road to Blois.

"They're going to be really surprised to see me get down after my letter of the day before yesterday," I thought, smiling. "That letter expressed so many regrets; it was surely the most sincere, the most openly tender I had ever written. I was so desperate at the delay. I was so bold in showing my feelings at this distance, since I did not believe I would be visiting them so soon! Will the Marquis have taken umbrage? Will she be frightened? Oh, no, she will have only been touched. Perhaps the letter is reaching her today. Perhaps at this very moment she is already rereading it to prepare an answer. She will blush more than ever when she sees me, and I, too, will be a little embarrassed at first. What questions the Marquis will have for me! and how many heartrending and morbid answers. But for her it will always be the old conversation continued, the intimate atmosphere, general obliviousness, and invisible and peaceful sadness that things exhale, and which falls at more serene instants in copious dew!"

Travel was slow then. Since we had reached Orleans rather late in the evening, we were going to sleep there, but I could not hold still. I asked for a horse and guide and pushed on towards Blois after supper. Morning came when I was three leagues from town. I changed to a fresh mount to get there. Around seven o'clock in one of the high streets, not far from the chateau, I knocked on the door of an old-looking house that I seemed to recognize, so quickly did these places seem familiar and present to me. The maid formerly at Couaën opened the door and happily called out my name. She ran up the stairs before any question on my part and took me into her mistress' apartment. She was in fact already up standing by the bed of one of the children, who looked ill. She uttered a cry of surprise when she saw me, but hardly asked after me at all, telling me that this very night her son had had an attack of coughing and shortness of breath. As soon as it was day, they had gone for a doctor, whom she was awaiting impatiently. My first and inevitable reaction was to feel hurt: perhaps when she saw me, she would have rather seen the doctor. She begged me to examine her son and give the medical opinion she thought me capable of. Her shining eyes consulted mine. Her haggard cheeks burned more than the little invalid's. I reassured her in complete sincerity since I could not detect any symptom in the child to justify so much alarm. The Marquis, who had been alerted to my arrival, came in a few moments later, and I gave him the events of the last few months, especially the Duke d'Enghien's assassination, with details he had not received. That is how that day and the next few were spent. Madame de Couaën made no mention of the letters I sent, no more of the last than the earlier ones. I was offended and felt forbidden to remind her of what had been so dear to me. Her child's illness completely absorbed her attention, and once she was somewhat reassured by the second day, her repeated questions, if we happened to be alone, bore solely on the danger that the Marquis and the rest of us ran as a result of the conspiracy being uncovered and the measures threatening. Instead of vague sadness without a cause, of which you may think you yourself the proximate cause, instead of floating reveries where you sketch your visions like clouds in the sky, she offered me pain and anxiety that were real and positive. And she displayed this pain artlessly. But human love, which pretends to devotion, is so unjust in its turn, so preoccupied with itself that I begrudged her preoccupation and fright.

How could I reproach her for acting like a wife and mother? The letters I thought bold had not astonished her at all, and she had not thought them strange. She had accepted without distrust something not without connivance. The letters, like an ordinary friendship, had nourished her like a delicate but plain and commonplace dish. That is why she did not find them worth mentioning. She did not suspect all those artful maneuvers of self-love, more than tenderness, these attentions that only the mind remembers, these tendencies that back off in fright and cleverly return for more excitement. She believed, she accepted everything from a friend and did not overflow with kindly gestures presuming he had faith himself. When she had seen me come in at the height of her anxiety, once she had uttered her first cry of surprise, she turned to me immediately, as another part of her own soul, and let me see her in all her distress, without either dreaming of keeping herself under control or pretending she was less distressed.

I begrudged her commendable maternal sensitivity. It not only wronged what I pretended to be for her, but also kept her awake and was damaging her beauty! There are moments of blindness and brutality in a man's love, to the point where he will hold against his beloved the consuming concern which makes her wither and pale and lose her looks because of him or far from him! Women are never like this; they do not conceal their grandeur in love, their virtue in the abyss, their title to immortal forgiveness.

As for the Marquis, after many half-finished conversations, we left for an afternoon together. When we were just outside the town, on the heights overlooking the road and the landscape, he made me repeat for the 10th time all the details I had been able to gather on the murky assassination attempt. I could hardly explain such fixation solely from interest in the victim. Finally his soul was bared in these words: "So, indeed, he triumphs. His rivals disappear. Destiny hands them over one by one. He already uses and abuses. He has princes shot. Moreau, Pichegru, Georges, what will he do with you? Comrades, each plays out his role! To you, so illustrous, will perhaps go the blood-soaked role. I will play the heaviest and sorriest! But I accept it and will it in its entirety. Limoëlan, I shall have my martyrdom, too! Mine is to wait and survive. to watch each movement of the victor until he falls, because he shall fall. Now he is beyond the page, tomorrow the emperor, absolute master over all our heads. Well, before tomorrow he will have begun his descent. The imbecility of the masses will follow him, will carry him a long time yet. My prediction shall surely be right. I will take note of his steps, each step downwards, each symptom of his fall, the budding signs of vertigo. He may seem to be ascending still, but reality is quite the opposite. In view of the end I will be patient. I will put up with that long tyranny like the officer of an imprisoned garrison without his sword, watching every last skulking soldier of the conquering army file past. Rather, I shall count on him, dependent upon himself, on his faults, his obstinacy, his anger. Someone who would assassinate a Condé will answer me. Oh, nothing will escape me from the lining of his mantle on parade to the smoke from his camps! No mother shall follow her son's marches on a map with more anxiety than I will follow his. I will inscribe joyously blow after blow of his victories, Pyrrhic victories where he shall perish. Year after year, he shall crush new generations beneath him like relay horses. But he shall have his turn. Unknown, immobile, annulled, without respite, I will mark all the points of this grand game. If he is disturbed from time to time, I will think it is I, hidden though I am, who has him charmed. Amaury, I see my revenge!"

While speaking in this state of exaltation, his face pale and splendid, Monsieur de Couaën really looked like a sublime martyr of hubristic earthly passions of the pure race of Prometheus bound. But whatever exasperating residue I had from the recent political attempt, I could not feel ulcerated to that point and embrace such implacable presentiments except to lament them. The very sight of this calm countryside, the idea of the holy day, during this Good Friday added to the strange, nearly offensive effect of this speech. I felt incapable of staying in a house with such rebellious and endless self-torture, just as I had felt rebuffed a short while earlier by Madame de Couaën's too fixated and instinctive sensitivity. Between the corrosive hatred and vulturous behavior of the one and the frequent obliviousness and slow maternal consumption of the other, what could I do? How futile the gift of my being would be! What good could I be for them with my repressed delicacy, my jealous susceptibility and my varied resources of intelligence and heart, which in any case could only adorn and comfort? Returning to town in this frame of mind, I went that very evening, without mentioning it to anyone, to reserve a seat in the diligence for Easter Monday.

It was only on Easter day, when I announced my departure at the dinner table, that I heard Madame de Couaën address to me the words held back up till then: "Really, tell me when you are coming to us for good?" She seemed to have made a violent effort to utter this, and the brusqueness of the tone she used hid badly whatever interest she had and jarred with the sudden blush covering her forehead at that very moment. But my impression was too fixed by then for that belated question to make me change it. I replied to her and to the Marquis, with a show of eagerness, that I would not fail to run back as soon as possible after the fateful trial and the debates I wanted to attend for all of us. So I left Blois the next day, joyful, relieved, inwardly angry, my feelings warring within, sending into my sky an exciting whir, thousands of amorous bees. "Let's love, let's love," I said to myself over and over. "The season of procreation approaches, seeds are pushing out everywhere, and the flight of my youth is not over yet. Let's love with love, let's love someone who can love in return, who perceives, suffers, and dies from love, who prefers to all else the abyss in us! Lasting, pure friendships with young women are not possible, I can see, except on the condition of frequent insensitivity and forgetfulness on their part and a perpetual diversion of their tenderness to persons other than ourselves. Since in staying attentive and lively, such friendships, so austere advisors say, only pretend to be innocent, let us dare more or better, let's have friendships that are completely guilty!" So reading a book, valuable in itself by a heart already too stirred up, chanced to aid delirious conclusions.—And the image of Madame R———reappeared at that moment more fresh, like after a winter's sleep, sometimes in silent tears as I had seen her that evening in her opera box, dying of languor at not being loved, sometimes in the enchantment of a ball, letting herself be imagined as giddy and frivolous as happiness could make her. In turn she became the frail pale reed who could be easily carried off, a mocking, fleeting imp, precious but hard to seize, or again, a discreet sphinx prudent and rather cruel, with a secret that her fine lips would scarcely utter, but which I wanted to snatch away.

CHAPTER XVI

By now we were in the first breaths of spring. As soon as I got back, I visited Madam R———. She received me cordially with her habitual tinge of subdued sadness and her typically misted forehead. I went back in the afternoon the next day and the days following. Still the same sadness and the same damp "clouds" with a flash just as subdued. Little by little we resumed our past bond without any overt discussion. She no longer lived alone, and the aunt who reared her had come to live nearby. But usually I saw her alone at that time of day in her narrow blue-toned salon where the blinds were often half-closed. Our conversation from the very first, even if ostensibly on the subjects of the moment, basically and customarily returned to her discouragement and deep ennui from a purposeless life and to her hope in love that I tried to persuade her to seize again. Behind the insignificant facts, and in our most trivial ways of passing judgment, we knew unerringly how to respond to our thoughts. I offered her books to read. I brought her first, if I remember correctly, some touching productions of Madame de Charrière. We had lively discussions about her characters, particularly Caliste. One day when she had expressed herself serenely during the conversation, as I rose to leave after a few less indirect words on my feelings, by chance I had moved to one of the half-opened windows. A lilac bush grew against it, a white lilac, I believe, and already past its prime, although it had barely bloomed. She pointed that out to me as an allusion to herself. "Well, just open the blinds," I said, "and let in the sun."

She soon left for Auteuil, and those trips I had made every day last year for another, I now made again, alas, for her. Everything I saw reminded me of my infidelity. I suffered, but I deadened as much as possible the injurious contrast with memory. She did not much like to go out walking in the woods, and when we did, I meticulously avoided certain paths too filled with inviolable tokens and murmurs. Attached to the house she lived in there was a rather extensive English-style park which sufficed for a lazy stroll. One day in the beginning we discussed our favorite theme where I criticized her early disillusion-ment of passion, languor of soul, and avoidance of sunshine. But she claimed that if one has passed the most decisive and beautiful years of life regretting and weeping, it makes little difference if one's tears and regrets continue more or less for some time, because the brilliant charm is broken forever, and there is already a chilling shadow cast over all that could happen. It is better that something requiring sparkle and freshness does not happen. Those were approximately her exact thoughts.

"Yes," I rejoined, "you mean that in life there is a gown of graceful and charming illusions that one dons only once; that feelings that lacked outdoor sun in their proper season, even when they ripen later, lose their firmness and never reach their golden color; that souls bathed for too long in their own tears are like grounds saturated with rain, which always stay damp and chill even after the sun comes out. You think that these grounds have no replenished thickets or stalks ready to bloom; that if lightning struck, nothing would be illuminated and that there would never be an altar there. Well, what you say is partly true. You say what I have often felt and feared in myself. But I have also told myself that one or two or three years in tears are only dew in youth, a better morning dries it all; a fresh breeze restores us. We forget, we exhale, we renew. We really have, think about it, several youths. Often enough we believe that youth is composed of the beautiful years and their gifts. When you are despoiled, you take to bed in a coffin and cry over yourself. But once the sun shines, we come to life again, the heart blooms, and we are amazed by these flowers and lawns that cover over the sepulcher of yesterday's sorrows. Each returning spring is a youth that nature offers us and through which she tries to test our power to enjoy and our capacity for happiness. It is not wise to resist too much. On that mysterious slope where unknown dancers gambol, where a charming star shines, we climbed once or twice, perhaps without seeing anything that could be imagined from below. We got weary and climbed back down, our heart and feet bleeding from the brambles. Henceforth the star shines in vain, the bouquet on high lights up in vain. The most moving voices, the lightest white clouds invite us in vain. You watch incredu-lous from below and decide not to risk any flight, forbidding yourself what inspires all."

This last word struck her, and taking up the thread with a smile less sad than sly and tender, she applied this truth to herself:

"Well so be it! One no longer wants the risk of climbing."

This was said in her salon, and I had to leave so she could dress for some visit she had to make. About a half-hour later, returning from a walk around the village and woods, I went back to her house and since I did not suppose she had returned, I went into the park to pace back and forth while I waited for her. But I espied her there herself at the end of a path to the back. She had stopped, pensive, and seemed to be studying a singular effect of light, which in the midst of a rather darkened landscape illuminated just the summit of a little green hillock crowned with a bouquet of acacias. We were at the end of April, and there was a soft seasonal sky, half-veiled in every direction by a curtain of fluffy, somewhat heavy clouds. The sky seemed very low, lightly bordered across the horizon like a covered dais, but diminishing in opacity and veiling at the center, and there only, completely clear in the middle at the spot where the vertical rays of the daystar had the strength to pierce. It was truly a sky of quiet celebration and burgeoning hopes. One of those skies, which if seen in a painting, we would accuse the painter of making unnatural and bizarre. Perhaps in a painting, static as it is, such a sky would really look artificial while in the heart of nature, which harmonizes all, it is a pure beauty. She was there admiring the reflection of that unique fall of light and its magical play upon the little greening hill. I ran up behind her, and at the moment she turned toward me, I pressed her:

"Shall we go up together?"

"Go where?" she asked surprised.

"Up there on the lighted hill," I replied pointing. Quickly, as if struck by the invitation, she took the hand I was holding out, and like two children we ran to get to the spot. But before we were half-way up, the light on the summit had disappeared.

Well, my friend, there in abridged form is the entire outcome of the principal error I had to tell you. I could even limit myself to that frustrated project as an emblem to indicate the attempt at passion aborted. But that would give you too pleasant a picture. I must make you feel more keenly the efforts and impotence of striving, the lacerations and the brambles.

When passions like this begin, it only seems like moving along a gentle slope. If you are tired, you can always stop early enough. What is so lovely to climb could not be painful to come back down. The hands that you give each other are not knots or chains; they will be able to stop in time to hold on without any bleeding traces remaining from the grasp. That is not the case at all, as experience teaches imprudent souls all too quickly. Whatever judgment you make at first, all these liaisons that look inviting, all these trials of tenderness are rudely charged against us. They do not follow along without punishing us. If the engagement is light, the change is crushing and bitter. When the attempt leads to rupture, the mark remains and makes a scar that is painful or encrusted. After a certain very small number of first images, the heart becomes a speckled mirror, where the happiest objects are only reflected through a permanent net.

There was a memory against us that neither of us could remove but which we avoided awakening, the memory of a woman absent and betrayed. On many occasions, I found Madam R——— perceptibly preoccupied, as if forewarned, not only from scruple and reproach of faithful friendship that she must take herself to task for but also from the fear that despite all my attentions, I might truly be found elsewhere. One evening, after singing an Ossianic romance on the harp (the song brought to the lips secrets of the soul), she came over to the open window where I was standing and pointed to a brilliant star in the sky. I asked her if she wanted to be my star and guide my life.

"Why do you ask," she said, "when someone else has had that role for a long time?"

But denying the woman who should never have been eclipsed in my heart, I declared that up to then there had never been such a star in my night and that no one had agreed to shine her light on me, although I had long sought such a person. While she listened with an unfathomable expression, a sharp gleam (was it pride or love?) sprinkled soft lights on her damp and sorrowful brow. I redoubled my entreaties and vows. I denied once more. She came closer, looking at me directly. Both gentle eyes glistened with tears. Like the star above without its veil! From that day forward, I spoke to her openly about what she inspired. My vows retraced the past. I told her, by means of a few omissions, my long struggles about her and that letter written one evening in the height of the Georges crisis. "I felt so unhappy then," I told her, "and so little loved as I would like that I was in a hurry to die." To lessen her fears of rivalry by taking them to more than one object at a time, to show her how earlier I had always had my affection more divided than she knew, I revealed something of my attachment to Mademoiselle de Liniers, but as a knot completely undone. She loved to listen and followed my stories with shrewd and patient sensitivity, obviously pleased with the influence she had obtained. She showed her sense of triumph by an occasional sly smile and appeared even more flattered by such confidences than seemly for a loving heart. This was because, despite a basically melancholy disposition and a languid manner that appeared inviting, she was not a naive sort for whom love conquers all. If in the paths in the park, or during the return from some evening out as we walked together, somewhat apart from the others, I would murmur constantly the word she had allowed me to utter and pressed the hand she did not pull away, she was the first to be startled, surprised at herself at such a sudden change, to be so responsive to such language. In such an instance where some other woman, lured by the feelings I was expressing, would have been silent or confused, she took the time to study herself and her disturbed frame of mind. She was immediately aware of each furtive advance I made and viewed it from a distance, always comparing herself to what touched and encompassed her, moved, no doubt, but not subdued. To the most pressing confessions, those most calculated to make her surrender, she responded only by a rare rejoinder, sincere but discreet. She had once been loved with overwhelming passion, or so she implied, but she maintained a stubborn silence on the details and outcome. Was her husband away when that took place? Did the first injuries in that singularly cool relationship come from him or her? I never got very far in that affair. For his part, he stopped off at Auteuil rather often when he was accompanying his ministry chief back from Saint-Cloud. He had dinner with her once or twice a week, always maintaining appearances impeccably, if perfunctorily. I got along well with him, although I was in no way close to him, and he seemed neither surprised nor shocked to find me there.

What had happened to my faith in the ways of God, the faith that had seemed to be coming to life again in my heart? How far away it was, in flight to nothingness, banished with no more ado than a shadow! At certain moments in a peaceful—or dreary—interlude in life, it is not unusual for a kind of religious atmosphere to form around us, a kind of nurturing mist that gathers and closes in around us. You are bathed in it, feeling refreshed already. The young branches open to drink the invisible sap. But let the storms come, as mild as bold blasts of spring or more burning beams of sun, and the mist immediately clears away. That is the way my finer feelings fled. Durable, living faith needs both atmosphere and solid rock, and I had only the atmosphere.

A few hours each morning were salvaged from dissipation by my studies, which had resumed in spite of everything, by one or two courses I was following, and a fair amount of random reading, principally philosophical. As soon as I arose, however, I usually wrote to Madame R——— in the first flush of desire, a letter *à la Saint-*

Preux, which I gave to her later myself. For even though there were
no obstacles to our seeing each other, I loved to send her every bit of
the fresh loot I had collected in our short separation, all those scattered
foolish pearls that a somewhat amorous imagination can shake loose
at will. To this pearl necklace of my awakening, to this bouquet
plucked from morning thoughts succeeded more serious diversions at
the Jardin des Plantes, the Collège de France, and the Bibliothèque
Sainte-Geneviève. Towards two o'clock, when I had done my duty by
Francis Bacon's *Novum organum* or Xavier Bichat's most recent
writing, Adam Smith's *Theory of Moral Sentiments,* or Malebranche's
Entretiens métaphsiques, I hurried either to her home on the Chaussée
d'Antin or at Auteuil, to that pensive Herminie whom I compared to
Tasso's (it was in fact her name). The rest of the time I was at her beck
and call. Often we stayed inside even during the most inviting sunny
days of May. She did not like the country, even though she had rushed
to move in. And when I arrived, sometimes having already eaten, I
would find her still drowsy and heavy-eyed, her shades still drawn,
her windows still closed. Yet for her this was not, as it would have
been with Madame de Couaën, a vague and encroaching reverie like a
deep lake, mysteriously rising. Madam R——'s mood as I examined
it was a languor composed of a multitude of sad and specific details,
small instances of suffering, a myriad ill-closed wounds. She held a
grudge against society. She envied situations replete with homage. She
judged her own situation mediocre and entirely too inferior to that of
so many others she had a right to equal. It was natural enough
perhaps. If she had seen herself from the first more consoled in her
affections, she would not attributed so much value to these vain
appearances. But these petty miseries had had time to filter drop by
drop into her solitude like raindrops on a leaky roof, and she had
deepened their ruts and wet spots. From the threshold of her life of
silence and shadow, she was secretly anxious to come forward and
regain her rank of youth and beauty. At military parades, perform-
ances, and parties, where we went more and more, I saw her indulge
in the tactics of bedazzling like a sickly flower that tries to find dawn
in each belated dusk. But her long mornings remained entrenched in
the miserable pains of habit, contaminating the blessed winds of
genuine pleasure. At first I attributed this veil of vapor, which some
days did not lift at all, to lack of love alone. Soon I discerned better
the density and complexity of some drama.

Georges' trial was to get underway. I had promised both my
friends and myself that I would be present. Indeed, that was the
alleged pretext of my staying on in Paris. I could not begin to tell you

what frivolous chain of circumstances kept me from doing it. I missed the first session rather than delay going to Auteuil and escorting Madame R———. And so it went for the second session and the following, until through inertia and shame I had almost made a decision to stay away. I reproached myself for being a coward and an ingrate. I felt I was violating my word of honor. I could not break out of that inexplicable impasse until Madame R——— wanted to attend a session and required my company. We went precisely on the day of the summations. Although she had all the compassionate interest that women generally have for this kind of drama, it was not in the spirit of somewhat idle curiosity or in the guise of an escort that I had sworn to go receive the last acts of my friend, *my* general as I called him. The lawyers' speeches lacked grandeur, were far below what their role called for. Georges' defense attorney in particular seemed feeble in subterfuges. Georges was evidently submitting to it with a Christian irony that repressed any other irony. But the sight of those three tiers of defendants was solemn, redeeming the proceedings. My thoughts kept returning to it. Georges headed the first row, Moreau, the second; the absent corpse of Pichegru was spared no conjecture; Enghien already killed. What a foreboding aggregation! What regal, martial prey trapped by the same net! That group alone to be burdened with dreadful fates when everywhere else the Empire was in the making, and we were sated with lucky omens and pompous signs. I imagined the burgeoning Empire like a great Carousel, a limitless Champ-de-Mars, beyond the consular arena. And at the entrance of that new track, passing through the massive triumphal arch that served as the portal, the Consul-Emperor at that moment was under the dark and restricting vault. He was pausing there just long enough to let his lictors crush, without his apparent involvement, all the bodies in the way on either side, while he and his cortege would emerge to the acclaim of the crowd. There are, my friend, narrow, dark vaults like that, convenient for the violence they hide and seem to elicit, blood-filled vaults that form the floor of the arcs of triumph where human ambitions pass. That is the entrance where every Caesar enters and fatally grows large!

When Georges' lawyer had finished, the defendant rose to shake his hand to thank him for his efforts. We had not exchanged glances, but at that very moment our eyes met. Georges was continuing to thank his lawyer, and since I was in the same direction, I could believe that he recognized me somehow and was sending me a grateful good-bye. Choked, breathless, I pulled Madame R——— after me, and we left. That was the only time I saw Georges.

However, Madame R—— rebuffed every attempt at political mourning, which she little understood. Some time later I had to accompany her to the first large imperial banquet that took place at the Invalides. She was predisposed towards these imperial displays, trying to gradually bring me over. I could detect that she was already ambitious for me in the same way she was for herself. Political virtue cools off quickly in breath of a throaty murmur. But since it was the moment when the heads of Georges and his confederates still resounded on the pavement of Place de la Grève, as I thought about it all, I felt pain, confusion, and sharp attacks against my weakness. Other matters disturbed me as well. About this time I received news of Mademoiselle Amélie and her grandmother. I was still moved. One of their Norman neighbors, a man at least 10 years my elder, was their bearer. Our perilous common ground of taste and disposition made us friends immediately. He had no apparent reason to come to Paris but it was actually to pursue a passion whose object was far from recalcitrant. He was a charming man on whom nature had bestowed many gifts. He was affable, sensitive, prompt to offer his services on many a matter at the very first hint, a little fickle, slightly spoiled, not at heart but by good luck and pleasure. He had been one of the gilded youth of untold pleasure-seeking. But through it all amiable, well-mannered, at home in society, a connoisseur of letters and even a delightful poet. In short, a mixture of facile tenderness and gallic wit of a better era, with some singular receptiveness to religion. We got along famously. We were quickly confidants. I told him about my perplexity. He took it to heart with fresh interest, as appropriate for a friendship that does not want to grow stale, even next to love. He advised my embarrassed feelings with penetrating remarks, showing his superior experience. His liaison and example were not without influence upon me, emboldening me with Madame R——.

But no matter what I did, I could not get the exile at Blois out of my thoughts. Every two or three days, when I went to the little convent and saw Madame de Cursy and heard this worried good woman talk as usual about the health and worth of her niece—never suspecting that I was not just as worthy—it was such a cruel reproach for my inconstancy to hear these confidences. Every letter I wrote or received—or that Madame R—— also received sometimes—put back into motion that underlying cord whose weakest vibration extinguished everything else in me. I spoke to them about Georges' trial as if I had been there. But since in any case I could not express my sentiments freely on that subject, I could be summary. Often in the midst of these factitious exercises, a sign of affection in distress or a sincere appeal escaped from my pen. This happened especially following the lopsided comparison I made between the two women in spite of myself, or when I considered the numerous lacunas and something moderately deep and frail that I had already noticed in Madame R———. How many times, as I returned in the evening from rowdy quarters with Mlle de Liniers' neighbor, entirely too much an accomplice of my detestable progress, we would stop on the Pont-des-Arts, then quite new, before separating. I would exclaim, pointing in the direction of Madame de Couaën, "Ah, she alone, now and forever, I love the best, and she would love best in return!"

CHAPTER XVII

There is the lover who cherishes oblivion, silence, woodland sites—or any other kind of solitary site—whether in the presence or thoughts of the beloved. What does this true lover care that his love is unknown, that society expends itself in idle speculations or malicious interpretations, while the vulgar express their admiration, his equals show false compassion, his rivals in fame say he is languishing and wasting his strength, her rivals in beauty insinuate that she is secretly fading from boredom and desertion? What does he care about turbulent evening festivities, the victorious trumpeted noonday processions, ever-renewing spectacles where the curious eye or spirit wanders? If no one knows about his love, it is understood and crowned in their two hearts. If he is unaware of the rest of the world, he reads an entire body of infallible knowledge into his cherished abyss. If his love endures unaltered for many years, in a glance he sees come and go the woodlands and sparkling springs and Asian paradises. If he takes a single step or if he travels, everything enchants him in equal measure but only because he sees everything through a single tear. I was never granted such a love myself, my friend, but I was granted enough to experience more than one trait and to believe in it. Two lovers who love each other truly, so a simple creature gifted in matters of the heart has written, in the midst of society and things which for them make up just an unreal, unstable surface, are like two inspired adolescents. With their arms around each other's necks, they look at the images their free hand nonchalantly traces. Everything is mere image to them. Such a love exists; God has let us meet a few earthly examples now and then. Some fine souls were touched by it, like a stroke of lightning selecting a temple in serene weather. Tender and even painful miracles sometimes result. Because such celestial love affairs only fall to rise again soon, otherwise they would risk being lost or changed. Such love affairs are born only on the condition of dying quickly and taking their victims with them. Dear God, grant remission for your creatures so consumed by love!

But there is a different kind of affair, more customary in worn and weary souls, which commonly usurps the name of love affair. Vain, pleasant, a mixture of grace and malice which makes use of all the sought-after social refinements, it is only a more ingenious pretext for pursuing pleasure, a silken thread quivering, often broken through the labyrinth of society. A lover in such an affair is not the least bit oblivious of his surroundings. On the contrary, he is very anxious, spying, shivering and shuddering in the winds from without. He likes to show himself in love and to give cause of illusion or envy to those who are really in love. Instead of seeing everything as a mere image, he himself is only a mobile image, which he displays and parades in front of others who, though more or less like him, he presumes to equal or eclipse. Look for him in the crowd only on tumultuous occasions! He desires with no object, he invents pitiably, and bored with himself, expends his ingenuity in keeping distracted. Sap, flood, flame, perpetual rejuvenation in the same thought, ardor ennobled by sacrifice, even blamable obliviousness, but consumed and distraught with love? Never! He is not really in love.

Unhappy are the lovers eaten away by longing. More unhappy still are those who could conceive of a larger love and feel a few genuine sparks but cannot keep them. It is like the electrified dust raised by lightning. It immediately falls. However, the dim, worrisome memory that follows leaves a residue of anxiety on the singed terrain. That after-memory will aggrieve the lovers at the heart of the vanity and apprehension that overwhelm them at the beginning of better projects. They want to love. They want to make each other believe they are in love, but they cannot. Madame R——— and I were a little like that.

She especially, if I may say so. I should like to depict her fully without harm to her dear memory, and if I can be a faithful narrator, I shall succeed in being fair to her sensitivity and innumerable admirable virtues. What intrigued me the most about her, after her first sad moods were conquered, and underlying her obvious satisfaction in captivating and pleasing, was something timorous, distrustful, secretive from habit and fear, a calyx wary of her perfumes, a stalk worried by every zephyr, a spring so long restrained that it was stingy in its flow. If I begged her to answer my letters accumulating in her hands by a few frank and open pages, she would promise to do so but rarely get around to it. But I discovered that she destroyed almost anything she first wrote in a moment of passion. Every morning when she awoke, she tore up the notes she wrote after midnight. One day I came across one, unfinished, and forcibly snatched it away. It was ecstatic, almost delirious. But her sangfroid returned quickly and repressed everything. What few notes she gave me she still found a way to get back, usually on some pretext or other. I obeyed, trembling and blushing as much for her as for me from that petty affront. Either from a sense of her own weakness and protection of her virtue, or from a lure of coquetry, or more likely an indeterminate mixture of all that, she constantly refused me the facility of meetings in sure places without witnesses. We were certainly free to have long talks in the country. Her aunt bothered us very little. But in Paris we were left much less to ourselves. She often stood me up at outings we had arranged together. The beginnings usually went well. We met where agreed, but having gone alone to visit somewhere, instead of setting out at once for the spot where I was waiting, she would elude me at another. One day, when she had come to see Madame de Cursy at the little convent, she passed in front of my room, which I wanted to show her. But she was opposed, letting me see an obstinate and irritating suspicion. Madame de Couaën, innocent and bighearted, would have entered in a minute.

On the other hand, Madame R——— seemed confident, fragile, and melting wherever we had only a brief moment, like crossing from one room to another, at the turning in a thicket at Clarens, or on a threshold where we would separate. When I reproached her for these insulting contradictions, she agreed, blaming her disposition, which was too weak and inadequate for good as well as evil. My passionate letters were dear to her. She would wonder in rereading them if she really deserved them. She confessed she was at least proud to have inspired them. And she was proud for herself, rather than naively fulfilled and happy. But her affection had also accents of very simple language. She almost wished I were sick, sick enough to be in bed, without danger, however. Oh, how she would then tend me with her own hands! How she would prove to me her unrestrained devotion. Madame R——— was truly touching, and I pardoned her when she said things like that, her tender silken brow bent over her pale hortensias.

"Where were you running a little while ago?" she asked one evening, when I had not seen her during the day and hurried into the park where she was, but rushed right past her without catching sight of her. "Where were you rushing off to?"

"I saw a slender white form in the shadow and thought it was you, but it was only a lily—a tall white lily which from here, you see, with its slender figure and pallor in the dark greenery, I mistook for the dress of a girl."

"Ah, now you are trying to excuse yourself with a lily," she cried, with a show of scolding. "I'm willing to forgive you this time for having passed by so close without seeing me. But watch out. If that happened twice, that would prove you weren't in love. Or something in the air would have warned you."

Later, during the winter, one evening I followed her from afar without taking the trouble to catch up, since she was being picked up at someone's home. The next day she told me she had recognized me.

"How could you," I asked, "under my hood, at that distance and in the dark?"

"Oh, I don't make that kind of mistake," she replied. "I didn't see you, but I felt you."

Such a remark, as you can imagine, compensated for many a lukewarm reaction. I related them to my new friend, an experienced judge of such gracious matters. In return he showed me letters still damp from the language that lovers use, and I bore away from these emotional conversations, interlaced with the essence of poison, a surcease of nefarious titillation and emulation.

Madame R——— had no trouble getting me to accompany her to military festivities, the ceremonies of that dazzling Coronation winter then underway. When I saw those elite young men, distinguished by heroism, I could tell that she would have liked me to be one of them; it would have enhanced her status if I had. She cited illustrious names of my party who no longer disdained this career of peril and honor. The subtle salutes their sabers addressed to the women on the platforms or balconies went straight to the heart. Why wasn't I down there filing past my peers, head held high, already decorated and famous, to salute her with the flash of my sword, so that she could acknowledge me and show with a proprietary gesture that proclaimed for all to see, "He's mine!" I was shaken. I chomped at the bit, like a reined-in courser who hears the squadrons. "Oh, before those last events," I would reply, "that would have been my place and my vow! But after that, now, how is it possible? After Enghien, after Georges—never!" And I lowered my brow like someone somehow vanquished. She said nothing, and I would be envious the rest of the evening. At the theater, at the most sought-after performance of operas, it was the same. I should have liked to enjoy myself. But when she saw the elegant and triumphant members of her sex, saw sometimes an entire audience rise and idolatrously applaud the late arrival of one of the current queens of beauty, she herself would be overcome by envy and gloom. Instead of being intoxicated at being alone together in those cramped boxes where her aunt, even though present, hardly infringed upon us—exactly like our situation in society, isolated, half hidden, not too ill at ease, seeing without being seen—instead of that, we looked at each other in sorrow and tears in no way meant for each other. Was that love?

On my side it was hardly more than a distinct predilection nurtured by the extended opportunity, in appearance quite proper, but motivated, I regret, by my resolution to keep my senses and soul separate. On her side it was an affectionate course of least resistance, piqued by vanity. We advanced only by a thousand tricks and ruses which cut, badger, and harass. At balls she enjoyed from time to time arousing my impatience and fears of rivalry. Once, at the marriage of one of her relatives, to which she had had me invited, she kept herself surrounded the entire night by noisy young men and cousins from the provinces, playing the queen of the country. Although I had complete leave to visit her or accompany her every evening, we had thought up some romantic fantasy that had me watching beneath her windows overlooking a quiet street, every evening at midnight. Then she would lean over her little balcony a moment to throw me some sign of adieu—a wave, a scribbled note, the corsage at her bosom. I never missed that rendezvous and watched beneath that casement like a stubborn sentinel, rain, snow, every phase of the moon, motionless or prowling, a suspect creature for the rare passers-by who prudently moved away from my shadow. Most often, then, I took my leave around eleven and sighted her soon after. During the interval, I had followed the least movement of lights in the dwelling, the departure of visitors, her half-hour of solitary practicing on the harp—like a prelude to the rising of the Evening Star. I had caught even the sounds of the voice singing, her shadow and that of her chambermaid, whom one sensed stirring around unloosed hair, and that little corner of raised curtain which she had used a short while earlier to verify my presence. But as soon as she had appeared and received my sign of homage and let the token fall from her hands, I gestured her to go back in as quickly as possible because of the coldness of the season. Then her window closed again. Nothing remained for me to see except her roof beaming white with snow and the trembling of the silvered tile. On other evenings, however, she forgot—somewhat deliberately, I think, that I was there. She practiced longer on the harp, and the sounds that burst out with more prodigality and expression seemed to insult my long waiting. It happened once or twice, even when I had not seen her during the day, that she did not appear at all, as if we had not agreed to it. But I in my tenacity kept on waiting. I had earned as a result of walking along the wall the stupidity of a sentry who is not relieved. I walked imperturbably over my own tracks, but I no longer knew why I was there. Then suddenly remembering and seeing that her light was out, my rage and indignation against these cruel tricks or against a forgetfulness no less outrageous overwhelmed me. I would dream, next to that much too inaccessible balcony, some timely means of invasion, and I would walk home through Paris, my head full of some enterprising violent project to scale her wall. Oh, what do you say to the ardor of that soul so nobly exhalted! What a glorious winter that was, the crown of my youth!

Moreover, for my friends at Blois I had no further excuse for keeping exclusively to Paris any longer. In one of the letters the Marquis wrote (for during the past few months it was he, not she, who wrote), he said, "We think you may be neglecting us a little, dear Amaury. Madame de Couaën accuses you of slipping into new routines, and even I wonder whether Madame R——— or some other hospitable hostess has not supplanted us in your regard." When I received that note, I would have liked to leave, to give at least a week to the past, to bereaved friendship, to regrets and to the support of a crumbling illusion, to a reparation—incomplete by far—of a sacred mausoleum. But Madame R——— kept watch over that point in particular. She was a coiled spring that barely needed to be touched, and she would cut off all sighs and smiles, bristle with all kinds of distrust. A week in Blois would have set back and erased the effort of seven months of perjury. She only had to see me sad in a certain way and she suspected the cause, becoming instantly changed in tone and singularly embittered. Thus I postponed mentioning that short trip from one day to the next and in the end never dared take it.

It would soon be a year since they had left Paris. It was already two years since leaving La Gastine for the last time; I had asked Mademoiselle Amélie in embarrassed and covert terms for a period of two years to see clearly what to make of myself and decide my future. I learned that she was to come soon to spend a few weeks with a friend of her mother's. What was I going to have to say to her, and how was I going to mask so much confusion? What new clarity had I acquired during these two years? What opening had I achieved? A vacillating, stuttering will, less articulate than ever! A false, disloyal position, not only towards her but towards the two other hearts, equally wounded! not one energetic act, not one direction followed for my happiness or that of anyone else, not one straightforward way out of the impasse!

Oh noble young woman, standing untiring, chained so firmly to the threshold of your first hopes, you remind me of a young Jew at the edge of a fountain or a well, your hands folded in your sleeves, waiting for a faithless servant to return to place the heavy urn on your head. Or perhaps no longer waiting but remaining, still watching, never calling, never importunate even in the most secret of desires, your hands resting on your gentle Madeleine, who is less wild now and has never found you shedding a single tear! Oh simple sublimity of will and duty! What an effect it had on me every time I remembered you that way. It seemed to me that despite the lapse of two years and when I ought to express myself on her future, it was still not on her behalf that this self-sacrificing person engaged me, not her heart dedicated to self-forgetfulness and the service of others. It was on behalf of Madame de Couaën, with reproaches and shame for this abandonment. It was this sharp pain that brought Mademoiselle Amélie most to mind. Believe me, I did not lend her thoughts unworthy of her. I interpreted what she truly felt, what she would have felt if she had known everything. Sometimes I thought I could hear her saying, "Ah, for her, at least, for her, I would never complain of being left behind, I would not have blushed for you, my friend. But if she were abandoned, too, she could be prey to pain like mine! Ah, have pity on that maternal breast that has no place to hide such anguish, have pity on that wifely brow that no suspect shadow must darken! Forget me, have pity and kindness for her, if I still have any right to ask!"

In the Marquis' last letters, it was more a question of his wife's health, and vague expressions of anxiety kept recurring. Madame de Cursy spoke to me endlessly about it, and her little community prayed for her beloved niece. The name of Madame de Couaën, uttered by chance in the circles I frequented, had become a sharp and burning torture. Several time people who had always seen us together the year before asked what was between friends once inseparable. Often when I entered a group, I heard someone ask Madame R——— *sotto voce*. She never failed to report it to me with an air of injury, as if I had caused her some affront. At a dinner at her home one day, when there was a rather large number of guests, the general conversation turned to Madame de Couaën. A lady who had run into her when passing through Blois recently said she was hardly recognizable, very thin, turning pale from one moment to the next, with bright blotches on her cheeks. I was thunderstruck by these details. Madame R——— had gotten up on some pretext and left the room. When she returned, she found my face undone, struggling with tears I was trying to hide from the guests. A few minutes later, as we were moving to the drawing room, she came close and snapped, "Anyone can see you love her!" When she was jealous, the most sudden change took place. The name Herminie no longer fit. The moist, ashen silk of her brow, the warm matte ivory of her cheeks gave way to a light, hard, metallic green. Her voice had clear vibrant accents; her laugh was throaty and mocking. She was wildly coquettish that entire evening. The best comparison would be to the malicious bronze sphinx I mentioned before. I wrote her about it the next day. I justified my tears and tried to prove that such behavior was beneath her, who in my place could not have kept them from overflowing. She readily agreed, dropped her guard, and resumed her soft glow. But true confidence was not really reestablished. Rather, it never was, at any time, established between us.

CHAPTER XVIII

Such perplexities, my friend, which cannot be conveyed unless you have lived through them yourself, should not be measured by apparent motives. Perplexities that were complicated still more by my dreary, sordid consolations, which had the immediate effect of attacking the will at its core! A life twisted and torn in the most sensitive parts of its being! A paralyzing confusion of a nature born for the good, adolescence ensnared in the trap, wanting to love where he had no right and no longer knowing whether to end in open virtue or in brash, self-centered disorder! The agony, the impoverishment, and lament of tender fallen souls! Oh, I well knew that false situation and its absurd depth, that disgust with everything it engenders, that inextricable entanglement that soon bruises a brain hitherto clean, healthy, and strong at every sensitive point, that perpetual lapse in the principle underlying all action, that slow mute defeat when we should be in our valiant prime! It is like a battle we continuously fight in ourselves without being able to declare ourselves on one side or the other, and the prostrate soul, the prize in the fight, is also the battleground and as such subjected to all the frustrating retreats. At the end of each day the soul does not know which side has claimed it. These are the long mornings attached and nailed to one spot, as if by some obsessive mania, in a chair or in the curtains, one's head in one's hands, one's eyes hiding from daylight as if unworthy of it, one's face buried in the bolster. It is futile to try to study. You may open a book at random, but your mind is so far away that you almost read backwards. You hear a few drops of rain falling one by one on the ashes in the fire. You see your real limbs livid beneath an eerie light. Inertia mixed with anguish. The causes of this anguish are no longer present but persist like a lingering fever, when you count your heartbeats. And if you think about it again, an awakening, a confusing shock of all obstacles, all difficulties and impossibilities, but no way out, no opening that could be used to return to peace and equilibrium, to resume order, in sacrifice to someone. A slow flood rises and stirs in all our depths our Augean stables. No torrent to cleanse them and carry them away. As for our Soul, it is seated in the foreground but in the pose of Theseus tortured, waiting like a dumb peasant for the foul river to flow on and dry up. This is where a sojourn in false situations leads when you condemn your youth to them. They bear with and in them a terrible expiation. Such misery is worthy of contempt, my friend. But you should remember, if you were tempted to blush a little too much over it and to berate a soul already too beaten down, that these false situations merit no more contempt than so many other miseries and agonies we have brought on ourselves on this earth. Concerning respect from our fellowman where action is prized above all—movement and bustle even in evil and which would blush at the confession of any agony if a God gets what is due Him—there would hardly be any encouraging word to be drawn. I can hear already the harsh reproaches and the haughty ridicule elicited by scandalously abject weaknesses. From a Christian point of view and in the eyes of God, these weaknesses—do you see? trembling, drenched in sweat—are no more petty than so many acts and results you might take pride in, so many hypocritical, self-proclaimed triumphs, like those burning hells of rivalry and hatred, those secret, external agitations of the Whigs and Tories of every variety in the various stages of fortune, honor, and power. Before God, before my brothers in God, my friend, I confess my weaknesses, I crush and humiliate them in all shame. Before other human weaknesses which would proudly assert primacy, I raise them up, or at least I support these weaknesses as sisters of the other weaknesses, and when such a weakness is ours, more inactive, more paralyzed, well, that is the way a shred of spiritual scruple can enter some souls, an infirm element which no longer has the strength to be good, but which is aware of the good and hence hindered from transgressing a line, which suspends and neutralizes and which, if chased from our flesh, takes refuge in our bones to break us and groan.

I probably would have decided, I really believe, to leave for Blois without telling Madam R——— ahead of time, without taking leave of her, simply writing to her one evening that I had taken upon myself, despite everything, to condemn myself to a week's exile there. However, a black-sealed letter from the Marquis tragically dispensed with such an effort. The Marquis informed me of the sudden death of their son. Mute on the depth of his own wound, he spoke about his wife and the alarming state to which this blow had reduced her. He requested me to petition permission for them to return to Paris for two weeks. He wanted both to remove his wife from the site of the first moments of sorrow and to consult some doctors. I rushed to Monsieur Desmaret, who took care of the matter with the Minister Fouché. The order from the police was sent the same time as my return letter to the Marquis.

This child whom our friends had just lost so grievously was the elder. He was barely seven, having been born in Ireland, Kildare, before the couple came to France. Young Arthur's precocious talents had freely developed and a pervasive inner beauty made him a rare creature, doubly precious. He looked like the beloved O'Neilly lineage: white skin, black hair and eyes, a brow caressed by dreams, a very reflective and sensitive disposition by nature, like his mother and grandmother. He even had a birthmark at the base of his neck as only his grandmother had had. Not even his mother had inherited this imprint. Madame de Couaën had pointed it out to me one day when she was undressing him, kissing this sign with emotion and respect. His younger sister was just like Wordsworth's Lucy, as her godmother Madame Cursy had pointed out: withdrawn, serious, more taciturn than silent, given more to disdain than to daydreaming. Her blue eyes and rather long upper lip indicated that she would resemble her father more and came from the old Couaën roots, which for a long time had hollowed out its nourishment from the dark and isolated cleft of its rocks but had prevailed, vital and strong. These two children were devoted to each other, and young Arthur rendered a almost tender cult to his sister, like a knight or a poet. At Couaën he braided her coronets from the flowers in the meadow or along the canal and for hours on end could adorn her with them. She let him do so, seated, motionless, with the gravity of a young queen. Once, because they had been seen for several days plunging all by themselves into a pathway from the garden to the woods, we were curious enough to follow them. They had made a little square of their own, surrounded by lawn, and had had the gardener plant a beautiful jasmine in the center. They had heard their mother speak of Ireland and Kildare so often that their heads were full of it. The little girl would question her brother as if he would know more about it than she, since he had been born there. So Arthur had the inspiration to call this chosen spot "Kildare," like Andromache in Epirus in memory of Pergamos, like all exiles in fact. With a loving notion of metamorphosis, worthy of poetry by children—or angels—they had the jasmine stand for their grandmother Madame O'Neilly, whom Madame de Couaën talked about sadly in front of them. Every day they went to talk to the jasmine and sing slow melodies. In the morning bouquet they offered their mother, Arthur and his sister inserted some petals from this tree so that the bouquet would contain a remembrance, a vague greeting from their grandmother, but without their mother knowing it so that her sorrow of absence would not be directly awakened. In the end all that was found out. Doesn't it seem to you that the boy, through an instinct of spirituality and prayer, seized an inspiration from expiring lays, a breath of a baptized Ariel? After that I would call Arthur "our young bard," all the more so when I found him one day when his absence had everyone worried, sitting alone on the mountain, his tearful eyes turned out to sea without his being able to explain to me either why or how he was there. His father absolutely adored him. When he held him between his knees, he studied him, coaxing him to speak. The Marquis' usual somberness seemed illuminated by the boy. Still I could not keep from finding in this tender and poetic child much of the paternal genius, a germ also of wandering thought, a vague dream of fame perhaps as much as tenderness, something of a fixity or stubborn and devouring melancholy. The noble father used to smile at such moments, no doubt at the thought that the child would someday be a flambeau, an illustrative exemplar who would reflect on the race hitherto unknown and upon himself. May the fathers who receive from a famous son the brilliance which eluded them and which they would have deserved first be blessed and doubly sanctified!

After leaving Couaën, Arthur had been rather sad and peaked, heartsick. The good care at the little convent had not made him forget the beach and the woods. In the beginning he would often ask his mother, when Madame de Cursy could not hear him because since he did not want to hurt her, "Mama, will we see the sea again soon?" Madame de Cursy, crossing through the garden during mass one day, came across the children singing in unison, like vespers, this little poem of Arthur's:

> Dear God, give us back the sea
> And the mountains of Saint-Pierre,
> Give Grandma the jasmine tree,
> In our little garden there.

His sister's disposition became more difficult also, willfully capricious and imperious. Madame de Couaën and I had some discussion on the direction these children needed. But untrained, effortlessly excellent, she could discipline only by a motherly kiss. She could barely bend to a need to discipline. And although I offered to take over this task, would I have had the perseverance and disinterest to carry it out? During my short stay at Blois, Arthur, taking advantage of a moment when I was alone at his bedside (for he was sick then), said, "Why don't you stay with us anymore? You make us unhappy." I do not remember what I answered. He said no more but looked pensive and did not question me further. Little Lucy, prouder or less sensitive or even more discreet, would not have asked.

Now when I depict these two beautiful children with traits that make them distinctive from other children, I do not pretend such traits were always in evidence and made them complete models. Oh, by no means! Often Arthur the bard was noisy, haughty, or rebellious. Often his regal sister was impudent and talkative, moved to tears by something trivial. Often they were boisterous, blending in our eyes with all the charm and contradictions of childhood.

So it was one of these dear creatures our friends had just lost. I was there in the group waiting for them when they reached the little convent in the dead of the night. Between us there were only clasped hands, silent embraces, speaking of nothing, mentioning no name. My first impression was that she was less changed than I had feared and still beautiful.

The next morning, I saw first one, then the other. With him, as soon as I dared touch his immense wound, he stopped me with a gesture, forbidding and irrevocable. I stammered and did not pursue the subject. I immediately realized that in his sorrow there was more than that of a father for his child. There was in his grief the concept of the male child, the firstborn carried off, mourning for a dead name, something wounded elsewhere than the entrails, a portion of bitterness that could not be avowed because its source was in an ancient prejudice deeper than nature. For that reason there was no consolation, not even any language possible on the subject. He loved his daughter, so much like him in her tender season, his own strong image retraced in gentle and beautiful lines, but she could replace nothing in his eyes. Only a son could hide the abyss in the tenebrae. Was he the kind of man to desire another son, to form a hope all over again? If the physicians reassured him on Madame de Couaën's health, if in his pride of race, he had just requested hope of a male heir from Arthur's mother . . . in this illumination, my brow clouded over with shame, and I hoped with all my heart that the doctors found her ill and judged that her condition was mortal.

She was in fact very ill. In daylight I could see that she was suffering and weak. She at least was all mother and nothing but mother. She brought up the subject first, threw herself weeping on her daughter, whom she kissed. The little girl, standing gloomy beside her, seemed to bear all that affliction and contain it; poor child, she felt it, too. One word from Madame de Couaën revealed beneath the open wound the damage of a deeper melancholy. "This blow," she said, "was a punishment upon me for having desired something outside the prescribed circle, outside the family, and the family has been struck on the inside by this severe call to order." I tried vainly to combat this interpretation which seemed morbid to me and which was not Christian, strictly speaking. But she did not have thoughts lightly. This one had taken root during her entire forsaken stay in Blois and had constantly obsessed her. Her son's death had only confirmed this preexisting fear.

She told me how the prepared corpse had left for Couaën with old François and how the Marquis during the lamentable watch had done everything himself, had looked into everything himself, taken care of the shroud, nailed the coffin with his own hands without permitting either companion or a helper.

From the first day I felt the awkwardness of my new situation. When it was my usual time to see Madame R——, I had to leave Madam de Couaën. Neither her former rights nor her recent bereavement were going to hold me back an entire half-day. Another woman had control of the moment. Madame R—— came to show her friend sympathy. The first visit passed well. Madame R—— wept copiously and spontaneously gave in to feelings inspired by such a crushing spectacle. But other visits were not so simple. Vanity returned, and rivalry slipped in. She and I avoided any special show of attention, but with a gesture or a glance she skillfully marked her ascendancy over me and indicated the understanding we had. I went to the little convent every day before two. Then Madame de Couaën vainly tried to hold me back; I escaped and flew to Chaussée d'Antin where, still bleeding from serious and afflicting impressions, I often found a suspicious welcome and a thousand jealousies on the alert. All these little grievances entered and accumulated, breaking their thorns in me, so to speak. If there resulted no great shock at the time, they turned up later with accrued interest. Whether through basic friendship or a secret desire of surveillance, Madame R—— spent several evenings with Madame de Couaën during that fortnight, sometimes by herself, sometimes accompanied by her aunt. I was very much taken up with lectures on animal magnetism during those months; still I managed to leave in time to take Madame R—— home, but sometimes just barely, without taking much part in the conversation. Madame de Couaën took note of this arrangement and was hurt.

This was seen especially in her sad smile when she said goodbye. She tried to make it as benevolent as she could, but with her sad heart her smile looked like a crease in her pale face. Oh you who have aged and suffered too much in your soul, if you want to disguise the bitterness of your care, do not ever laugh and don't force a smile!

One evening when Madame R——— and I had let slip arrangements for a proposed outing, Madame de Couaën, who was standing near us by a window on a magnificent cloudless, moonlit night which augured a sunny day, asked me to escort her the following morning on a walk and to some shop or other. She asked me as if to show that she was neither annoyed nor jealous but simply asked as a sister who wanted her turn after another sister. I had a brief moment of hesitation, partly because Madame R——— was in earshot and partly because the request really interfered with what I had planned. My almost imperceptible reaction was apparent to Madame de Couaën. She immediately withdrew her request, calling herself indiscreet for attempting to exploit me. It took all my entreaties to smooth over that reaction of mine and to encourage her to make requests again.

It had been only a year during the same season, in the same places when we used to walk together. I felt bound and gagged by other ties. I told myself to watch my words carefully. You create a shadow of honor that you try to follow in violation of any law. The open terraces, the chestnut trees and the marble status sparkling beneath deep frost, the same borders along the sanded pathways that the one o'clock sun brings to life, all these would see many changes in us. At first I wanted to take a different tour of the garden. She insisted on the old tracks. What had become of our promises, our happy plans? Her daughter walked alone by our side.

She seemed to want to subject herself slowly to the contrast between the impressions of now and then, and to extract some austere moral. She did not try to arouse any explanation from me, nor did she seem to expect one. But calm, sensible, with her touch of native imagination, buoyed by a deep inner flood, she spoke often and almost alone, revealing gradually beneath the sky a nocturnal lake of buried thoughts.

She said that there comes a day in the life of the soul when one is fully thirty. Then things appear as they are. The illusion of love, which in the form of a beautiful blue bird flew in front of us, flutters and retreats, inviting us to advance, but seeing us in the meantime, deeply engaged in the forest and brambles, flies away for good. From time to time it can be distinguished in the sky, perched on a star which invites us to follow. Then whether one would live thirty more years, and thirty more again, on this earth, it would always be the same. The best would be to die, God willing, before exhausting this uniformity, for one would be more useful for those here below in praying for them.

She said that for the loving soul there is a very painful struggle. This is when the bird of hope that was thought lost forever comes down for one more moment to rest; when you are twenty one day and thirty the next, and twenty again, and when illusion and reality chase each other in us several times in the space of a few hours. "But now I am thirty forever," she said.

She confessed to having always had a world of her own, an enchanted palace in the mist, an endless green land, peopled with affectionate genies and dreams; to having lived an intense inner life, completely trusting and resistant to things for a long time. But it was finally completely over with her, more abruptly than with other people, with a single blow.

She said also, I remember, that your illusion or love at twenty is like a necklace strung with pearls. But at thirty the pearls fall off; only the thread is left, which in a steadfast heart at least is indestructible and lasts through this life and the next.

And while professing this bitter knowledge of Job from the gentle lips of Naomi and with a breath of a tireless soul, she was still frequently bothered by the effort of walking. To sit down I would find benches warmed by the sun, as I had hoped once to do for her mother in Kildare. And then we would resume our walk in the sun.

One more thought which still came up in the course of her lament and which had no fear of disclosure was that there is one very difficult day of discovery when after having believed someone needed her and that someone was inseparable from her circle, her heart was disabused. One particular evening when everyone else had retired, she threw herself on her knees with her face in her praying hands and asked God to take care of her and bring her peace, no longer being able to pray directly for the happiness or unhappiness of another.

She reproached herself for having neglected God too much until then, of having approached the sole efficacious and permanent Consoler too seldom. She would have wished a convent at Blois for herself and her daughter, because she feared, she said, to be completely useless, like a stranger, to Monsieur de Couaën, purely a cause for his habitual anxiety.

I tried to interject in her effusiveness a few words of hesitant

refutation, that there is a kind of illusion also in too much disillusion-
ment, that often appearances are worse than the intentions they
indicate. But she appeared neither to hear nor need to. She kept on
speaking: no bitterness, no fine and subtle allusions, but a full and
general application of her words to *faits accomplis,* in forgiving form
and with irrefutable judgment. When this entire plaintive hymn was
exhausted, and we were ready to leave the garden, a charming child
passing in front of us caught my eye, and I thought I recognized
Madeleine de Guémio. I was suddenly struck by the recollection of
Mademoiselle de Liniers, who could be in Paris. I said as much to
Madame de Couaën, and to make sure we hurried toward the two
persons walking ahead, accompanying the child. Mademoiselle de Liniers
(because it was indeed she who had recently arrived and was walking
with one of her mother's old friends) turned around and recognized me
at the very instant. She and Madame de Couaën had never met, but they
had written to each other and liked each other. Mademoiselle de Liniers
had already learned of the dreadful loss. The two women, hardly named
to each other, embraced with feeling. When young Madeleine saw that,
she gave little Lucy, astonished and grave, a kiss on the forehead.
Everyone promised to get together. I asked Mademoiselle de Liniers for
permission to call. And we all withdrew—each, alas, with an increased
burden of disturbing thoughts!

That very evening, as we had gathered at Madame de Couaën's
and Madame R——— and her aunt had just arrived, the conversation
turned to the discussion the Marquis and I were having on politics. He
was speaking with intensified bitterness of the Empire, that insolent
mystification, the immense ruin that the height of the scaffolding was
preparing us for. Ordinarily when the Marquis slipped in that direction, I redirected the thrust of his cold blast, respecting the stormy
convictions embroiling his unconquerable soul without trying to
tamper with them. But that evening, whether his predictions seemed
too sweeping and untenable, especially given the clemency and accu-
racy of Madame de Couaën's ideas, whether Madame R———'s
presence caused me to feel bitterness and self-love as I listened to him,
without my being able to explain how it happened, I found after a few
minutes I was openly contradicting him. I did not justify the Empire.
I touched only on the brilliance of its arms, its force, its actual solidity
and sufficient bases in the nations, all evident reasons, indeed, so self-
evident that I appeared too easily to be wise and clairvoyant. But I
said all that in an argumentative tone, impatiently and rebelliously, and
that was the first time I had done this with the Marquis. Astonished by
this new contentiousness, which astonished me no less than him, he

erased his fiery invective and began again with singular gentleness and immediate clarity in the discussion I opened to him, surprising me at every instant by his blend of blind hatred and condescension, and by the firmness and penetration of certain views emerging from assertions quite passionate but collapsing by themselves. It is an experiment I first tried on Monsieur de Couaën, and which I have had many an occasion to verify, my friend, how men of a high degree of intelligence and genius often reveal the most abrupt deviations and defects. You think you hold them and they escape. You study them for years. You determine the formula of their character and nature, like a tricky curve. An unforeseen perspective, and you lose the move. "I praise him, I condemn him until he realizes that he is an incomprehensible monster," Pascal said. What the illustrious thinker said about man in the abstract, man in general, is no less true for each individual of note. The more the individual has inner faculties and strengths, when religion does not have the upper hand, the more the false and true mix in him, in bizarre coexistence, and emerge one in the other at the same time. Corruption and contradiction of a fallen spiritual nature is more visible in these great examples, just as the turmoils of physical nature are more visible in the lands of volcanoes and mountains. What chaos, what enigmas! What unnavigable seas are these souls of great men! You bump against an absurd* crag, and suddenly you find to one side the depth of an Ocean. You were in despair over them, and suddenly you are forced to admire them. Their greatest parts lie near defaults that would seem mortal. At any moment, if you clutch them closely, you must revise your opinion of them. You do not get used to that until much later, because at first you want to create the whole man for yourself.

In that particular discussion, moreover, the Marquis was only half wrong. The opinions he advanced on the Empire were exorbitant, intolerable to hear, a true revolt for the ear of judicious good sense. But they contained a penetrating idea. It is said that any error is only a truth transposed. Any enormity in minds of a certain order is often only a large view taken outside of time and place, keeping no genuine relation to surrounding objects. The special quality of some ardent eyes is to cross and suppress intervals with a glance. Sometimes it is

---

*"An absurd crag" as one would say a "crag of absurdities," a deaf crag. Just as one says an "insane foam." Homer, speaking of Sisyphus' torture, dared to say "impudent rock" and was criticized by Marmontel. I make no pretense of justifying Amaury's expression; I am simply explaining it. Note by Editor [Sainte Beuve in his narrative persona].

an idea, several centuries late, which these vigorous minds imagine is
still present and viable. Sometimes it is an idea, in advance of its time,
which they believe is imminently realizable. Monsieur de Couaën was
like that. He saw 1814 from the vantage of 1804 and was clairvoyant.
But he judged 1814 possible from 1804 or 1805 on, and from thence
quite a chimerical accumulation. There is a white point on the horizon
which everyone would swear is a cloud. "It is a mountain," says the
eagle-eyed travellor, but he adds, "We'll reach it this evening in a
couple of hours." If at every hour of march, he cries enthusiastically,
"We're nearly there," he shocks his companions with the beam in his
eye and makes eyes that are less piercing and more used to the plain
seem more reliable.

Engaged as I was against Monsieur de Couaën and after the first
heedless bound, I tried to retreat and come back down honestly from
the assault on that citadel. But the direction of that discussion was set.
One negation entailed another. All my objections of long standing
gathered together in opposition in spite of myself. Or indeed, when
everything seemed to be falling off naturally, I myself prolonged it,
looking for an opportunity to make amends. In the end, discontent,
feeling hurt for having hurt others' feelings, I left, since I did not have
to escort Madame R——— that evening. Madame de Couaën, quietly
disturbed by that scene, followed me out of the antechamber to the
top of the little stairway. She was no longer the calm woman of the
morning in her tranquil, lamenting psalmody. She pressed me to tell
her what I had against her, whom I had a grudge against, what I had
in mind. Her cheeks were on fire, she was holding my hands. I felt
her extraordinary agitation. It was the second time I had seen her in
this inflamed light, in that convalescent home on the boulevard, from
a few foreboding words I uttered while the Marquis was writing. I
reassured her in words as confused as her own, and I fled, prey to a
thousand impulses.

But scarcely had she gone back in (as I learned from her later)
than, addressing Madame R——— or the latter's aunt, she said, half
as a question, whether the ladies had not seen me often during the
long year just past. And the aunt, quite innocently, replied not, "Yes
often," as Madame R——— would have, but instead, "Oh, my God,
yes, every day." That fatal sentence said everything.

The next day the consultation with the doctors took place. The
celebrated Dr. Corvisart was to be among them. I went early, somewhat timidly, to confront the faces of the night before. I found
Madame de Couaën composed and circumspect. The Marquis was
cordial. I drew him aside when I came in and expressed my excuses

for my conduct the night before quite frankly, but much less urgently than my shame made me feel. It seemed cowardly and cruel to me to have caught that noble rage off guard, to have pitilessly made him return to it, and not to have respected a depth of inviolate sorrow in its vehement rambling. Monsieur de Couaën stopped me short before I had finished, "Amaury," he said, "fight me, refute me to extinction, so long as you love us!"—And I did love him, as I experienced then and more and more subsequently. I loved him with a friendship all the more deep and bonded for our natures and ages being less akin. When he was absent, this forceful man always had a large part of me. I left for him in the bottom of the heart a bleeding part of my self, like Milon leaving his limbs in an oak tree. And thus I carried away the bursts of his heart in my own flesh.

However, if I am to believe a few remarks made by Madame de Couaën during the following week and even a few direct indications which I noted, sometime by the occasionally more brusque tones of the Marquis, a kind of impatience when I was present, which was revealed in two or three minor incidents, the effect of that unfortunate discussion was not so soon erased. That vehement spirit conceived and kept umbrage of some sort. It was a strange thing! When I had confided in a rather open letter to him the peril and scruples of my soul, he had not believed it, at least he had not been scandalized. And so here it happens that after a long absence, after entirely too-evident neglect and unfaithful affection on my part, through an accidental political contradiction, he developed suddenly a jealous streak, as if, in this type of pride, watchfulness in the tenderest feelings could arise only when a shock was administered to the proudest feelings. What is special in this was that the proud, shocked side had manifested no emotion, had kept no trace of rancor, and that everything had gone to engage and do injury at the heart of a dissimilar idea. But on the other hand, perhaps that was on his part only the result of rapid stock-taking and that he told himself that indifferent and disoriented as I was in politics, I must have been changed and shaken in other more secret feelings.

Whatever the cause, you will admire, my friend, the inextricable consequences of my faults. For me, one more concern was to be linked to these friends crushed in their exile. I found a way at the last moment to embitter the dark mourning of one, to darken the angelic resignation of the other, to place more stones on the path of their bruised and weary feet.

The same morning I paid a call on Mademoiselle de Liniers without finding her home. There are days when all is in suspense, and destiny silently accumulates its weapons. I saw Madame R——— only as briefly as possible. In the evening I returned to the convent to learn the doctors' decision. The Marquis, more reassured, gave me the principal points, which appeared to me to indicate that a heart ailment was likely. He did not leave me alone with Madame de Couaën the entire evening. I felt extreme foreboding. I saw myself seated among three people suddenly brought close without understanding one another. Not a one of them made an inviting gesture, yet they held me with a strong, narrow bond. I was going, I was trembling from one to another in inexpressible solitude, like a straw at the mercy of the wind, like a magnetized needle feverishly hesitating among three different poles in a triangle around it, like large hailstones that endlessly attract and repel opposing clouds. Fruitless goings and comings, exhaustively febrile in the dull intervals—that is all too true of the story of my life in my most productive years.

In the circles of Hell, not far from the region of the tepid, or perhaps at the bottom of the ramps of Purgatory, there is a plain that is not described, the only spot that Dante and his divine guide did not visit. Three ivory towers rise at diverse extremities of that plain, generally beautiful and lighted on their crests from afar, but separated by ravines, swamps, barely breachable torrents, and each a day and a half's march from the others. A penitent pilgrim walks among them. But he arrives always at the foot of one tower after the sun has set and the gates closed. He leaves again, sweating and breathless, towards one of the other towers, but forgetting the time, alas, when he pauses in the mud and marshes to alleviate his fatigue, and arrives the day after only when the sun has set. And he leaves again until he reaches the third. But it, too, has just closed, and he begins again. That is the punishment, dear friend, for those like me who have used up their youth and not expiated their loss.

The next day (for I must keep you panting upon my tracks), frantic for some explanation and some wind that would direct my uncertainty, towards one o'clock, hoping to find her alone, I went to see Madame de Couaën. A carriage in front of the outer door bothered me from the first. They could not tell me the name of the visitor. I went in. Mademoiselle de Liniers was seated beside her new friend on a low chair. She had taken off her hat. It looked as if they had been exchanging confidences. Madeleine and Lucy standing at the other window made a gentle contrast with the maternal duo, absorbed as they were in some game, their curls intertwined. Poor children! If only they might forever be unaware of how painful and sublime it sometimes is when two women are taken with each other. Mademoi-

selle Amélie, of a whiter, snowier complexion than those last days at
Gastine, did not blush when she saw me. She was prepared for it,
completely out of consideration for Madame de Couaën. She received
nothing from the shadow of that face, finally known, which she
seemed to serve and adore. The latter, who did not know the purest
and most hidden part of the sacrifice, acted with noble Amélie as if
by compassionate divination, which immediately reveals kinship to
beautiful, fully tried souls. Their discussion was simple, sparse, easy
to foresee; it was a melody where veiled sentiments sighed. I spoke
little, I was moved, but not ill at ease. In that new pose they appeared
to me without contradiction, without tearing my eyes between their
two hearts. Suddenly there was a knock on the door: Madame
R———— came in. I realized that something was taking place at that
moment, unknotting my life, that a conjunction of stars was operating
above my head, that it was not in vain, dear Lord, that at that hour,
in this withdrawn place, three creatures who had failed to meet before,
who, no doubt, would never meet again, closed their circle around
me. What a change was introduced with the arrival of Madame
R————! Oh! what people said continued to be very simple and
apparently affectionate. But all these vibrations came to me. It was
clear to me that the two first sister-souls backed off with the shivering
of a wounded dove as soon as the third one arrived, that the third felt
the unease also and with trembling, although she was slightly aggressive. It seemed to me that the pious union of a concord drafted gave
way to discord, a painful riddling, and that we began, the four of us,
to gasp and bleed. That is what I grasped. For someone who knew
nothing, there was no difference in facial expressions and the tone
would not have been apparent. The Marquis soon came in. Mademoiselle de Liniers rose and left after a few minutes. And it was done:
something in these destinies brought together for an instant was
broken and cut open, henceforth not to be found together again. I did
not know what it would be. I discerned nothing of the conclusion,
although I firmly believed in it.

The results, to be sure, do not happen outside us, dear God, but
by the action of single external movements, by the operation of certain
lines that fatally cross, tie, and unknot; there is no more enlacing
magic, the magicians have stopped, and man, whom your Christ
delivered, intervenes. But the movements from outside that your
finger traces serve to bring about genuine results, living results, which
are born in us with the common efforts of your Grace and our desire.
Your Grace and our desire prepare, provoke, and hasten the results,
often expressing them in advance and giving them meaning. You

sometimes offer us, Lord, when you deign to do so, the intention and the canvas designed on the loom, as if to the weaver's apprentice. We have to put in a hand to finish it. Our will must say *yes* or *no* to your formidable proposition. Or else our mute indifference is already a morbid way to bring an end to it all. I was certainly slow to understand and act in the present time. However, eventually I understood. But at least starting from that first moment, the celestial canvas, the supreme design, the enigma of that emblematic encounter among four destinies remained suspended in my eyes night and day, like an object of fatigue and torment, until I read the luminous sense.

At the thickest part of the human forest, by divers parts and amid brambles that conceal the entire horizon, three rivals had arrived at the same point at the same time, three white faces preferred in turn. There I was also, unrehearsed, in the midst of it all. One had smiled repeatedly, one had spoken gently and casually without showing astonishment. But through that tranquil speech, a solemn change took place in the environment. The paths, which just a short while ago had been invisible, had gradually become like a crossroads of four dark roads. The three women greeted each other and each took one of these roads. And there remained only the most rugged and wild, where no one went. Was this one mine or was I to follow a different one? This image of my new situation became sharp in my eyes first of all. The desolate crossroads in the forest made me a fearful desert. Coming back down from my vision of Isaiah, I spread gloom even to the most lighthearted creature. 'Madeleine, Lucy," I said to myself, poor children who played together once like two sisters, will you ever see each other again?''

The Marquis' residence permit was drawing to its close. He showed no interest in extending it. I saw both of them, that whole week, often both morning and evening, but in our residual intimacy some kind of dull impediment had come into being. One day the Marquis had left me chatting with Madame de Couaën. When he returned a half-hour later, he found me still there, and in a tone of voice which seemed different to me he blurted out, "You're still here!" As for her, in those moments we were alone, she resumed her heartbroken, resigned manner, with accents of ingenuous trust. "Have you really changed with us?" she repeatedly asked. "Is it really true that someone has taken our place? What? every day for an entire year?" And she quoted Madame R———'s aunt. Her recrimination against the woman who claimed to be her friend was limited to "It is not nice on her part, for I knew you first." Alas, she did not know that another, that very girl of the recent mornings, had known me still earlier. I had time before the departure to have Madame de Couaën read a new work that had deeply moved me by its striking report of situations and sufferings of our own kind. It was the story of Gustave de Linar and Valérie. The more written works faithfully retrace a real event, an isolated case in life, the more they are likely by that very fact to resemble a thousand other nearly identical facts that human existence conceals. Madame de Couaën read it and was extremely touched by Gustave and Valérie, on the Count's noble character, on little Adolphe who died in the cradle, on so many secret resemblances. I tried to make her understand that led astray by passion like Gustave, I had sought only a Bianca close by her; that it was a liaison of a rather fragile bond in which I wanted to numb myself; and that besides, no irreparable infidelity was consummated yet. She listened to me but without being open to my obscure arguments and conceiving no other fidelity but the infidelity of the heart. Nevertheless, she was grateful to the gesture I was making to repair the breech. And then she would almost immediately reproach herself, with a backward glance after the mortal blow, which had, she said, punished and warned her.

The day of her departure, she entrusted to me a note of farewell and apology for Mademoiselle de Liniers, as she had not been able to call on her. She said she would send me a keepsake as soon as she got home. The Marquis spoke to me of spending a few weeks with them the following spring. But this second departure, although more decisive and heartrending than the first, left less of an impression on me. Our soul is only virginal once—for sorrow as for pleasure.

On the following afternoon, I went to see Mademoiselle de Liniers, but she was not home. I left the letter for her, but not only that letter. After many a struggle and many a draft, I had enclosed a note of my own in words to this effect: "The person I saw after two years so indulgent and admirable, will she remember that at the preceding farewell, this term of two years had been cast into the future like a limit where one could hope to see each other again? Oh, I have not forgotten either. But I would have to confess, covering my face, that during this space, the heart which ought to have pushed unremittingly to that goal did not know where to turn. How many weaknesses, errant desires, new duties, originating in misdeed and incompatible among themselves, abysses that innocence cannot even suspect, have turned my life into a whirlwind, a conflict, an almost perpetual reversal. How my own trouble has troubled me and offended several people in my midst. How at the present moment I have more to repair than I possibly can. How any regulated happiness has become impossible, inconceivable for me. How I would offer, besides, only a collection of regrets, imperfections, and defeats to a woman who could not possess too much unique affection and chaste sovereignty. Oh how I wish that she pardon me, forget me! that she at least let me believe her suffering on my account is that which time will cure, and that she not despise me, however, as an ungrateful wretch! An invisible thought, a silent witness will always follow her from afar in life and will seize each of her movements with apprehension. In my nights a prayer, every time I pray, will rise for her. 'My God,' I will cry, 'grant that she be happy, grant that she not mourn me. Let the wound I have caused serve only as a seedbed for your wisdom and love! Grant that she obtain a little later all the lot here below, which, without my fault, she would have a claim to. Grant that she still believe in happiness on this earth and trust in that!' —This is what I shall tell Heaven for that injured noble soul. And if my life becomes composed and pure, if I succeed in repairing some of the damage around me, in all the good I shall ever do, grant that she know it! If she remembers me to God, that will mean so much." I left this letter and did not return again. I had no answer and did not expect one. Once, during the following week, I met or thought I met Madamoiselle Amélie. It was at dusk. I was crossing through a group of trees in the Tuileries, pondering, brow bent to morbid thoughts amidst the black trunks and bare leaves. Several women were coming from the opposite direction and crossed my path. They had passed before I had the time to recognize them and bow. Was it really she? did she recognize me? did she see me turn around, greet her too late? Thus end so many human attachments, including the dearest: moving apart, into the shadows, with the uncertainty of the last farewell.—I did not see her again after that evening, my friend, but we shall speak of her again.

Four days after Madame de Couaën's departure, the courier who had served her came to my place with a little package she had entrusted to him. I trembled as I opened it: it was a medallion of her mother, containing a lock of black hair. I realized it was Arthur's. The courier I questioned was expansive with tales of this sweet angel. She had not seemed to suffer too much during the trip. No letter, however; just relics of her mother and her child, of the saint and the innocent, taken away, what she had that was the most eternal and wept over, was not that gift from her a secret, wordless language, inexhaustible, permissible, the only faithful language?

CHAPTER XIX

Once again I was alone with Madame R———. The nature of my affection for her was no longer what it had been before that double confrontation. All flattering dissimulation had vanished. She, however, seemed little changed and had become once more rather tender and quiet, encouraging in her demeanor, except for slightly more frequent lapses into suspicion and sadness. My express intention was to conduct our liaison circumspectly until she herself gradually let go. I wanted only to avoid striking her too soon; her existence was already precarious, and experience had taught her to withstand injury. I was therefore preparing to be free in this quarter in the near future. The two great sacrifices represented by the keepsakes I had beneath my eyes made me feel duty bound. Before God and before myself I needed to take that first step towards a reparation.

But in this kind of commitment, plans for ending in a friendly fashion, along an imperceptible decline, offer a final prospect no less illusory than the gleams from the summit at the beginning. You vainly trace a graduated course of compassion and prudence; there will still be convulsive shocks to endure. There is only one way to loosen bonds: break them. Since I saw Madame R——— almost every day, my intention soon vacillated in its details. Vanity conspires with the senses. The facade of love I once thought I felt for her had disappeared. But at times, when she was very close to me—an enfeebled, faintly fragrant flower—I still desired her. Self-esteem especially whispered that I had certainly gone to too much trouble, kept watch too many nights for such meager results. By being near her, I had wanted to distract myself from my purest passion and my most impure pleasures, to assemble in a single choice liaison just enough soul and sense, just enough delicacy and vice. But what had I obtained in return? Would I never have in my possession anything but blurred female faces, never a woman sufficiently loving and beloved, a woman who was a name for me and could murmur mine! This last thought was a bitter goad that always made me rear and kick. At the time spring was budding. The air was already fragrant; the earth, already festive. Perilous springtime, what did you have against me during those splendid years, returning so beautiful—and so often? My disposition was like all sensual dispositions whose will is not grounded in a higher order. For a long time I was at the mercy of every current of wind, every phase of the moon, every passing cloud (even when I was shut up by myself and did not see them), every burning ray of the sun. Even today the secret shading of my soul rests on such things. On those first warm days in Paris, which was then populated by bedazzled youth and soldiers of every division of arms, women were like birds on the wing. They preened in clothing of a thousand hues from early morning onwards. They made the boulevards and the walkways look like cloisonné. And in the evening at nightfall, in the faubourg streets, young women of the people, women in the shops, sat in their doorways bareheaded and bare-armed, fluttering giddy and wild at the sight of plumes and helmets, as if they were getting ready to celebrate some holiday of the Good Goddess Nature. In the soft mist, which veiled every one of them in a sparkling luster, they were all beautiful. If those days had lasted, not a single creature would have been saved because the world is saved, according to one of our saints, only because modesty was granted to women.

Such spectacles, on which I repeatedly feasted my eyes, brought back to me an exalted feeling of physical triumph, of material and physical action, an ideal view of the life that three-quarters of the illustrious heroes and subalterns lived at that time: parades, combats, and cavalcades. To sweat on the Champs-de-Mars, get drunk on trumpets and flares, to conquer worlds and women, to glitter and roar, spilling blood in skirmishes, but also sowing your spirit along the way, with no thought of living to thirty-six. This life of lather and boiling blood, which is the frenzy of our first youth, became again for me during those brief canicular hours the only life worth leading. That other life, dark and mortifying, in which the things of God and the soul are glimpsed from here below, even though I might have aspired to it an instant earlier, was no more perceptible to me than Venus, the shepherd's star, in the noonday sky. When emerging from a moral crisis, a sorrowful lapse or loss, there are two roads available to a man: collapse and sensual diversion to a point past satiation; or purification, widowhood, beneath the soul's sober, constant watch. At such times I gave in to the body, lost in the common, mechanical finality. I would enter Madame R———'s house in midday, after letting myself be blinded by the sun and quenching my thirst in the martial fanfares at the Carrousel, after sating my hunger with the coarse bread beyond the dark paying portals (*homini fornicario omnis panis dulcis:* "all bread is sweet to a fornicator," as the Sage says in the Apocrypha). I would begin to extol that glorious life of action she had seen me reject up till then, although she had occasionally advised it. I engaged in alternatively bold and tender moves she did not know what to make of, unprepared as she was for such abrupt interventions in her morning mood. That was when my last attack would begin, contemptible, implacable, without fervor and without excuse, inspired by the most sordid sentiments.

The numerous slights of guile, animosity, and possessiveness that she had made me swallow would most conveniently come to mind at such moments and would gradually squelch all my pity. She had not shown pity for anyone else, I would say to myself. I acted like a wild boar that rolls in prickly thickets to arouse its own rage. There had always been a part of her past unknown and unconfessed, something in her former life, which she kept from me, impenetrable. In the other two women I loved, I had experienced nothing like that. The first, Mademoiselle Amélie, had offered me from the beginning only the first simple spurts of a brook I could channel with a glance through the prairies at the foot of familiar hedges. The second, whom I met later, Madame de Couaën, had an earlier, missing portion beyond the seas through which her sweet gentleness had reached us, but she herself had told me many a time about that childhood life of filial love with its first storm. I felt as if I had been there with her because those pictures had been painted in my memory and relived in the same order. I could have sketched the flow of the Curragh river where her fresh life had bathed. But here with Madame R——— no stream of a charming and easy destiny that could be conjured up at will, reconstructed in the imagination through shared anecdotes. No distant groves, no river banks always named to become ours as well. Once a rather near boundary was reached, there was a deaf, stubborn closure as if by prudence, discretion without any exception and without any air of mystery. As for me, I have, on the contrary, always so much enjoyed going upstream, querying at their origins the very lives I have crossed only at a single point, so that I could recognize in the most humble destinies the birth, the first flowing bounded by the little valleys and dark depths, at the threshold of a thatched cottage, in all their special interaction with their surroundings. The more such destinies are simple, natural, and domestic, the more they appeal to me, the more they interest and amaze me. The more I become beholden to God—like seeing a lily in the field.

And from the disposition of Madame R———, which should have engendered only feelings of compassion—or at most a need to distance myself from her mute, closed life, my mind was never more than one step away from harsh irritation. The stubborn and increasing defense she opposed to my assaults by removing all intoxication from my heat of passion, only encouraged my calculated violence. As frail and broken as she might appear to be, she had a great strength of resistance in her reticence. She was not a woman whom involuntary distress overcomes at a given moment, and upon whom the impure gods of Mount Ida voluntarily lower a cloud. Her presence of mind, her virtue, keeping watch in the most extreme peril—yes, her virtue, I must concede it, a virtue generally less rarely encountered than complacent seducers would have us believe, a virtue that would not be suspected initially, in view of the lighthearted beginnings, a virtue that society gives little credence to and which it has often calumniated before the woman has even surrendered. In this sorry struggle, moreover, each effort made me increasingly disenchanted. I plucked, I tore, with bleeding nails so to speak, this elusive and rebellious stalk which has no value for the sensual man unless it trembles and bends by itself, showering blossoms and shedding leaves. I felt my criminal pleasure being destroyed and degraded in advance, and that rage propelled me to new attacks. Gentle, sensitive, courageous woman, have you forgiven me?

The wrath of the sensual and weak man has its form of access, its very special spitefulness. Wrath is not an attribute of the proud and powerful alone, although most often it stems from offended pride. In such cases it broods, grows more gloomy in absence. It ulcerates, hollowing a burning pit of hatred. But very tender souls are inclined to wrath also since such persons are very sensitive, very susceptible to pain, vulnerable to the smallest slights. The substance of the soul in this case is like flesh that is too palpitating and delicate, swelling and reddening as soon as a nettle pricks it. Among sensitive souls, tender rather than gentle, many are irritable in this way. I was subject to such wrath all the time. But when tender souls are debased by pleasure, a pleasure which leaves them discontent and bruised, they suddenly acquire a deep hardening, compatible with this irritability, leaving them even more open to their wretched wrath. If they are not to become harsh and cruel, they must keep themselves under strict surveillance. And if their rage is aroused, it is acute, fretful, convulsive, devoid of dignity, quick to attack, refined in outrages, bursting with gall, like the fit of a weak creature, like all people who abruptly reverse their natural bent. The author of Ecclesiastes says "all malice is but little to the woman's malice." Generally speaking, there is no wrath more instantaneously cruel and pitiless than that of tender dispositions. Madame R——— often became the occasion and object of those hideous outbursts.

The detours of the heart are so strange, the mixture of virtues and flaws so inextricable that there are women who are more afraid of appearing to abuse a suitor than to do so in reality. At times Madame R——— was like that, almost glorying in the misconduct that the people around her supposed was consummated, displaying in public countless familiar gestures and signs of the ultimate concession, while in private her virtue erected the greatest obstacles. Then, at other times, returning to a more natural and decent coquetry, she wanted to appear insensitive, almost indifferent to me, insinuating that I was an infatuated admirer for whom she had only friendship and that I was in despair but was unable to get over it. This came to me from two or three sources at the same time. At this insult, I ran straight to her house, and as I rushed through the streets, I even cursed aloud. I became aware of it from the astonishment of passers-by who turned their heads away as if meeting a madman.

My friend, until we have for good the same transports of the heart and the same speed of foot that we have in evil, until the first news of a unknown suffering brother, an affliction to visit, a burden to lighten sends us running through the streets murmuring along the way our projects of love, overflowing with words of mercy so that the passersby turn their heads away and consider us mad, we will not be men by the sublime folly of the Cross, converts of Christ the Lord.

One morning having arrived suddenly at her house, more bent upon vengeance, I imagine, or simply with my brain more or less calcified by the sun, after a few jocular preliminaries, I began listing my grievances in staccato, bristling propositions, suspect outbursts of that grim gaiety which hurts those who love us. But soon I passed all bounds, and as she redoubled her defense and reserve, I no longer contained my brutal egotism. To some incredulous response from her, I dared to declare crudely why and for what reason I had loved her, what my attentions and hopes had been; that I was mortally angry with her for having disappointed me, for increasing my pathology while denying me the remedy; how much I hated her for what I suffered physically when I was close to her. Then I talked about the sorts of loves and infamous pleasures she reduced me to, but said I knew how to force her or leave her and make her repent. I said all that in dry, hissing, sharply articulated speech, punctuated by striking her most beautiful and beloved pot of hortensias. Each blow I struck loosed a shower of petals. She stood listening, arms crossed, pale, almost violet, silent, in a long gray morning smock. But infuriated by her impassive silence, intoxicated by the sound of my own rage, I moved closer. I stretched out my hand and dug furiously into her hair, which was loosely knotted at the nape. I held her head back in this strained position, spitting my invective slowly in her face. This frail reed did not bend; it did not even stir. She stood tall, absolutely still, smiling contemptuously at the pain and insult like an enslaved priestess whom the conqueror cannot drag over to him. In the end, exhausted and ashamed, I dropped my hand. Her hair fell over her face and shoulders. The shell comb I had broken fell to the floor in pieces. Only then did she look heavenward and with a tear on her cheeks break the silence. "Amaury, can it really be you who is treating me this way?" These atrocious scenes were quickly followed, as you can well imagine, by others. I would fall prostrate at her feet, and with many a sigh, make every appeal for her forgiveness. A faint, tender blush enlivened her complexion. Her head, which she had held up stiffly, leaned weary and slack against the cushions I put out for her. Her forehead misted warm with perspiration. What she would have needed, it was plain to see, was reassurance and conviction, and I would say to her with my tear-filled eyes fixed on hers, "Is the love of two creatures in this world nothing more than the privilege of causing each other the most pain?" But these pompous words were still lies: between the two of us it was worse and less than earthly struggles of love. These scenes were not even the flitting fires of her venom and the affray of her jealousy.

On other calmer days and when I could somewhat resume my original plan of gently disentangling myself, when I was sitting next to her in intimate conversation, I would often interrupt myself to say, "Whatever happens to me, whether I still keep on seeing you or stop altogether and never return, please believe in my affection for you, unchanging and true, my eternal esteem." This word "esteem," which was not my exact thought, would make her thank me warmly and weep with gratitude. But all these repeated emotions left ineffable marks on her. Before my excesses, she would not admit the idea of parting, when I would casually broach it. From this point on, she obviously began to fear it, to believe it actually possible, and even on occasion to desire it.

My friend, do not conclude that I am going too far in my confession, that I intentionally sully the picture to remove the first attraction and render the entire episode more odious than necessary. My friend, what I dare tell you, has it not happened to many others also? Have I not, on the contrary, remained on this side of a great number of wretched acts which are concealed? Is this not the way so many of these most disappointing sophisticated liaisons are usually torn apart? even among the most envied classes? You see balls where a self-indulgent couple glides, loge balconies where they lean with an air of loving accord, gestures of infatuation, arch smiles which the world can see, or in the woods on strolls and morning hunts—all on the graceful ascent of that hill. Adolescents pass at the foot of such terraces resounding with harmonious laughter; they meet those mad cavalcades when they stop for a moment and scatter on the green carpets at the shaded borders of a clearing. Then these adolescents return home through the meadows completely consumed with such spectacles and write in the novel of their own desires an endless fabric of happiness and charm. But we do not know about the knots and crises in these apparent games of love. But we do not see these women, apparently obeyed in all respects—often the very same evening—in tears, pale and noble beneath insult, struggling against wandering hands. How many jealous swords are pulled out, threatening and bullying in a nocturnal surprise to make a faithful mouth lie, to subjugate a half-nude breast! How many of the most tender and beautiful brows have been dragged by the silk of their hair on a parquet or soft carpet, and dare not utter a cry! How many are wounded by withering names, by words that gnaw through a lifetime! How many wake up from defeat, rejected coldly by polite egotism, more insulting and cruel than rage! Society prides itself in this kind of crime to observe at least the forms of delicacy. There are those, they say, who would as cheerfully leave their name at the homes of these immolated women as they would after a ball or a formal dinner. Society particularly boasts that among some of the well-bred, quarreling is decently conducted and parting permits no outrage. Society lies. Impure cunning has its gross tricks which betray it in the end. The slime in human hearts rises and muddies everything in these final struggles, in these shocks where factitious passions are despoiled and made to confess. The egotism of the sensual nature produces itself hideously, whether it boils in the foam of rage, or whether it drips in slow and icy dregs. At the turn of the smiling slopes, you reach the depths of swamp or quicksand.

You recognize, my friend, the truth of these bitter observations. You yourself, alas, no doubt, are party to them, you could furnish examples as well as I. Oh, at least, if as it sometimes seemed to me I detected in certain obscure expressions of yours, you have, besides this chaotic misconduct, some better, preferred attachment, if the heart of some rare creature, a heart moved by the spirit of love, has faltered, has hidden herself, has doubled her trembling or glowing because of you, oh my friend, do not be afraid of me, I shall try to fit my advice to your circumstances and without capitulating before God, show you the pathway back. I shall say to you, "First of all, make this beloved a haven against stray pleasures which coarsen, against worldly pursuits which disperse and desert. I am not one, as you know, who would block off any Beatrice from the approaching footsteps of a mortal pilgrim. But remember, my friend, never abuse the heart that is given to you, make this cult of a chosen creature into a translucent and more tangible form of divine Love. If some Good Friday evening, in a church, at the grill of the adored Tomb, you find that chance has put the two of you kneeling within view of the other; if, after the first glance exchanged, you can abstain from any further glance out of pious respect for the dreaded Sepulcher, oh, how you will feel then that you have never loved more fully than in such sublime moments! Are there real obstacles between you, my friend? Accept them, bless them, love absence! Make your thoughts of God your habitual rendezvous; that is the natural milieu for souls. Communicate forever in the same spirit of grace, each beneath a wing of the same Angel. If she has already died, intercede for her, and at the same time beseech her to intercede for you. Here is the prayer: 'Dear God, if she needs succor, let me be the succor. If she no longer needs succor, let her be mine!' Consider through your love for her, all human female creatures as her sisters; this gives you so many different ways to love them as pure children of God. When you fall back into evil ways, think on this, that she will learn of it sooner or later, that she will have to repent on your behalf, and that the spirit of grace will be made contrite in her. The pain and shame you feel from this will make you return more quickly from your faithless conduct. All ways are good and justified, I trust, that bring sheep back to the valley of the Good Shepherd. Thus, my friend, to the task—and courage! If you truly love, if you truly are loved, whether or not you have fallen into this mutual ruin so dear to lovers, raise yourself from the very fact of love. Repair, repair! Carry with time your human affection, kindled still, into the years eternal, do not let it be sullied like our bodily organs and get burdened down with soil. Age will come for you. Your loving laugh will be less endearing; your brow will be more bare. Her hair will grow whiter; each year will leave its snow. Take refuge now in the site where nothing grows old! So live that no matter how heavy your limbs grow or how deformed your features get, time that weighs down both your bodies will, in the same rhythm, make your souls lighter. Old age, which comes after the delectable moments of our final youth are sacrificed, will find again, up to the end, the torrent of the invisible sap and will feel thrilling quivers as it approaches eternal springtime. Two people who have lived for each other with privation, disinterest or expiation, and have repented, can look at each other without fear, and despite unchanging wrinkles smile at each other, up to the cold onset of death, in tender adieu.

CHAPTER XX

Anger, it is said, is like a fast-moving grindstone. In an instant it can crush all the good wheat in our soul. In leaving these violent scenes with Madame R———, coming away alone, my brain feeling more crushed than if a heavy wheel had passed over it, I threw myself into all those stultifying acts that displace pain and substitute a new remorse. Thus, by an inevitable enchaining of this disorder, anger made me vulnerable to acts of lust, which by hardening my heart, increased its numb leaven of rage. It is said that the dissolute are compassionate, that those inclined to uncontrollable behavior appear ordinarily very sensitive and prone to weeping, but that souls that work to remain chaste lack such resources for tenderness. That in no way contradicts, my friend, what I contend about the hardening of the heart and the facility for violence which follows pleasure. St. Augustine compares these strange fruits of a softened stem to thorns on bushes with soft roots. St. Paul, as Bossuet has noted, puts on the same row and in the same camp men without benevolence, without chastity, the cruel, and the lustful. I will not speak here of sinful women and Samaritan women who often keep to one side secret fountains of tenderness and repentance. Pagan wisdom, expressing the same kinship between apparently contradictory vices, has Marcus Aurelius exclaim, "What lusts have brigands, parricides, and tyrants never tried!" This is because in the sensual man there is never but a semblance of compassion, a surface of tears. His eyes water easily before pleasure. They sparkle and glaze from a vague nitency. You would say he is going to love everything. But catch him on the way back, as soon as his desire is quenched, how he closes up! how he grows gloomy again! The brilliant surface of the thaw refreezes on the ice. While the chaste man is sociable, good at all times, of a loving, disinterested humor, of innocent glee that he exudes even when alone, and who talks happily with the birds in the sky, with the trembling leaves in the woods—the sensual man finds himself once more personal, bizarre like his desire, sometimes attractive and of a fascinating mobile sparkle and sometimes, as soon as he has succeeded, sullen, glum, furtive, hiding like Adam after his fall in the thickets of Paradise, but hiding alone and without Eve. This is because he has spent prodigally in the goal of rapacious pleasure dispersed in equal feelings on everything; he has spent once and to a bad end his treasure of happy joy and fraternal charity; he flees for fear of being convinced. Oh, during those days of abandonment on the precipice, who can tell the flights, the savage instincts, the fear of men, where the slave of delights falls? Who can tell, unless he has accidentally come across such a man, the sinister expression on his forehead and the harshness of his glance? Often, in the evening of these tarnished hours, wanting, however, to get my bearings, to rehabilitate myself in my own eyes by some conversation that would engage the spirit, I would set out towards a house where I had friends. Once at the door, I would propose to go to another, not daring to go up the steps of the first. I would go off, come back, go off, come back, twenty times without going in anywhere, without knowing where I was, stumbling on each threshold, so much is one's humor the most unsociable, so much does one's will vacillate.

Yet by dint of dispersion and recidivism, I had reached a deep feeling of exhaustion and arrest. There is a moment in us, more or less hastened by the use we make of our youth, a moment when on all points of our being an inner voice rises where a universal lament makes itself heard. This first "halt there" resounds in the realm of the spirit as well as in the domain of the senses. No system of ideas is presented which bears us away in its turbulence. The sole sight of a beautiful woman no longer distracts us from ourself. Starting with the day when this double delay begins inside us, our first youth is over. It pretends to stay on for some time, to still mount, but in reality it is decreasing and retracting. If we are wise even if we have not always been, this is the time to take the upper hand and grow stronger. The time of infatuations and anathema is over. Our greenness grows ripe. The coursers, reined in, grow peaceful. They are still vigorous, and one can still make them plow. But if we violate this first natural warning that Providence indicates, if we pass beyond and smother within the inner murmur of universal lassitude, we are preparing for the most desperate struggles, the most fatal falls, the most arid disorder. This melancholy and enfeebled feeling that I have told you I experienced other times when I came back in the evening, across vast squares, along quays white in the moonlight, I no longer found it after that, my friend. The beautiful iron bridge where I had passed noisy and triumphant in the afternoon, my feet ringing like Campaneus, saw me in the evening, my head hanging low, my feet dragging, with a soul as defeated and annihilated as Xerxes' when he recrossed the Hellespont. The serenity of the air, the scarf of vapor of the roaring river, the city in its pale azure mist, all that sidereal brilliance which sowed fields of infinity in my head, all was for me only a crushing phantasmagoria I could not decipher; my lusterless eyes saw in that legion of splendors only countless torches, sepulchral lanterns upon a stone vault.

Returned, however, to a sentiment of self by the excess of my nothingness, I meditated some great reform, a flight, a retreat far from that city of peril. I was tempted to go throw myself at the feet of some priest to get him to pull me out of my abasement. I felt that I could not attach the rein I needed myself. But in thinking it over, I see that at the time I felt more shame about my own degradation than I felt remorse before God. Because instead of going straight to Him in that state of humiliation, bathed in the sweat that He could have perfumed with a single drop of His grace, I said, "Let's wait until my youth has returned, my brow mopped dry with a reflowering of its gleam, to have something to offer God, to sacrifice to Him." But as soon as a little of that flower of youth seemed to have reappeared, I did not bear it to Him.

In the darkest of that inner rioting, three distinct beings always stood out. When I would return to my own rooms, near my stove, constructed as a bizarre altar, I would turn my back, ignoring my candle, press my forehead on the marble and remain for hours before going to bed in a state of a semi-wakefulness, contemplating a torrent of thoughts emanating from my self and with a monotonous flood gnawing and wearying my half-closed eyes. Gradually these three mysterious creatures appeared in my night, and here is how the most familiar vision took shape: I was alone in a crepuscular light, alone in a kind of deserted heath, in that forest crossroads I have mentioned before. The crossroads became bit by bit a known, real patch of heather, or at least one I vaguely remembered, like Couaën or La Gastine. Three women, all three growing paler, not holding hands, approached me. If I looked at one of them, she began to blush, and the other two grew still paler. If I advanced towards one, near enough to hide her view of the two others, the latter began to droop and die, and I was forced to pay attention to their lament. If I put myself in the middle without being closer to any one of them, even avoiding to look them in the eye, they all three grew paler together, making me grow pale with them and stop the flow of my own blood vein by vein as they fainted away together. A languid breeze then rose from the reeds and broom, weak, trembling, dry, having the chill and odor of death. It repeated in my befuddled ear a sound that could be, as one chose, Lucy, Herminie, Amélie. I could not tell which of these three names was hinted in the tenuousness of that sigh, and my malaise increased, and we all melted in drooping as if after an excessive fast or an enfeebling potion, when suddenly, my knees having given way on their own, the notion of praying entered my heart. Kneeling at the side of the most luminous white figure, you can guess which one, my friend, but looking to heaven this time, I would pray for all three, I asked that one would be cured, that another would forget, that the other would remember. And with fervor joining in, then it happened that I soon saw in the clearing of clouds a transfigured reflection of the three images, or rather the realities for which those images here below were only a shadow. The image towards which I had turned and whom I then looked at in the azure, advanced towards me and offered a greening branch, and the others, slowly retreating, seemed to smile at her and pardon her. And the little earthly breeze that sighed the three names became a symphony of angels but a single name, the softest of the three, the most celestial dominated, as if it has been sung in the spheres upon a thousand lyres! . . .

One morning, when I had gone to see Madame de Cursy, I read a letter from Blois, which had arrived that very instant. Madame de Couaën had put in a kind note for me at the end. Her entire letter expressed feelings of resignation and calm, of the happiness possible even in suffering. After those regards for me, she added, "Tell him, my good Aunt, you who know so well the sweetness that comes from voluntary acceptance, tell him what the pious heart gains in happiness by simplifying its life." Yes, I wanted to simplify my life, accept its recent ruins, reestablish its foundation on high and sacred grounds, where I could see the morning star at each awaking. When I returned home full of such thoughts, I found by coincidence a letter from my amiable and worldly friend who was writing from his estate where he had returned. Sudden catastrophes had overturned his passion, overly embellished until then. The north wind of misfortune was bringing those wings, so long aloft, back to God. He sent me news of Mademoiselle Amélie, who lived close by, whom he had recently seen and who had struck him by her redoubled abnegation and constancy. Madame de Greneuc had become more sickly, and Mademoiselle Amélie refused to leave her. After a few regrets on his own years, dissipated so far from duty, he added, "My friend, believe in the shipwreck of passion. Withdraw from those Sirens while there is time. There are periods of time, especially in the spring, in the first breezes in the forest when all the souls we have loved and hurt return to us. They return in the leaves, in the scents in the air, in the barks bleeding sap, the scars simulating half-written messages. They besiege us, they penetrate us. Our hearts are their prey on all points. Poor souls, you get your revenge. Oh, such bitter swarms, such stifling clouds! So many Didos fleeing silently through the myrtles! All my paths are peopled with shades!"

This outburst of painful advice, added to the sober, saintly message of Madame de Couaën, this precise convergence of two opinions coming from so far apart at the same time, struck me as an unequivocal sign. Merciful Lord, You were allowing this dear friend, who had been a deceptive model at certain moments of my fall, to be one of the instruments of my return, crediting him in your mercy with the beginning of the rectitude he effected in my heart! I had been to see Madame R——— the evening before. I resolved to have gone there for the last time. The next morning I wrote her not to be surprised if she did not see me, as an unforeseen matter would keep me completely occupied for the next few days. She replied with some anxiety as soon as she received my note. She sent someone to find out about my health and motive. I was courteous in my replies but elusive. I spoke in vague terms about a situation suddenly developing, of a likely trip to Brittany. She understood then. She wrote nothing further, and I did not see her again. If Monsieur R——— read my letters, he could have inferred from a few words I let slip that I had been overcome by a spell of religion and so explain my bizarre disappearance. Madame R——— went out little, and without an artificial goad, happily spent the entire day in her cozy boredom. I avoided her street, her quarter, the walkways where I knew she might occasionally sit. I never encountered her, no, not even at nightfall, in the uncertainty of the shadows. Later, two or three years later, I heard that Monsieur R——— had obtained a high post in the magistrate. Once, (I was already a priest), a gossipy person whom I had met at their house and who spoke to me in greeting as if I had never stopped seeing them every morning, after having asked me for news of them and being astonished by my ignorance, informed me that their relationship was reestablished and that she had had a son who gave her much joy.

When you meet, after many years, people you have lost sight of in the meantime and who had a father, mother, wife, cherished children, you hesitate to ask about them for fear of causing a sad response or a silence. And if you act oblivious, you often bump into tombs. But even when you know that these people have not died, you should hesitate after long absences to question friends about their friends. Because almost always these friendships that you knew in full bloom have had an opportunity to change and die. You stir up the ashes of a withered past; with a word you bring back grievances, faults, hatreds, everything slumbering in the ashes. You reopen tombs.

Thus I went about simplifying, pruning branch by branch the obstacles in my life. But was it enough to retrench the half-dead branches if I did not have the strength to grow new ones, which could bear excellent fruit?

In breaking with Madame R———, I broke with all the ephemeral attachments to a society I had cultivated only because of her. My first feeling, once my resolution was firm and my answers dispatched, was a suffusion of infinite deliverance, of burdens lifted. I went out for two entire days, walking in gardens through paths frequented or deserted, with renewed gaiety and a singular taste for all things, like a prisoner who finds again free space and the use of leisure time. There was mixed in my joy, I am sure, something suspect of vengeance carried out. But this first aimless vitality, this white foam of the soul which the instant of emptiness had made spurt out, soon evaporated, and I found myself, with my depths, in the presence of myself. The second phase was less sharp than the first. It was still calm, but calm without serenity, without a partly open sky, like the calm I experience when I write you about the sea that yesterday was agitated. The winds have fallen but the waves in their acquired momentum still struggle, heavy, clapping, rocking. It is a calm that is sticky and nauseating. I experienced that for some time after the spent passion for Madame R———; the released waves of my soul dashed against one another with a thud.

Oh divine Hand who alone can calm the waves, you were my resource when I was weighed down. I entered further in this restorative disposition where I had tried my strength so many times before. But it still was not without many alternatives and vicissitudes remaining. How should I describe them for you, my friend? More than a year from that moment would pass in an irregular succession of hail and sunshine, drought and bloom. The harvest I saw greening would fail to mature. Burgeoning grain, buds ready to open, cut off their stem in a single night! How many struggles before reaching that true springtime of the just on this earth, a springtime that itself is hardly more than a stormy and unpredictable March! I shall not detour you, my friend, in an infinity of alternatives. I shall list only the principal groupings. Promise me only that you will not tire too quickly of these poor oscillations of my soul. Remember your own. Take heart, seeing such weakness that did not perish.

I had occasion to meet at the little convent a respectable ecclesiastic, who without being a superior intellect, in no way lacked a staunch and pleasing mind. Above all, he was a man of practice and unction. The idea of the good to be done in active charity came principally from him. He had returned to France around 1805 and had known Abbé Carron, a product of Rennes like himself, quite well in England. He frequently discussed that edifying life with Madame de Cursy, who had likewise known Monsieur Carron in Rennes before the Revolution. The long stories that they both loved to relate about that saintly priest had a great influence upon me. The most direct remedy, the sole remedy for inveterate passions, is the love of men through Christ. Mercy and love redress the two contrary excesses, the sovereign cure of all pride and sensuality. Mercy or pardon or injury is pride conquered; love is sensuality redirected. The divine word Charity includes them both.

Abbé Carron, about whom I repeatedly questioned Madame de Cursy and the good ecclesiastic, was one of those marvelous natures whom God in his predilection has endowed with an instinctive gift of alms, prayer, and the nurture of souls. He was a flowering offshoot of that gentle family of Saint François de Salles, Saint Vincent de Paul, and the Bourdoises. He revealed in innocent laughter a great simplicity of doctrine and a childlike candor. Abbé Carron united a special sense of spirituality with extraordinary gifts which he humbly hid in his heart. However, here are two surprising stories he had been brought to tell for a fruitful end to the ecclesiastic who told them to me. One day in Rennes before the Revolution, as vicar of one of the parishes there, he was stopped on leaving church towards evening by a girl he did not know. She asked him to hear her confession. It was late. The church was going to close. He told her to come back the next day. "No, please," she replied, "who knows whether I'll still be willing tomorrow." So he heard her confession, and as a result pulled her away from the disorderly life several considerable men were dragging her into by finding her convent shelter from their reprisals. A few days later he was sought in the evening to administer the viaticum to a dying man, but he was to let himself be driven there without inquiring about either the name or place. The priest, armed with his God, obeyed. When he arrived at a rich-looking house, he was taken in without a word, through a series of apartments up to a room where a bed with closed curtains was indicated to him. Then he was left alone.

Only then he approached the bed and, partially opening the curtains, found a body stretched out lifeless, a weapon at his side. He thought he had been called too late and without trying to penetrate the mystery, he recited prayers for the dead while waiting until someone came to lead him back. Finally several persons came in, and he told them the situation. But at the sight the men were overcome. They fell stunned at his knees, confessing that it was his life they had wanted, that they were the seducers of the girl he had removed from their pleasures and that the dead man, full of life only moments before, had planned to strike him dead when he approached. Terrified by the divine sentence, they rushed to become Trappists.

Another day at the confessional, taken up with a penitent for whom he had few hopes, Abbé Carron, after making his exhortation, pushed the bar of the grill rather brusquely, thinking there was little to be done with such a painful and rebellious soul. But in opening the bar of the opposite grill he heard a voice speaking to him: "I do not come to confess but to tell you that whatever be the aridity and difficulty of a soul, you are not allowed to despair of it, nor does it give up its right of return to God." Abbé Carron had reported this himself to the good ecclesiastic.

The ecclesiastic had also learned this story, not from the Abbé himself, but from one of his most worthy penitents, formerly an officer in the Condé's army, Monsieur de Rumédon. When the latter was in Jersey and confessing for the first time to this holy man, he was suddenly seized during the final exhortation with an involuntary reverie. Abbé Carron then broke the threat of his exhortation to ask, "Why are you thinking such a thought?" and gave Rumédon the precise points of his distraction.

These marvelous stories, which I had them tell me over and over in all their details, and which combined in circumstances of untiring charity that art of alms, was Abbé Carron's own genius. They found in me a docile soul, happy to believe them. I considered it quite simple and legitimate that things like this happened with the beneficient natures whom nothing stopped in their flight to the good, neither dungeon walls nor distances. The furrow they trace is illumined beneath their steps, I said to myself, they already have the agility of an angel. The invisible finger writes mysterious letters in every life. But you need a certain celestial day, a certain degree of burning for the letters to become manifest. A miracle is only this unfathomable burst of letters, ordinarily dim. From my earlier philosophic excursions I had learned to recognize in the theosophist Saint-Martin, in the midst of a perpetual incense of love, mysterious relationships, communications from one mind to another, a view facilitated through the interstices and crevices of the visible world. All these bits of the beyond came back to me, letting me know that this was only a waiting period in the vestibule of that dwelling. I rose to the Christian meaning of things. *Nunc videmus per speculum in aenigmate:* now we see in a glass darkly.

By a singular coincidence I cannot omit here, the saintly Abbé Carron, whom I am discussing, and who, even absent, became one of my spiritual directors, I saw only once in my life, but I saw him in this very dead-end street of the Feuillantines, near the house where we talked over his good works. I think it was in 1815, shortly after the 100 days. One of his priest friends, little known then but illustrious since, was lodged with him: Abbé Lammenais. They stayed together until the older man died. Thus alms met doctrine; eloquence set fire to mercy.

There are men whom God has marked on the forehead, in the smile, on the eyelids with a sign, as if with a pleasing oil, whom He has invested with the gift of being loved. Something fragrant, of which they are unconscious, emanates from them and attracts. They come forward and immediately there is an aura of charm. Scholars with furrowed brows smile at the sound of their name and grant them long hours of talk in their sacrosanct studies. Misanthropes make an exception in their favor, and tell their bitter grievances, their hatred of men to them alone. Wayward girls love them and clutch their mantle after seeing them only once, begging them to return with hands in prayer. This attraction is already no longer that of evil; they seem to cry out: "Save me!" Honest women long for their company. The worldly and fickle are all indulgence for them and touched by a kind of respect. When such men enter new houses, children spontaneously run to their knees after a few minutes. The confidences of the wretched seek them out. Noble hands and friendships which do them honor come to them on every hand, along with offers of young hearts to be guided and requests for good advice. Oh, ill-fated is the servant burdened with these gifts, ill-fated if he makes use of them, I will not say to deceive, to charm and betray (the last an infamy), but if he makes use of them at random and for his own pleasures, if he does not make fruitful for the good of all, this talent for love, if he returns late to the palace of the Master, without bringing in his wake a long file of the praying and consoled!

This was how I represented these thoughts to myself after these conversations, when Abbé Carron appeared to me at the head of a flock of sick and poor; in the ardent vows I made following his trail from afar, my face watered by copious tears. The precious gift of tears had come back to me. I had certainly lost it, my friend, during that preceding year of dissipation, frivolous intrigues, stubborn pursuits, and wrangling. Such types of anxieties, a Saint has said, make the invaluable gift melt as easily as fire melts wax. But four or five days after the break with Madame R———, walking alone beneath an inner mist, somewhat abated, I suddenly felt as if a deep spring had broken loose and was churning in me. My eyes began to flow rivers of tears. The pure scenes of Couaën, my early days at la Gastine, when the blond bees would fly off at my approach to the orchard hedges; my childhood especially, my uncle's house, my window facing long roofs rusty with moss, and the visions in the azure, all that was virginal and docile in those days of mine was returned to me. I had the foretaste of what eternal youth can be, a soul's perpetual childhood in the Lord.

When I was thus content with my days, to which I mixed old readings with incomparable flowers of the deserts, I went more and more often to see Madame de Cursy, who took pleasure in seeing me so felicitously changed, although she never had known the depth of my oblivion. I followed my path, while reading, up and down the boxwood of her narrow garden, like Solomon as a child studying wisdom among the magnificent lilies of the valley. If she was writing to Blois, I begged her to bear witness to me, showing that I was simplifying my life. Her own conception of it was already a recompense. You will not begrudge me this movement of perceptible joy sanctifying itself to the fear of You, my God!

But I haven't spoken of the breezes and hailstones which still assailed me before I got there or which struck me during the best of my hopes. You cannot pacify with a single stroke what you have left untrammeled for so long. I had days without a link to the preceding, which put the entire future once more into question, those days that start off wrong in the morning and make you believe firmly in evil and the Tempter. I have rarely, my friend, taken things by the lugubrious side, by the side of Hell and Satan, by the creaks, rages, and flames. Rather it was the good, love, increasing attraction to the Father of us all, the modest trembling of the Chosen, the half-consoled sadness of penitence, it was that especially that I like to propose as an image and that I would like to imprint on the world. However, sin is not swept out of our bones. Ancient corruption still infects us, and if we think it is conquered, it makes us remember. You go to bed with the sun in a state of prayer; you have lived for weeks on honey and wheat prepared at their best. You have tasted these delightful states of mind which half-days of fasting bring. And yet here you are waking up in mad gaiety, burning thirst, uttering as if spontaneously blasphemous, impious words. Among the numerous demons, the old Fathers distinguish one they call the harbinger, because he runs in a sunbeam to tempt scarcely awakened souls, and he is the first to descend from the chariot of dawn. The pestilent words disturbing my breath came from him. Oh, let us stay pure forever, if we are! Let us never soil our imaginations or our lips! Because there are moments which the most secret soul mounts, where the pit of the abyss in us is forced open. Bridegroom, have care in your dreams not to let escape some shamefully dark words in the arms of your bride! In illness, if delirium overtakes us, let fear the escape of some debauched words which make our mothers and sisters blush and reveal to them our lairs of tenebrae. Oh, you who are pure, stay pure in heart, to be sure that only pure sounds, prayers learned earlier, verses of the Psalms mingling with holy oil, brush your lips in the death agony.

In those days my will lurched from morning on like a drunken woman. Insensate and depraved desires plowed through me. But other times, only towards noon when the early morning had passed rather well, when a vague ennui, disgust with my quarters, an errant need so well known to the hermits of the Thebaid that they called it the Demon of Midi, pushes you outside, fragile convert, already wearied. Smiling images of places, shady spots in our preferred hills and our Tempes stir our familiar phantoms. We recall the same hours we once spent in tender conversation. King David, a little past noon, went up to the marble terrace of his palace and saw Uriah's wife bathing on the terrace opposite. He was hit by that arrow which flies at midday and which must be feared, he cried in his penitence, as much as the ambushes of night: *a sagitta volante in die, ab insursu et daemone meridiano.*—You cannot keep still. Farewell study and the cell you thought you were making! If you were on the Syrian desert like Jerome, you would take a few steps and roll in the burning sand, you would roar like a lion thinking about the women in Rome! But Rome is all around us. You go into town, on the unshaded bridges, through the abandoned squares that a rain of fire is grilling. You wipe off the noonday sun, finding it still too tepid for the price of inner burning. We defy the sun to make us forget her, and we finally go back in, broken, sweat streaming, happy to be beyond all thought. And the return lasts only a moment. After a quarter's respite and nap, thick robust forms, violent Praetorian delights, forms you have scarcely glimpsed once, a year before, two years perhaps, and which either satiated us then or even displeased us, return with a sharp, arid savor. That is one of the misfortunes of having fallen before. It might seem

that once seen and rejected, these women would be forgotten, arousing
no love in us! An error! They leave their trace in the senses, bizarre
recalls that come back to life at long intervals. For a moment we want
to find everything again. Nothing is arrested. The failure of the first
impressions has already compromised our nascent feeling of chastity.
The rest is precipitated. You undo all your virtue at once. You take
pleasure in spoiling all your sources of happiness.

And what happens to the rest of that week cut in two by a torrent?
on which an avalanche descended? How on the following day do we
take up the book we were reading at the page where our pencil noted
some ascetic sentence, where the Sage of Ecclesiasticus told us to
attach the Lord's precepts like rings on our fingers in order to see them
always before us? where Saint François de Sales proposes chastity, the
lily of virtues and its white beauty? Such weeks end in a thousand
scattered serpents or barking dogs, like the belly of the Siren. When
you tell a little girl of five that she will hurt her teeth eating candy,
she'll answer, "Oh, I'm going to lose these teeth. I'll pay attention
when I have new teeth." We are all more or less like that child. At the
first backsliding, we push our defeat to the end. We wait for new days.
We set solemn delays for our return: Easter—Christmas—next week.
We sign a lease for our vices, and we renew the terms endlessly out of
consideration for the impure guest. We act like the unruly student
who befouls all the more the notebook he is completing because he is
promising to fill out the next notebook better.

But the Tempter did not always descend glorious or furious,
carrying away my soul on the chariot of the sun, bearing it into the
burning arena. He glided thus along more reserved tracks in the depths
of that valley of Bievre where I climbed book in hand, or above the
Vanvres, gentle, silent, beneath the cloud of my dreams. Let us learn
how to recognize and fear the least clouds.

There were other days where without preamble, cloud or ardor,
the Tempter surprised like a thief in waiting, like a hostile savage,
crouched on the ground, whom you take in the distance for a bit of
brush and who rears up to attack.

Yet again there were days when seizing adroitly hold of my
ingenous joy, which was born of a better conscience, he imperceptibly
scattered me, sent me a nosegay of violets to carry, to frolic and play
through the perils, like in the dew, and look nonchalantly or keenly
on everything as if I were on a balcony. But he let me return safe and
sound so that the next time I would think I was invulnerable.

Sometimes, he wore the cloak of the Good Shepherd and advised
me early in the morning to errands of friendship or alms. "This

demon," one of the Fathers says somewhere in Cassin," suggests honest and indispensable visits to brothers, to the sick, close by or distant. In order to get us outdoors, he knows how to indicate pious duties to carry out, that we must cultivate our family more, that this devout woman with neither family nor support needs to be visited and has a claim on our care, that it is a pious work to procure for her what she does not expect from anyone, if not from us; that this is worth more than remaining in our own cell, useless and idle for the Other." And he would even suggest to me in the morning visits to poor or respectable persons beyond distracting districts, which I would have to skirt.

Because in those days, my friend, I tried especially to cure my egoism of the senses by the spectacle of living misery, knowing that nothing runs more counter to the genie of sensuality than the spirit of alms. But how many times, at the strongest of the best resolutions, swearing to spare up to the last denier for a good Samaritan work, returning from some visit with my eyes still wet with tears and murmuring the name in memory of which I wanted to edify my life, how many times was it sufficient for a simple accident to overturn everything! And I fell again from the step thrice sainted of serving the poor, from that parvis of alabaster and porphyry where Jesus washed their feet, into the ignominy of pleasure. We are nothing without you, my Lord! Charity without the regular channel of piety is like a fountain in the sand which quickly dries up.

Yet what emotions comparable to those of pure charity once you have felt the refreshment, and against what other emotions ought we exchange them? Here is one of the naive joys that Abbé Carron had told the ecclesiastic, one of the joys that comprised a period in his life and which, transmitted, made one in mine. I always recall it when I want to imagine something of the assiduous felicity, delicate and disinterested like the Angels'. During the early years of his vicarate at Rennes, Monsieur Carron was called into a family which had fallen gradually from a former opulence into the direst distress. The resources at his disposal were modest and insufficient. His relations with the parish were still very guarded. In returning he was thinking of a way to some other more efficient benefactor to help. It was Holy Friday. The night before he had heard about an English Protestant recently established in the city. He decided to write to him, and once back home, did so, marking the principal circumstances of that family's distress, invoking the solemnity of a week so sacred to all Christians, without, however, identifying himself. A few days later, having returned to the family, he asked if anyone had come in the meantime. He was told no. He continued to visit from time to time and believed that his letter had had no effect. Nevertheless, he suffered a little from it and made some rather pained reflections on the incomplete character of charity of heretics. But one day, about a year later, he heard a new name pronounced in that family, he inquired and by questioning realized that it was his rich foreigner who had seen the justice of that appeal and had answered it that very day he had received it, Easter. But the poor people had not dared confess this surcease of help to Abbé Carron, fearing it would slacken his concern for them. Monsieur Carron's joy in learning that his appeal had succeeded was immense, the most transporting he ever had, he said. He came back with bounding heart, accusing himself of having doubted a brother, praying for his conversion to the complete truth, having more than ever faith in the final union of men.—If all marvelous stories about Abbé Carron seemed almost natural to me, this last one, so natural, seemed the most marvelous still. Weigh an atom of these luminous joys against those molded only with blood and mud!

In the last days of combat, at each reprise of darkening delights, I had a longlasting feeling of decadence and ruin. To shake off the painful impression, to deceive a little this precipitous flight from myself and my youth—in the plain of the environs, several leagues away—or by the veiled April sky, having in my face a slight gentle and ripening wind, or on those less warm and gentle days of a lingering autumn, immobile days, without ardor, without a breeze, when it seems that the brittle season dares not budge for fear of wakening winter, I spent the afternoon hours wandering across the wide spaces, emboldening myself in liberty and solitude, I tried to believe that I had never been more avid, more inexhaustible, for all the vows and infinity of love. I said to myself, striking my forehead like a young ram against the enervating breeze: "It is springtime, a new springtime approaching in me, and not winter!" And on other days where nothing was committed, experiencing to the core a deep appeasement, a sentiment of tranquility rather than ruin, instead of acquiescing and blessing, and recognizing with joy that the ferocious age was expiring, instead of being happy at that indifference, like that of Alipa, which would have let my spirit and heart reign, I was sorry for myself. I found myself less in the face of the universe, irritated, humiliated by all that dust of beings which flew in the clouds and which my first energy would have thought itself capable of inflaming. There were spots on my scalp where thinning hair was hardly growing back. There was, in my heart, empty spots where natural desires were drying like dead grass. I asked again for the smoke and inner darkening with the inextinguishable spark. I would have snatched the immortal brew from pagan gods and fabled lovers.

And then sometimes a morning, sometimes an evening, all would suddenly go back in order, just as everything had been overturned without a sure cause. The lily of virtue rose on its stalk, the savory and calming honey distilled its indescribable sweetness. After a happy fortnight, what lucidity! what peace! what facility of conquering! At the least suspect thought, my senses themselves shivered with fear; another excellent sign, a deep fright traversed my flesh. I believed at those moments in grace from on high, as previously I had believed in evil and the Tempter.

CHAPTER XXI

I am in calm seas; I approach the great bank. A little more effort, my soul! A little more indulgence, my friend! we are escaping from dark and hidden navigations.

My studies and my reading became increasingly Christian. But it was not dogmatic study, a logical or historical demonstration which I proposed for myself. Chiefly because I did not feel the need of it. Persuasion to Christianity was innate in me, like the milk of the first nursing. I had been unfaithful with the revolt of my juvenile exploration of philosophy. But subsequently it had been my life, rather than my spirit or my heart, that had stayed away. Every time I returned to healthy living, I spontaneously became Christian again. If I wanted to reason on some high question of origin or end, of human destiny, it was in that order of ideas that I naturally placed myself, it was that atmosphere of the Holy Mountain that I breathed like native air. From the moment that things invisible, prayer, existence and divine intervention resumed their meaning for me and gave me a sign, from the moment that they were not pure chimera of the imagination in a universe of chaos, Christianity at that point reappeared invincibly true. It is, indeed, the sole visible and consecrated side by which one can embrace things, adhere with a staunch faith, enter into a regular relationship with them (through ritual), and render homage at each step to their incomprehensible authority. Christianity is the human support of all divine communication. To love, to pray for those one loves, to do good on earth in the sight of the absent we mourn, in view of the cherished shades and their satisfaction on another plane, to say a more ardent *De profundis* for those one has once hated, to live in each thing according to the filial and fraternal spirit, to have also prompt indignation against evil, but without animosity for the sin, to believe in grace from on high and in our own freedom—that is

the intimate side of Christianity. In my readings, theological questions, when they came up, bothered me little. However, I applied
myself to study them and get them in my grasp. But apparent
contradictions, the excesses in human opinions mixed with pure
doctrine, did not disturb me. There was a natural separation in my
mind; a parting between the essential and unessential; the rust on the
bark got deposited by itself. The primitive fall, the dispersed tradition,
and the wait of the Just Men for the Messiah, the redemption by the
Son of Man, the perpetuity of transmission by the Church, faith in
the sacraments, these were points my spirit did not contest. The rest,
which could be cumbersome, was easily postponed, or still hovered,
to be viewed with simplicity, and only as required by the particular
case and effective practice. So I did not construct a system. Besides
the facts of science and secondary certainty, the truths of observation
and detail never struck me as incompatible with the higher givens. I
believed that things were much more reconcilable among themselves
than commonly supposed, and I was ready to admit each fact true
provisionally, even when the link with the ensemble was not readily
apparent to me. Mademoiselle de Montpensier———, a daughter of
kings, without being a great theologian, had a very cultivated mind
and a beautiful intellect. Somewhere she made the admirable remark
that after having thought a great deal on the happiness of life, after
have carefully read histories of all ages, examined the customs and
distinctiveness of all countries, the lives of great heroes, the most
accomplished heroines, and the wisest philosophers, discovered no
one in all that assemblage who had been perfectly happy; that those
who had not known Christianity sought it unconsciously, if they were
especially reasonable, and without knowing what they lacked, were
well aware that they lacked something. And those who on the contrary
having known it, she added, despised it and did not follow its precepts,
were unhappy in their persons or in their states. I myself hold, my
friend, rather similar conclusions. I noticed that all that is truly happy
or morally good in men and their acts is so in just proportion to the
quantity of Christianity therein. Examine carefully, for example, and
what seems perhaps to be a vague verity, in general terms, will become
penetrating in detail, if you look closely. This verification that I loved
to make vis-à-vis great men of the past, or, more directly yet, on my
contemporaries, and on those I observed at close range, in my mind
equaled many a laborious historical demonstration on Christian truth.
I took up passions, faculties, virtues one by one. What was the best
use and perfected state always brought me back to the Apostles. I

took, I still take sometimes, one by one, men I have known and, trying to avoid as best I can temerity or subtlety of judgment, I say:

"Elie has a noble disposition, a nature that is tender but still firm, open and easy in intelligence, raised effortlessly, at the least equal to all situations, generous and prodigal with grace. His manner is as enchanting as if he came from the race of kings. If he speaks, he is fluent. If he writes, his pen is golden. He is an obedient practicing Christian. And yet near him, in the long run, you feel a chill, a slippery surface interposed between his soul and you, frivolous, indifferent, contradictory judgments where it is a matter of inviolable rights and flagrant equity for the greater number. This is because he has his own competency, his plan of insinuating prudence. He is never disturbed; he concerns himself with long-range, secondary goals; or perhaps with him it is only an old habit caused by his long sojourn with the amiable Fathers of Turin. He is Christian, as I said. But any time you draw from the chord of his beautiful nature a sound somewhat out of tune or off pitch, you have touched a part of only mediocre Christianity.

"Hervé is a Christian, too. He has a thousand virtues. At an age when the heart begins to slow down, he has kept the warmth of soul and nonchalance of adolescence. He whom you would be ready to revere is the first to fall in your arms, soliciting fraternal friendships. But how does it happen that in knowing him better, loving him more and more, something in him still troubles you and at times obscures the overall good impression, like a stubborn wind that scorches your lips in the minds of a green countryside? It is because his impetuousness in his ideas is extreme. He rushes in with an ardor that you first admire but which soon wearies you, burning and altering. It is his only flaw. The perfect Christian would not go overboard. The perfect Christian is calmer than that, especially in what he thinks. He is more guarded about his own concepts and his discovery of the evening before concerning the regeneration of men. He is more reassured on the independent and perpetual ways of Providence. He reserves almost all his fever of anxiety for the charitable works of each day.

"And the other, Maurice, likewise so good, so poor all the time, so disinterested, he believes in an idea superior to himself, he devotes himself to it as if to a thing outside himself. He invites you first of all to devote yourself to it also, and he forgets that he is the author of this idea he undoes every morning, remakes, and repairs. If he lived a little less in that confused and turbulent plenitude that repulses you, would he be more self-aware, if not more Christian?

"And suppose they thought more about being more Christian,

would we see one with his true dignity of character, that vain and
infatuated stiffness; that other with his integral and amiable qualities,
that somewhat egoistical pettiness which crumbles and cavils, which
retrenches at the least excuse; the last with the generous heart, that
dishonoring proposition which chases away any divine thought? With
each fault, great or small, but real, that a friend lets you perceive, you
can say: if he did not have this flaw, would he be more Christian?

"And if in thinking about one or the other of your Christian
friends, you are tempted to day, 'But he is too lax and too benign in
his character, too credulous, too much the simple lamb with other
men. I have found his real flaw: he is too Christian.'

"Have no illusions. Reform your concept of this slight failing, his
excessive simplicity, strengthen his character, sharpen his discernment,
occasionally illuminate this docile Timothy's eyelids with a spark of
victory. Grant him that holy perspicacity the Apostle calls more
piercing than the sword, that can even divide the spirit from the soul,
bone from marrow, thought from intention. Yes, if need be, let a
breath of the fighting archangel circulate in his blood. Let also his
thought be agile enough to traverse hearts, fine enough to pass one
way or another between the inner plate of the mirror and the quick-
silver painted on it. Add all that, and if he keeps his other virtues, you
will have him still more Christian."

And if these good, praiseworthy friends of our acquaintance,
whom I have been pleased to choose surreptitiously one by one, in
order to see them confirm the words of the Apostle by their very
faults, shock us in the end by the spots we see in them, what does that
mean my friend, except that we in our turn are not the Christians we
should be? The Christian, remember, is not so easily disgusted or
annoyed by these inevitable shocks. With a more acute discernment
of faults, he is more tender and tolerant. He is not rebuffed by the
smell of secret wounds. He remains constant and faithful; at the same
time he is detached in the usual sense. He almost thanks his brethren
for their faults that enlighten him on his own. Above all, he pities
them. He inflicts at first the pain on himself. He is ingenious and
modest to help them mend: *cum modestia corripiens eos.*

The ecclesiastic in question had inherited from a relative who had
just died a splendid library of sacred works. I went with him to see it.
It was in Rue des Maçons-Sorbonne, on the first floor of one of those
sunless houses in which Racine must have lived, the same perhaps
where he had climbed so many times the uneven stairs, with the large
ramp of gleaming walnut. The library filled two vast rooms and
included, among other volumes of theology, a large number of Jansen-

ist works, or, indeed, the complete collection of that group. From the famous *Augustinus* of the Bishop of Ypres to the last number, dated 1803, of the *Nouvelles ecclésiastiques* clandestinely printed throughout the 18th century, there was nothing missing. I could go there to browse at my leisure and put aside what I wanted to borrow. I soon learned in detail the history of the Abbey of Port-Royal-des-Champs, and such a recent example of primitive austerity made a great impression upon me.

Oh winds that passed over Bethlehem, rested on the Bridge over the smiling solitude of Basilia, burned in Syria, in the Thebaide, at Oxyrinth, on the Isle of Tabenna, winds that somewhat warmed your African breath at Lerins and in the Mediterranean Isles, you brought together one more time your ancient perfumes into this valley near Chevreuse and Vaumurier. You paused a moment on the hearth of aromas, in a refreshing oasis before dispersing in these last storms!

In Port-Royal there was a spirit of contention and quarrel which I was not looking for and which spoiled its purity for me. I entered as little as possible into this dead and corrupting division, which man in every epoch has introduced into the abundant fruit of Christianity. Happy and wise is he who can separate the ripened pulp from the bitter membranes, who knows how to moderate silently Jerome by Ambrosius, Saint-Cyran by Fénélon! But this contentious spirit, which had promptly embittered all Jansenism in the 18th century, was less sensitive or less arid in the first part of the reformed Port-Royal and during the generation of its great men. It was to this era of study, penitence, beginning persecution, endured without too much complaint, that I attached myself. Among these solitaries whose familiarity I entered, in a manner of speaking, after the illustrious, the Arnaulds, the Sacis, the Nicoles, and the Pascals, there is one I especially want to describe to you because I imagine you know little about him and yet, like Saint-Martin, like Abbé Carron, he soon became one of my invisible masters.

All have and all become more or less in the lives of such masters. But there are strong natures that dare more, that take more easily upon themselves and soon walk alone, looking from time to time behind them to see whether they are being followed. There are others who particularly need guides and supports, who look ahead and to the side to see if anyone has preceded them, if anyone is signaling to them, and who first look around for their counterparts and superiors. The most admirable and divine type of these filial weaknesses is John, who needed to fall asleep and lean on the shoulder and chest of the Savior. Later he grew strong and inhabited Patmos like the heights of

Sinai. I was a little like that, first unstable, imploring, and mismatched in the midst of the riches such natures have. I was in a hurry to be attached and supported. Thus, in the active and warlike world, I would have been ecstatic to be Georges' groomsman, Monsieur de Couaën's aide-de-camp. I would have sunk my body and soul in some valorous destiny. Impassioned to follow and go forth, I would have unthinkingly, by default, chosen Nimrod over the true shepherd. Natures like that, dedicated to others in the role of affectionate followers or companions, have been found throughout time and in diverse situations, like Hephestus to Alexander, the Abbé of Langeron to Fénélon. They would often be discouraged and would sink to the ground if they did not find support. John of Avila was dying of despondency when Theresa raised him up. But there are also those who wander and get lost in the complacency of friendship, like Melanchthon led by Luther. In the Letters themselves there are tender souls like that, *second* souls who marry an illustrious soul and indenture themselves to that soul's fame: Wolff, someone has said, was Leibnitz's priest. In the holy Letters, Fontaine followed Saci and the good Camus, Monsieur de Geneva. Ah, when I happened to enter these piously domestic confidences one step at a time, how my admiring and understanding nature expanded! How I should have liked to have known firsthand the authors, the inspirations of these narratives! How I, in my turn, envied those who were servants and secretaries of the great! The title of acolyte of saints and famous men seemed to me, as in the primitive Church, to constitute a sacred order. After my recent disappointment with the turbulent guides of my external life, I was all the more avid to create invisible masters for myself—men who were absent or already dead, not known to me personally—humble themselves and almost forgotten, quiet initiators of piety, intercessors. I made myself their submissive disciple, and I listened to them with delight in my thoughts. Because that is what I did with Monsieur Hamon, I should like to speak of him now.

Monsieur Hamon was a physician at the Faculté de Paris when, at the age of thirty-three he sold his worldly goods and retired to Port-Royal-des-Champs. Always poor, dressed like a peasant, sleeping on a board instead of a bed, eating only bran bread pilfered from what was fed the animals, stealthily giving his meals to the indigent, he led a life of continual humiliation, mortification, and escape. He nullified his knowledge that profited only the sick. To see him, you would have thought he was a common creature, some peasant of the neighborhood. In the 1664 persecution of Port-Royal this false impression, inspired by his simplicity, let him remain in the monastery at the call of the captives to whom he rendered all due cares of body and soul. This man of worth, versed in letters as well, had made a friend of young Racine, then a student there, and liked to give him advice in his studies. Racine always remembered him. He valued this sainthood crowned by God in the shadows, and in his will asked to be buried at the feet of Monsieur Hamon at Port-Royal. The image and restitution of the true reign. Oh you who have spent your life in humbling yourself like the most humble, behold great poets, shouldering fame, who die in the Lord, asking for the blessed privilege of being buried at your feet in the attitude of the most faithful squire!

I found in this precious library all Monsieur Hamon's writings, and I read them all. Their composition and style are negligent. He would be entreated to be more careful. He wrote only to his defending body, on the order of his illustrious friends and directors, and their injunction did not reassure him on his own inadequacy. He repented of producing and of violating the religion of silence, which suits, he said, the sick and which should be broken only by the groans of prayer. The good opinion of those he considered his superiors was cause for remorse, like a punishment from God and a fear: "How do I know if God is not punishing me for my vanity of times past in permitting my supervisors now to hold me in too much esteem." He would happily repeat with the *Philosophe inconnu* that out of respect for high truth, he would have sometimes preferred to pass for a vicious and sullied man than as the intelligent contemplator who seemed acquainted with them. "Great and respectable truth," Saint-Martin exclaimed in a fit of adoration, "has always seemed so far from the spirit of men that I feared more appearing wise in their eyes." Monsieur Hamon was usually like that. He tells himself in a narrative or confession, indicted for his own use, some circumstances of his life, the first occasion that led to his writing. With what emotion I read the details that recalled to me the places I frequented so often and the alternatives so familiar to my heart! "The first time I saw Monsieur de Saci," says Monsieur Hamon, "I asked him if there would be anything wrong in writing something on a few verses in the Psalms. He was highly approving, but the problem was beginning; I didn't know how to go about it. As I went to Paris, a day when I had done nothing but run around without praying to God and in utter dissipation, all sorts of wicked thoughts having obtained free entry in my heart and with so much impetuousness that it was like a torrent

---

We obtained with some difficulty this small Hamon opus, and we have been able to reproduce the passages completely.

dragging me along, I found I was completely beside myself when I got home. Since I was close to the church of Saint-Jacques in the quarter, I went in, at the end of my strength. It was a refuge for me. It was very deserted after dinner. I stayed there a long time because I was so lost and interred in the tomb I had dug myself that I could not find myself again. When I began to open my eyes, the first thing I saw was this verse of from a Psalm of David: 'be thou my strong rock, for an house of defense to save me' (33:iii). I applied myself to that with all my strength because I was terribly weary of my self and my phantoms. Since it seemed to be that I had been edified therein, I resolved to write it down, etc."

My heart still palpitating from my reading, I entered the church of Saint-Jacques-du-Haut-Pas, the very church where I had heard mass from the first morning, from the first Sunday I had spent in Paris. In thinking back on that distant day so illuminated now, I was like a man who climbs up his mountain as far as his point of departure but to a rock opposite the first. The dangerous torrent still growls in between. In this church, I approached near the place where Saint-Cyran is buried in the sanctuary. Monsieur Hamon had not failed to kneel there before me, and I repeated his other sentence, "Nothing takes us so far away from peril as a good tomb." What was Monsieur Hamon's peril compared to mine? What were those *wicked thoughts* that he so bitterly accused himself of in his somewhat distracted courses? compared to the frenzies of my assaults? And I meditated yet another sentence of his: "You have to dwell in the desert a long time and dwell there profitably in order to dwell in a city as in a desert." Thus I put together a life of retreat in the fields, a few leagues from Paris in Chevreuse also, near the dilapidated walls of a monastery, not leaving it for the big city but once every two weeks, on foot in summer, for things needed for study, for library books, to visit two or three serious friends cultivated with reverence, always returning by nightfall. I found once more, precisely in these simple projects, the chaste and puerile impression of those days when I dreamed of learning Greek in Paris, beneath a humble, gray roof, *Jansenist*, as I would have said then. It seems that with each small progress we make towards the Good is attached as an inner reward an early buried memory that awakes and smiles. Our Angel of seven years quivers and throws us a bouquet. I felt in those moments my affection redouble for these innocent stones and streets where I had strewn so many thoughts, where so many slow reflections had accumulated like moss along the way, like an invisible vegetation, gentler and more tufted to the eye of the soul than a lawn would be.

Lacking an establishment, the idea of visiting, at least as a pilgrim, Chevreuse, the ruins of Port-Royal, and of looking for the trace of the men I revered, could not fail to occur to me. I had, if you will recall, already visited Aulnay with similar intentions. Once or twice, then, the days of my prowling around the ruins in the environs, I set off for this desert, by way of Sceaux and hills beyond. But my unworthy feet would soon tire or I would get lost in the Verrières woods. A simple pebble thrown across the path can disturb our dearest hopes so much that I never carried out the trip I so much desired. In the end what difference does the material reality of the place make as soon as an impatient desire has constructed it for us? The thought and image were alive in me; I never opened one of those books printed in Cologne, with the Abbey of Port-Royal-des Champs engraved on the frontispiece, without recognizing the city of my hopes, without stopping for a long time at the bell tower of the fatherland.

In the number of special rules that I had picked up from Monsieur Hamon, there were some which never left me and which were added as precious verses to my habitual viaticum. While I was so sensitive to the idea of places, I found him recommending that we not be too attached, of not imagining them, above all, as the essential framework of our good life. He reminded me of that saying in the *Imitation of Christ*: "*Imaginatio locorum et mutatio multos fefellit*" (The idea that we make of places and the desire to change them are a snare for many). He cites Saint Augustine: "*Loca offerunt quod amemus et relinquunt in anima turbas phantasmatum*" (places that charm our senses fill our souls with distraction and reverie). "That is so true," he said, "that some people are obliged to close their eyes when they pray in churches that are too beautiful."

Some of his maxims, in our time of quarrel, I frequently took as advice: "We see so many seeds of division everywhere that it is very difficult not to add to it even in taking hardly any part, except by speaking little and praying much in the privacy of our own room." Elsewhere on the subject of inevitable divisions and shocks, "I see indeed that I had to get used to making myself a room that could follow me wherever I went, where I could retire, as the Gospel says, for shelter from the bad weather outside."

Considering how much I loved to judge others, to distinguish the innermost nuances, and to go back in time to the roots of intentions, I, who without seeming to, burrowed like an avid physician through human breasts to seize the forms of the hearts and the juncture of hidden blood vessels, I had good reason to apply this advice to myself:

"I found myself," said Monsieur Hamon, "so weary and sore of judging, of worrying over others, that I could hardly pray God enough to deliver me from this fault which kept me from converting once and for all. I resolved to stop judging anyone, seeing with what pain I had judged people who were better than I . . . . Because if I deserved to have someone define me, I could be defined as a man who, when he says something good, always does the contrary of what he says." Thus, Monsieur Hamon took hold of me, penetrating my secret avenues. I saw in myself, moreover, some singular, fortuitous relationships, as when he exclaims, "I have no relatives; I had only an uncle whom God took away." Such resemblances added to our union. He prepared me by the attraction he felt for those stronger than he and became a way to reach the universal apostle Saint Paul. Oh, they are dearer than all the others, those unexpected guides, unknown, come upon on the byways, through which the stranded and lost come together, just before dusk, the sole sacred way!

Saint-Martin, Abbé Carron, and Monsieur Hamon made me feel in a miraculous way what it means to edify my life and bear the gift of spirituality. This gift consists in finding God and his quick intention everywhere, even in the least details and the smallest movements, to keep a certain connecting spring beneath one's finger. Then everything takes on a sense, a special enchaining, an infinitely subtle alerting vibration, a beginning of new light. The invisible network, which is the spiritual base of Creation and second causes, which is continued through all events and makes them play within Creation like a simple blossoming on the surface, or, if you prefer, like hanging fringes, this deep network becomes perceptible at several places, and is always certain at the very places it is in hiding. Henceforth there are two lights. Terrestrial light, that of the sages of human interest and scholars in the secondary sciences, is only like a street lamp when the stars are out, when the glowworms give the ground an enamel sheen, when the moon in the firmament peacefully admires the moon on the waves. In the inner disposition of spirituality, there is a perpetual watch. Not a dot around us remains indifferent to the divine purpose. Every grain of sand glimmers. A step we take, a stone we pull up, a piece of glass we put to the side of the road to keep it from cutting children or the barefoot, all becomes significant and a source of edification. All is mystery and light in a melange of delight. *What do we know? God knows* it is there in every result, fecund doubt, and the reassuring idea that survives. Cheering explanations abound. Some trivial incident, which earlier you would not have noticed at all, opens the door to loving, adoring, infinite conjectures. "Sometimes," Saint-Martin says,

"God secretly prepares for us a thing that can be useful and even pleasant, and at the moment it will arrive or happen, God inspires in us the desire for it coupled with the urge to ask it of him, in order to give rise to our thought that he has answered our prayers, and to make filter through us some sentiment of his loving kindness, his obligingness, and his love for us."

That is how it happened, my friend, that while an exaggerated diadem was being inaugurated after the storm beneath the splendor of the victories, I was following my own imperceptible path to one side of the great influence that seemed to invade everything. I was feeling the effects of other truer, deep, and direct influences. The infiltration of celestial dews grew in me through the sun of the Empire. As I got used to this universe of the spirit, I appreciated more its circles and extent. I felt better, in the presence of my heart alone, the immensity of the conquests to be made, the difficulty of maintaining them. And just as the Archbishop of Cambrai said he was a large diocese unto himself, I was for myself an entire Europe to fight and pacify, that year when Austerlitz was in the offing. Nevertheless, who would have thought that these three men of such slight renown whom I have mentioned would have usurped so much sway over a soul, otherwise so responsive and open to an epoch ruled by the memorable Man? And how many others whom I do not know were in situations more or less like my own, with their immediate, singular inspirations, which owed nothing to that Man. Let us not magnify, my friend, the action, already incontestable, of these colossi of power. The proud ocean waterspouts, as high as they rise and as far as they go, are never but one more ripple on the surface, compared to the infinity of hidden currents.

After a few months of this life, which episodes of bad behavior rarely interrupted, I had become calm and rather happy. There was even in this uniformity of my days a kind of sweetness, so quickly acquired that I reproached it as suspect. The thought of wounded creatures, Madame de Couaën in particular, would arise suddenly in midst of the most peaceful hours and during my solitary twilights. Oh, how new tears would overflow. My soul, strengthened by abstinence, recomposed the ideal passion more strongly. During these reopened springs of bleeding tenderness, I had the ardor of a less vague healing, of a more expiatory penance, of an austere happiness of which she was better informed and which she blessed. I wanted to put between her and me something apparent, but understood by her alone and by God, simultaneously both unbridgeable and eternally communicable, both a sacred barrier and a canal. When, in these rapid waves, I hurried to the foot of altars and prayed for her during the tributes of the Hail Mary, I imagined that at this very instant she was no doubt praying for me, sad hearts intent in this way to be open to each other. I realized that this was only a daybreak that would have to be pursued. The thought of the sacraments, which stabilize and consume immediately, struck me as indispensable. The Order even came to mind without surprising me as the magnificent terminus of my desire. It seemed to me that I would never more be more expiating, more contrite, and more acceptable at the feet of God than when, having climbed to the last step of the altar and holding the host in my hands, I would add a permitted name in the commemoration of souls.

At the most ecstatic of these pious moments, I sometimes had troubles of another kind, as if to show me all the inconsistency and versatility of a heart which thinks it has only a single evil and believes this illness is nearly cured. I learned one day, through someone I met through some rather embroiled compliments that she paid me, that my absence had been noted in the world I had left and that there was talk of extreme condolences on the loss of so much charm and on this devout infirmity in which I had fallen. But the person speaking to me had not given credence to such a motive of withdrawal, she added knowingly, because she knew I was a young man of exceeding wit. There was nothing in all that I could not have foreseen, and it was clear that after my brusque eclipse people had to gloss it a bit here and there. But when what I had easily concluded was confirmed more precisely by that person's comments, I became disturbed, embittered, revolted for an entire day. Capricious sensibility of the heart! Fénélon was right, "We should forget human forgetfulness!" Yes, their forgetfulness. We excuse it; we even envy it. The sages look for it, the poets sing it. But however much we love forgetfulness, how badly we tolerate a frivolous social judgment, the distant echo of a single jeer!*

> My naive soul, you're hurt to be told
> Unfounded criticism, even a witticism,
> At your expense by casual friends
> Who should have left you alone
> Combating conflicts on your own.
> You imagined 'out of sight, out of mind'
> With discretion, repaid in kind.

We found a very similar sentiment in an unpublished poem by one of our contemporary writers. It seemed appropriate to cite them here as a harmonious response to the text:

So you're upset, but before you get
Plunged in self-pity and rage,
Let us look within to see whether
Lacking one fault, we don't have another.
Revellers racing along the Styx
Fête the means before the end,
Kid gloves hiding their dirty hands,
Fasting long for the feast.
Our calmer life is its own excuse.
Now we can flee sensual self-abuse.
Yet we're still a ship trapped by sludge
Without a wind to let us budge;
We complain if the starry sky's too clear,
So much we loathe fleeing stimuli here.
Rather than give in to wounded esteem,
For an accusation when we're not to blame,
O my soul, we should look within
And first descry and repent our sin,
Confident that God will let us in.

Un mot, qu'on me redit, mot léger, mais perfide,
Te contriste et te blesse, ô mon Ame candide;
Ce mot tombé de loin, tu ne l'attendais pas:
Fuyant, jeune, l'arène et ta part aux ébats,
Soustraite à tous jaloux en ta cellule obscure,
Il te semblait qu'on dût t'y laisser sans injure,
Et qu'il convenait mal au parvenu puissant,
Quand on se tait sur lui, d'aller nous rabaissant,
Comme si, dans sa brigue, il lui restait encore
Le loisir d'insulter à l'oubli que j'adore!
Tu te plains donc, mon Ame!—Oui. . . , mais attends un peu;
Avant de t'émouvoir, avant de prendre feu
Et de troubler ta paix pour un long jour peut-être,
Rentrons en nous, mon Ame, et cherchons à connaître
Si, purs du vice altier qui nous choque d'abord,
Nous n'aurions pas le nôtre, avec nous plus d'accord.
Car ces coureurs qu'un Styx agite sur ses rives,
Au festin du pouvoir ces acharnés convives,
Relevant d'un long jeûne, étonnés, et collant
A leur sueur d'hier un velours insolent . . . ,
Leur excès partent tous d'une fièvre aggissante;
Une vie plus calme vie aisément s'en exempte;

Mais les écueils réels de cet autre côté
Sont ceux de la paresse et de la volupté.
Les as-tu fuis, ceux-là? Sonde-toi bien, mon Ame;
Et si, sans chercher loin, tu rapportes le blâme,
Si, malgré ton timide effort et ma rougeur,
La nef dormit longtemps en un limon rongeur,
Si la brise du soir assoupit trop nos voiles,
Si la nuit bien souvent eut pour nous trop d'étoiles,
Si jusque sous l'Amour, astre aux feux blanchissants,
Des assauts ténébreux enveloppent mes sens,
Ah! plutôt que d'ouvrir libre cours à ta plainte
Et de frémir d'orgueil sous quelque injuste atteinte,
O mon Ame, dis-toi les vrais points non touchés;
Redeviens saine et sainte á ces endroits cachés;
Et, quand tu sentiras ta guérison entière,
Alors il sera temps, Ame innocente et fière,
D'opposer ton murmure aux propos du dehors;
Mais à cette heure aussi, riche des seuls trésors,
Maîtresse de ta pleine et douce conscience,
Le facile pardon vaincra l'impatience.
Tu plaindras nos puissants d'être peu généreux;
Leur dédain, en tombant, t'affligera sur eux,
Et, si quelque amertume en toi s'élève et crie,
Ce sera pure offrande à ce Dieu que tout prie!

CHAPTER XXII

However, I was soon to receive stronger shocks, and quiver to more resounding echoes. Because whatever I may have told you about my spiritual abstraction and my capacity for isolation in the heart of those momentous years, I did not pass through them completely unscathed. Around me reared in rapidly passing seasons thousands of obfuscating trophies; beneath my eyes they assembled invincible rays. The autumn of that illustrious year, when I was so taken up in detaching myself from the outer world, brusquely took up arms against my projects of peace and silence. War unexpectedly burst into flame again between France and the powers in coalition. This time the aggression was still coming from the other countries. A single cry, a cry of the insulted demigod, broke out throughout the Empire and pierced for the moment the retreat where I was fighting my mute enemies, where I was following my invisible angels. During the three months of that campaign I lived in a kind of electric cloud, which hovered overhead and enveloped me in a storm, discharging its thunderclaps on the hills of the horizon. I had a heart as swollen in my chest as the ocean when the moon is at the equinox, and I could no longer find my proper level.

One circumstance in particular aggravated this effect and complicated my emotion with an even more personal interest. Among the Senate decrees at these junctures was one that called to arms all conscripts of the last five years, and although I was very certain that in not coming forward, I would not be sought out, I could, strictly speaking, have been included in the first of the five classes. The idea that I was escaping only by hiding made me blush, and making an appeal to my piety, even to the support of my secret vow, I wondered whether I did not have a solemn duty to volunteer.

Scarcely was the campaign begun and the news of the first successes learned, it was worse, and my trouble increased in the universal anxiety. I prayed only at infrequent intervals. An extraordinary flood of that youthful age, sufficient unto itself and supporting to all else, mechanically pushed me outside the bounds of faith. I fell again into chaos and purely human conflict, dreaming only of excitement and fame, burning emulation, bestirring myself with all the others, galloping in a rain of bullets and dying quickly. Every new noise in the morning sounded like the Invalides cannon already celebrating some new victory. No longer under the pretext of paying a friendly call or seeking alms, but with bellicose murmurs and in the hope of news bulletins, I let the Demon of Midi drag me out beyond the river. The final form of my delirium! Morning spent in idle expectation and also ineffable prestige! You would have said that some dull mist had since passed into the skies as if upon our souls. There was more sun then than now!

One day—Ulm had already surrendered, and a forest of Austrian flags had just been ceremoniously presented to the Senate—while I was walking near the Luxembourg, I met an officer I knew, Captain Remi of the cavalry, attached to the headquarters staff of Marshall Berthier. He had been part of the deputation that had born the conquered flags. Having received a rather light wound in the arm in one of the last engagements before Ulm, he had been selected for this honor guard. He was all aflame with the marvelous campaign and the magic rapidity of such a complete triumph. He was impatient to return and was two days later to set forth for Strasburg, although his wound had worsened considerably during the return to Paris. But he counted on getting there in time, he said, for the huge forthcoming battle, which the arrival of the Russians would decide. I went on my way wishing him the luck of heroes, and hardly had I lost him from view than I regretted not having been free and open with him, not having told him my remorse at being idle, my desires to wage war. "Who knows," I thought, "if a confiding word would not have levelled the mountains under which I have tried to bury myself; if Berthier's aide-de-camp would have been able to arrange for the next great battle to become one of the new directions in my life, or at least my immortal tomb?" And this thought, as might be expected, bored away in me during the following days. But I thought the captain had left and did not try to find him.

Captain Remi was a person whom I had liked from the very first, even though I had only seen him from time to time. I met him for the first time at General Clarke's, at the time I came to Paris and was seeking support in Monsieur de Couaën's case. He had since left that general and gone under Marshall Berthier. I had seen him at long intervals while out walking or at balls, and we always talked with some mutual enjoyment and interest. He was handsome, open, sensible, motivated with a rather serious taste for self-improvement and bringing into diverse matters that precocious and simple aplomb of a man who has waged intelligent wars. He was hardly more than thirty at most, being in the draft of 1796. I sensed in him a depth of political and patriotic opinions that are attractive in a soldier. An excellent officer and in love with his profession, he did not go into the Empire blindly. In short, there was a reciprocal attraction which had made us rather close.

Two or three more weeks passed, and I still had not succeeded in losing myself on the paths of pacific kingdoms. One morning, having gone out to distract myself with a horseback ride at the Fountainebleau barrier, I crossed on the main highway a few leagues from there, the first column of Austrian prisoners, which had been moved from the frontier to the interior. The aspect of the conquered put me in mind again of my wounds and defeat, conquered myself, so to speak, a man whose sword had fallen from his hands without being able to fight. Everyone was beginning to be in a state of expectation, expressly waiting for some great event, because the Russian army must have joined the remnants of the Austrian army. I returned anxiously to town and shortly went to the Palais district on foot. But on leaving the Feuillants terrace near Place Vendôme, I met Captain Remi himself, pale, undone, as if getting up from sickbed. I approached him with surprise. "What, you're still here?" I cried. And he told me how the day after our earlier encounter, hemorrhaging and fever had set in and that the stubborn fever had left him exhausted, but that finally he wanted only a little more strength to recover. "I am leaving tomorrow, this very night," he added, his eyes shining, "and perhaps I will still get there in time." We were in front of his door. He invited me to come up. Once settled into his mezzanine flat, seeing his noble sadness, I no longer hesitated to tell him about mine: "If there is time for you, there is also time for me," I burst out. "Your hope brings me back to life. Tell me, can I come, take part with you in that battle between Emperors you are racing to?" And I explained to him my plans, so often repressed, which were stifling me. In the vacillating hope he wanted to manage for himself, he was encouraging, indulgent, and pretended that nothing was easier to carry out.

"I receive your engagement," he said. "You know how to handle a horse. I will keep you with me at first. You will enter afterwards, if it seems like a good idea, the Velites corps which has just been formed . . . Yes, this very night, we are leaving, we are going by post as far as

Strasburg, and from there full speed to the army. Six days should do."
He was looking to support his own hesitation in reassuring me. Such
a speech overwhelmed me. I went back to my rooms, I took my arms
and the very sword that Georges had touched. I went by the hotel of
Madame de Cursy to warn her not to worry about my absence, that I
would be in the country the two weeks before winter set in. When
morning came, my new companion and I were rolling towards
Strasburg.

He was, as I mentioned, an upright man, with a firm military eye
but with freer ideas and a more open horizon than most soldiers.
Regarding this eternal grand battle that we pursued, that we almost
named in advance, that we delayed, that we agitated in a thousand
ways, he said, "I simply must be there. In the first place it will be
illustrious and splendid, and will hold honor for me. We shall certainly
have enough others within a few years, I know, but this one is still for
justice, necessity, and defense. Later, I fear, it will more likely be one
man's ambition. So I want to be there, especially for this one.—And,"
he added beneath his breath, "stay there!" I glimpsed in him then a
pang in the heart, something like an old loss. He was accusing himself,
as far as I could understand, of not having been faithful enough to a
memory that should have remained unique in his life. He spoke of it
to me only covertly, moreover, in clasping my hand. The image of
Madame de Couaën, so languishing herself, and that impending loss,
passed before my eyes. "I, too, would like to stay there," I said, and
a long silence followed. Day was ending; my companion fell into a
light sleep, for he was still weak. As for me, watching the trees pass,
more and more funereal as they rose with the first stars, the hour of
infinite regret, I murmured this vow beneath my tears, "Oh, yes, let
us die before we love, for fear, in surviving, of being unfaithful, of
sullying by mean distractions that we reproach ourselves with in the
act of surrender, the mourning that should be kept inviolable."

In my turn I was overtaken by sleep, and when I began to wake
up in stages, it seemed to me that in realizing where I was and where I
was going I was continuing an absurd dream, a sick man's nightmare.
But either the speed of the horses or the morning air coming through
an open window decisively rechanneled my thoughts, so while confessing myself the most fickle of souls, I readjusted to the situation
rather quickly.

We trembled in advancing to learn some great news of victory.
Already a confused rumor, the harbinging "they say" that seems to
travel by night on the wings of the wind or on a horse of the dead,
was beginning to quiver, to intensify around us at each post we

passed. The captain, on these bits of information, remade his strategy calculations for the twentieth time. He unfolded his pocket map and on the basis of the last bulletins, explained to me the positions of various corps, the barely effected juncture, by his calculation, and surely incomplete, of the Russian and Austrians, the probable causes of delays due to the fatigue of some many forced marches. Our heads, bent over the same map, bumped at each jolt. When we entered Strasburg, everything rustled with tremendous hope but nothing was certain, nothing was official yet. We hardly gave ourselves time to get down and almost went from the carriage to the saddle. That was how we would now follow the route. We touched Kiel, Germany and the willows of its low bank were before us, when at the head of the bridge, just as we were beginning to cross, a courier whom the captain recognized immediately as heading for the Emperor came off galloping. The captain called to him by name and went towards him. Three messages, *great victory, armistice, peace in a week* flew like lightning. The captain turned pale as death, staring straight ahead, silent, led by his horse. But in the middle of the bridge, at the old boundary, I was the first to stop, saying, "For myself, who never saw a battle in my life, and who am destined never to see one, it is not fitting that I cross the Rhine, the warriors' river. But you, my dear captain, your revenge is assured; it will be glorious. Be comforted. Adieu!" and without further words, without dismounting, we kissed on both cheeks. He left for Germany, free rein, like a desperate man. He was killed at Wagram three years later. I was gloomy going back into Strasburg and returned from there straight to Paris. After the captain's pale face at the courier's news, I thought of Monsieur de Couaën. And at this harsh news I saw him with cold sweat running down the veins of his brow and that special tremor of his thin lips. For myself I was not particularly surprised. In all that, I recognized what I call my destiny, what upon coming out of such vertigo I no longer dared call the will of God. Humiliation drowned me and covered my head with a lake of 100 cubits. Did missing Austerlitz, did breaking my good bonds cause this confusion? What is certain is that I would not have found myself worthy then to have aided in silence the least of the brothers in the kitchen court of a monastery.

However, oh my God, your ways were guiding me! I was ashamed of myself, but you were less ashamed. I had contempt for myself, the fugitive impotent to ravish the world, to be rejected by events and things, and you were more ready than ever to welcome me. After so many errors and inconstancies, I had only the abject remains of myself to offer you, but you did not disdain these remains, provided they hid a spark. You act like Lazarus, oh my God, and you receive almost with gratitude the crumbs from the table of the Prodigal Son, the rags of the sinner's body and soul!

I landed one evening in a Paris still resounding and illuminated. My friends, that is, Madame de Cursy and the priest, were not surprised by my brief absence. I resumed my former life but without the security or the happiness of the first charm. I saw indeed that this last assault had been a disguise of my secret leaning, which, in order to reengage me fully in the world, had unexpectedly offered the glorious aspect in the form and arms of a warrior, that it was always the phantom of the senses, the intoxication of pleasure, but appearing to me this time in the camps like Armour and with a helmet that bore a silver eagle.

Napoleon had just returned to the capital. The entire army would follow him, and the general rendezvous was planned for the first days of May. The fully staffed Guard was already there, and the bare-armed caressing, the permitted orgies and squandered glances of a triumphant peace animated the city. It was time for me to take a stand. There comes a moment in conversion when in order to heal we need to put between ourself and relapses the sovereign obstacle of the sacraments. It will not do to approach them too early or too frivo-lously before they are truly sacred to us, for fear of worsening the situation by violating them. But the hour comes when they alone can place the seal, ratify the pact that a prudent heart concludes with the eyes: "I made a covenant with mine eyes," says Job (30:i) and make sure one is not the sensual man Ecclesiasticus speaks about in the ancient law: "All bread tastes good to him; he will never weary of returning and biting in to the end." It is not too much, towards that end, that a God in entirety, God of body and soul, be put between the ancient idol and ourselves. I was especially one of those, as I have told you, for whom religion depends less on the convictions of the intelligence than on practical conduct. In reasoning I found nothing to oppose religion, but I either did not act or acted badly, and that was worse. And if I did not take care, I was going to be mollified in the presence of a truth that I recognized and that each day I would become incapable of grasping. I wrote to my dear friend in Normandy these very words, which I find in my daybook of the time: "My intelligence is convinced, or at least, raises no objections. But," I added, "My manners and my practice remove and reject me, despite the partial efforts I attempt. Age is coming and youth is leaving with each passing day. The more rigorous years stretch out before me. I would like to reconcile my ideal love with religion, so as to strengthen each by the other. But inferior senses undermine that beautiful alliance, and I fall again *passim* both discontent as a lover and demoralized as a believer. Here is my wound . . . , this wound of the senses which always reopens at the moment I think it is healed." I had jotted down these words for myself before I sent them. They were the unfeigned summary of my extreme situation, that limit I was desperate to cross. Oh! it is a bad situation, my friend, when morals stay the same while the spirit is convinced otherwise. You continue to live badly, you are persuaded that you live badly. Nothing enfeebles nor dilutes the spirit, nor takes away the faculty of true faith, nor disposes it to universal skepticism, so much as to be thus a witness in its conviction of more or less multiplied contrary acts. The intelligence is enervated in contemplating the defeats of the will, like a man at a window who would have the cowardice to contemplate a murder in the street without running to the defense of the victim who is his brother.

A letter from Monsieur de Couaën inviting me to spend a few weeks at Blois, in a voice of gentleness and friendship that I had not had from him for a long time, helped determine me. I dared neither refuse nor go. I hastened to put the idea of Madame de Couaën in all security and purity on an altar behind ballustrades of cedar, invisibly inscribed on plates of gold. At last, what will you say, my friend! after that last trial, and when I felt so low, everything above was ripened and prepared. I believed I was abandoned, and all was imperceptibly lifting me up. One day the good priest, the first to bend my thoughts, spoke to me of the Seminary at ———, where the superior was a good friend of his, and the simple, practical life they led there. Each breath of spring that year, those moments once so feared, felt propitious to me. The first dews that the earth drank, bloody a while ago, regenerated my soul. This soul, until then so sorely detached, fell silently, of its own weight, like a ripe olive in the Master's basket. I resolved to confess, and when I had done so, at the end of two weeks, leaving Paris, I entered with special permission, although the course of study for the year was half gone, at the reburgeoning Seminary of ——— where the superior was the intimate friend of my good priest.

CHAPTER XXIII

When you enter a seminary, especially one in the country, you experience immense peace. It seems that the world is destroyed, that wars and victories have been over for a long time, and that the heavens, thinly veiled, without a dog-star and without thunder and lightning, enclose a new earth. Silence reigns in the courtyards, in the gardens, in the corridors peopled with cells. And at the sound of the bell you see the inhabitants emerge in a swarm as if from a mysterious hive. Serene faces match the whiteness and cleanliness of the house. What the soul feels is a kind of loving intoxication of frugality and innocence. I would have little to tell you about my individual feelings during that stay that you could not easily imagine, my friend, after all that went before. I prefer to retrace something about how I spent my time, the order and use of the passing hours. Moreover, those varied and regular exercises effectively arrested all violence in thought and filled our souls with equanimity. Rivers artfully detoured, deliberately channeled, almost become a single peaceful canal.

We rose at five in the morning, winter and summer. In addition to the bell that woke us, a different seminarian each week entered our cells saying *"Benedicamus Deus,"* and we answered from our bed, *"Deo gratias."* It was our first word, our first stammering towards the light. On certain high holy days, like Christmas and Easter, we used another formula, which I no longer remember, but which had this sense: *"Christus natus est, Christus surrexit."* Perhaps those were the very words: "Christ is born; Christ is risen."

At five-thirty, we went down to the common room where we knelt for prayer, and then we remained for meditation, standing, kneeling, or seated, if we felt weak. The general rule was to be alternatively a quarter-hour on the knees and a quarter-hour standing, and the clock placed in the middle of the garden faithfully marked all quarter-hours during the entire day. This exercise lasted an hour altogether. At six-thirty, we went to hear mass in the chapel, which was in the middle of the garden, so that in summer our white surplices made a silent line through the parterres and covered walkways fragrant in the morning air.

We returned to our cells at seven o'clock. There, alone with our books, our narrow table and chair, our modest bed, we put this little domain in order for the rest of the day—for most seminarians made their rooms themselves. I did my own, too, my friend, gaining thus a better picture of the life of the poor, and could relate in thought to so many wretched lives in the miserable hovels of the cities, so many struggling hands like mine at that moment. I felt pity for the large family of mankind and I wept. These household chores were brief, then I studied as I pleased. Once in our cells, we were our own masters and answerable only to our conscience. I found there with my crucifix all my paltry rooms of former years, now bright and pure, all my Chartreux vows carried out. This perpetual passage from communal life to solitary life, from absolute rule to freedom, was very appealing. The soul's double instinct sometimes to flee, sometimes to seek company, was satisfied.

The first meal took place in the refectory at eight. As much bread as a person wanted, a little wine, that is all there was except on the two days of Corpus Christi when each had a cake, and on those days, because of the joy, the wine was white. After the meal, which lasted a bare quarter-hour, we returned to our cells. At nine we had a class in theological dogma. The students, seated around the room on benches, listened to the professor on a shallow riser. Through questioning he completed the preceding lesson. He explained that of the following day and responded to more or less lively objections. The dogma course was divided into distinct treatises and included all Catholic truths in its outline: True Religion, the Church, God, Creation, Incarnation, Holy Sacraments, etc. I was submissive, attentive, and although accustomed to the fantasizing of reading, I forced my intelligence into the furrow of this solid instruction.

The class in dogma lasted one hour. At ten o'clock we went to the chapel, which took a quarter-hour, including the time to go there. This little exercise was partly voluntary. Some went back up to their cell before going, others went immediately; occasionally you could cut. But don't you admire this disposition of time, how many slender pipes and adroitly managed channels were used to bring the waters of the spring down the hill to water the garden of a soul!

After staying in our rooms until a quarter to twelve, we heard the bell call us to *individual self-examination.* This was done on our knees, each reading to himself a chapter of his New Testament. Then, after a pause, the Superior read an examination phrased as an interrogation, for example, on a virtue: "What is charity?" "Have we been charitable?" For these exercises and all the others, morning mediation and mass excepted, we wore a simple cassock with a surplice.

At noon we went to the refectory for dinner, which was quite frugal, unless it was a high church feast day, when the meal was more festive and abundant. There was a reading. The two other meals, morning and evening, were taken in silence. The reader first read a passage of the martyrdom of the saint's day, and there were sometimes naturally sublime passages, for example, the date of Christmas which is designated in all eras, the year of Rome, such and such Olympiad, etc., and afterwards that magnificent narrative which remained suspended: *Christus natus est in civitate Bethleem* (Christ is born in the town of Bethlehem). After the martyrology, the reader read from the Holy Scriptures, and finally took up the history of the Church in France. Dinner lasted a half-hour. From the refectory we went to the chapel to say the angelus, and, upon leaving the chapel, we could break silence for the first time during the day. This moment had a quickening pulse and was always a pleasure. We scattered out through the garden walkways—not in all, however; one was section reserved for outsiders, and we could enjoy it only once a week, or during the vacation period. Most of our sanded paths were straight and had a bench at either end with a painted wooden statue, austere statues that chastened our reveries and sanctified the excess of foliage by their presence. In the restricted section there was a darker, even humid, walkway, where outsiders seldom penetrated. I had secretly dedicated it to a thought. I went there only once a week, Wednesdays, and I usually took a bouquet I had just gathered to the Virgin's statue in the back. There were two other attached paths in which I said a special prayer as I walked. But I would return to the Virgin several times and meditated longest in the largest of the three paths.

The hour of recreation was when outside visitors could see us. I had none to receive except my dear friend from Normandy, who made two or three trips just to encourage me. I showed and explained everything to him. He was enchanted with the calm each step of the way and by the economy of time and place. As we strolled around, I told him my favorite stories about Monsieur Hamon, Limoëlan, Saint-Martin, and Carron. His own gift for the spiritual was sharpened in listening to me, and he replied with other anecdotes, no less marvelous, which he had read or which had taken effect on him or around him, by stories about the poor, like those of Jean the almsman, by narratives of apparitions of Christ, as he called them, which had happened recently but sounded like the era of the good patriarch of Alexandria.

"All that spreads out, holds good, corresponds," he was saying, "and you learn things that make you sell your furniture and keep just a single plate for your table." And then there were, as we walked through our pious gardens, happy cries which escaped him, of a blessed painting and of a beauty naturally discovered. He who had written me so many times on the bitterness of spring was holding forth on its sweetness. "Winter is becoming too hard for me now," he said one day during a visit at the end of autumn. "Oh for one more spring, one more spring! When you've kept a single grain of the Gospel, springtime with God surpasses being in love!" I had him admire our covered walks, our trellised arbors, the impenetrable shade of our walkways, not revealing to him, however, the one my heart kept for itself. And he spoke to me about his own house, which I had never visited, a silent house, also, he said, clear, light, airy—on a hill—green grass, magnificent daisies. And he depicted springtimes there, sometimes coming abruptly, quickly, in gusts, like assaults of a storm, and sometimes, more frequently, gathering strength gradually: "With order, without sudden attacks, crises, while the hazel-nut flowers fringe the entire forest and the holly gleams and sparkles in the sun beneath the large trees which have not leafed out yet." And he added irrepressibly, "Oh, there are holy things in life, my friend, and how many treasures our passions keep us away from!" At times he was tempted to stay with me and said so. But I reminded him that his path was already laid out, and we separated affectionately. Thus his worthy life became more steadfast, and he went down the end of his youth through beautiful slopes.

It was during the same recreation hour that we read the letters we had received at the table, distributed by a seminarian assigned to that task. The friend I've just mentioned, Madame de Cursy, and my spiritual director formed my entire circle of correspondence. I wrote once a week to Madame de Cursy, only once or twice a year to Monsieur de Couaën. During recreation, we played ball, our only customary game. Once a week, Wednesday, the free day, you could play billiards, chess, or hearts, backgammon, badminton, or boules. I never played.

Recreation was over at one-thirty with a group recitation of the rosary, a 15–minute exercise. The second half of the day was spent like the first in cleverly distributed pauses and reprises: an hour and a quarter in the cell, an hour in ethics class by a different professor, another visit to the chapel at four, collective spiritual reading before supper, after supper, evening recreation, finally prayer with a reading on the meditation subject for the next morning. We went to bed at nine. Thus our days passed, each resembling the other, my friend, like beads on a rosary, as we used to say, except for Sunday and Wednesday. Sunday there was no class. We went to the village parish church to hear high mass and vespers. We had more time to spend in our cells and a few minutes of recreation after Vespers. I said there were no dogma and ethics classes on Sunday, but we did have one on the Holy Scripture in the morning.

Wednesday was the big day. During the entire winter, our recess did not begin until noon and had nothing very cheery about it. We took a long walk in the countryside after dinner, and those at the boarding school in town, affiliated with the seminary administration, often came to use our gardens and play games in our absence. But, starting with the first Wednesday after Easter, recess began at seven in the morning and lasted until eight-thirty in the evening. We were completely in control of the garden. The game room was open. Silence was no longer observed, not even in the refectory. It was delightfully festive for the rebirth of spring, but how many inevitable, stubborn ulterior motives in my heart, alas! At eight o'clock the older students of the boarding school came in. They heard mass in our chapel. After which, the two houses became one congregation. Those who knew each other got together to chat. The lovely imbalance of ages, not too extreme, however, added interest to the conversations. There were brothers who were already men, and brothers who were adolescent. There were no ranks in the refectory. Everyone sat where he wished, and in that universal confusion, only the cell remained inviolable. One could not take another person there without express permission. Before dinner personal reflection took place as usual, and after dinner an uplifting reading. In the evening after the boarding school students had left, we lined up in no particular order and said the rosary aloud amidst the linden lanes, now already dark. Those who came last were guided in rejoining the march by that harmonious distant murmur. Like the buzzing of innumerable May-bugs in a flax field, or the murmur of dilatory bees behind a hedge. One time the procession, which by chance had moved off to an unaccustomed section, reached my secret walkway. What emotions assailed me as I approached! The redoubled shadows veiled my tears, the noise of coughing muffled my sobs!

The Wednesday regimen was that followed during vacation, which lasted most of August and all of September. Every day we took a long walk. In the evening we were allowed to sing songs bearing on the events of the day or remarkable incidents during the week. The one who wanted to sing climbed on a bench, and the singer-improviser next to him. The crowd applauded these scenes, which were always innocent and seemed to echo the South, a facetious vestige of the Middle Ages, and did not lack either a lively strain of rustic, popular culture.

We sat for general examinations on theology before Easter and at the end of the Year. Those who were to be ordained sat for another examination at the bishopric, or rather before the bishop. Ordinations were preceded by a week-long retreat, during which all exercises were suspended. We filled our time with edifying reading, and there were sermons morning and evening. Each seminarian had to pass five ordinations: tonsure, minor orders, subdiaconate, diaconate, and priesthood. The tonsure was the simple stage, purely a sign that had no consequences. It concerned only a lock of hair, the lightest, airborne part of our self. The minor orders, four in number and which were conferred on a single occasion, had their true meaning in the primitive Church. Then one really became in turn porter, that is, keeping the keys and ringing the bell; reader, keeping and reading the sacred book; exorcist, having the power to eject demons, because in those days the possessed who sheltered vanquished gods and oracles abounded; acolyte, serving and accompanying the bishop and carrying his letters. The subdeacon is allowed to touch the chalice, the deacon had the right to serve the people the blood of Christ, in those days when both bread and wine were used in communion; but the priest alone consecrates the bread and wine and makes God enter therein. Only he gives the sacraments, except communion and the orders, reserved to the bishop, and even he can delegate this authority to a priest. The most serious and solemn of our ordinations was that of the subdeacon because this requires the vow of perpetual chastity. This was the moment when our life was indissolubly bound to the duties of the Catholic hierarchy. The consent of the future subdeacon did not result simply from his presentation to the church beneath the eyes of the bishop. All candidates, arranged in two lines, waited for the bishop. After having warned them of the responsibility to which they wanted to dedicate themselves, he would say, "May those who consent to receive this burden come near!" One step forward was the irrevocable sign of the will and the perpetual bond. Some drew back and turned around sadly. Oh, I certainly felt, my friend, all the meaning of that word. How I weighed in putting my foot forward the entire immense weight of that burden! The ceremony was barely finished at two in the afternoon after having started at seven o'clock in the morning. In the interval elapsing between general communion and the end of mass, the ordinants were offered a little wine from the gold chalice to keep up their strength. When it was over, there was a tremendous effusion of joy, cordial embraces, a general animation which was like nothing else, because it was simultaneously tranquil and lively, a coming and going in all directions in the courtyards and lawns to meet each other, a reciprocal penetration of purified intellects and somewhat above the things of this earth. The ordination of priests takes place at two principal times of winter and summer, Christmas eve, and Trinity Sunday.

The seminary's feast was the presentation of the Blessed Virgin at the temple, November 21. The bishop came to say mass and afterwards, seated at the foot of the altar, he received each seminarian, who approached and dropped to his knees to repeat from the 16th psalm, *"Dominus pars haereditatis meae et calicis mei; tu est quio restitues haereditatem meam mihi."* (The Lord is the portion of mine inheritance and of my cup; thou maintainest my lot.)

All in all, the life of the mind was much less cultivated than the life of the soul. We enjoyed the first seldom but the second, often and much.

My friend, I have outlined the generally pleasant aspects of regulation and regularity. Underneath you would perhaps have found less happiness than there seemed to be. You would have found sad, bleeding or troubled souls, struggling against themselves, against tendencies or misfortunes, some blemished souls also—few in number, however, in my opinion. Mine was one of the most mature and affected, no doubt. I used to tell that to myself with a kind of satisfaction, not from pride but from charity in seeing all these blossoming young pieties. But who knows whether someone besides me was not also more advanced in the fatal knowledge and, like me, keeping it hidden?

I was able to discern at least one among us who was suffering deeply and who one day during a walk let his secret escape to my breast. He was a young man who had been reared lovingly and spoiled, you might say, by a mother who was good, but moody and violent. The mother's violence had developed in the young man's nature more serious angers than children usually have and frequent suicidal impulses. Between those two creatures so viscerally attached to each other there had been many frightful scenes. As the child grew up, these scenes became rarer, it is true, but took on a more guilty, occasionally impious character. The beautiful years of his adolescence had been withered as if by a poisonous shadow. He took refuge in a resolution never to marry for fear of begetting a son who would be as violent towards him as he reproached himself for being against his mother. The mother had groaned a great deal over that resolution without daring to complain about it. When she died a little while later, she forgave him for everything. But he could not forgive himself, and once in the seminary, tried to dedicate his celibacy to Him who engenders neither anger nor ingratitude. While not intimate, I had become linked at least in a friendly way with that melancholy young man. I frequented also two or three Irishmen, more from an attraction to their country than by any personal appeal. I had obtained permission to speak English with them, and I owed to their company the means of keeping up a language that has become so necessary for me.

As for doubts, struggles of the intellect vis-à-vis the truths we were taught, I had little to do. What I had to combat and repress was a kind of pleasant reverie, a too-complacent letting go, a semi-Martinist frame of mind too enamored of the roads not taken. I triumphed better for having enclosed myself in the transmitted word and by following the procession of the faithful step by step.

But I will not take up any more of your time with these three years, my friend. What I wanted to tell you especially about the melting passions and love of pleasure is dried up. So, crossing that interval of happy monotony, I shall transport you to what was just ending over there of the sorrowful events where I had left you hanging. Thus the end of the voyage approaches. While I was plumbing with you my former depths, the vessel where I am was laboring, skimming many a sea night and day. In vain the winds pushed it back and by their obstinacy gave me leisure for my narrative. Now its speed carries the day. The gray latitude of Newfoundland can be fully sensed. The birds of the next continent are already appearing. We have seen flying west the first of the vultures announcing land. In five or six days, young friend, a confidant so dear he made the heart of the confessor weaken and gush, before the end of this week, we will have to take leave of each other.

CHAPTER XXIV

On Trinity Sunday I had been ordained. New relationships formed around me. I could appreciate the extent of immense duties, which bordered my road all along the way and cast sharp shadows over it. I had returned briefly to Paris after my ordination. The last personal attachment I had maintained no longer existed. Madame de Cursy had died at the end of the preceding winter, about three months earlier, without my being able to see her again, and the little convent, sparsely inhabited with a few very old and infirm nuns, offered a widowed solitude where death, once introduced, was going to stay. During the last year also, I had learned that Mademoiselle de Liniers, yielding to her grandmother's deathbed wish, had finally agreed to accept what is called a good match. She had married someone much older but high in rank and responsibilities. How sincerely grateful I was to her, angel of sacrifice, for obeying a dying woman and resigning her heart! For several weeks I had had no direct news from Blois. I feared that Madame de Couaën would be getting weaker daily despite turns for the better which reanimated hope and masked her decline. After presenting myself in Paris to my ecclesiastical superiors who distinguished me with a thousand favors, I decided for a number of reasons to make the trip to Rome. But before leaving, I had an ungovernable desire to see my native countryside again, my uncle's farm, and—I did not dare say it even to myself—the towers of Couaën. It had been seven long years since I had left the blessed shelter of those woods. There was no longer a living creature to attract me, but I needed places, beaches. Clothed in a new ministry, I wanted to bless the field of my forefathers' death. I wanted, as a grown man, to bow in tears to my cradle, to refresh myself a little in the virgin shades of childhood, to repent along the adolescent path of lust. Before undertaking a painful yet untiring march among the well-travelled roads, I was impatient to make this detour to inhale the savor of the heath, to immerse myself at the height of the season with the flowers scattered throughout my sharpest years and for the unending memory of a few souls.

So it was on a beautiful afternoon that I dismounted from the diligence at the closest town and set out immediately on horseback along the hedges, moats, fields of wheat reddening in the sun—not getting more golden as elsewhere. Here and there I crossed a few flocks of small black sheep on the short, flowering lawns to reach my uncle's house, mine since his death, my dwelling through childhood and youth until I left the countryside. From the clearning I could see that the windows were nearly all festooned with swallow nests, a sign of absence, and tall grass in the courtyard. Dogs I did not recognize darted out barking at my approach and did not stop until they saw my cassock. In this serious land even dogs recognize and respect the habit of the priest and cleric. Finally the gardener appeared. He and his wife for years had been in the lodge by themselves and every morning, by my old standing orders, opened the shutters and swept out the dust as if I might arrive that very day. A casual note from me had been their law. I was overcome with emotion when I entered these unused rooms where everything had been religiously kept in the last arrangement, as it was during the funeral period. The chairs were placed with respect to such custom, the center table waiting for the evening wake. In a corner some frames were leaned against a wall but not hung during my uncle's lifetime, even though they were on the point of being, and now never would be, an exact image of so many plans and hopes. On a wooden hook, the same large-brimmed straw hat for whoever would go to the garden in the heat of the day. I looked at everything again, I climbed back up to my room near the attic, where as a child I conversed with the clouds in the sky and branches on the roof. An open cage still hanging at a window recalled an early sorrow, the story of a bullfinch that flew away. I rushed back down and buried myself in the garden and meadow, through high ferns, actually as high as young pine trees. I lost my bearings and found them. At each step things sometimes seemed smaller and farther away, sometimes larger than I had imagined. But it was always more tufted, more sylvan, more abundant than I had thought in a healthy wild aroma. Skirting the pond and the stream, image of holy waters in solitude, I drank a large swallow of that source of my heritage, so limpid, alas, and neglected for so long, which, while the master went astray elsewhere, had never ceased to ripple and bubble for the least bird and blade of grass. At that moment I lacked only a friend to whom I could say something of what oppressed me, on whose breast I could let my tears fall and who would offer comforting words. Who has not wished for a friend who would have remained behind us in our childhood paths, whom we would find again after ten years at the end of the same walkway, a breviary in his hand? A friend who was witness and keeper of our youthful desires, the faithful chaplain of our first vows and virginal ardors? All that we had promised ourselves once, the evening of a holy communion; all that we planned with tears in our eyes in chattering together along a grove of hawthorns—he held to it, he did not budge, he did not go beyond the next town, he studied, he prayed, he climbed one step each year. There came a moment in his life when those who the eve before blessed him he blessed in his turn, where he came back Levite of God, into the house of his father, seeing each bow as they met him. And all that took place without stormy interruption, without crisis, absence, like a simple turn of the seasons making the trees grow higher and loading them with leaves. Especially on the day when one returns by himself to the deserted family roof, who has not dreamed of such a friend?

There is a prudent human maxim: "Travel often down the path that leads to the home of a friend. Otherwise thistles will grow amidst the grass." This advice is good for friends we meet late, for those with whom mutual advantage, frivolous or delicate attraction, an interest or common goal links us. But there are childhood friends, friends who are made at an age when souls are formed, before they have taken on their virile hardness or before the bark has thickened. There are friends whom we never see, whom we find again only after ten or so years, whom we do not need either to cultivate or reestablish, and who are always the surest, the dearest to the heart. Grass no doubt grew on the path in the meantime; it grows there as in a forest. But when we pass there again after so long a time, it is only softer, and even the brambles have their charm in the heath of the native valley.

I was choking on tears, suffocated with memories, for lack of a friend to help me bear them. How long the night was! What an active and magical insomnia beneath those family draperies, strewn with old flowers and figures. Each painted flower, each figure played on my thoughts like a composition of souls of the dead. The next morning in broad daylight, having retraced the same paths in the dew, I felt that it was too much, that to expose myself to a second sunset on that horizon that was so charged, would be enough to make my soul burst open. I had decided that I would visit only that house and Couën, no place else: neither la Gastine or anywhere else in that neighborhood. So I left, immediately after lunch, on a small native horse with my portemanteau on the rump behind me, telling myself that nobody expected me, and I turned toward the chateau two leagues away, in a hurry to cross in a straight line that inundating sea of souvenirs and fragrance. My plan was to stop for only an hour or two and to return to the town and then go on to Paris as quickly as possible.

I was recalling, as I dismounted at certain spots in those hollowed trails, the day I went there for the first time, uncovering the mysterious road, as now I was recovering it. Oh, my presentiment had not misled me. It was there indeed that the first branching off of my life had taken place. Did not everything I had become depend on this first trip? In the time that elapsed since, destiny had developed for me, unswerving from the propulsion of that beginning. The wheel of my human fortune had poured to that side. It was nothing striking in the eyes of the world, so few events and so barely visible! but an entire series of sentiments, passions, errors so intimately linked to it. A tender nature, simultaneously emotional, rich, weak, running through its phases, undergoing its storms, up to that divine port from whence this tender nature would repair blessed, armed, strengthened, I was hoping, with its storms from outside, to be feared more than those from within. Well, that it is an abridged version, I thought, of most obscure human destinies! This is what a vanished youth means, something indefinable and enchanted which gets lost in distant promises! What would I have made of those burning years, enjoyed only once, if circumstances had not also pushed me toward these visible sites?—Instead of that, nothing. Nothing and just as much, alas, in reality, than if the result had been more brilliant. Just think of the troubles, the thoughts, the vicissitudes, the struggles! What an inner life! And is not that the story of many people both past and present? How many lives with no doubts and how many youths, capable of glowing, likewise! What an immense number of schemes, forestallings, struggles, and hidden sufferings! That is what life is. The bulk of society is that alone. The face of society changes, is renewed, differing through time, but beneath the novelty of form and appearance, poor human beings, generations first young, then withered, like the leaves on a tree, as the old poet says, the same today beneath the breath of God as in the times of Job and Solomon, poor human creatures, the perpetual and monotonous revolutions of our hearts. These revolutions burst out more or less outside us; sometimes they are mixed with what is called history, but the burst has nothing to do with their being fulfilled. All races that succeed one another on this earth are born to flourish in their season, agitated and tossed by practically the same breeze. Blessed are they, blessed are they who respond, well before winter, to their only springtime, unchanging and sacred. And I was telling myself these things on the constant renewal of the same human passions, along the hedges continuing to green, at the heart of festive and unchanged nature. As I came closer to the chateau, which I could espy at a certain turning of the path, I felt as if I was returning to touch my point of departure in order to come closer to closing the circle of my first destiny. I was disturbed along the way as if by one last anticipation. But my trouble did not foresee everything.

In passing the first barrier and crossing the court of the farm, I was surprised to discern an air of activity at the chateau, and not the dreary abandonment, the uninhabited aspect I was expecting. The window of the room I had occupied for so long above the entry gate was wide open. When I passed the second barrier with my horse, which I was leading by bridle, I saw, through the grate of the garden gate, other shutters opened as well. At the noise of the horse beneath the vault, someone advanced from the inner court. It was Monsieur de Couaën. Imagine our astonishment, especially his. Although we had been apart for years, the dominant feeling of his welcome was surprise and a slight embarrassment flitting across his face.

"I was in the environs," I stammered, at first as if to justify myself. "I wanted to see once again the places where I did not realize you still lived. How does it happen that you are here?"

"As a matter of fact, we did not return until last night," he said. "Madame de Couaën had such an acute desire to breathe again this air that was almost her native air with its sea breeze that I had to give in to her request. An invalid's request, for she is ill, more alarmingly than ever," he added. "So I wrote Monsieur Desmaret for permission, and he sent it at once. She is very weak and worn out by the trip. I shall go prepare her for seeing you."

I was impressed by that miraculous coincidence of her desire to see Couaën again with my own, which had also come up suddenly, perversely, and irresistibly. "What," I said to myself, "the same day, perhaps the same hour, she at Blois and I at Paris, without any communication, without any predetermined aim, we would have felt suddenly such a violent and inexpressible temptation to visit these same places, to breathe in their air. And after so many years of absence, privation, and rigorous prudence, we would be face to face again, by pure chance and at the risk of mortal trouble! —No, it is not this. Blind secondary causes, which man calls chance, do not have that kind of power to play around us and call back into question the peace in our souls. No, it is only something the invisible Hand could prepare because He wants to effect some great good from it." And a tender yet lofty thought seized my heart, born with a shiver of holy fright, and I was trembling when I followed the Marquis into the tower room he was taking me to.

She was lying on a chaise longue, near an open window, the same place I had first seen her sitting on a footstool embroidering. When I entered, she no more turned than she had then but, alas, now it was weakness and not dreamy distraction. Her daughter, already big, about 11 or 12, stood between the chaise longue and the window watching her mother. I advanced to her quickly. I grasped the hand she held out to me, and I felt her very dry and frail to the touch. As for her face, it was as pale as it used to be, but blurred and diminished by the white lace surrounding it. Soon, as she spoke, a little color returned. Some black locks escaped upon her forehead; her eyes, still sparkling and looking larger because she was thinner, contrasted with her withered cheeks. However, stretched out like that, calm, still beautiful, in that warm peach perfume that came in with the sun and hovered around her, if I had not known the slow years of illness, I would have taken her for a convalescent.

"Monsieur Amaury (because I still want to call you that)!" she exclaimed first, in a tone of voice in which I discerned both delicate effort and consoling intention. "Is this really you we see again? What grace of God leads you here?" And she spoke to me of events in the interval, of the great decision I had conceived and carried out and which she had, she said, so much admired. She spoke of what she had written often to that good aunt we had lost, and what satisfaction it gave her aunt, who loved me like her own kin, to know that decision before she died. After these mutual regrets about Madame de Cursy, I spoke to her about her daughter, so grown up already, her attentive companionship, and her precious education pursued in the leisure of these long days and lonely nights. An idea abruptly occurred to her. She asked whether I had known nothing about the arrival of someone at the chateau before entering, and when I told her that I knew absolutely nothing about any arrival and that I had come solely to see again for a single hour, while I was passing through, these places so impossible to forget, she replied with an involuntary movement that she minimized as best she could with a smile, her morbid thought (exactly like my own), "How singular it is. I could even believe that Heaven expressly sent you. And, actually, Monsieur Amaury, who knows whether someone won't have need of you soon?" All of us were silent after that sad sentence. Monsieur de Couaën had a perceptible start; it could have been sorrow, discontent, or embarrassment. It could be he was embarrassed by my presence, that he was especially shocked by the idea of my ministry. He was the first to cut short the conversation, speaking of the exertion Madame de Couaën had to be spared, and we both left her room.

The heat was oppressive. He led me to the end of the grove, where we could sit down. I could assess the frightening progress of unhappiness in Monsieur de Couaën over the years. He was eternally prey to his mute mourning for his son on the one hand and to his covert, opinionated, envenomed duel with the head of the Empire on the other. He did not allude to the first point, but I could see from a few bitterly resigned words he let slip on Madame de Couaën's condition that this loss was less for him a new sorrow beyond compare than a wakening of the old. Thus, when one has once borne up under the greatest sorrow possible in this world, the rest, when they come, cannot fill further the overflowing vase, they can only agitate it and stir its depths. In striking the ulcerated heart, the most they can do is reopen sections of the immense old wound.

As for the other object and pastureland of his active animosity, he reached it quickly and discussed it as if there had been no interruption since our first conversations, paying little attention to my changed state, and with some kind of mania, common to great characters who have not found an outlet for their energies and have expended it on themselves. He was grateful to me for listening to him without dissent, and the shadow of jealousy which I first thought I saw on his face dispersed in a glow of friendship, while he entertained me with his hatreds. There was a fascination in his words which exerted an influence attracting me as before, although I sensed more strongly than ever something outrageous and false—inevitable in disappointed men. His face showed me that kind of altered transparency, even more striking than before. The more he was carried away by his idea, the more he blanched, so to speak, so that he no longer looked the age he was four years earlier but like an old man. I could imagine that I saw stretching out the lines of the wrinkles and his barer temples the cleated claws of a vulture. I could make no better comparison than to see him like an old captain in a conquered country who resists a siege by himself, forgotten, but unvanquished, tall but grown stiff, having become a little like the rocks of his crenelations, incapable of anything after the defense and half mad as a result, as was said, I think, of Barbanegro after Huninga. Or like a wounded man who holds violently on to his entrails and blood and uses all his living breath to wait for his conqueror's death.

At the height of our conversation we were disturbed by a sudden darkness and thunder, a torrent of rain we had not seen coming and

which did not give us time to go back inside. Burrowing for shelter in
the depths of the foliage, we waited for a letup when soon, believing
we heard voices repeatedly calling for us, we broke out through the
downpour. They were calling for us through the gardens. As soon as
she saw us, young Lucy, terrified, threw herself in her father's arms,
crying out that her mother was dead, that she had just passed away a
moment ago. We ran to the bedroom and discovered that Madame de
Couaën had indeed lost consciousness and seemed lifeless. The outbreak of the storm had brought on a crisis. While we tried to bring
her back to consciousness, Monsieur de Couaën ordered a doctor
fetched from the city. Recalled to the responsibilities of my position,
I for my part asked to have the parish rector alerted. Madame de
Couaën had been placed on a bed. After extended efforts and a very
painful struggle, she came to. Her first thought in seeing us was to
smile, but she could not keep from saying that she could not stay
long. She was sufficiently aware when the rector, who had hurried,
came in. She recognized him by his garb, never having seen him
previously, and she understood why he had been called. It was
then, in turning towards us without the least trace of embarrassment
interfering with her weakened voice, without the least blush altering
the uniform, morbid pallor of her brow, that she declared that since
God seemed to have sent me on purpose, if Monsieur the rector and
Monsieur de Couaën would be so kind to grant her the favor and
would consent, she would like to have me hear her confession, give
her communion, and prepare her for the death she felt approaching.
The rector, who knew who I was, hastened, after two or three
questions to me, to acquiesce to the sick woman's wish and yielded
authority to me. However, Monsieur de Couaën's brow clouded over.
It passed quickly, and he himself came, taking my hands convulsively,
implored me to accept. I had a moment of extreme self-doubt. Yet
when I considered how many miraculous coincidences had occurred,
I had an illumination. After the first trip to Brittany, as a consequence
of my first desire, I could approach the present scene of this second
desire, so ardent that I had been unable to keep from leaving my
uncle's home that morning; I could not fail to recognize the direct line
traced and see a luminous indication of the ways of God. I bowed in
assent, replying in a few words choked by tears, and I left the room
to withdraw in prayer before those hours of formidable ministering.

Scarcely had I repaired to that room where I used to stay and
which had been prepared for me again, than the burden of it all
overcame me. I fell crushed, my forehead on the floor, and I beseeched
Him who strengthens and moves, who gives a brazen buckler to the

heart and incorruptible softness to the lips; He who knows above all
how, whether young or old, one speaks to virgins, widows, courtesans
and wives, how one consoles mothers on their deathbeds; the Same
who without shame listened at Jacob's well to the Samaritan woman,
He who is Simon's house felt the tears and perfumes of Magdelaine
pour over his feet, wiped by her tresses, without repulsing her,
without being disturbed by it, saying aloud that what she did was
good; He who judged that Martha's sister, seated at his feet for a
whole day, made the wiser choice; He who inspires and arms confessors, sending the least of them, provided they are sincere, a reflection
of his virtues, a majesty that has nothing ferocious, a condescension
that is in no way carnal. Reviewing at random the examples that
seemed little suited to give me authority, I beseeched Him, this God
of the weak and dying to permit me to be less hard, less threatening
than had been a repentant Abelard repentant to a despairing Heloise
imploring, that He would make me less complacent and less easy than
perhaps had been Fénélon with the *la penserosa* of the *Torrent*; but He
would let me attain rather a stance both more clement and more
austere, like Saint Jerome exhorting Saint Paula and St. Francis closing
the eyes of the Baroness of Thorens. I prayed that He make me
serious without constraint, sober without aridity, suddenly fortified,
endowed with unknown lights and accents, master of my tears,
commanding my old idols, capable, without being too shaken, raising
her soul high, engendering her in God without too much trembling,
presenting her immolated like a sainted prey, without her glimpsing
too much of it. The soul of the pastor/priest will soar like the eagle, if
he is shown the way: "Let my soul, therefore, easily sublime by Your
Will, Lord, rise and climb!" I cried, "let her rise, like the zealous,
pitiless eagle who ravishes the dove in her nest but brings her to you!"

Among the three sacraments that I was preparing, confession,
extreme unction, and communion, there were still two--the first two—
which I had not yet ministered, since I had scarcely been ordained six
weeks. It was therefore with this creature of so much predilection I was
going to begin to practice the conferred roles of judge and purifier.
The cedars of Lebanon themselves would have trembled. The rector
spoke to me briefly. I went over all details precisely, and then he went
to get the host and holy oils from the church while I heard confession.

When I returned to the tower chamber, I was wearing the surplice
the rector had left me. She was lying on the bed, completely clothed
in a modest position, hands clasped together, her head slightly raised
upon the pillows. She appeared to have reached a state of non-
suffering, as often happens with invalids in the final moments. The

lines of her face were emphasized yet calm. Nothing in her, except for weak and feverish shortness of breath, betrayed the venom of approaching death. Everyone left the room. The door remained open. The day had become beautiful again, softly refreshed, and tinkling bells, inviting the dying to pray, reached us from time to time through the sonorous air of the evening breeze. I put myself in a position so that she could speak without bending over too much and without my having to see her. The crucifix was placed on a cushion, at the other end of the bed. She could see both the crucifix and me. It was thus that her confession began in as general terms as possible, as suits the article of death.

Angels from heaven, powers of love and fear, with your centers and your swords, redouble your guard around my heart, so that what it heard and replied in God's name in these moments remains under seven seals, so that this tabernacle of flesh has neither rent nor sigh, so that what the heart received from the mystery rests inviolable, with no possible confusion with the rest of my memories and terrestrial conjectures, or rather that what was heard never be linked to my human memory, so that this scene remain for me only ashes, perfumes, a distant little lamp amidst surrounding shadows—like, in fact, a tomb!

When confession was over, everyone came back in the room. Preceded by the bell, the rector came in with the vial and the holy ciborium. Candles were lit at each corner of the bed. A table was set with a white cloth expressly for the holy vessels. Some glowing coals were brought in on a silver warming pan to burn the flakes imbibed as soon as they were dipped in the oil. Because the invalid's state did not compel urgency, the best order could be followed. I had to begin with extreme unction, which is the complement of penitence. After the absolution of faults committed and separate acts, extreme unction reaches each organ at its origin and root, corrects it, so to speak, and reintegrates it. The servants were either on their knees or holding candles. Young Lucy, kneeling on a chair at the foot of the bed, was withdrawn, silent, admirable in her attention, expressing a form of self-reflecting sorrow quite beyond her age. The Marquis was standing, stooped, his arms crossed upon his chest. His drawn face twitched convulsively from time to time, almost dry-eyed, with no appearance of praying, but the height of silent desolation, the picture of crushed yet forever unbending resistance, the great invalid whom then or never I should heal, too. Clothed in the violet stole and accompanied by the rector, I approached Madame de Couaën. After having instructed her where she was to answer "Oui, Monsieur," I began the application of the sacrament, making the annointments in the sign of the cross on the seven designated parts of the body.

What I felt inside while I was passing in order, repairing with the blessed paintbrush the eyelids, ears, mouth, neck, hands, and feet of the dying woman, beginning with the eyes, the keenest, promptest, most vulnerable sense, and into the double organs, starting with the right, the keenest and most accessible; what infinite and appropriate ideas each brief formula that I articulated placed in my mind; what, to put it better, the blessed rain escaping from my hands rolled in a holy storm within me, has no word in language, my friend, and could only be matched by chords from the pipe organ of eternity. But if you wish, you can easily sketch a shading of a crying out to you, in a broken and weakened echo of an incommunicable thought:

"Oh, let it be given on the eyes first, the sense of sight, the noblest and keenest sense; to these eyes for what they have seen, espied or the too tender and treacherous in other eyes, of the too mortal; for what they have read and reread that is too attaching and too cherished; for what they have poured in vain tears over fragile objects and faithless creatures, for the sleep they have so often forgotten in the evening in thinking over what they have seen!

"On the sense of hearing also, for what the ears have heard or let be said that was too sweet, too flattering and intoxicating; for the sap that they steal slowly from deceiving words so that they may drink the hidden honey!

"Next on the sense of smell for the too subtle and voluptuous perfumes of spring evenings in the depths of the woods, for the flowers received in the morning and all day long breathed in with so much guilty pleasure!

"On the lips for what they uttered that was too obscure or too open; for what they did not reply in certain moments or what they did not reveal to certain persons; for what they sang in the solitude that was too melodious or too full of tears; for their inarticulate murmur, for their silence!

"On the neck at the base of the breast, for the ardor of desire, as the consecrated expression goes *propter ardorem libidinis;* yes, for pain and affection, rivalries, for too much anguish in human tenderness, for tears which choke a throat that has lost its voice, for all that makes a heart beat or gnaws at it!

"On the hands also for having clasped a hand not bound to them by holy bonds; for having received tears too scalding; for having perhaps begun to write, without ending, some unallowable response!

"On the feet for not having fled, for having sufficed for long

solitary walks, for not having wearied soon enough in the midst of
conversations that stop only to start again!''

But let us pause a moment, my friend, to take in the majesty of
this moment. There was one place where I used French with those
present, to caution them to participate with full attention and cooper-
ate in their minds with the sacramental act, to remind them that we
shall all in our turn come to this supreme passing, and that we would
need to merit passing with as much calm as that surrounding us then.
Then I cautioned her to bless her daughter, her people, and to offer
advice and adieux. She did so. First with her daughter, towards whom
I raised her right hand, already unsure of its movements. This hand
rested on the girl's head at the height of the crown, like an alabaster
dove. The girl's face was hidden in the coverlet, which smothered her
moaning. Madame de Couaën recommended God's counsel through
prayer, as her daughter would not have a mother's guidance, and she
wished for her a gentle disposition as a recompense for so many pious
duties. Without removing her hand from her daughter's hair, she
asked the Marquis' pardon in the name of the dear child she was
confiding to his care,—pardon for her connubial neglect, the heavy
burden she had caused him, the possible consolation she had failed to
give him. He came abruptly forward from the foot of the bed where
he had been standing up until then and before she had finished, and
with no other response, he seized that limp hand from his daughter's
hair and bore it to his lips with an impassioned tremor. Then in a
feeble but clear voice she addressed her servants. She accused herself
of having overly neglected them during her absence. She sought their
prayers and asked them not to forget her in death, calling them by
name one after another, beginning with old François. The whole room
was a single sob. The communion service followed immediately. God
granted that my voice remained steady, my eyes contained themselves,
and my heart was not swept away by this torrent of sorrow swelling
around me. She and I, if I may risk saying so, were the calmest of all,
as we had to be, the most firmly directed, borne only by the flood of
this sorrow and as if raised higher towards heaven in the imperishable
bark. When communion was over, the rector left, taking the holy
vessels back to the church. The Marquis, his daughter, and I remained
alone around the bed. It was a new scene of adieux, but more pressing,
more internal. She asked his forgiveness again and conjured him here
as she had earlier to let the spirit of sweetness and pardon be established unreservedly in his heart. "If you do not forgive everyone," she
said, "yes, all strangers, whether peasants or Emperors, it will be
because you have not completely forgiven me. Forgiving a dying

woman entirely is forgiving, in memory of her, all who live. A cherished woman lingering as a sweet and forgiven idea intercedes perpetually in the heart." She played with this thought in a thousand delicate and sublime meanings. Returning to her daughter, she made more specific her advice to be prudent and live a well-ordered life, singling out her haughty turn of character as an especial danger but mingled with a thousand tender words of praise and adoring encouragement. I received my share in these intimate words:

"Monsieur Amaury, let me die, grateful to the point of tears for so much devoted service and so many efforts over yourself!" And she asked me to bless her, more particularly as a simple priest and friend. Somewhat let down from my earlier elevation, it was hard to me not to break down. It was then, after speaking to each, that she expressed the desire to be buried, not in the parish sepulcher of Couaën but in the chapel of Saint-Pierre, beneath a central flagstone near the lamp, and that a mass be celebrated for her there twice a year. Moreover, she wanted to be enshrouded in the very clothes she was wearing, by the scruple of this desire to spare the living from those most sorrowful attentions that are a veritable death agony; happy she could spare us without putting this subject into words, alas! Once her wishes were so clearly put forth, she felt very weak. Night had come, and she sank into a drowsy state. All conversation ceased. I remained next to her bed reading the Psalms in French, in a voice she could hear if she were not asleep but which would not wake her if she were sleeping.

The doctor from town was not long in coming. He confirmed that she could not have been weaker but was completely conscious. There was nothing to try except a few spoonfuls of tonic that he prescribed. The rector himself returned to help the sick woman with his prayers, and throughout the first part of the night he, the doctor, Monsieur de Couaën, Lucy, and I filled that silent room, already funereal, where two tapers still burned. But after midnight, because there was no symptom of a change, I got the Marquis and Lucy to go get some rest. The doctor went into a nearby room, close enough to hear the slightest call, and the rector also left with the intention of not returning until morning. So I found myself alone with the personal maid, sometimes completely alone, near the bed where that soul kept watch at the supreme watch and gently breathed in and out. I redoubled my prayers. In the fullness of my heart, I added spontaneous prayers to those I had in the text beneath my eyes. If I stopped a moment or let my voice die, a slight movement from the dying woman alerted me to continue, that she still called for prayers. Towards morning, however, while the others were still absent and even the servant had left for a few moments, I was reading, with ardor, several short verses of the ritual rushing over my lips in a hundred pleading exhortations. Suddenly the tapers paled, the letters hid from my eyes, morning light entered. I heard the sound of a distant bell and the song of a bird, tapping the window pane with his beak, burst forth as if responding to a familiar signal. I rose and looked at her, transfixed. Her entire posture was motionless; her pulse was not beating. I brought to her lips, like a mirror, my brilliant ebony crucifix that Madame de Cursy had left me. No sign of breathing showed. I lowered her half-closed eyelids with a finger. The eyelids obeyed and did not rise again, like things no longer alive. With the first tremor of morning, in the first light of blanching dawn, at the first swing of the bell and the first trill of the bird, that wakeful soul passed on!

Admirable, dear soul, flown away forever in that moment, since that hour when you entered the invisible, where, save for a more or less slow final expiation, you have certainly been promised to the plenitude of divine joys, since that moment when your spiritual eyes were instantaneously unsealed. The gall of death, like the gall of Toby's fish, gives complete clairvoyance to all it has touched. You know what we feel, what we do here below, what we have done and felt in former years, in the very years where you lived near us in your corporeal envelope and judged us with such indulgence! Oh, do not blush for us overmuch. I who helped you, raised with effort and authority to that height, from the moment you are there, I fall back, I bow. It now for me to pray to you. Succor us, beautiful Soul, before God. Ask him for us to have the strength that we have communicated to you, perhaps, but, alas, without having enough of it ourselves, and since mortal infirmity has need of a signal, a call, a souvenir in order to walk unwaveringly towards the sure paths, intercede with the Master to keep yourself our keepsake in the beyond, the visible cross at the angle of the road, to keep you by preference the spirit of warning and the heaven-sent angel!

When the Marquis came in shortly afterwards, I advanced to meet him, pointing with one arm to the inanimate body, putting the other arm around his neck:

"Now she lives a better life," I said, embracing him. The day was painful and long indeed. We took turns in the mute chamber, he, his daughter, the rector, and I. In the wavering taper light, the intoning of a slow prayer by the rector or myself wavered also, monotone and sad. At dinner I tried to break the dreary silence in talking about examples of saints on the deathbed and benedictions that encompass the living, but I felt it extremely difficult to take, vis-à-vis Monsieur de Couaën, the superior tone of my sacerdotal habit.

As silence was returning after a pause, Monsieur de Couaën said, "My dear Amaury, I have decided to raise and keep a lighthouse near the Saint-Pierre chapel. It is a rather dangerous spot. Fishermen on our coast often break against this cliff. The lighthouse will have a guard and at the same time the chapel will be better protected." It was the first time I had heard him worry about the shipwrecked fishermen on the coast. He seemed to be listening to a distant noise of waters filtering into the entrails of the cliff.

I spent the evening and part of the night keeping watch near the mortuary bed, but when it was nearly morning, Monsieur de Couaën strenuously imposed my retiring in order to be ready for the religious offices during the day. As a result, I had been resting somewhat heavily for some time when old François came to wake me and warn me that they could hear his groans and smothered bellows in the tower room where he had ordered that he be left alone with the body. They did not dare open or enter because of his prohibition. I went down immediately and as I approached I too heard lugubrious, dull roars, like a mother rolling upon a lifeless body of a child. I went in. He had his face against the bed, embracing the object. The coffin he had had brought up remained open nearby without his being able to make himself place in it what had been the tenderest part of his flesh. His cries ceased when he saw me. Perhaps he was unaware he had made them or had been heard.

"Let us know how to separate ourselves from these corruptible remains which are not the soul we grieve."

And taking with precaution the body under the arms, as you do with a sick person you are afraid of hurting, as the holy women did for Jesus, I engaged him to do the same with the waist and feet. He followed my directions, and the burden was then placed gently in the coffin. I said, "Let us dispense with alien hands."

We put the lid in place. I put nails on my side; he put some on his—because he had already readied all the instruments himself. The result was that we did together what he had been determined to do alone.

The interment took place in the morning. The rector celebrated those services. I had said a low mass earlier, exclusively for the soul of the deceased. During the service, the Marquis dominated the assemblage from the height of his venerable head, alone at the bench closest to the choir, standing against his son's marble. The cortège began to move from the church towards the chateau and the mountain, skirting the furthest garden, the canal, and the landing for the mill, the favorite spots of former days, crossing the ferruginous stream, and taking the high road, quite rough in the full heat of day. The news of the arrival and death of Madame de Couaën had not had time to be widely known. There were only a few peasants from the village and the nearby hamlets, a fair number of women, a few girls. The Marquis wanted to go to the end. His daughter had stayed in the chateau. Still wearing my surplice, I climbed the mountain next to him, giving him my arm sometimes, for the climb was painful at this hour. Through the uneven shade the sun beat down upon our bare heads. The pallbearers climbed slowly in front of us, breathing heavily. Oh, sun, bear down upon the two of us, more cruelly still. Stones and pebbles, bruise and cut our feet still more. This is where we last climbed seven years ago, I prey to suspect excitement and adulterous delectation, he prey to acrimonious ambitions and envious hatred. Oh, let both of us following this body be broken in our wounds today! and let him return as cured as I, henceforth by the same grace! But sun, you are not yet heavy enough on our heads. Path of ascent, you are not hard enough; nor you, pebbles and rocks, sharp enough on our feet. Because we need to have our sweat pour like blood today. Our sweat should rain along the old tracks until they are as fertile as furrows.

Once at the summit, the greatest spectacle, and for some time, an unaccustomed spectacle, opened up before us, a perfumed, flowering heath, humming with a thousand noises in the heat, an immense, pure sky framing a brilliant sea, and cut clean with the black anfractuous rocks that were like a glorious border. Everything as far as Couaën, to the extent that I had attention to note it, had seemed smaller, more abridged than before. Only here did I find again the same eternal grandeur. Thus I thought, "This climb we have just finished resembles life. Beyond and at the summit, this is what the soul discovers. But the soul that discovers these things in God from this life must keep walking, like us, beneath the fatigue of the day and the sun while the sainted soul of the dead can forego fatigue and pain." And while walking I prayed for her whose spirit so happily inhabited this heath in the times of the terrestrial fatherland, and which, liberated now, was returning to hover over us.

In the inside of the chapel everything was ready. It was only necessary to put the body beneath the middle flagstone in a kind of small cellar and to throw dirt upon it. But at this sight, tears and thoughts assailed me. With the rector's permission, I advanced to the threshold, and before all those present in a circle, before that sea and that majestic sky, not far from the stone guard-tower, in a language to be understood by all present, I cried,

"Winds of the West, sighs of the Ocean, blow without too much rage, bring sometimes in your storms a breeze from her fatherland!

"Waves of the sea, stop gnawing so furiously against this cliff and leave everything upright!

"Halcyons, crows, seagulls, birds who leave in autumn for the great banks, stop here in your regrouping. God will bless your passage and strengthen your wings!

"Vessels, sails in distress, be trusting. God, we beseech you to keep them from breaking on this bristling gulf, and keep the new lighthouse from sending deceptive signals!

"Dear God who is in the winds, waves, elements, who presides over things and human destinies, see that only the good, clement, and blessed happen around these mortal remains of the Woman who was so good, so tried, so penitent; let her have the rest we pray for her!"

And turning towards the crowd, I dismissed it. They broke up in silence. We made our way behind, the Marquis, the rector, and I without engaging in conversation.

Each of us spent the rest of the day in his room, tending to his wounds and sorrows. I had seen the Marquis touched, I had heard his groans in the morning, I had seized the tears on his cheeks when I had spoken outside the chapel. I had felt in returning his arm tremble in resting on mine. I waited anxiously the moment we would be alone and naturally in conversation to strike the last blows on him by virtue of my duties and my heart. After dinner, which took place for the sake of form, and very late, he, young Lucy and I went out through the gardens. Without having realized it, we reached the avenue leading to the mountain. The Marquis affectionately sent his daughter back in, and we continued walking. It was then, after a few minutes of inner struggle and hesitation, towards the middle of the climb, I abruptly began,

"Marquis, permit me to address you for once in these environs with the authority vested in me by Him to whom I have pledged myself and from the heights of the revered memory of those no longer with us. Tell me, what have you felt during these last sad days? Drowned in a true affliction, what have become of your cares of the eve before, the ambitions of this earth, the insurmountable obstacles you fought, those duels against all odds with the powerful? The victories of tomorrow, which will belie your hopes once more, could resound in your ears at this very moment without your hearing any less the silence of death, the solemn and infinite roar of the waves.

This iniquitous power that wounds you and that another power will replace when it falls (because in the end it will fall, I am sure of that). This other power in its turn will soon be an iniquity. Tell me, will you feel your pride offended at that moment, and do you dream of festering and cursing? Let true sorrow have at least this fecund effect on us, to cure us of the false and sterile sorrows!

"All this disorder in human results, this inequality in fate and luck, this ill-luck of chance which you accused seven years ago on this spot, all that is what it is only because the revolt of will creates and maintains it. I would want no other proof that evil was first introduced into the world by man's will to revolt, but in seeing how much this evil, while persisting in its appearance, ceases in reality, is converted occasionally into good, is lowered to the grasp as a fruit of merit and virtue, as soon as the thunderstruck brow bends, as soon as human will is subjected. The universal complement of all our insufficiencies, the corrective of all inflections, the concordance of all that swears and cries out, the light in the chaos, is to will in one sense and not in another. It is to accept.—Yes, it is the will for sorrow, death, and what is worse for some souls, obscurity, injustice, misunderstanding. All these evils veritably cease to exist as soon as we decide they will, or at least they exist only to become the healing sources of their bitterness. Consider, Marquis, and see whether if looked at one way, you would not have cause to bless and praise, perhaps, precisely for not having succeeded at the measure of your desires. Because what would you really be if you had succeeded and surged forth, if this world where you wanted to take part had let you board it, if you had seized there the important role that you dreamed of since youth? What is the reef of all great characters of your kind, once engaged in practical activity? Forced duplicity towards men, expedience in means, excess by intoxication, pretext for reasons of State. You are getting red, forgive me! It is only because instead of that, you have kept the grandeur and simplicity of unfrequented paths, a kind of ancient ingenuity, faithful companion of your despair. Oh, there is no excess in you, and I would want only to cut away the hatred!"

And I continued, seeing him under my sway and listening: "Oh, if you introduced within the sole element lacking, the breath of freshness which never comes too late, the dew which manages to nourish even in the rocks and sand (and I pointed to a spot of sand and greenery, a kind of fragrant warren where we walked)—Let these dead who are dear to you remove from a part of your nights, a part of your soul, these hatreds of here below and these prolonged emulations which attest to a great nature but which also precipitate it, imprison it in ferocious caverns that embroil it in the brambles. The girl, so serious already, so struck, who is made in your image, is she destined to finish growing enveloped by you in a shadow more dense than the cypress?—Learn how to accept in spirit what is, will it! Just pray, pray; give free rein to this simple thought. I will tell you thus: 'Noble Sicabra, half despoiled in the midst of the age, bend down! Make yourself one of us all, a widower, a heartsick father, a child of mortal misery! A tear, long denied and devoured, which finally falls, humble and burning, from a pupil of stone, counts more before God than torrents loosed by facile tenderness; an iron knee that bends snatches at the vaults of heaven as it sinks!'"

He was still silent and as we were coming back down, I perceived a star in the sky, at the same place as during the former and final promenade. Near the little tower, on the terrace, his daughter, recognizable by her straw hat, seemed to wait for us as had her mother once. I pointed to the star: "The souls of the dead are like this. One leaves them in the West in the dust of the tomb and suddenly one finds them again in the star of the East!"

"Ah, yes," he burst out, letting down his guard, "You were right, my friend, *Lucia nimica di ciascun crudele*--I have lived too much in hatred." And we fell in each other's arms at the name of Lucy, and remained mute for some time, except for our sobs. Did his daughter see us embracing from up on her terrace? What did this sight mean to her? Did she think about it later? I do not know. Do we know what the daughters of women we have loved think of us in their hearts?

No doubt the Marquis was not cured of his malady from that moment on. You do not wean ambition in a day any more than you wean pleasures. But a new, peaceful element was introduced. A salutary effort took root, and more and more with age that great soul brought himself under control. The meaning of his cross was given to him. From then on he had the measure of his suffering.

As for me, I had accomplished what I owed to my ministry, but I was at the end of my strength. Affection so repressed had its revenge, and I was not going to be up to it beyond that. It was time for me to steal away. Early the next morning, the day following the funeral rites, I went down and saddled my horse myself, making him leave softly at a walk as far as the courts and the barriers, leaving the chateau without saying good-bye—and then leaving Brittany as fast as I could—and France a few days later.

CHAPTER XXV

My friend, you know everything. The rest of my life has been only an application, to the best of my abilities, of general duties and feelings towards men. Many assignments, trips, study, divers activities. But what I felt was proper to me, what was original and distinctive in my destiny, the part marked in my name before God, in the universal tribute of human misfortune and sorrow, the secret taste by which I would recognize my tears among all others, here is what is eternally attached to the circumstances of this story for me. Almost any man, whose youth was sensitive, has likewise had his story where the principal quality of his soul, and in some respects, the natural savor of his tears, was produced, where he brought his dearest offering as the price to pay for initiation to life. But the majority, far from sparing and respecting this first inner accomplishment, shake if off, offend it, denature it, and in the end usually profane or eliminate it. That ambitious man who persists miserably and grows old in his ruses, he had, no doubt in a better age, a first, noble treasure of suffering, some graven image, some adored sepulcher that during some generous moment he promised himself he would visit forever. But he quickly wearied of it, he let it fall by the wayside, and it covered over with earth after a few seasons. In the end he built over it the apparatus of his intrigues, the tiresome scaffolding of his power. The poet himself, who built a mausoleum on the spot of his first great sorrows, too often risks forgetting about the soul in the marble monument; his idolatry for the statue hides the ashes from him. That dried-out, frivolous man, that social climber we avoid, he perhaps had his story like the ambitious man or the poet. He began by feeling, but he subsequently added so many tasteless layers and deceptive ploys to his first best feelings that he got lost along the way before finding anything. So, it is not best, after having undergone in your youth such a wrenching and tender calamity, to cling to it, keep it secret, unique in itself, to purify it in silence with simplicity, to take refuge there at intervals in the active life to which the rest of our years are destined, to have it always in our depths like a sanctuary and tomb to which we are led on every road, by special paths known to us alone, to return there unceasingly with an undefinable emotion, with a singular accent dear to men, which brings them without their knowing the source and which disposes them on any occasion to be touched by our words and to believe our beliefs?

At least I tried to have it this way for me, letting that mysterious, distant star cast upon all my days a faithful reflection, which is none other in my eyes but a softened reflection of my cross. In what will soon be the two decades that followed the last crisis, my life had been rather diversely taken up with the divine work, rather peripatetic, more fixed on the goal than tied down to any place. Emerging from emotions like that, while still young, having so much to watch in myself, in old and recent wounds, I had to fear any burden that was too heavy, any regular responsibility for souls. Rome on several occasions held me for a long time and strengthened me a great deal. That city of meditation, continuity, eternal memory was especially good for me. I needed that immense cloister, that slow and permanent celebration, and the calm of the emtombed saints. Rome is the best place after a shipwreck to appease the last waves in the heart. Rome also is the best vantage point for judging, as from the most deserted and stable ocean cliff, the turbulent foam of the world. I have often returned to our France, but without desiring too long a residence or functions attaching me, feeling more master of myself, more capable of good, somewhere else. I saw Monsieur de Couaën many times after that evening on the hill, but never in Brittany. In fact, he never got used to living there on a year-round basis. When the time of his right of séjour expired, he neglected, despite Monsieur Desmaret's hints, to request a complete pardon. A kind of sad habit and a few advantages he saw for his daughter kept him at Blois until the first Restoration. During the 100 days he went from Brittany to England with his daughter, by then a grown and accomplished young lady. He saw Ireland again, found again what was left of his kindred, as well as who remained in his wife's family. It was during that trip that beautiful Lucy found favor with a young lord of the country, son of a Catholic peer, and married him two years later. Today she lives partly in London, partly in County Kildare. At the time of her marriage I gave her as a present my uncle's farm with the land attached to it, reserving a modest little section for my own use when passing through. She probably attaches little value to this gift, less than I attach to it, I who have no such interests. Being small when she lived there, she did not know it, and perhaps she will never visit it. But it is an inexpressible happiness for us to give pledges to the children of beloved women, now dead, and to reassemble on them the sweet testimony which in part they neglect and in part they ignore. Didn't one of our poets say

> Les jeunes gens d'un bond franchissent nos douleurs.
> Que leur font nos amours? . . . leur ivresse est ailleurs.
> (The young leap over our pain.
> Our heartache means nothing;
> They've something else to gain.)

Upon returning to France after the 100 Days, the Marquis refused election to the Chamber of 1815, to which he would have been nominated unanimously. He feared, in the presence of grievances, and in the shock of so many passions, the reawakening of his own resentment and the travail of the old leaven. He died in 1818, about a year after his daughter's marriage, upheld by the hope of his religion and believing firmly that he would find again his wife and son. It was my great sorrow not to be with him at that moment.

What more can I add, my friend, about the other characters of this story? Did I know, given my absence, alas, the detail or outcome of their destinies? You leave the port together, or rather, having left from adjacent ports, you meet again on the same seaway. At first you celebrate, you preen, you spend time together while waiting the first wind; you even leave in the same squadron born by the same breeze, until the evening of the first day. Then you get further apart from one another, losing sight of one another, almost carelessly, by nightfall. And if you meet once again, it is to cross paths quickly with the risk of some storm. And you lose sight of each other again forever. Mademoiselle Amélie, whose marriage I reported to you, died a few years later, leaving a son. I do not know what happened after that. My fine Norman friend continues to live in his retreat, nearly happy, his strengthened character seldom disturbed. Like a heart that has been well regulated for a long time, he sometimes complains that he is still beating. If I were not writing these pages to you, I would address them to him.

I was not in France when Monsieur de Couaën died. It was my first trip to America, which I shall see again soon, but remain for the rest of my days, no doubt. I stayed three years that time in active duty, escaping thus from that retreat, too absorbing in the long run, of Roman life, or in the spectacle of the envenomed quarrels in France.

As you know, it was after my return from that first voyage, one evening on Mount Alban, a little above the Convent of the Passionists, not far from the ruined temple of Jupiter and the broken triumphal avenue, and the two beautiful lakes rather near there at our feet, that our destinies, dear friend, came together. I came upon you alone, motionless, taken up in admiration. Opposite, the magnified setting sun and its flames, overflowing the sea at the horizon, drowned in confusion the Roman plains and gilded the eternal coupola, sole visible monument. Your eyes swam in luminous tears. I approached without your noticing, you were so ravished by the space and blinded by the splendors. However, I spoke to you, and we chatted, and from the first everything in your blossoming spirit charmed me. After a few days of conversation, I understood what your weakness and idol were, your dangers and desires. I saw into you as into myself, but still young, still half inexperienced, vis-à-vis the bitterness you had experiences. I was flooded with tenderness and sadness. My heart, which I believed closed forever to new friendships, opened again for you.

You were sometimes astonished when you knew me better, my friend, that I had never tried to seize and exert a regular influence, and to make a visible place for myself by writing, preaching, or something else, an the grave moral and religious questions that divided and continue to divide our country. My distances, without speaking to the talents that not distancing would have required, held firm thanks to two principal causes. The first is that never having approached your active world in my last days in your milieu, having observed it rather from the outside from afar, from beyond the Atlantic during the three years of assignment, or from the heart of the deserted squares of Rome, along the monastery walls and in the isolation of my old sorrows, I thought I discerned that the real world was really vast and resistant to direction, that one did not usually imagine when in the hurricane eye. And I have a greatly reduced idea of the importance of what once was most frantically sought in your milieu, and consequently I am also much less prey to the alleged governing impulse of such and such a voice in the melee. In the second place, I have also doubted that this public influence, noisy and risky where so many suspect ingredients slip in, so many vain impulses, was the most healthy. It often happened in my divers paths and in my wandering detours, for example, at the heart of those religious Orders the world despises and considers dead—it often happened that I discovered so much intelligence and soul, almost unrecognized, without fanfare, without an external setting, but useful, profound, having an influence that is completely good, sure, continuous, precious to their surroundings, that I have reconsidered my doubts on the advantageous predominance of the apparent leaders. My cherished secret vow would therefore have been the first row before God among these rather obscure but active lives, among this people of nameless benefactors, dispersed here and there. The most beautiful souls are those, I said, that while acting, most nearly approach invisibility, like the most perfect glass being that lets light pass through it intact without keeping any behind, without signaling by a thousand pompous colors that it is present.

In such agitated times and from an observer's threshold, I could not avoid being subject in certain secondary areas of my perspective to variations that age alone would suffice to bring, regardless of lack of vicissitudes and upheavals in the environment. I learned to suspect my opinion of the day since that of yesterday was perceptibly modified, and to be unhurried in advising others for a transitory application of something that tomorrow perhaps I would disavow or repent. Variations which are thus composed gradually, slowly, and silently within us, have a weary sweetness and all the charm of an adieu, while if they occur with emphasis in front of witnesses who will reproach us, they become wounding and harsh. In a period of youth and impetuous ascent, we are brusque and quickly contemptuous towards all that we reprove after having believed in and loved. The stone where the night before we rested our head serves almost immediately as a lower step for climbing higher, and we crush it underfoot, insulting it with our spiked heels. At least later on, when we are already on our descent of the hill and want to sit on the stone and leave it behind, let us not insult it. And if we turn back to it, if we touch it at the turning of the road before moving off, let our hand pat it as a friend or give it a farewell kiss!

As for the essential beliefs, in those years of attack and diversity on everything around, have I not had more serious shocks, my hours of agony and doubt in which I said, "My God, why hast Thou forsaken me?" No one ever escapes such hours entirely. They have their access of tenebrae even in the heart of faith, in the times of Job, Christ, Jerome, Saint Louis as well as our own. Even with our knees on the holy rock, we become again more wavering than the reed. Nor have I been exempt from frequent assaults in those special wounds which you have seen me taking such pains to close, which quivered at certain moments—and do so yet. This still requires an inner effort, the daily struggle of every mortal. But every time I gave in to the controversies of the day and wanted to contribute my thoughts and opinion, it meant I had just lost by an imperceptible detour the keen and present sentiment of the faith through the echo of words, loosening the hold of my intimate, scrupulous self-reflection, judging it more insignificant, and since the result was bad, I concluded that what brought it on was not sure, while on the contrary I never felt myself so confident or vigilant as when I kept silent and practiced my faith.

What struck me most on my first return from America was the situation of that France, to which I have always been attached like a child and for which I bled beneath my stole during the years of invasion, was that after the Empire and the excesses of military which had prevailed, we abruptly passed to the excesses of speech, to the prodigality and bloating of declamation, images, promises, and to an equally blind confidence in these new weapons. I mean to speak here, you understand, only of the moral disposition of society, of that facility for illusion and sudden change which characterizes us. Unintelligent restrictions of power have only increased and will only increase this characteristic. This almost universal precipitous whirlwind of minds, if I had not for many years been on guard against it, (beginning with Monsieur Hamon's advice), this credulous precipitous whirlwind around me would have sufficed to put me on guard, and would have made me enter into my silence even earlier. Increasingly every morning brings with it a question of its illuminating insights which are only social discoveries. There must be in this new vortex serious repercussions, mortgaged miscalculations for the future. In my pain I often imagine the unflattering image of society in its material aspects like a chariot mired in the mud, which, once a certain momentum is achieved with age, most men despair of ever seeing move and no longer even desire to do so. But each new generation comes along, swearing before God that nothing is easier, and it gets to work with a generous lack of experience, harnessing everything to the right, to the left, crosswise (the places in front already taken), arms on the wheels, making the poor old cart creak everywhere, and many a time running the risk of breaking it. People quickly tire of this game. The most ardent soon get rope burn and drop out. The best never come back. And if later, a few manage to harness themselves as ambitious men at the front of this apparatus, they pull very little in reality and let newcomers take hold as awkwardly as they themselves did at first and get exhausted the same way. In a word, aside from a certain initial generosity, the great number of men in the affairs of this world follow no other goals than the false principles of a crafty experience which they apply to advance their name, their power, or well-being. Whatever the struggle, whatever be the idea at stake, it is always complicated in approximately the same terms: on the one hand, pure generations erupt with the ferocity of pagan virtue and are soon corrupted; on the other hand, mature generations, if that is still the right word, are tired, vicious generations who were pure at the beginning and who reign henceforth, foil the interlopers with the ease of established and masked corruption. A small number, the more inspired, after the first disillusionment of lofty conquest, hold to the antique and unique percepts of charity and kindness toward men, acting more than speaking, hold to this Christianity, so to speak, to which no new moral invention has yet found a syllable to add. However, my friend, I am far from denying, through these constant obstacles, a general and continuous movement of society, a realization, less and less gross, of some divine percepts. But the law of this movement is always and by every necessary extremely obscure, the felicity which must emerge from the means employed remains very doubtful, and the intervals to be crossed can be prolonged and impeded almost to infinity. We are all born in the hollow of a wave. Who knows where the true horizon is? or the land?

But at the moment I was writing that, just as if to answer my doubts, came the cry "Land!" I have just climbed up on the bridge. After the first summits are perceived, the seaway first effaced, soon distinct in its length, the land appears before our eyes. The black and brilliant dots, vessels enameling this immense bay have come into view. The highest hill of the shore gradually puts on its forest. Then the uneven hills are shaded in turn, and after a particular double turn, we are entering the waters of New York. On my earlier trip I disembarked at Baltimore. Oh America, your banks are as spacious as the solitudes of Rome. Your horizons have stretched out like Rome's. In grandeur only Rome can be compared to you. But you are limitless, and its frame is austere. But, young, you swarm in every direction in your deserts of yesterday, and Rome is fixed. You burst forth in thousands of swarms, and one would say that Rome forgets herself in thought. In the destinies that will come to pass and the roles that you represent, will you be enemies, my queens? Will there not come a day when its immutability and your life should united in some unknown manner? the certainty risen from its calm and your inventive agitations, eternal oracle and incessant freedom, the two grandeurs forming a single whole here below and giving us back an animated shadow of the City of God? Or at least if the spectacle of a too magnificent union is refused to the infirmity of the world, at least is it true that you contain, thus as it murmured on every side, the final material form that human societies must don to reach their full term of perfection?

What I know is that there will be in this form of society or any other the same passions as before, the same principal forms of sadness and pain, all kinds of tears, penchants no less rapid and deceptive reefs of youth, the same ancient moralities applicable still, and almost always futile for the beginning generations. This is my fertile role. I am dedicated to this field to be eternally worked in the nature of Adam's sons. Salutations, America, whatever you are. America who becomes henceforth my terrestrial heritage, my last fatherland amongst the fatherlands of exile and passage. Adieu, old world and what it contains of friendships turned toward me and cherished tombs. Active, tireless life commands me. A burden I cannot put down is imposed upon me. I have the chief responsibility, for the first time, of the governance of many souls. Can I with such a sight ahead of me, still cast a single backward glance? Can I worry about the echo of these memories in a heart? Should I now, my friend, let these pages reach you? Or should you read them only after my death?

In New York Harbor, August 182—